Four-time RITA® Award nominee **Joanne Rock** has penned over seventy stories for Mills & Boon. An optimist by nature and a perpetual seeker of silver linings, Joanne finds romance fits her life outlook perfectly—love is worth fighting for. A former Golden Heart® Award recipient, she has won numerous awards for her stories. Learn more about Joanne's imaginative muse by visiting her website, www.joannerock.com, or following @joannerock6 on Twitter.

Sarah M. Anderson may live east of the Mississippi River, but her heart lies out West on the Great Plains. Sarah's book *A Man of Privilege* won an RT Book Reviews Reviewers' Choice Best Book Award in 2012. *The Nanny Plan* was a 2016 RITA® Award winner for Contemporary Romance: Short.

Sarah spends her days having conversations with imaginary cowboys and billionaires. Find out more about Sarah's heroes at www.sarahmanderson.com

D0582874

EXPECTING A SCANDAL

JOANNE ROCK

HIS BEST FRIEND'S SISTER

SARAH M. ANDERSON

MIX
Paper from
responsible sources
FSC C007454

This book is produced from independently certified FSC™
paper to ensure responsible forest management.

For more information visit www.harpercollins.co.uk/green

Printed and bound in Spain
by CPI, Barcelona

MILLS & BOON

First Published in Great Britain 2018
by Mills & Boon, an imprint of HarperCollinsPublishers,
1 London Bridge Street, London, SE1 9GF

Expecting a Scandal © 2018 Harlequin Books S.A
His Best Friend's Sister © 2018 Sarah M. Anderson

Special thanks and acknowledgement are given to Joanne Rock for her contribution to the Texas Cattleman's Club: The Impostor series.

ISBN: 978-0-263-93598-1

51-0418

EXPECTING
A SCANDAL

JOANNE ROCK

To the A Team nurses at All Children's Hospital in St. Petersburg for your commitment and caring, for making a difference every day and for taking time out to share your stories with me.

One

Adjusting her glasses on her nose, Abigail Stewart hoped the funky red-and-black zebra frames distracted from the sheer desperation that must surely be visible in her eyes.

She didn't want the assembled Royal Memorial Hospital committee to see how badly she needed the commission for the sculpture she'd just proposed for the children's ward. Or how much it upset her to be back inside a hospital for the first time since her sister's death. Standing at the head of the hospital's boardroom after her presentation, she smoothed the hem of a fitted skirt that pinched her pregnant hips under the gauzy red top she'd chosen to hide her baby bump. At five months along, she wouldn't be fooling anyone for much longer. But considering the scandal attached to her baby's conception with a lying jerk posing as Will Sanders, the powerful head of Spark Energy Solutions, Abigail wasn't in a hurry to field questions about it. She was only just beginning to wrap her head around being a single mom in the wake of a hellish year that had cost her a beloved younger sibling.

A year that promised to go downhill even more, since Abigail would definitely not make the next mortgage payment on her house if she didn't nab this commission. She'd taken too much time off in the past year to help her mother cope with losing Alannah in a kayaking accident, depleting her emergency savings.

"Does anyone have questions about the art installation I'm proposing?" Abigail forced a smile despite the nervous churn in her belly.

At least, she hoped that rumble was nerves and not belated morning sickness. For the last two months, *morning* had been a relative term.

"I have a question." The deep, masculine voice at the back of the spacious room caught her off guard.

She'd thought all of the committee members were seated at the large table with a good view of the projection screen. Yet, at second glance, she saw an absurdly handsome man in green scrubs sprawled in a chair by the door in the back. From the leather shoes he sported to the expensive-looking haircut, he had an air of wealth about him that the scrubs and slightly scruffy facial hair couldn't hide. Even the phone resting on the table beside him cost more than her monthly house payment. She'd been so focused on getting her video up and running that she had somehow missed his arrival.

With a crop of thick brown hair and deep green eyes, he had a body that a professional athlete would envy— his broad chest and strong arms were supremely appealing. And for a woman five months pregnant and battling morning sickness along with a case of nerves to notice—that was saying something.

The hospital administrator who had invited Abigail to present to the committee gestured the newcomer toward a vacant chair at that table, where one presentation packet lay untouched. "Thank you for coming, Dr. Chambers, please join us."

"Sorry I'm late. My last surgery ran long." He rose and tugged the plush rolling chair out from the gleaming maple table, joining eleven other members of the committee in judging her. "And, Ms. Stewart, I'm sure you're very talented, and your gallery of works is certainly impressive, but I'm afraid I don't see the point of a statue in the children's ward when we are in need of more staffing and more on-site equipment."

Her stomach dropped.

The rumbling of reaction around the table gave Abigail a welcome moment to collect her thoughts before responding. She'd thought the commission was a foregone conclusion, whether she won it or another artist did, so she wasn't entirely prepared for the question. But since no one else jumped in to answer, she needed to field it fast.

"I believe the funds for artwork are designated strictly for that purpose by the benefactor who provided the grant." She glanced at the hospital administrator in charge of the committee, Belinda McDowell, who served as Royal Memorial's development officer. When the older woman didn't correct her, Abigail plowed ahead. "So the funding isn't something that can be reallocated."

Dr. Chambers stared back at her, his jaw flexing with thinly veiled impatience. Did he think art was so inferior to his field? Her spine steeled with some impatience of her own.

"Assuming that's the case…" He glanced at Mrs. Mc-Dowell for confirmation. At a nod of the woman's steel-gray bob, he continued, "Why a statue? Will children really appreciate art at that level, or would we be better served giving them something more age-appropriate that stands a chance of engaging them?"

Resisting the temptation to open his presentation packet for him and point out where she'd addressed this very question, she told herself she was being touchy because she needed this job so much. The visibility, the credibility and the portfolio development were all critical, even without the benefit of the income. Making a living as an artist in Royal hadn't been easy, even before Alannah's death.

"The statue would be a starting point since the hospital board would like to unveil the first element of a larger installation in the children's ward at a party later this month." She lifted her own presentation packet and flipped it open to the page with her proposed timeline. "There are some further details on page six."

Okay. So she hadn't been able to resist temptation.

But Dr. Green Eyes was single-handedly turning her presentation on its ear. He scrubbed a hand over his short beard, looking skeptical.

"Are there any other questions?" she blurted too quickly, realizing belatedly she was probably being rude.

Damn. It. How had she let him rattle her? Probably had something to do with the hospital bringing up bad memories. Or her too-tight skirt and her surprising reaction to the doctor. She'd thought, after the colossal mistake she'd made in sleeping with her former boss at her temp job, she'd effectively sworn off men for a while.

It bothered her to feel very feminine flutters of response to superficial things like an attractive face. Or a beautifully made male form.

That rich male voice rolled through the boardroom again. "Can good art be crafted in such a short time?" Dr. Chambers asked, now scanning through the pages of her presentation folder. "Do you really think you can meet that kind of deadline?"

Could she? It wouldn't be easy, of course. She had ten days. And she sure didn't appreciate the implication that "good" art was measured by how long it took to create it. Brilliant works had been crafted over the course of years, and others in the span of hours.

"Of course," she returned coolly. "Although, obviously, the sooner the committee reaches a decision, the easier it will be for the chosen artist to meet the deadline."

The committee leader, Belinda McDowell, rose. "And we hope to give you a response as soon as possible, Ms. Stewart. Thank you so much for coming in today." With a curt nod, she dismissed Abigail before turning her attention to the rest of the group. "I have one more artist I'd like you to meet if you can all remain for just ten more minutes."

Dismayed that she was already done with her portion of the meeting, Abigail hurried to gather her things before she headed toward the door. Had she blown the most important presentation of her career?

Passing Dr. Chambers on her way out, she felt her gaze drawn to him in spite of herself. Maybe because she wanted to give his chair a swift kick for finding fault in her presentation.

More likely, her artist's eye wanted to roam all over those intriguing angles of his face, the sculpted muscles of his body. At least, she hoped it was her inner artist that was having those ridiculous urges. Because if it was some kind of womanly desire for her surgeon heckler, who'd been about as charming as a Texas diamondback, then she had bigger worries than a depleted bank account and a baby on the way.

She needed a doctor all right. But only because she ought to have her head examined.

Vaughn Chambers flipped through the two artists' presentations side by side at a table in the hospital's doctor lounge later that afternoon. The lounge was busy at this hour during shift change, with colleagues darting in and out to grab coffee or a bite to eat. But Vaughn had positioned himself with his back to the room, earbuds in place, a coping mechanism he'd started using more often since his return from a military medical deployment with the United States Army Reserves.

Despite being the heir to an oil empire, Vaughn had never been willing to simply follow the path chosen for him. Instead of taking the easy route and accepting a CEO seat in the family company, he'd pursued a medical career. Inspired by his grandfather's military service, he'd been compelled to make a contribution of his own, signing on after he'd already secured his medical degree. He didn't regret those choices, but he was still paying for them.

He refused to let his service rob him of the career that meant everything to him, but coping with the aftereffects of his time as a brigade surgeon in Afghanistan had all but consumed him for months after he got home. Now, he understood the strategies for dealing with the post-traumatic stress. But since trauma was his surgical specialty, he could never fully insulate himself from the situations that triggered bad days.

Like today.

Vaughn stilled his restless knee under the table with effort, forcing a quietness in his body that he wasn't feeling, while a groggy resident struggled to make a fresh pot of coffee at the snack table beside him. Vaughn's patient this morning had been a stabbing victim, helicoptered in from a nearby ranch where a couple of cowboys had gotten into an argument over a card game. The surgery went well, though slowly, considering all the areas that needed repairing. But then, Vaughn had always been a rock during surgery, shutting down everything else in order to focus on the work he'd dedicated his whole life to perform.

The aftermath was what killed him, when he could no longer compartmentalize by focusing solely on the surgery at hand. And today, of all days, he'd had to sit in on a committee meeting about a new art installation right after he'd emerged from the operating room. He should have just blown it off. Except his colleague, Dr. Parker Reese, had asked him to attend as a personal favor. Or maybe Reese had been trying to do Vaughn a favor, nudging him back into the world outside a war zone, since Parker was one of the few guys who knew what Vaughn was going through. Either way, he'd promised. So Vaughn had dragged himself into that boardroom, adrenaline level crashing, knowing he wasn't at his best.

Now, drumming his fingers on the lounge table as

he stared at the two artists' presentation packets, his eye landed on a photo of Abigail Stewart. Her long, espresso-colored curls fell over her shoulder as she smiled in a candid shot that captured a far more light-hearted woman than he'd met today. Sunlight behind her—like dawn breaking—made her glow. Her dark eyes glanced at something just off to the side of the camera, and whatever it was made her laugh. The photo wasn't your standard head shot, but made sense for an artist. She practically vibrated with warmth and vitality in the image.

Something he'd stomped during their brief meeting. He'd known, even as he questioned her after her presentation, that he'd been abrupt. Tactless. But that was because he'd been battling to keep himself together. Normally when he got out of a more difficult surgery, he either escaped under the headphones, or he booked it back home to decompress with his service dog, Ruby. Today, neither option had been available. So he'd launched his reservations about the art project at Ms. Stewart with zero filter.

A clap on Vaughn's back startled him. He whipped around too fast, too fierce. He could see it in Belinda McDowell's wide-eyed expression, her tiny step back.

"I—" The seasoned hospital administrator was an endlessly competent woman, a tireless advocate for Royal Memorial and a consummate professional.

And Vaughn had just spooked her because he was having a bad day.

Damn it.

"Sorry about that." Yanking off his earbuds, he turned on what little charm he could scavenge, smiling broadly. "I must have been falling asleep." He gave a rueful head shake. "Good thing my residency days are behind me. I'd never cut it."

The administrator thrust an envelope toward him. "No apology necessary. I'm very grateful to you for agreeing to pay a visit to Ms. Stewart so she can begin work on the art installation."

After the presentations, the committee had voted unanimously to select Abigail Stewart to begin work on the statue for the children's ward as phase one of a larger art installment. And because Vaughn had regretted the way he'd approached her, he had volunteered to deliver the news personally.

Ah, hell. Who was he kidding?

He couldn't deny that he had volunteered because she fascinated him. In spite of the rocky start to their meeting. In spite of the day he was having that reminded him he might never be normal again. Something about Abigail Stewart called to him.

"It's no problem to drop by her studio. I have to pass through downtown on my way home anyway." Accepting the envelope from Mrs. McDowell, he glanced down at Abigail's name typed on the front. "What's this?"

"Half of her commission payment, which were the terms we discussed in the meeting," she said crisply, nodding to a couple of the older cardiologists who'd been on staff at Royal Memorial for decades. "Please remind her she is welcome to work on site as often as she requires. There is a security badge and parking pass for her in there, as well."

So he'd be seeing more of Abigail. Possibly a lot more. With only ten days until the Royal Memorial summer gala, the artist would have her work cut out for her. Vaughn would have a ready-made excuse to see her again—often—at the hospital. If he chose. He wasn't sure how he felt about spending more time with a woman who cut through his usual defenses on the job, and elicited an elemental response in him in spite of how much he normally shut down at work.

"Of course." He laid the envelope on the table near his phone. "I know we want to give her as much time as possible, so I'll head over there as soon as I check on one last patient."

He wanted to see his stabbing victim before he left the hospital. There were too many emotions dog piling on this day, making him antsy and ready to leave.

"Thank you." Mrs. McDowell checked her vibrating phone before silencing it. "And do be sure to get some rest, Dr. Chambers. You're an important part of our staff."

She turned efficiently on her gray heel and strode off, leaving Vaughn to stack up his papers. He paused before he could slide the presentation packets into the file folder, Abigail's photo catching his eye once more.

The noise of the lounge—residents laughing, an older doc dictating his notes in a monotone—all faded as Vaughn focused on the woman's image. He leaned closer to her photo, studying the lines of her face. She was undeniably attractive. Sultry, even, with those dark eyes, endless curls and kissable lips. But there was more to it than that. Vaughn had been approached by plenty of women since he'd returned from Afghanistan. And not one of them had tempted him out of his self-imposed isolation.

He'd almost been worried about the lack of interest, except that he knew PTSD was a long haul in the recovery process and he'd made definite progress since he'd started working with his golden retriever. Ruby had helped him sleep more soundly, waking him before his nightmares got out of control, preventing people from crowding him when he went out. Hell, Ruby had given him a reason to get out of the house in the first place, and that had been good for him. He'd figured the rest would follow in time.

Today, despite the adrenaline letdown and the cold sweat on his back throughout that interminable meeting, Vaughn had felt a definite spark of interest as he'd watched Abigail Stewart in that boardroom.

A welcome sign of some normalcy.

No matter that he wasn't in any shape for a relationship, he planned to at least see what happened when he saw her again.

Two

Circling her studio like a restless cat, Abigail cleaned and organized, too keyed up to work after the tense meeting at Royal Memorial. She'd tried drawing to decompress when she returned to her home-based art studio, but she couldn't concentrate. She'd ended up scrapping the little sketch she'd started once she realized her charcoal was bringing Dr. Chambers's likeness to life on the paper.

Now, she straightened her chisels in the storage block of wood, arranging them the way she liked—short-handled tools in front, longer blades in the back. The exercise wasn't strictly necessary, but she felt like she ordered her mind when she organized her world. And she needed that right now. Normally, sketching or painting helped her to wind down and readied her thoughts for the bigger work of her studio—wood carving. But today her inner muse was still sighing over the meeting with the surly surgeon, and she could not afford to ruin the beautiful piece of elm she was working on by accidentally carving the doctor's shoulders into it.

Not that the women of Royal, Texas, wouldn't line up to admire those spectacular muscles. Maybe it could be Abigail's breakthrough piece. But since her normal milieu tended toward fantasy creatures and more abstract pieces, she wasn't sure a set of broad male shoulders belonged in her catalog. They definitely didn't belong in her romantic musings when she was four months away from giving birth and eager to make peace with her sister's death. Somehow, she had to find a way to honor Alannah's life and move forward. She'd hoped maybe the Royal Memorial project would help her with that, but if Dr. Chambers had his way, she was already out of the running.

She turned up the folk music she'd been favoring for her creative time lately, hoping to quiet the demons while she got her studio in order, but the buzz of her doorbell cut right through the drums.

Setting aside a small carving knife, Abigail rose from her workbench and edged around wood blocks and logs in various stages of drying around the sunny backroom that she used for making her art. She'd knocked down a wall and moved the kitchen in her house to accommodate the needs of her work. When she tugged open the side door that had the buzzer, she fully expected to see a delivery of some sort. A new awl, maybe, or the used palm sander she'd bought on eBay.

Instead of a cardboard package, though, she found the man who'd preoccupied her thoughts all afternoon.

"Dr. Chambers." She felt the hum of awareness immediately. It didn't matter that he wore a ridiculously expensive watch and drove the low-slung, European-made sports car sitting in the driveway behind him, even though she'd told herself she was done with rich playboys, like the father of her child.

The vivid green of the hot doc's eyes watched her with interest. And, she guessed, radiated less animosity than he'd demonstrated back at the hospital. He'd left behind the scrubs she'd seen him in earlier. Now, he wore dark dress pants and a fitted blue button-down shirt open at the collar, a nod to the heat of a Texas July, perhaps.

The close-trimmed facial hair hid some of his face, and she guessed he would be even more overtly attractive when clean-shaven. Maybe that's why he wore the beard. Sometimes that level of compelling good looks could be a distraction from the substance beneath. Abigail would bet the women he worked with noticed him either way.

"It's Vaughn." He thrust out a hand, the silver Breitling watch glinting in the late-afternoon sun. "And I hope we didn't get off on the wrong foot earlier."

The words caught her off guard, even as she took his hand briefly. The contact hummed up her arm and tickled its way along her shoulder.

"Abigail," she said automatically, even though he clearly knew who she was. She hesitated, feeling awkward as she pulled her hand back. "And I'm surprised to see you. Unless—"

A surge of hopefulness made her tense. He wouldn't have come all the way out to her studio to deliver bad news, would he?

"You won the job." He relayed the information with a

curt nod, as if he was reading the results of a CAT scan to a patient. The words were so spare and utilitarian, but the impact was tremendous. "I thought I'd deliver the news personally—"

Abigail didn't hear the rest of what he said, a wave of relief rolling over her so fast she nearly stumbled backward from it. She clasped her hands together and squeezed the good news tight as a giddy yelp of laughter leaped out.

"Thank you!" She did a little dance in place, sandals slapping out a joyous rhythm. "You have no idea what this means to me."

She would keep her house and the studio she loved. The commission was enough to smooth the way for her baby's first year without having to worry about money every month. And, perhaps best of all, she would have a beautiful piece to dedicate to her sister's memory. The tree sculpture would be for Alannah. A tree of life and hope.

On her doorstep, Vaughn stared at her feet, tracking the happy hop like he'd never seen anything like it before. "I thought it was the least I could do given my demeanor earlier—"

She waved away the concern. None of it mattered now.

"Would you like to come in?" She saw the folder beneath his arm. Guessed there might be a check inside that paperwork. How surprising that the ornery surgeon had ended up being the bearer of the best news she'd had in a long, long time.

The briefest of hesitations.

Maybe the rich doc wasn't used to spending his time in an artsy bungalow downtown. With her folk music still blaring inside and her watercolors taped in all the windows, her work space was definitely on the eclectic side. Or maybe he just didn't like art period. Today, she was too relieved to care.

"Sure." Another clipped nod as his expensive leather loafers climbed the wooden steps. "Thank you."

Abigail backed into her studio and turned down the volume on her music, eyeing him as he moved deeper into her space. She'd never had a man here in the two years since she'd relocated to Royal from Austin. He had a way of filling up the room, even though her studio was airy and open. Vaughn's presence, while quiet, loomed large.

He took it all in, his gaze missing nothing as he followed her to the drawing table, where sketches lined the walls around it. She gestured to one of the chairs there, an armless seat she'd made herself of reclaimed wood.

"Have a seat. Can I get you some water? Sweet tea?" she asked as she headed into the kitchenette in the back corner of the studio. She would have gladly cracked open champagne if she wasn't five months pregnant. Not that she kept champagne on hand. But this new commission changed everything for her.

And even though she hadn't appreciated the doctor's contentious approach at the time, he was here, offering her the job that would keep her afloat—financially, creatively and maybe emotionally, too—at the most critical juncture of her life. She couldn't help but feel a softening in her attitude toward him.

"No. Thank you." He sat forward in the seat, all business. Withdrawing the folder from under his arm, he laid it on the table. "I brought the contract for you to sign, along with the initial payment."

He slid the papers out of the folder, carefully positioning them between her morning watercolor of a nuthatch on a tree branch, and an afternoon charcoal sketch of…him?

Oh. *No*. Horrified she hadn't tossed the paper in the basket, she rushed back toward the table, hoping to move it before he noticed.

Had he already noticed?

"I. Um. That is—" She was by his side in a split second. Standing too close to him. Hovering over him. Sounding completely inarticulate.

"It's all very straightforward." He glanced up at her. Frowned. "Is anything wrong?"

She couldn't tell from his expression if he'd noticed the half-drawn image of himself. Leaning forward, she slid her scattered papers together in a hurry, knocking the check on the floor and bumping his thigh with her knee. Awareness of him made her senses swim.

She'd been careful to leave her artist's smock over her dress, so she didn't think he'd noticed her baby bump. Not many people in Royal knew about it, after all, and she guessed the flash of male interest she'd seen in his eyes would disappear once he learned of her impending motherhood. Was it so wrong to want to savor that attraction just a little longer?

"Ah. No." She shook her head, imagining she appeared about as innocent as a toddler with a hand in the cookie jar. "Just sorry about the mess."

Her cheeks burned. All of her was feeling rather warm, actually, and it wasn't just because of the awkward embarrassment. Her skin tingled beneath the hem of her skirt where she'd brushed up against his leg.

Backing up a step, she tried to act casual even though

her heart thudded too fast. He picked up the dropped check and returned it to the table.

"Your studio puts my office to shame." He studied her with green-gold eyes that tracked her every movement.

"I was straightening up when you arrived." She hurried over to her desk and shoved the papers in the top drawer before returning to the table. Taking the seat beside him, she tried to collect herself.

Hit the mental reset button.

To cool down and get her thoughts back on track, she turned the contract toward her and started reading.

The meeting with Abigail Stewart had gone from interesting to downright fascinating. The tension between them had shifted since the stressful morning meeting. He credited that to several things. Being further removed from the surgery that had threatened to give him flashbacks definitely helped him to relax more around her. Add to that the fact that Abigail was obviously thrilled she'd won the art gig, which put her in a happy frame of mind.

Best of all, he'd spied a half-finished sketch on her table of a man who bore a striking resemblance to him.

He would have written it off as a coincidence since he couldn't be certain, of course. But then he'd seen the way her eyes locked on the drawing and her rush to remove it. There'd been a flare of unmistakable embarrassment. Awareness. Hell, the electricity between them had spiked to a shocking degree in those moments when she'd been close to him. The attraction had been a revelation considering how resolutely—and easily—he'd ignored dating since his deployment.

The heat Abigail stirred wasn't going to be ignored.

Vaughn watched her read over the contract he'd brought, and lingered on her lovely features as she pursed her lips or tilted her head. For a moment, she traced a line of text with her finger, as if to slow her pace or concentrate. Dark curls pooled on the table beside the paper, the silky waves calling to his fingers to touch them. Test how they would feel against his skin.

She'd changed since he'd seen her at the hospital earlier. She wore an artist's smock over a loose summer dress. The pale green cotton printed with daisies peeked out of the smock at the hem, the kind of simple summer staple that was probably comfortable for working. Yet on Abigail, the outfit was as seductive as anything he'd ever seen a woman wear. The low-cut neckline visible above the square-necked apron revealed ample curves, and a gold medallion knocked against the table as she bent to read the papers he'd given her. Beneath the table, she crossed her long legs, and her sandaled foot brushed his calf for an instant as she moved, sending his imagination into overdrive...

And damn. He shouldn't allow his thoughts to roam in that direction until he knew more about her. What if she was married? Had a significant other? He didn't see another car in her driveway, and her ring finger was bare, but that didn't necessarily mean she was available.

Surely the drawing she'd made of him meant something, though.

"There." Abigail signed her name with a flourish. "All set." She pushed the paperwork toward him, straightening in her seat. "Would you like me to show you around the studio before you go?"

He couldn't decide if that was a genuine invitation

or a politely worded hint for him to be on his way. He used to be better at reading social nuances. These days, just keeping his own emotions in check took focus. And although he was anxious to get home and decompress from this day, he had to admit he enjoyed this time with Abigail.

"I'd like that." Leaving her advance payment on the table along with the security badge and a few other documents, he slid the signed agreement into his folder. He'd give it to Belinda tomorrow to make copies. "It's not at all what I expected," he told her honestly, hoping to learn more about Abigail if he spent a little time with her.

"No?" She glanced at him over her shoulder as she led him past a shelf full of paint cans and chemicals, her dark eyes challenging. "Did you envision me sitting around my garret with a bunch of wine-swilling pseudointellectuals while we debated the novels of Kafka?"

He laughed out loud, surprised at the sound. "Not quite. But I definitely didn't envision this many axes." He stopped near a bunch of sinister-looking hatchets and hand tools leaning against the wall alongside ladders in varying sizes.

She paused beside him, her embarrassment from earlier in their meeting long gone. She smiled with something like fondness as she looked over the tools of her trade. The whole place smelled like hickory and apple wood, a welcoming scent that reminded him of fall bonfires.

"Wood carving can be strenuous labor, but I love it." She straightened a few small blades on a shelf nearby. "I still work in other media, but I've been obsessed with wood for the last few years."

"The tree sculpture you proposed for the children's

ward will be made from wood?" He hadn't read the specs of her work very carefully, and besides, she had a great deal of artistic license in the project, so it wasn't as though the hospital was dictating precise details for the project she crafted for the installation.

"Yes. I have a perfect length of bay laurel in mind. It's been drying for years, and I've always known that I wanted it for a tree of some sort."

"Years? How long have you lived in Royal?" He didn't remember hearing about her work until after he returned from his deployment.

"It's been a little over two years." She stepped carefully around a short sculpture of a bird with an ox's head, moving deeper into the stacks of raw wood.

"Do you mean to tell me you that you brought some of this with you when you moved?" His gaze wandered over all the huge logs of varying sizes.

"I brought almost all of it since I had access to a lot of wood remnants where I lived in Austin. I haven't found a good source here yet." She moved aside some of the limbs with relative ease, making him realize that she had the larger hunks secured with ropes hanging from the rafters so they wouldn't fall. She spotted the bay laurel she had in mind for the hospital sculpture and showed him some of the features.

"You should come out to my place sometime," he said when she finished, even before he'd worked out if she was single or not. "That is, if you want to check out the trees."

"I don't take any fresh wood. Only fallen pieces." She stepped carefully from her place among the knotty branches and gnarled slabs in every shade and fiber. "Do you think you have any downed trees on your property?"

"That's not the sort of thing I typically look for when I go riding. But I've got over two hundred acres, so there's bound to be something if you'd like to take a look sometime."

"Really? You wouldn't mind?" She brightened, the same happy expression lighting her eyes that he'd seen when he first told her about the commission.

He liked seeing her smile. Hearing the way her pleasure warmed the tone of her voice. He found himself wanting to get a whole lot closer to her and all that warmth.

"I'm not on call at the hospital this weekend. Come by anytime." He withdrew his phone to message her with his contact information, dragging her phone number from his electronic copy of the commission contract. "I just sent you the address."

"Thank you. I find inspiration just being out in nature, so I'd be grateful for the chance to see any of the woodlands." She showed him a few more features of her studio, ending with the sunny corner where she liked to paint.

His eye roamed over the paintings she'd taped up around the windows and walls. There were dozens.

"You paint, you draw, you carve," he observed. "You don't ever feel like you're spreading yourself too thin?"

As soon as he asked, he wondered if the question was too pointed. If he sounded critical again, the way he had in the meeting earlier. But the query was honest, and some of his bluntness was simply a part of his personality, long before the PTSD had hit him hard.

She shrugged, not seeming to take offense. "You repair everything from gallbladders to head trauma. I like to think I take that same kind of holistic approach to my expertise, too. It's all art, so it's all in my body of work."

"There are so many paintings." He ran a finger over one image of a woman's back. Or at least, he thought it looked the curve of a feminine spine. The colors were muted and the image was a close-up, so he couldn't be sure. Yet there was a sensuality to the flare of hips, and the subtle shape of an hourglass.

"I paint them quickly in the morning sometimes for a warm-up, just to get ideas flowing." She glanced up at some of the paintings above her head, a rainbow of color on the wall behind her.

"How about the drawings?" he asked, thinking back to the sketch she'd done of him. "What makes you decide to use charcoals instead of paints?"

Her hesitation made him think that she understood exactly what he sought to discover. *What had made her sketch him?*

She took her time answering, threading a finger under a loose curl to skim it away from her face. A prism hanging in a nearby window reflected flashes of light on her skin. "I'm inclined to draw when I'm unsettled. I often use the charcoals to vent emotions—nervousness, anger... grief."

Her voice hitched a bit, alerting him that he may have touched a nerve. Regretting that, he sought to reroute the conversation, not wanting to lose the tenuous connection he really wanted to strengthen with this woman. He couldn't remember the last time he'd had an in-depth talk with anyone outside of the workplace.

"It's good you've got a productive outlet for that." He wondered which of those negative emotions had driven her to sketch him. No doubt he'd upset her earlier in the day. "Too many surgeons I know detach so thoroughly that they become—" Jackasses? That seemed a harsh way to define some of his colleagues. "Dedicated loners."

"You wouldn't be able to perform your job without some ability to detach." Her hand alighted on his forearm in a gesture of comfort.

The contact was a social politeness. An expression of empathy.

But damn if it didn't light up all his circuits like the Fourth of July. For the space of two heartbeats, her touch remained. He looked down at the place where she'd touched him, her fingers already sliding away. He missed the warmth immediately. Craved more of her caresses.

"Detaching isn't a problem for me," he admitted, unwilling to confess how deeply he wrestled with the fallout from that skill. "Sometimes that makes me far too abrupt, as you witnessed firsthand in today's committee meeting."

He watched her face, locking on her expression before he continued. "Were you venting negative emotions about that when you drew the picture of me?"

Perhaps she'd been expecting the question, or maybe she'd simply been more prepared to revisit the topic after her initial embarrassment about the sketch. She lifted a brow, her gaze wary, but she didn't flush with discomfort this time.

"You noticed that and didn't say anything?" She shook her head with a rueful laugh and leaned up against a built-in counter with cabinets below and shelves overhead. Paintbrushes in every size imaginable hung on a rack over the shelves. "I guess you are good at detaching. If I saw someone had made a picture of me, I would have been quick to ask a hundred questions about it."

His gaze traveled her body, where her position drew all the more attention to her curves.

"I was curious." He shoved his hands in his pockets to combat the urge to touch her. "I just didn't think it was the right moment to ask."

"Truthfully, yes, I felt frustrated about the meeting when I returned to the studio. I didn't have any preconceived idea of what I would draw. I just sat down to blurt out anything that came to mind." She met his eyes directly. Openly. "I was surprised when I saw you take shape on the paper."

He wanted to think he'd ended up there because they had a connection. An undeniable spark.

Because the longer he lingered in Abigail's sunny studio, the more he felt his normal boundaries crumbling. And while he wanted that—craved following up on the attraction simmering between them—he wasn't sure how he would handle anything beyond simple lust. The realization made him edgy.

She filled the silence that followed with a sudden question. "Would you like me to finish the drawing?"

His throat went dry. The question had gotten complicated in the space of a moment as he started to recognize that Abigail wasn't going to be the kind of woman who would be open to a purely physical relationship.

"I wouldn't want to keep you from your work." He couldn't think of a more eloquent retreat with Abigail moving toward him. Touching him again.

"Not at all." She took his hand briefly to lead him toward a chair near her painting spot, her touch fanning the flame inside him, making him think about so much more. "Have a seat and I'll finish up. You can see what it's like to watch an artist at work."

In the space of five minutes, Vaughn realized he'd somehow used up all his emotional reserves today. All of his ability to detach. Because that simple touch from Abigail sent all the wrong messages to his brain. He hadn't given himself the outlet of a sexual relationship since he'd returned from Afghanistan. And now, the consequences of that had him on sensory overload, when he'd already battled the aftermath of a hellish surgery this morning.

A perfect storm of too many emotions without enough time to process them. He should have taken the time to go home and pick up Ruby before he came here. Having his dog beside him would have helped.

But he was already sitting in the seat Abigail had shown him when she returned with a heavy pencil in one hand and her half-made sketch in the other. She set both on a low table nearby, then moved closer to him, her gaze all over him. Studying him.

Seeing inside him somehow.

"Do you mind if I position you just a little?" she asked, already setting aside the folder he'd been carrying.

He wasn't sure if he'd agreed or not. His forehead broke out in a sweat. Warning heat blasted up his back. He wanted her.

"Here." Abigail set her hands on his shoulders and gently shifted them toward her.

She stood close, her knee brushing his thigh as she moved him, her breasts at eye level. She smelled like cinnamon and oranges, a spicy, tangy fragrance that would be burned into his memory forever. Sunlight kissed her face as she lifted his chin with one palm, her eyes taking a critical assessment of his features while he battled lust and a whole knot of other things he couldn't come close to naming. Hunger for her gnawed at him. Hot. Persistent.

"I've got to go." He clamped a hand on her wrist. Too hard at first. But then, realizing his responses were all out of whack, he gentled his hand. Released her. "I'm sorry, Abigail. I forgot that I said I would—" He rose from the chair. Sidestepped her. "Upload my notes on a critical-care patient after some—" His brain worked to come up with something vaguely believable before he did something stupid. Like kiss her until they were both breathless. Senseless. "Technical difficulties at the hospital."

His voice rasped drily as he grappled for control.

"Of course." She nodded even though she appeared as perplexed as he felt. "I'm sure I'll see you at the hospital when I start work on site."

"Right." He didn't reiterate his offer for her to come by his ranch. He needed to get his head on straight first. "I'm sure you will."

Backing out of the door, he lifted a hand in a quick wave.

"Thank you for coming by. I couldn't be more excited about the project," she called after him.

But Vaughn didn't answer. He was down the steps and seated in his truck in no time, slamming the door behind him while he turned over the engine and blasted the air-conditioning on his overheated body.

He didn't know what the hell he'd been thinking, pursuing this sudden attraction he was clearly not ready to handle. Maybe some other day, when he wasn't already depleted from a surgery that had brought back too many memories. But for right now, he needed to put some distance between him and a woman who stirred a surplus of emotions. No matter how much he thought he had mastered detachment, Abigail Stewart made him realize he'd only succeeded in getting damn good at lying to himself.

Three

A few days later, Abigail wondered if it had been presumptuous of her to accept Vaughn's offer to search for pieces of fallen wood on his ranch outside of town. Driving out of downtown toward the address Vaughn had given her, she knew it was too late to turn back now. She did really want the chance to walk through the trees and find inspiration, along with some different kinds of boughs for the oversize statue she was creating for Royal Memorial. That much was true.

But there was no denying her interest in the lone wolf doctor who so fascinated her.

When she'd texted her request for when she'd like to come to his property, the response had been almost immediate, making her wonder if he was just that prompt. Or if he'd been thinking about her, too. She was intrigued to see him again even though she knew she needed to tell him about her pregnancy.

Now, turning down the road that passed the Ace in the Hole Ranch, where she used to work for the man she'd believed to be Will Sanders, she couldn't stop the flood of memories. The main house was massive, with a deep front porch and multiple rooflines, plus an open breezeway connecting to a guest cottage. The crisp, white-painted home and dark shutters were immaculate, the trimmed hedges in perfect alignment. In the years she'd lived in Royal, she'd never seen the rolling lawn allowed to grow a millimeter too long. At night, it was really something to behold, with the many windows lit from within, and landscape lighting that illuminated the prettiest features.

Working at the Ace in the Hole had been rewarding if only to step onto that gorgeous property every day for a few weeks last winter. Her actual duties had been straightforward enough—organizing files and transferring them to more secure storage for Will.

Or, more accurately, the man who'd been impersonating Will Sanders, his former friend, Richard Lowell. Not many people in Royal knew that Will Sanders had returned to town to crash his own funeral. The FBI was now involved in the quiet investigation since they hoped that they might lure Rich Lowell back. Abigail knew about it because she'd received a letter from an attorney asking her to attend the funeral, since she was named as one of Will's heirs. She'd nearly fainted when Will walked into the service himself.

None of that changed the fact that she'd had a one-night stand with the man who'd impersonated Will.

And now, she needed to let Vaughn know about the pregnancy. She was trying to move beyond the anger and frustration surrounding the father of her baby. She still worried about what she would tell her child about his or her daddy down the road. That he was a felon? A sociopath? Guilty of more crimes than she even knew about?

Shuddering, she touched her belly protectively and felt an answering flutter. The shifting movements of this life inside never failed to amaze her since she'd started noticing it in the last few weeks. Amid so much grief this past year, those signs of vibrant renewal felt like the most precious gift in the world.

Pulling up to the gates of Vaughn's property, some of those happy feelings faded, however. The gates were huge. Imposing.

And the most definitely ensured privacy.

She knew many doctors earned a good living, but an electric gate with wrought-iron scrollwork outlining the house number suggested a whole different level of wealth. The arched entrance was a good ten feet tall on the sides, swooping up to fifteen at the peak of the arch. She pressed the call button on the keypad and Vaughn's voice answered as the gate mechanism whirred softly, pulling open to the paved road that must lead to his home.

"Glad you found the place, Abigail," he said, through the speaker on the security system. "You can park in front of the house and I'll meet you there."

"Okay. Thanks." Her voice sounded flat. Because she was intimidated? Or because she'd hoped to find Vaughn living somewhere more…accessible?

She knew it wasn't fair to hold it against him that he'd done well in life. But after seeing how Will Sanders's money had corrupted someone into impersonating him, she sure didn't take any pleasure from the wealthy trappings that other people might find appealing.

Rounding a bend surrounded by live oaks, Abigail had to admire the old growth buffering the home from the roadway. There were walnut and maple trees, ash and pecan.

And then, there *he* was.

Vaughn Chambers stood out in front of his ranch home built of sandstone, the dusky browns and tans of the rock walls blending with the hills and trees so seamlessly it looked like a part of the landscape. A planked porch wrapped around two sides, with the main roofline continuing down to the porch, a trick of building that provided plenty of shade to homes in the summertime. The darker roof and wooden porch columns set off the lighter stone. Three dormers graced the main roof, giving the house a modest-sized second floor and a huge footprint on the main level. A detached garage with huge, dark wood doors looked big enough to hold a monster truck. Or, more likely, multiple vehicles.

The house was lovely, and couldn't be more different from the manicured beauty of the Ace in the Hole. Vaughn's home had a rustic, natural appeal.

As for the man himself, her breath caught to see him again. The short beard and moustache appeared freshly trimmed today. His thick brown hair was darker and spiky from a recent shower. He wore a gray T-shirt with jeans and boots that looked like they'd seen real work. A golden retriever sat at his feet, its long fur brushed and gleaming in the July sunlight.

"What a beautiful dog!" She was grateful for the animal, a welcome topic of conversation to hide her nervousness.

"This is Ruby." He scratched his canine behind the

ears, the affection in his voice obvious. "Ruby, meet Abigail."

"May I pet her?" She liked to ask first even though the dog appeared well-trained. Her sister had once startled a stray in her eagerness to pet it when they were kids, and she had a scar on her leg from the bite for the rest of her too-short life.

How daunting that a hundred and one things every day still made her think of Alannah. Her chest went tight with the familiar squeeze of sorrow.

"Sure. She's a social dog and she likes a good scratch on the haunches."

Bending closer to Ruby, Abigail stroked the silky fur. Her knee brushed up against the animal's collar as she patted one side of her back, the movement jingling the silver tags. One had her name engraved on it and, she guessed, Vaughn's contact information on the other side. It was the second tag that caught her eye for the red caduceus and the Service Dog—Full Access notation.

Vaughn had a service dog?

She knew it was rude to ask about it, a working-dog etiquette tip she'd picked up from her friend Natalie St. Cloud, who owned the Cimarron Rose B and B in Royal, where Abigail occasionally stopped for a meal. Natalie had an autistic son who had a service dog, another golden retriever, and the animal had made a world of difference in their lives.

Straightening from petting the dog, Abigail swallowed the questions pinwheeling through her brain. If Vaughn had noticed her reading his dog's tags, he didn't indicate it. He gave the dog the command to "free play," and Ruby sprinted over to a pair of weathered gray barns on the side of the house near a large, fenced pasture.

"I'm glad you're here." He turned toward her again. "I regret the way I left in a hurry on Wednesday."

The hint of hunger in his green eyes made her feel things for him she shouldn't. She really needed to tell him about her pregnancy. End this heart-fluttering tension between them and focus on her work and her baby.

"It was kind of you to make the time to stop by personally in the first place." She took a deep breath, prepared to tell him the truth.

"Would you prefer the walking tour or a horseback version?" he asked and gestured toward the barn before she could get the words out.

She loved riding, but it had been years she'd been in a saddle and wasn't sure how she would fare. Five months pregnant might not be the best time to try refreshing her skills.

"Maybe I'd do best on foot today. My horseback-riding skills are decidedly rusty."

"I have a utility vehicle with a cart attached. If you see something you like while we're out, you can just let me know and I'll use the cart to pick it up for you later."

"That would be great." She had planned to simply use the day for inspiration in creating her own tree for the children's ward, but she appreciated the offer of bringing some pieces home with her. "Thank you."

They started down a worn path between the house and barns. Ruby remained close to Vaughn's side even though she wasn't on a leash. The golden retriever didn't dart off to examine butterflies or sniff interesting fence posts. Clearly, the dog was tightly bonded to Vaughn.

Abigail enjoyed walking with them both as they entered a wooded area on the southern side of the ranch. Part of her delight was being in nature, something she missed in her downtown bungalow. With the earthy scents of green and growing vegetation around them, she breathed deeper, her fingers trailing over tree trunks and brushing against mossy logs. But another aspect of her pleasure had to do with Vaughn's very male presence beside her. His warmth and strength. The simple consideration he showed for her when he lifted a low sapling branch out of her way or pointed out a rocky patch in the terrain.

"I didn't get to ask you something the other day." Vaughn held out his hand to her to help her across a rivulet.

She accepted his offer, squeezing his fingers for balance as she hopped over the water, his touch making her far too aware of him. "What's that? After our first meeting, I can't imagine you holding back on any question you wanted to pose," she teased lightly, telling herself not to let the brush of his fingers affect her.

"Are you seeing anyone?" He stopped beside her, his boot cracking a twig underfoot as he pivoted to look at her, his hand still holding hers.

Everything inside her stilled. Because with that question, he was making it clear that she hadn't misread the signals he'd sent. If she hadn't been expecting a baby, maybe this could lead to something more. Something special.

Her heart thudded so hard he probably felt it in his hand where her palm grazed his. Staring up into his eyes, she allowed herself a flash of if-only thoughts, where this moment would play out differently.

And then, she forced herself back to reality.

"No. I am definitely not." With a resolute shake of her head, she stepped back, disentangling their fingers with more than a little regret. "But my life is about to get very complicated, Vaughn, because I'm five months pregnant."

Too stunned to hide his shock, Vaughn dropped his gaze to her slim figure. She wore three-quarter-length yoga pants and a blue-and-white floral blouse that covered her midsection. Now that he thought back on it, all the times they'd met she'd been wearing loose tops or, like the other day, her artist's smock.

He'd just assumed she was single when he didn't see a ring and felt—*thought* he felt—the sparks between them. Damn. Damn. Damn. He knew it was rude to stare and, belatedly, he forced his eyes to meet hers.

"I had no idea." He shook his head, feeling like a first-rate idiot as a bird whistled and circled overhead. Ruby pressed against his leg, her head lightly nudging his knee. "I never would have guessed—"

"Well, I haven't made a habit of advertising it yet since I'm still trying to come to terms with what this pregnancy means for me." Abigail rubbed one hand over her other arm as if to ward off a chill, even though the day bordered on being hot. "Would you mind if we keep walking?"

"Sure." He nodded, his hand scratching Ruby's head automatically as they stalked deeper into the woodland portion of the ranch. "You're not...with the baby's father?"

She shook her head. "I'm not even sure he's alive." Her words were halting. Troubled. Then, as she slanted a look his way, something fierce lit her dark eyes. "But even if he is, he won't be a part of my child's life."

"He won't?" Vaughn knew she might not have a legal

say in that since the father could sue for paternal rights. If Vaughn had a child, he would move heaven and earth to make sure he had a role in the baby's life.

Not that he would ever be a father after the way his world had changed forever. Besides, from the vehemence in her voice he suspected it wasn't the right moment to speculate about possible legal action involving her baby.

"Are you close with anyone in the Texas Cattleman's Club?" she asked, surprising him with the quick turn of conversation. Her tone was different now. Confiding. Confidential.

How sad that he felt like they were getting closer on the same day she pulled away. He still couldn't believe the woman he was so attracted to was carrying another man's child. He was too shocked at the news to figure out how he felt about that.

"I'm not active, but my father still is." His dad had asked him to stop by the club more than once since his return from Afghanistan.

His parents didn't really understand how hard he battled the PTSD, or that Vaughn didn't socialize more than strictly necessary. He pointed to a turn in the path through the woods, silently showing Abigail the way while she continued.

"Then you might know—and your father most likely already knows—that Rich Lowell was impersonating Will Sanders before the imposter faked Will's death."

Vaughn had heard rumblings, but not the full story. Will Sanders was a man who had it all—including a prestigious family with deep roots in Royal, and with the Texas Cattleman's Club. He owned one of the largest ranches in Royal in addition to being CEO of Spark

Energy Solutions, an energy company with ties to oil, gas and solar.

Or at least, he was CEO. Before his supposed death eight weeks ago.

"I heard something about Will Sanders walking into his own funeral this spring, but the story was too incredible to believe." Vaughn wondered how Abigail knew about it. The story hadn't been in the local news outlets even though Will Sanders was a high-profile member of the community.

And then, he understood. Abigail wasn't a member of the TCC. So if she knew about the FBI investigation that was allegedly probing into the impersonation and embezzlement schemes of a man posing as Will Sanders, it could only mean she'd been questioned. Or was close to one of the main parties under investigation.

She halted beside him, her brows lifted, as if fully expecting he would have put the pieces together.

He stroked the top of Ruby's head, taking comfort from her presence when he should probably be offering support to Abigail. "Is the man who pretended to be Will Sanders the father of your child?" he asked.

The hum of summer insects in the meadow nearby penetrated the woods, filling the air with a rising, buzzing sound, an ominous underscore to his question.

"Yes." The terse reply communicated a wealth of resentment.

Or was it something more complicated than that? He couldn't read her expression, but there was a plethora of emotions there.

"I'm so damn sorry." He spotted a place he'd wanted to show her, where a fallen log made a mossy seat beside a rushing brook. No doubt, this day wasn't going to be the kind of prelude to romance he'd hoped for, but he couldn't pretend he wasn't still drawn to the compelling woman beside him. He took her hand again, craving the feel of her in spite of everything. "Come sit for a minute."

"I don't regret this baby for a moment," she confided as she followed him toward the creek. "But I hate that I won't have a happy story to share with my child about his or her father. Quite the opposite, in fact."

Abigail's artist's gaze seemed to take in every detail as he led her under a low-hanging branch to show her the bend in the brook, perfect for dipping your toes on a hot day. The whole glade smelled like balsam and loamy earth.

"He deceived you along with the whole town." Vaughn couldn't imagine how devastated she must have been. But according to local gossips, Abigail hadn't been the only woman taken in by the fake Will Sanders's charm. The lowlife had been married to Megan Phillips and had an affair with a woman while abroad on business. "That's a lot to process in addition to the baby news."

He felt protective of Abigail, damn it. Was that why he kept hold of her hand, or steadied her waist when she stepped up onto the log? She deserved his care.

But as he sank to sit on the fallen tree beside her, Vaughn knew he was lying to himself. He would take any excuse to touch her. Get closer to her.

"Our night together should have never happened in the first place." She wrapped her arms around herself, her feet dangling just above the brook's edge, while Ruby settled along the back of the log, faithfully watching Vaughn's back, the way she'd been trained. "I was doing temp work at the Ace in the Hole last winter. I didn't even know him that well. He told me he was separated from his wife, and I believed him."

Vaughn wasn't sure how to offer comfort. So he just listened. Waited. The rush of the water filled the silence while a soft breeze rustled through the hickory tree overhead. He couldn't deny a sense of relief that her relationship had been just one night and not a deep, emotional relationship. Yet at the same time, he knew it was irrational of him to feel that way since he barely knew her.

"I was working late that night because it was my younger sister's birthday." Her voice changed. Softened. "Alannah." She glanced over at him, blinking fast before she looked away again. "She would have been twenty-four. Only she died ten months before that, and I was really…struggling that day."

Whatever he'd thought she might say, it hadn't been anything remotely close to that. Understanding made his chest ache for her. He related to that kind of loss all too well.

His arm went around her shoulders. Behind him, he felt Ruby shift. Even his dog nudged Abigail's back, whimpering with the kind of empathetic emotion that animals keenly understood.

"Honey, I'm more sorry than I can say." He tipped his cheek to the top of her head. "She was taken from you far too soon."

He didn't even want to think about some bastard taking advantage of her grief. Because as much as Vaughn could admit he liked the feel of Abigail in his arms, he would never use her vulnerable state for leverage. That was just…so damn wrong.

"I knew right away that the night with Will—the imposter posing as Will—had been a mistake," she confessed, her voice muffled against his shirt before she straightened, then swiped quickly at her eyes. "I should have taken precautions the next day, but I was still so weighed down with grief. If anything, I felt worse." She shook her head. "It had been months since she drowned in a kayaking accident, so I thought I'd been coming to terms with it a little more. There was just something about having her birthday come and go that really set things back."

With an effort, he dropped his arm again, not wishing to overstep, the way that jackass boss of hers had.

"There are good days and bad days when you're grieving." He knew firsthand.

"Yeah." She nodded, startling a little as a frog splashed into the water beside them. "And that was a bad few days. By the time I hauled myself out of it, I realized I missed the window when the morning-after pill was most effective." She tipped her face up to a patch of sunlight through the leaves. "I don't know. Sometimes I wonder if, subconsciously, I didn't mind the idea of having a baby. Nurturing another life when one so important had been taken from me."

"Whatever the reason, you've got a child to plan for." He had more questions about that, but he knew it wasn't his place to ask her those things.

It surprised him how very much he wanted to, though. How was she going to manage her work with an infant to care for? After the statue was completed in the children's ward, she still had a commitment to develop a bigger, interactive installation.

Her art involved chisels and saws. Power tools that

make her studio off-limits for a child. She would have
to hire help.

"I do." She nodded, a dark curl blowing against his
shoulder as she shifted on the log beside him. "I'm going
to focus all of my energy on preparing for this baby and
creating a sculpture so beautiful and moving that my
sister would be proud."

Her smile dazzled him, even more so since he could
understand the bittersweet emotion that came with it.
Ruby settled again behind them, her tail wagging slowly
through the pine needles and dried leaves.

"That's a healthy way to express mourning." How
often had his counselor told him he needed more constructive outlets in the early days of battling PTSD? He'd
never found one. But maybe he could make another kind
of positive step. He could share something of his journey
that might help Abigail, even though that kind of thing
was tough for him. "I know that, actually, because I've
never been successful at finding my own. Healthy ex-
pressions of grief, that is."

The admission was awkward. But not as difficult as
he'd imagined. Something about Abigail's presence relaxed him a fraction, taking some of the edge off his
too-sharp emotions.

"I'm sorry, Vaughn." Her hand reached to cover his
where it rested on his thigh. "Did you lose someone
close to you, too?"

Too many.

He mulled over the best way to answer the question
without ripping open his own hard-won control. He focused on a water bug swimming circles in a still patch
of water off to the side of the brook.

"I took a yearlong deployment in Afghanistan with

the army." The simple statement didn't come close to conveying what the experience meant. How deeply it had affected him. Changed him. "I can't claim the same blood ties to the guys lost during that time to the bond you had with your sister. But there's a definite brotherhood with men you spend your rec time with. Guys you share meals with."

Each piece of information hurt to share. As if speaking about that time made him relive it. Which was foolish, since he relived the worst of those times often enough in his mind.

Ruby must have sensed the tension because she left her spot on the ground behind him to sit by his knee, her face lifted to his. She was such a good dog. And he appreciated her helping him hold it together in front of Abigail.

"You don't need blood ties for that connection," Abigail assured him, her fingers threading neatly through his, filling in the empty places. Squeezing. "I'm sorry you lost brothers over there."

She tipped her dark head to his shoulder, and he breathed in the sweet, tangy sent of cinnamon and oranges.

The ache in his chest eased a fraction at the feel of her against him. He closed his eyes for a moment, while dueling songbirds called to one another overhead. He tried to steady himself because he wasn't the one who was supposed to be receiving comfort. He was supposed to be offering it.

"Ruby has been a big help," he admitted, wanting to put the rest of his brokenness on the table for the sake of honesty. Abigail had already battled the disappointment of one man's deception. He wouldn't make the same mistake of hiding the truth about himself. "She's a service dog, and she's trained to give me extra assistance for dealing with PTSD."

"I noticed her collar," Abigail confessed, "but I know it's rude to ask about it."

He smothered a chuckle.

Abigail lifted her head, confusion in her eyes. "What's funny about that?"

"Remember the way we met?" He wanted to touch her again. Stroke her hair. Pull her into his arms. But he knew he needed restraint after what she'd shared. "I was incredibly blunt and tactless. You owe me a rude question or two, Abigail, to even the score. You can ask me anything."

He could tell she wasn't sure how to interpret his shift in conversation. But he couldn't linger in those dark places. It was all he could do to share as much as he had with her today.

"I don't know if I have it in me to be rude. Too much of a good Southern girl." A small smile curved her lips.

She was so lovely. And in spite of everything she'd shared with him today, he still wanted her. He wanted to know how she tasted. What her lips would feel like on his. How the rest of her would fit against him. That was wrong on so many levels, especially given how hard he battled his own demons. He was in no shape to offer Abigail the kind of steady presence she needed in her life right now. But that didn't change the fact that she would be in his dreams tonight.

He wanted to stroke her cheek. Run a thumb along her full lower lip to test the feel of it. To see her eyes widen with awareness.

"Be candid, then. You can ask me brusque, tactless

questions anytime you like." He was joking. Trying to make her smile and doing his damnedest to evade any more conversation about his time as a brigade surgeon.

But something in Abigail's expression made him think she was taking the suggestion seriously.

"I do have something to ask you." She still held his hand, and at some point had moved closer to him, too. Her voice was a soft stroke of breath against his cheek. "Something frank and honest."

His heart thudded harder. He really should let go of her. Show her around the woods the way he'd promised. But she mesmerized him with her sultry dark eyes and her tender heart.

"Just this once, Vaughn, will you kiss me?"

Four

Too stunned to trust his ears, Vaughn waited a breath. A heartbeat. The brook at his feet rushed over rocks, babbling with far more clarity than his thoughts.

"A kiss?" He needed to be sure, as much as it pained him to ask, to risk her denying the words.

For an answer, she raised her free hand to his face, tracing his jaw through the thick scruff of beard that he'd worn since his homecoming. One more barrier between him and the rest of the world.

"It's been a long, long time since I've had a real kiss that wasn't about drowning sorrow and forgetting." She spoke with an earnest sincerity that slid right past his defenses. "I just think it would be nice to have a taste of…what might have been."

He could have resisted his own impulse to taste her, but he damn well couldn't deny her request that made him want to move mountains to make her happy. To please her.

So he lifted up a rusty prayer for restraint as he threaded a hand through her silky hair. He cupped the back of her neck. Drew her toward him. He moved slowly, giving her time to change her mind. She thought it had been a long time for her? He'd bet it had been even longer for him.

And every instant of those achingly lonely months without a woman's touch turned on him now, sending a roaring heat blazing over his skin. Sensual hunger reared up like a ravenous beast. Ruthlessly, he tamped it all down to brush his lips tenderly over hers. Once. Twice.

He breathed her in. Felt her breath catch. He skimmed a touch down the side of her neck while the whole world fell away around them. He wanted to bring her home and kiss her whole body this way. With the sweet reverence she deserved after the year she'd endured. His beautiful warrior.

Except she wasn't his. And she never could be.

Breaking the kiss, he closed his eyes for a moment longer, unwilling to look into hers and see all that he could never have with her. He was too broken to share a life with anyone, let alone a woman who had a child on the way. She deserved so much more than the scraps of himself that he just barely held together.

When he felt her shift away from him, he looked up to see her brush her fingers over her lips, a gesture that made him want to haul her right back into his arms again. He steeled himself against the impulse.

"Should we finish up the walk?" he asked, holding out a hand to help her to her feet. "I think I see a fallen pecan tree over there."

She nodded, already in motion. Perhaps she needed to

get her thoughts together as much as he did. Ruby trotted between them, looking up at him with soulful eyes. Vaughn followed more slowly, knowing he'd never forget the feel of Abigail's lips on his.

Back in her studio that evening, Abigail lifted her safety goggles and stepped away from her project to stare up at the giant tree sculpture she was making for the children's ward. She set down her chisel on a workbench, knowing she was getting ahead of herself with some detail carving down low on the tree when she still had big cuts to make on the top half. She planned to graft branches of varying kinds of wood onto the trunk, creating a tree that was larger than life and represented all trees. In her own mind, she knew it was a multicultural tree. An accepting tree with many outstretched arms.

But she let people see in it what they chose.

She had a long way to go to complete the project and tonight she was still rattled after that kiss and the time spent with Vaughn, unsure what it all meant. She was in dire need of an outlet, and her work usually provided the best kind of distraction.

Unfortunately, not today.

She had been lost in the moment when she'd asked for that kiss, affected by the warmth of the man and the beauty of the surroundings. Heartened by his understanding of a night she would always remember with some sadness mixed in with the miracle of conception. Telling Vaughn had been cathartic. She felt a connection to him that went far beyond their brief acquaintance. Maybe it was because he had experienced devastating loss, too.

Whatever it was that drew her to him, she'd had no

right to ask for that kiss. Her hand dropped to the swell of her belly where her child rested. She was a mother now, and she needed to start thinking like one. She could no longer afford to follow a moment's impulse, no matter how compelling.

The remainder of that walk had been quiet. She'd pointed out a few fallen tree limbs that she wouldn't mind reclaiming, and he'd told her about improvements he'd made to the property over time. Conversation hadn't been tense, exactly, but was definitely more reserved with the memory of that kiss between them.

No doubt, she'd scared him away with her revelation about the baby. Which wasn't necessarily a bad thing given her pregnancy and her need to turn a new page in her life. She was ready to devote her heart and her time to her child.

So why was she still thinking about how Vaughn's fingers had felt, sifting through her hair, stroking lightly down her neck? How his mouth had molded to hers gently, like he was tasting something precious?

Yanking the safety goggles the rest of the way off her head, she got the band snagged in her hair. With a curse, she stepped over to the window so she could see better to untwine the tiny snarl.

Outside, a dark gray pickup truck was backing into her driveway. With the tailgate down, tree limbs spilled from the cargo bed, a red ribbon tied around the longest end, the whole load strapped down and neatly clamped. A dog's nose poked out of the partially open window, as if to catch the scent of new surroundings.

Vaughn and Ruby had arrived.

A ridiculous jolt of excitement chased through Abigail even though she had just finished telling herself to draw boundaries with the sexy doctor. She carefully freed the knot and the safety googles from her hair. Then, setting down the eyewear, she caught herself pausing for a quick glance in the mirror.

Damn it.

Not allowing herself any time for primping, she went straight outside in time to see Vaughn open the door for his dog, leash in hand. Ruby hopped down the running board and onto the ground, wearing her service-dog vest.

"I hope it's not too late for a delivery," Vaughn called, reaching into the truck to retrieve two brown paper bags. "I brought you some dinner for a bribe."

The bags were emblazoned with the logo for the Silver Saddle, the bar and tapas restaurant inside the Bellamy, Royal's new five-star resort. Abigail had never felt like she had the budget to indulge in any of the restaurants on the property, and her taste buds anticipated the treat as much as her rumbling stomach.

What a thoughtful gesture. Her heart squeezed tight to this new evidence of Vaughn's warmth and generosity.

"Since when do you need to bribe women into accepting gifts from you, Dr. Chambers?" she teased, hoping to keep things lighter between them as she stepped toward the truck bed and ran a hand over one of the gnarled pecan-tree branches. "I can't believe you loaded all of this up today. You must have been working since the moment I left your house."

"I didn't mind. It was a good day for a project." He paused as another, smaller pickup truck pulled in behind him, taking up all of Abigail's small driveway. More tree limbs spilled from the second cargo bed. "That's my groundskeeper's sons. They gave me a hand with it."

Overwhelmed at the thoughtfulness of the gesture, Abigail was having a hard time holding on to the boundaries she'd planned to draw. Especially as two grinning young men sprang from the second pickup, asking where to unload the limbs.

"This is Micah and Brandon." Vaughn made the introductions and let Abigail show the men where to lay the pieces, in a covered drying rack she'd built on the side of the house for that purpose.

"Should we give them a hand?" she asked him while the workers began unbuckling the harnesses on the first load.

Ruby stood at Vaughn's feet, watching along with them.

"Nah, we'd only get in their way. Those two are on a mission to earn extra cash for their own landscaping business." Vaughn shook his head with a laugh. "I can't keep them busy enough."

"I'm thrilled," she told him honestly, watching the drying rack begin to fill with pieces of wood for future projects. Regardless of the reservations she had about getting closer to Vaughn, she couldn't deny that he'd gone above and beyond to help her. "The installation at the hospital is really going to exhaust my store of raw materials, so this couldn't have come at a better time."

"My pleasure." His smile, when he chose to wield it, could melt polar ice caps. "And I hope you don't think it was presumptuous of me to bring dinner. Honestly, I was starving by the time we loaded up the trucks, and I figured you might be hungry, too, after all the time we spent outdoors today."

She wondered about that, sensing there might be more to it given the way he'd seemed to retreat after the kiss.

Was this a simple olive branch to start over as friends? Or could that kiss have meant something more to him, too?

"I think it's very kind of you." Abigail hadn't eaten, either. She'd been too busy trying to distract herself from thoughts of the sexy doc by immersing herself in her work. Now, she couldn't help but think how much different her life would be if her baby had been fathered by someone like Vaughn. Someone thoughtful and caring. "After spending the first few months of my pregnancy feeling tired and depleted, my appetite has recently returned with a vengeance."

She figured it couldn't hurt to remind him of her baby, and where her allegiance would remain. She led him and Ruby through the house to the backyard patio, where a tiny flagstone courtyard was surrounded by plants and trees. While Vaughn began unboxing the meal, she retrieved plates and silverware from the house, along with cups and a pitcher of water. On her last trip, she remembered a bowl of water for Ruby and the matches for her outdoor lanterns.

A few minutes later, they sat across from one another at her wrought iron café table, enjoying the wealth of food Vaughn had provided. He'd moved one of her side tables from the porch down to the patio so they had more room. There were containers of bacon-wrapped dates, tiny crab empanadas, bruschetta with goat cheese and tomato, flatbreads with shrimp, crispy wonton chorizo ravioli and potato croquettes.

Vaughn had lit all four of the tiki torches filled with citronella oil to keep the mosquitoes away. The dancing flames combined with the feast made her feel like they were at a Hawaiian luau. She sat back in her seat, admiring the way the sky started to turn pink as the sun sank lower in the sky. The daylight lasted so long in the summer.

"That was fantastic," she declared, sipping her ice-cold water while Ruby sat beside Vaughn's chair.

"You didn't try these yet." Her dining companion passed a tray of more delicacies toward her. Tiny toasted puffs with a red sauce and a leafy green garnish.

"Everything is almost too pretty to eat." She reached for one anyhow, though. "What are they?"

"Cauliflower fritters with caviar." He lifted the water pitcher and refilled both their cups. "What do you think?"

A flutter in her belly made her smile, her hand reaching to cover the spot where she felt the phantom swirl of movement.

"I like it, and so does this baby." With each movement, her pregnancy became more real.

"You can tell?" Vaughn's expression shifted. Guarded, perhaps, but curious, too.

His interest touched her. She hadn't been able to share the joys of this pregnancy with anyone. Her mother made an effort to be excited, but she was still very mired in mourning Alannah, making Abigail less apt to share new developments.

So now, she pulled her chair closer to Vaughn's, wanting to share the wonder of something so miraculous. "May I have your hand?"

He swiped his fingers on a napkin, straightening in his chair before he rested his palm in hers. Abigail flipped it over so his hand faced down, then centered his touch high on her belly.

Warmth flooded her skin through her thin summer sheath dress. His large hand spanned her ribs, one finger trailing all the way to her navel, his thumb on her breastbone. Her mouth dried up, her heart pattering too fast, and he had to feel that. Memories of the kiss returned with new, heated intensity.

She lifted her gaze to his, losing the battle to maintain her defenses, wishing things could be different.

Then, the baby shifted.

A soft quiver of movement beneath his hand made his palm tense. Flex. His eyes went wide with a flicker of emotion.

"That's incredible." The awe in his voice made her remember why she'd wanted to share this with him.

It wasn't about getting closer to him, even though his touch made her feel breathless with awareness. She'd wanted him to feel the baby because that life inside her was special. Healing.

"Isn't it?" She let go of his fingers then, releasing him. "I haven't shared that with anyone." As soon as she said it, she realized how pathetic it sounded. "That is, my mother still lives in Austin and she's still working through her grief. So it's hard for her to be excited."

"I understand." Vaughn eased his hand away, but he rested it on the back of her chair, his fingers grazing her shoulder where the straps of her dress didn't quite cover. "It's only natural to want to celebrate something so profound. And while I'm sorry for your sake that Rich Lowell turned out to be a poor excuse for a man, I'm *not* sorry that his bad decisions gave me the chance to share something special with you."

Abigail held herself very still, knowing she needed to keep a rein on her runaway emotions. Vaughn was dealing with his own struggles—a serious disorder that might make a sufferer detach from all the things Abigail was feeling right now. So drawing him deeper into her world seemed unfair to him. To her. And to her baby.

Yet those wise intentions felt a world away with Vaughn by her side, his knuckle skimming her bare shoulder.

Mesmerized by his words, by the warmth in his green eyes, she couldn't think of a reply.

Just then, a rustle of movement and male laughter on the far side of the bungalow warned them of Vaughn's approaching workers.

"Dr. C." The taller of the pair, Micah, strode into the backyard first, holding up something shiny that glinted in the pink rays of the setting sun. "I wanted to deliver your extra set of truck keys before we take off. The wood is all stacked in the drying rack."

His brother trailed a few steps behind. Vaughn stood, thanking them both. Abigail used the moment to collect her thoughts. Give herself a mental shake. Standing, she began clearing the dishes, dismayed at how quickly sizzling attraction could stamp out good sense.

"I can help with that," Vaughn called, finishing up his conversation with the young men before covering the lawn with long strides so he could hold the back door open for her. Chivalrous. Thoughtful.

He brought Ruby with him to retrieve the rest of the leftovers from their meal and brought them to the door.

"Do you mind if she comes inside with me?" he asked. "I could set up a spot for her in the corner."

"Ruby is absolutely welcome indoors," Abigail assured him, making quick work of putting away the leftovers while Vaughn rinsed off the plates. "It's fun having her around."

She'd welcome a buffer of any sort if she was going

to keep herself from swooning at Vaughn's feet again. Or outright requesting more kisses.

"Thank you." Closing the door behind him, he settled the dog in a quiet spot in the dining room, then began loading the flatware in the dishwasher. "Ruby has been good for me."

He glanced over at her where Ruby made herself comfortable with her head on her paws. Seeing the two of them together today—how bonded they were—made her think it must be difficult for Vaughn to be apart from her for his long hours at the hospital.

"She must miss you while you're working," she observed carefully, testing the waters on the topic. Wanting to know more about him. "I'm sure you put in long hours as a surgeon."

He placed the rest of the dishes inside the washer with the same methodical care before shutting the appliance door.

"The weeks where I'm on call are the toughest since I go in at all hours." He rinsed and dried his hands. Turned to watch her as she wiped down the small island countertop. "Micah and Brandon will take Ruby out if their father is busy with other things, so she's in good hands."

"I'm glad you have extra help. She doesn't go to the hospital?"

"There are plenty of jobs where service dogs are allowed, but ICU is a very different workplace."

"You must miss her, then." Setting aside the sponge, she rinsed her own hands then stood near him, where he leaned against the granite.

Her kitchen had never felt crowded before, but with a tall, sexy doctor beside her, dominating the space, she was all too aware of the tiny square footage.

"Surgery is my job." His jaw flexed, his gaze fixed on a point beyond her shoulder. "It's the one thing I can perform no matter what else is going on around me."

If she'd missed the defensiveness in his voice, she sure would have seen it his tense arms. His rigid shoulders. Ruby must have felt the tension, too, since she rose from her seat to sit beside him, pressing her head against his thigh.

Okay.

Abigail had tested his comfort level regarding the challenges of his work environment, and found that was a do-not-cross line.

"That's another way our jobs are very different." Drying her hands, she retreated to a seat at one of the bar stools at the island. "Some days it feels like all the stars have to be in precise alignment for me to find the inspiration to create."

Rattling off a few of the things that could distract her when she was supposed to be working, Abigail was glad to see Vaughn's shoulders relax by degrees as she spoke. Even Ruby chilled out, going from a sitting position by Vaughn's knee to lying at his feet. Yet perhaps stepping on one of his personal land mines was a constructive reminder for her.

Vaughn Chambers was a magnetic man. Talented. Thoughtful. And charismatic when he wanted to be. But she couldn't allow herself to forget he wrestled demons in his spare time, and they weren't the kind that stepped aside to make room for a wishful heart like hers.

Five

Two nights later, Vaughn finished dictating his shift notes into his phone and sent them to transcription for updating his office files. Seated in a far corner of the nurses' station, he tuned out the noise around him. He'd already done rounds with the next critical-care team on duty, but inevitably he found a few additional thoughts cropping up before he left the hospital for the day. His knife-fight victim was recovering nicely, with no major organ involvement. There would be therapy for a sliced knee tendon and, later, elective surgery to repair a torn labrum in the right shoulder, a result of his attacker pinning his arm behind him. All things considered, the guy was damn lucky.

Vaughn, too. He hadn't lost a patient since returning from Afghanistan and wanted to keep it that way.

What he *hadn't* wanted was to advertise his emotional shortcomings to Abigail when he'd gone over to her studio the other night. He'd planned to end their day together on a high note by bringing her the raw materials from his ranch—and some dinner, too. Their kiss had played out so many times in his memory that he found himself wanting more even though everything in him warned that being with her was going to be complicated.

So he'd gone over there and tried to keep things light. Romantic, even.

It had been working, too. Conversation flowed easily through a meal she clearly enjoyed. He'd been relaxed and having a good time, too. Had sensed another kiss was imminent.

Then things took a downward turn when she asked about Ruby and his job. He hadn't shared the PTSD diagnosis with many people—period. So he hadn't developed an ease with talking about it, which must have come across in his surly response.

"Dr. Chambers, you're just the man I wanted to see," a deep male voice greeted him, hauling Vaughn out of his thoughts.

Troy "Hutch" Hutchinson was a maternal-fetal specialist and a good friend. The guy was not only a gifted doctor, but also a generous one, donating time to Doctors Without Borders for a long stint in Africa.

Vaughn shoved out of the rolling chair at the nurses' station, clapping Hutch on the back. "Did you have time to look at the patient in 2C?"

He'd had a seventeen-year-old accident victim transferred from a rural hospital late in his shift. She hadn't required surgery, but her condition was critical, especially because of an early stage pregnancy.

"I just checked on your car-accident victim and her baby looks good." He laid a file folder on the nurses' station counter and helped himself to an apple from a gift fruit bowl delivered to the unit earlier in the day. "You up for tennis one of these days?"

Vaughn hadn't played in months, but he'd spoken to Hutch a few times about getting together to hit. The other man lived in Pine Valley, but he belonged to the Texas Cattleman's Club, too, so using the courts there presented no problem. Which brought to mind another question he had for his friend.

"I'm free all the time. *You're* the one with triplets." Vaughn remembered how happy the guy was when his wife, Simone, gave birth to three healthy babies.

"Right. And my serve is going to be rusty after devoting months to baby-rocking." He grinned between bites of apple. "Not that I'd trade the dad duty for anything. But if I don't stay in shape, I'm not going to be able to keep up when they start walking."

Vaughn wasn't so sure about that. Hutch was a gifted athlete at every sport and a prized teammate at any sports-related hospital charity event. But he wasn't going to argue. Vaughn needed to make an effort to reconnect with the world, as witnessed by his ineptitude making conversation with Abigail.

"Good point. Name the time and I'll be there." Pocketing his phone, Vaughn waved his colleague farther down the hall, away from beeping monitors and nurses buzzing in and out of the floor's hub. "I have a quick question for you first, if you have a minute."

"Sure thing." Hutch walked with him, tossing his apple core in a basket on the way.

They stopped by the window overlooking the top floor of the parking garage. The lights were on since it was after 9:00 p.m. and one car drew his eye in the mostly empty lot.

Abigail's compact vehicle was parked under one of the streetlamps. He recognized the vehicle from the magnet on one side, advertising her artwork. The knowledge that she was here, working late, sent a surge of longing through him. He wanted to see her.

Needed to see her.

"Hutch, I wasn't sure who else to ask about this…" Vaughn had put in a call to Will Sanders, hoping to learn more about possible danger to Abigail from the man who impersonated him. "But I've struck up a friendship with a woman who was involved with Will Sanders's imposter this winter."

"Rich Lowell." Hutch's lip curled, his disdain obvious.

"That's the name I heard, too. Is that confirmed?" Vaughn hadn't gleaned much from Abigail the day he'd learned about her pregnancy, and he wanted to be sure she was safe. "Rich and Will used to be good friends."

"So I hear." Hutch leaned a shoulder against the window. He hadn't grown up in Royal, yet these days, he had a far better grasp on what was happening in town than Vaughn did. "But the police warned the TCC board to take extra precautions with any files Will had access to in the past year, including member profiles and sensitive data. Rich had access to everything."

"Do the police think he's still in the area?" Vaughn's gaze dropped to that solitary vehicle under the streetlamp again.

The nearest car was at least fifty yards away.

"They aren't ruling anything out. The FBI did DNA testing on the ashes that Jason Phillips shipped back after the plane crash that supposedly belonged to Will, and they definitely don't belong to Rich Lowell."

So Rich was alive. And a wanted felon.

"The guy could be dangerous." Vaughn's gut churned at the thought of Abigail being vulnerable to a man like that. He swore softly.

"I'm sure police have warned her to be careful. They've spoken to everyone who was close to the imposter." Hutch straightened from where he leaned against the window, his phone vibrating in his pocket. "And I hear Will is hiring a private detective to do some work on the case, too. Make sure nothing gets overlooked."

Hutch checked his message while Vaughn plotted the fastest path to the children's ward. He had to check on Abigail. An artist living alone in a downtown bungalow didn't have the resources that someone like Will did. She couldn't hire her own investigator or a bodyguard.

"Thanks for the update." Vaughn backed away, thinking the stairs were quickest. "And I'm not letting you off the hook for tennis."

Hutch grinned as he pocketed his phone. "You think I'm beatable after a few months away from my game?"

"No one's reign lasts forever." He levered open the door to the stairwell and headed down a flight to the children's ward, where Abigail must still be working.

He hadn't wanted to push for more with her when his head was wrecked and she was expecting another man's child. She had a lot on her plate, and so did he. But if she was in danger, all bets were off.

He would make damn sure he was there to keep her safe.

The tree needed more branches.

Abigail could appreciate that now that she saw the

tree sculpture in its new home in the Royal Memorial Hospital children's ward. Art took on a different appearance according to the surroundings—the light, the space, the colors nearby. And after paying a professional mover to relocate her half-finished piece this afternoon, she could see that she had more work left to do than she had imagined.

She didn't mind the extra effort. This project meant so much to her that she wanted it to be perfect. Abigail liked the idea of a tree with deep roots and extensive branches that reached out to draw in visitors. A place of comfort and reflection.

What Abigail *did* mind was the added expense of paying a mover to transport more raw materials to the hospital. If she'd been thinking ahead, she could have saved herself some money by incorporating everything she needed into one trip. Considering how long that commission check needed to last her, it was essential to start making smarter decisions to spend wisely.

She took out a pen and paper from her purse to write notes about which pieces would fit the sculpture best to add new branches to the tree. Then, lowering herself to the work platform she'd installed around the base of the tree, she tucked a foot beneath her and started a list.

The lounge was quiet tonight, making it easy to concentrate. When the sculpture was finished, the lounge would extend to the area around her tree, but for now, the hospital building crew had roped off her job site. It didn't stop interested people from hopping over to take a peek or offer a compliment, but it wasn't as though she had to work with many people around her.

By tomorrow, there would be plastic sheeting hung

up all around the sculpture so she could use her electric tools. For now, she scribbled.

She was so lost in thought, imagining a pattern of wood pieces grafted to the central trunk, that she never heard footsteps approach. She startled when a man's voice intruded on her note-taking.

"It's awfully late for you to be here." Vaughn stood close to the platform, dressed in street clothes—khaki-colored pants and a white button-down with a neck-tie that could have been a postmodern painting. A few splashes of color on a black field.

Her heart warmed to see him in spite of all her stern warnings to keep her distance. The tone of his voice skimmed her senses like a caress, hitting all the right places and making her think about kissing him again. It wasn't fair to feel so physically aware of him when she knew he might not be in a position for a relationship, battling his PTSD issues so hard. But she hadn't even opened her mouth to speak and she was already tingling with sensual want.

"I had to move the tree trunk into place today so I can do more of the carving on site." She shuffled aside her notebook and pen. "There comes a point in the pro-cess where it becomes risky to move the statue if I've already done a lot of detail work."

"I could have helped you." He stared up at the trunk and the preliminary branches—mostly raw, uncarved wood in bay laurel to match the trunk. "How did you get it all over here?" He lowered his voice for her ears alone. "You need to be careful while you're pregnant."

"I am. I hired a moving company." She ran her hand up one side of the tree where she'd done a little craving today, notching out some thick bark for texture. Better to touch the tree than the man who tempted her. "And I would have hired your groundskeeper's sons since they were so helpful with stacking the new wood, but I booked the movers the day I got the commission."

"It looks great." He pointed to a carved creature already hiding inside a hollow. "I really like the barn owl."

She flushed with pleasure at the compliment. "Thank you. I hope to add quite a few birds." Her birds were popular in the local antiques-and-crafts store, Priceless, where she sold a few of her works. "Although I'm not sure how many I will finish before the summer gala since I've realized I want the scale to be bigger."

"It's already huge." Vaughn stepped up on the platform and stretched his arms around the trunk as far as they would go. Less than half way around. "Are you sure?"

"Definitely." She flipped her notepad up to him so he could see what she'd drawn. "I started making a list of what I want to bring over here, but I ended up making a sketch of the revised branch scheme."

"I like it." He nodded, peering up from the sketch to the sculpture in progress. "But how will you notch in all those new branches?"

"That part will be time-consuming," she admitted. "And since it involves technical craftsmanship as opposed to artistry that will show in the final product, it's the kind of thing I could hire out if I knew someone skilled in carving."

Like furniture making, grafting on the branches involved making seamless joints. Fitting pegs into perfectly cut slots.

"I'll find someone who can help you." He shifted to sit down beside her on the platform.

His knee brushed hers, the touch sending ripples of awareness along her skin far beyond the point of contact. She'd worn a T-shirt with the simple cotton A-line skirt, a good uniform for a job site since it was comfortable enough while still appearing professional. The lightweight cotton wasn't much of a barrier for her leg next to his strong thigh. Her throat dried up and she took an extra moment to steel herself against the feel of him.

"That's all right, Vaughn. I told the art committee that I could finish this project in the allotted time frame, and I will. It just means a few more late nights." Possibly it meant seeing the handsome doctor a few more times, too.

What woman didn't enjoy being around a man who made her heart beat faster? Even if he should be off-limits?

"I want to talk to you about that." His voice was quiet again. Serious. "Have the police spoken to you about taking extra precautions now that they believe Rich Lowell is still alive?"

She hadn't expected this line of conversation at all. And although she'd been warned to keep the details of the investigation quiet, she guessed Vaughn probably knew more about it than her, considering his TCC connections.

Following his lead, she kept her voice quiet as well, needing to keep the conversation confidential. There was one young couple in the waiting lounge nearby. The woman read a book while the husband snoozed on her shoulder.

"I got a call from a federal agent last week." She hadn't known what to make of it at the time. Because as much as she resented Will Sanders's impersonator, she was unclear how much of a threat he posed to her and the rest of Royal. Yes, he was a horrible person, but she wasn't sure if he was outright dangerous to her. "She told me the remains delivered for Will Sanders's funeral did not match Rich's DNA and that investigators had every reason to believe he was alive."

"I heard." Vaughn's green eyes locked on hers, his expression grim. "Didn't she tell you to be more careful? What if he tries to contact you?"

At the time of the phone call, Abigail had just read a letter from her mortgage company threatening to start foreclosure proceedings if she missed another month's payment, so she may not have been as focused as she should have been.

Her life was so far from where she wanted it to be for her child. Guilt nipped. She touched her expanding belly, the smooth curve of new life more evident when she was seated.

"The agent told me not to reach out to him. And asked again if I had any idea of his whereabouts." She shook her head, remembering all the times she'd been asked that same question. How sad for her child's sake that the man she'd been involved with was on the run from the authorities, a completely inappropriate choice for a partner that would follow her forever. "I told her absolutely not and that I wouldn't try to contact him again if I did."

"But you're carrying his child." His hand went to her knee. A gesture of emphasis, perhaps.

Yet the warmth of his palm lying lightly on her thigh sent a shiver of pleasure through her.

"He doesn't know that."

Vaughn's eyebrows lifted, his hand sliding away. "You never told him?"

Her skin still felt warm where his hand had been.

"He was hardly in town this spring." She had felt guilty about her lack of communication at first. But once she'd discovered how deep his deception went, she was actually relieved. "Earlier this year, he was flying back and forth to Ireland. Then he was out of the country on business. Finally, I went to the main house once to try to speak to him."

Overhead on the PA system, a doctor was paged, the announcement blaring into their corner of the hospital, which was otherwise so quiet.

"When was that?" Vaughn asked when the speaker went quiet again.

She thought back. "The first week of May, maybe?" So much had happened in the last few months. "It was probably a week before the plane crash. Maybe a little less."

"And Rich wasn't at the Ace in the Hole that day?"

"I have a hard time thinking of him as Rich." She had never even met Richard Lowell, as himself—he was a man others in Royal knew well enough for his friendship with Will. "Don't forget, I thought Rich was dead in a boating accident and that Will had moved on after losing his closest friend." Her chest hurt remembering their conversation about that. "He told me about that accident on the night—on Alannah's birthday. When I was falling apart and feeling vulnerable. He made me feel like we were kindred souls, mourning people we loved."

Bitterness gave the words a bad taste. The more that came to light about Rich Lowell's deceptions, the more she realized how thoroughly she'd been played. He had taken advantage of her grief, maneuvering her right where he wanted her.

And she'd been too caught up in her own loss to notice. "The bastard."

Vaughn's quiet assessment of the situation mirrored her own.

"My thought exactly. But on that day, when I went to the main house on the ranch to confront him, he was there." She had been prepared to bargain for full custody. Offer to move out of town even, if that would help Will, since he'd never left his wife even though he'd told her that he and Megan were separated. Abigail had hoped he would want nothing to do with the baby. "I went in the back way, toward the office where I had done temp work. The desk and room where I used to work was empty, but I could hear arguing in Will's—er, Rich's—private office."

"Do you think it was Rich's voice?" Vaughn's hand shifted to rest lightly between her shoulder blades.

She realized then how wrong her first impression of him had been. That he was an arrogant. Brash and blunt. Since that first meeting he demonstrated a tenderness and empathy for her that made her understand what made him a good doctor. His patients must feel well cared for.

"I know it was Rich because I peeked inside the office door. It was open a crack." She'd been startled by what she saw. A very different side of the man who'd been her boss for two months. "Just as I reached the door, to see who he was arguing with, there was a thumping noise. Like a shove or a punch. And when I looked inside, Rich was fighting with Jason Phillips."

Vaughn swore. "Jason Phillips? The same man who sent the urn back with Will's remains, only they weren't Will's remains."

Jason, like Will, was also a member of the Texas Cattleman's Club. He was a key player at Will's energy company, Spark Energy Solutions, although Abigail didn't
remember his exact role. He lived part-time in Dallas
and part-time in Royal. She'd never heard him speak an
angry word before that day she'd seen him fighting with
the man who was impersonating Will.

"Is Jason a suspect in stealing from Will? Or do they
think he knew that Rich Lowell was a fake?"

A cleaning crew rolled a cart past the lounge, mops
and cleaners rattling as they steered their supplies over
a threshold. The two women pushing it were having a
rapid disagreement about whose turn it was to use the
floor-polishing machine. The argument faded along with
the clacking of the cart's wheels.

Vaughn tracked their progress, waiting until it was
quiet again before he answered. "I've heard Jason is
away on international business and can't be reached.
He could be Rich's accomplice. He could have double-
crossed him. Or he could have been completely innocent and his only crime was figuring out that Rich was
a thief. But I think it's clear you walked in on a very
dangerous situation that day."

At the time, she simply didn't want to be around men
who were fighting. She didn't want her baby around vio-
lence, either. But maybe she'd escaped something much
worse. A new wariness crept over her, making her grateful for Vaughn coming here tonight. For checking on her.

A chill had taken hold of her while they spoke. And
the only place that felt warm was the spot where Vaughn
touched. His hand still rested between her shoulders, as
he continued to rub lightly.

Unable to resist the comfort he offered, she tipped

her head onto his shoulder. Allowed herself to soak in the feel of his arm tightening around her, hugging her close. For the moment, she felt safe. Protected.

"I don't think Rich Lowell would come after me." She would be more careful anyhow, of course. "He doesn't know I'm carrying his child, and he would be wise to stay far away from Royal with everyone looking for him." If he'd stolen as much money from the real Will as she'd heard, he would be able to start a new life somewhere far, far away.

Vaughn turned more fully toward her, taking her shoulders in his hands so he could look into her eyes. "He might not come for his child, Abigail. But what if he knows you saw him fighting with Jason? What if you saw or heard something significant that day without realizing it?"

Fear sank deep inside her. She swayed slightly, and Vaughn reached to steady her. "But I didn't hear anything specific. I don't know what they were arguing about. I just recognized angry voices."

"I believe you, honey. And I'm not trying to frighten you. But I can't stress enough how important it is for you to be careful." He smoothed a path down her shoulders to her upper arms. "Have Security walk you out to your car at night. Install an alarm system at home and make sure you use it. But most of all, we need to call the police and let them know you saw Rich and Jason fighting."

Her mind whirled. Of course, he was right about all of those things. She wasn't just protecting herself. She needed to make sure her child was safe. And for that reason, she would part with the extra money for an alarm system, even though it would put a bigger dent in that commission check.

"I will." Nodding, she tried not to feel overwhelmed. But her plate had been full before with a baby on the way and a massive art project to complete. Now, installing a new system would take time. And how could she compare prices when she felt like she needed protection right now? "I can stop by the station tonight on the way home."

She could cross that much off her list anyhow, even though she was bone-weary.

"It's already late. You must be exhausted." He studied her for a long moment.

She could tell he was thinking. And how funny that she'd known him for such a short time and already she understood things like that about him.

"It's not a problem. If I had any idea that what I'd seen was significant, I would have reported it already." Shoving her notepad and drawings in her purse, she prepared to leave the hospital. "I'd better get underway, though. I want to be here early tomorrow to put in a full day's work."

"May I make a suggestion?" He waited for her nod. "I don't want to impose, but I'm happy to help."

He drew a breath, ready to roll out some kind of plan, but she shook her head.

"No. You've already done so much to help me. Just giving me this commission in the first place—"

"I didn't do that for you. That was your talent. You were the committee's first choice."

She wondered if that carefully worded answer meant that he hadn't voted for her project. Not that it mattered. She'd gotten the job that meant everything to her. "Then you helped me by giving me access to your ranch and delivering all those tree limbs that will fuel my art for a long time to come."

Sliding off the work platform she'd built around her sculpture, she hopped to her feet. Searched in her bag for her keys.

"My landscaper would have only created a burn pile with them otherwise. Giving them to you saves us the trouble." He stood with her, stilling her hands before she could tug her keys from her purse. "Abigail, there are four empty bedrooms at my ranch. Sleep there tonight where you have Ruby and me to watch over you. Then, we can have a squad car come out tomorrow to talk to you there. You'll get a good night's rest and then can give a statement in the morning."

Vaughn's hands held hers. Their gazes locked. Her throat went dry.

"Sleep…at your place?" Her voice scratched over the words a little, the invitation making her think all the wrong things.

All the things she'd been trying not to picture happening between her and the most appealing man she'd ever met.

"Sleep," he repeated, voice firm. "Trust me, I understand how the last guy you were with took advantage. I would never hurt you that way, swooping in to capitalize on a vulnerable moment."

Oh. She nodded stiffly, thinking it was probably a very sound plan. A wise idea. Good, rational thinking to help a pregnant woman get her rest and keep her safe.

"Thank you. If you don't mind, I will take you up on that." She liked the idea of having Vaughn by her side when she gave her statement to the police. For his friendship. His support. And yes, the tender concern he'd showed her. She couldn't deny that he was coming to mean a great deal to her.

"Good. I can drive you there." He checked his watch. "I'll have to be to work early in the morning, too, so we can ride in together." He walked her out to her car, stopping there just long enough so she could get a few of her things and lock it up again for the night.

And then he was on the phone with the Royal police—a call to someone on the force he went to school with, apparently—and arranged for an officer to come out in the morning. It was all helpful and logical. Kind and thoughtful.

Yet, as she slid into the passenger seat of the sexy sports car he used for work, Abigail couldn't help but wish that Vaughn didn't feel the need to be quite so honorable where she was concerned. She wasn't all that vulnerable, damn it.

If she wanted something more to happen between them, she was definitely in full command of her senses to make the decision. Not like that awful night back in February.

No one was taking advantage of her again.

A part of her wanted to plot a way to kiss him senseless as soon as they walked into his house. But the part of her that was five months pregnant reminded her she needed to think like a mother and not a woman with a fierce hunger for the man in the driver's seat.

Just sleep? She feared she was going to be too hot and bothered to even close her eyes.

Six

Vaughn wasn't the only one excited to have a visitor.

Ruby greeted Abigail with the full-on joy of the dog's off-duty personality. A happy, panting, tail-wagging, follow-Abigail-everywhere welcome. As grateful as Vaughn was for the service animal's training, he liked seeing the golden retriever simply enjoy their guest while he helped her settle into a downstairs bedroom. Abigail, for her part, seemed equally charmed. She had laughed with delight to see one of Ruby's unsung skills on display as the dog helped her "unpack." Abigail had brought a gym bag that she'd retrieved from her own car, a duffel she kept with clean clothes, a towel and toiletries.

When Ruby sat at Abigail's feet as she opened the bag, Vaughn mentioned Ruby's unique gift. Only when Abigail clamored to see did he give Ruby the command to unpack, and the dog carefully gripped the toiletry bag in her teeth, carrying it to a drawer Vaughn had opened for her. One by one, Ruby transplanted all the items in the duffle.

"She's amazing," Abigail proclaimed while Vaughn rewarded her with a treat and released her to play.

Even then, Ruby didn't venture far, wandering in and out of the suite while Vaughn double-checked that the room and attached bath had fresh towels and linens. Did the dog sense he needed a chaperone? He'd given Abigail his word that his offer for her to stay here was just to help her and keep her safe at a juncture in her life that had to be incredibly challenging. So, of course, Vaughn wasn't going to let himself linger in this room with her for long. He would keep his word. But he wouldn't court temptation, either.

The room he'd given her was spacious, with three walls painted in a soft tan, while the wall behind the dark wood headboard was lined with reclaimed planks, like an old barn. A giant pair of steer horns had been mounted above the bed.

"Can I get you anything else?" he asked after assuring himself she had clean towels. He stalked back into the bedroom, where she sat on the black painted chest at the end of the sleigh bed.

A stack of extra blankets rested beside her, not that she'd need them in July, but he'd wanted to make sure she was comfortable. She'd kicked off the pink tennis shoes she had worn with her gray floral skirt and T-shirt, the pink canvas a feminine touch in a room otherwise full of heavy, dark woods and Aztec-themed patterns in the rugs, pillows and prints on the wall.

"You've already been so generous." Abigail stroked

Ruby's silky ears while the dog rested her head on the chest beside their guest.

"A bottle of water? A snack before bed?" He knew he should let her sleep, but he also wouldn't deny a pregnant woman sustenance. "I didn't have much time for dinner, so I'm going to make something for myself."

Pulling her attention from his adoring dog, Abigail met his gaze slowly. There was something different in her expression. A determination, maybe. Or certainty.

"I'm hungry, too." She tilted her chin up as she came to her feet. Her skirt settled around her knees in a swirl of cotton knit. "Just not that kind of hungry."

He stilled. His heartbeat stuttered as his brain tried to take in the words and what they meant. Behind her, Ruby curled at the end of the chest. Content.

Clearly, his dog wasn't worried about whatever was happening here. But Vaughn wasn't so sure about himself.

"I brought you here to make life easier for you," he reminded her, remembering what she'd been through with Rich Lowell. "I don't want to take advantage of you on a day when you've had a scare. When the world is off-kilter."

He wanted to place his hands on her as she stepped closer to him. Comfort and reassure her. But with the sultry look in her eyes, he didn't fully trust himself. The heat that had been simmering between them threatened to bubble over at the least provocation.

"My world is not off-kilter." She halted just inches away from him in the center of the room, under the ceiling fan that spun silently on a low setting, the air teasing through her dark curls. She lifted both hands to his chest and placed them there. "I wanted to be here tonight, not just to be safe from the past. But maybe to erase some of it, too."

Her fingers stroked along his shirt, smoothing either side of the placket. The citrus-and-spice scent of her fragrance teased his nose. Memories of her taste threatened to level all his good intentions.

Heat rushed up his spine.

"Abigail." He held her shoulders, needing to keep her still another moment while he wrapped his brain around this. "I like you. Too damn much. I would never want you to regret this."

"The last time for me was so emotionally painful," she confided, her dark eyes wide. Sincere. "I was vulnerable and weak. Now, I'm sure of myself. And I understand this isn't necessarily going to lead to anything. I know you aren't ready for a relationship. I just—" She shook her head, brow furrowed.

"What?" His voice was ragged with need, but he tipped his chin up to see her more clearly. Wanting to understand.

"I want a beautiful memory to replace an unhappy one."

The certainty in her voice broke through his last restraint.

He wanted her more than he could remember ever wanting a woman before. She understood he couldn't offer forever. But he could damn well give her this.

"Then I'm going to make that happen, Abigail." He skimmed a touch around her waist, his hands aching for a better feel of her. "Tonight, we're going to torch those old memories for good."

Breathless, Abigail was glad Vaughn held on to her because her knees went liquid at his promise.

She'd made her desire plain. Taken control of her wants. And this incredibly sexy man pledged to deliver all of it. She shivered with longing as his hands spanned her hips, pulling her to him.

He felt strong. Immovable. His body was a testament to physical training. Yet he'd been so tender with his kiss in the woods. So thoughtful with her tonight.

Now, she wanted all that delicious male muscle around her. Enveloping her. Holding her. She arched up on her toes and kissed him, the scruff of beard a gentle abrasion to her chin and cheeks, depending how she shifted against him. For a moment, she breathed him in. The scent of woodsy soap and musky man, the sensual glide of his tongue along her lower lip.

Teasing, tempting, tasting.

Then, the kiss went a little wild. A groan of hunger from him. A sigh of pleasure from her. Fingers combing through his thick hair, she couldn't feel enough of him. She kissed a path along his cheek and his jaw, her body melting everywhere he touched her. Her dress felt paper-thin, the heat of his body setting hers aflame.

He walked them backward toward the bed, falling with her onto the king-size mattress, taking her weight so she settled gently into the soft red duvet printed with a gray-and-white Aztec design.

"Are you okay?" Vaughn asked, a soft whisper in her ear. "I want to be careful with you."

His teeth nipped the tender lobe, sending a quiver down her spine. Her hair spilled all around them, some of the curls still clinging to his shoulders as he angled back to unfasten her skirt.

"I'm perfect." She reached to work on the buttons on

his shirt, wanting to feel his skin without any barrier. "I want more. I want to see you."

His green eyes tracked hers, thoughtfully assessing. Or maybe seeing how serious she was about that.

"That feeling is mutual." He raised up on his elbow, then all the way to a sitting position. "But since tonight is all about you, I'll go first."

"Slowly," she blurted. Because she was having such an incredible track record with getting what she wanted tonight she might as well go for broke.

A darkly masculine smile made her feel faint with yearning. But he unfastened one button after another. Taking his time. "I like this sensual streak I'm beginning to see."

She tugged a pillow under her head to make herself more comfortable, watching his talented hands work. "I'm an artist, remember? I have a fondness for appealing lines and angles."

Stripping off his dress shirt, he wore a fitted white tank beneath it. He reached behind him to tug that over his head, tossing both onto the chest at the foot of the sleigh bed.

Vaughn clothed was a sight to behold.

Vaughn with no shirt was a vision of athletic male grace. Tattoos swirled and danced on his collarbone and chest. Tribal art in black work, she thought at first. But as she looked closer there were names inked into those graphic swirls. Dates.

Her heart squeezed in recognition. Understanding.

He was covered with a vibrant pattern of losses.

She didn't need to ask to know. Shifting to her knees, she leaned closer to kiss the places where Vaughn had etched a memorial to patients, maybe, and to the brothers lost in Afghanistan.

Too many.

For a moment, he allowed the gentle tribute of her lips on his skin, combing his fingers through her tousled hair. But then he edged away to meet her gaze.

"Do I get to see you now?" His hands bracketed her hips, thumbs retreating just a little way under the hem of her T-shirt, where he touched bare skin.

He sought to redirect her, she thought, unwilling to share stories about those names on his body. She understood about sharing loss in small doses. Understood how much it could hurt.

So she let him set the pace where his past was concern. Instead, she focused on his thumbs grazing her expanding waist, his touch causing delicious shivers. Pleasure coursed through her veins, thick and hot.

With it, however, came a hint of reservation.

"My body isn't the stuff of male fantasy these days," she reminded him, sinking back on her heels a bit.

"You, of all people, must know how thoroughly pregnant bodies have captivated the artistic imagination for centuries." He molded his hands to her body under her shirt, feeling the curve of her stomach and hips. "A woman is never more beautiful than when she's carrying a new life inside her."

Her throat burned a little at his sweet words. And gave her the courage to strip off her gray T-shirt, revealing her pink satin bra, a splurge she'd made with the commission check to accommodate her newly generous breasts.

"Slowly," he reminded her, his gaze fixed on her body, his voice rougher than it was a moment before. "I have a fondness for curves."

A smile pulled at her lips. She raised up on her knees again, confidence renewed. She flicked open the clasp on the bra, letting the cups part so she could shrug off the straps.

"So beautiful." The whispered reverence inflamed her skin just before he kissed one tight peak. Chased a circle around the center with his tongue.

Her body ached for him with a new, heightened need. Heat pooled between her thighs and she pressed herself tighter to him, wanting more.

She let her hands roam all over him, tracing the ridges of muscle and exploring the dips and hollows that came with them. She felt the hiss of breath between his teeth as he switched from one breast to the other, drawing on her harder, taking her fully into his mouth.

Allowing her hands to wander lower, she skimmed the intriguing planes of his abs before she ran into his belt. With impatient fingers, she made quick work of the buckle, the hook, the zipper.

And stroked a touch up the proud, thrusting length of him.

The guttural sound he made echoed the rough want she was feeling. She needed him inside her. Moving with her. Filling her.

But he clamped her hand in his, halting her touch before she peeled away his boxers.

"It's been a long time for me." His green eyes were stark with need. A sheen of sweat glistened on his forehead that hadn't been there a moment ago.

She kissed his cheek. Licked along his lower lip. "Me, too."

"Give me a minute." He slid off the bed and stepped out his clothes, leaving him gloriously naked.

With all the lights on in her room, she could see every perfect inch of him as he retreated into another room, returning a few moments later with a condom in hand.

At least, she thought that's what he flashed at her when he entered the room, but she was still plenty distracted by the sight of him naked. Never taking her eyes off him, she stood to let her undone skirt fall on the ground. Then, tucking her thumbs in the waistband of her pink satin bikini underwear, she lowered those, too.

"You are the prettiest thing I've ever seen, Abigail." He left the condom on the bed and cupped the back of her neck, hauling her close to kiss her. Then lowered her ever so gently to the bed.

He stretched out on top of her, the warm brush of hair on his leg a tickle against her smooth one. Her breasts molded to his chest. His erection a hot, silken weight pressing between her thighs.

He kissed her then, and things got serious. Awed. Humbled. Reverent. Wordlessly, she rolled on top of him, wanting to see him better. Needing to take ownership of this moment. This incredible night.

His thigh parted hers, a welcome pressure and heat to fill the ache that grew worse by the second. She fumbled with the condom, ready for everything.

She whispered his name, needing him now. He took the packet and finished opening it, sheathing himself while she kissed his chest. Lower.

"Abby." He breathed the nickname into her hair as he hauled her up his body again.

Then he came inside her, inch by inch, until her eyes fluttered closed against the bliss of it. She felt the slick perfection of it all the way to her toes. Her head lolled forward, resting on his chest for a long moment until she gathered herself. Moved her hips.

His groan of satisfaction spread through her, vibrating inside her. This time, when he rolled her to her back, she let him, ready to relinquish that control since hers was ready to shatter. She was close to release, and they'd only just started, her body starved for all that he could do to her. For her. With her.

She knew once with Vaughn would never be enough.

Meeting his green gaze, she watched him moving over her. Mesmerized.

Once, he leaned down to whisper her name in her ear, reaching between their bodies to pluck gently at the tender core of her. She flew apart instantly, wave after wave of pleasure breaking over her, drowning her in the sweetest release.

In the middle of it, she opened her eyes just enough to see him watching her. She found just enough wherewithal to lift her hips, taking him deeper. And in that moment, his body tensed. Spasmed. His own completion rocked him as every muscle went rigid.

They held each other for long moments afterward. At some point, he'd pulled one of the spare blankets over them while the overhead fan turned lazily above. At the foot of the bed, Ruby still snoozed, the occasional dog snuffle and sigh a reminder of her presence.

Abigail felt a beautiful languidness in her limbs. She lay her head on Vaughn's chest after they'd disentangled themselves. She hoped he wouldn't regret this night together. She understood he wasn't ready for a relationship.

Knew that he struggled to make emotional connections because of the disorder he battled. Of course it would be daunting for him to be involved right now.

And yet, a little part of her couldn't help thinking they'd taken a step forward together in spite of everything. He'd admitted he hadn't been with anyone else in a long time, making her think this had been special for him, too.

As exhaustion pulled her toward sleep after an eventful day, Abigail told herself not to read too much into what had just happened. She had only just begun to truly heal from her sister's death. From the devastation of learning her baby's father was an imposter, a thief and a possible threat to her.

She couldn't afford another hit this year.

Where Vaughn was concerned, hope might be a dangerous emotion.

Seven

Vaughn lay awake in the spare bedroom beside Abigail well past midnight, hating to leave her side too soon after the way the father of her child had checked out on her.

He liked being here, brushing touches over her hair while she slept. Seeing a hint of a smile curve her lips, welcoming his touch.

But falling asleep beside her meant the possibility of nightmares, and he didn't want to freak her out if that happened. Granted, the nightmares had decreased since Ruby came along. The dog was aces when it came to sensing trouble at night. She nuzzled his arm or his face, whimpering until he awoke. She usually alerted him before things took a turn for the terrifying. But if Ruby knew to rouse him, that was because he was already making noise or starting to wrestle the blankets. He'd disturb Abigail for sure.

So he laid there, contemplating his next move.

Sex had been amazing. Far more than a simple release, their time together had rocked him. He hadn't expected to be so thoroughly captivated by her. Or touched by the fact that she'd chosen him to help her erase her demons. That alone had been an unanticipated gift.

As for all the rest? He was still blown away hours later.

Tomorrow, he would stay by her side while she gave a statement to the police. He planned to place another call to Will Sanders to give the guy an update since—if their roles were reversed—Vaughn sure as hell would want to know about Rich fighting with Jason Phillips in his office. The information had to be significant.

And the more he thought about it, bad news for Jason. The last guy to get on the wrong side of Rich was Will himself. Will had paid for that by having his identity—and months of his life—stolen from him. Considering no one could reach Jason to speak with him personally, that didn't bode well for him.

Vaughn also wanted to find some skilled help for Abigail to work on the sculpture so she didn't exhaust herself during her pregnancy. He'd already asked Micah to meet them at her place in the morning. Abigail wanted to stop by her house before they continued to the hospital, and Vaughn figured Micah could either use the pickup to haul her extra wood pieces to the hospital, or he could help dig the ditch around her house to facilitate the alarm system she needed.

Actually, now that he thought about it, Micah better bring Brandon with him to get everything done. Vaughn scheduled a text to hit their phones tomorrow morning at six so they could plan their workday accordingly.

But if he wanted any sleep tonight for a full day ahead, he needed to retreat to his own room, behind a closed door. Sliding out of bed, Vaughn figured he would simply set an alarm to wake early and start breakfast. Maybe Abigail would never notice he'd left her side.

Calling softly to Ruby, he headed toward the door. He wasn't going to scare a pregnant woman with the hell that played out behind his closed eyes on a nightly basis. Which already had him wondering, how long would she be content to spend time with a shell of a man who had so little of himself to give?

After she'd given a statement to police the next morning, Abigail rode in the passenger seat of Vaughn's truck on the way to the hospital.

They were stopping at her house first, to pick up a few extra tools she needed and so she could change into something more work appropriate than the yoga pants and T-shirt she kept in her gym bag.

Despite the incredible night with Vaughn—a night she refused to regret—she had awoken alone. The sheets were cold on his side of the bed, too, so it wasn't as though he'd been beside her recently. She'd smelled breakfast cooking, however, so that had been thoughtful of him. But the aftermath of their intimacy had been awkward. She felt him pulling back. And while she wasn't surprised, given what she knew about him and his past, she couldn't deny feeling the sting of his retreat.

Plucking at her shirt, she tried not to think about the events of the past day with Vaughn. The morning was already relentlessly hot, the humidity thick and heavy just outside the air-conditioning of his truck. Awareness of the man beside her—and the nerve-racking mess of her past—made her skin burn all the more.

"Officer Grant made it sound like I would be questioned again about the fight I witnessed, didn't he?" She thought back to the early morning visit from Vaughn's friend in the Royal Police Department, a higher-ranking police official who rode over to the ranch along with a uniformed officer.

"With the FBI involved, they must be looking at a lot of different facets of crimes committed," Vaughn noted, his phone vibrating with incoming messages while they sat at a traffic light.

Her stomach cramped in visceral response to his words. How was it possible that she'd been involved with a man wanted for questioning by both of those federal agencies? Her life had turned strange and scary in the past few months, and she couldn't deny that she felt grateful for Vaughn sitting beside her now. And this morning, too, while she gave her statement to his police-officer friend.

She knew she couldn't depend on the handsome doc long-term, but for now, she distracted herself by glancing over at him. He wore a light gray button-down this morning along with gray dress pants and a pair of dark leather loafers with subtle stitch work on the toes that looked handmade.

She'd noticed that about his home, too. He must support private craftsmen with his purchases because he didn't own the kind of expensive items that filled high-end stores. She'd looked over the Aztec blankets in her room this morning—when she'd awoken alone—and saw they were sewn by hand and not a machine. They were high quality, of course. But definitely crafted by artisans.

That was different from the way Will—that is, Rich Lowell—had thrown money around. He used it to show his status, flashing cash as if there was an unending supply. Vaughn, on the other hand, while clearly well-off through his family's wealth above and beyond his thriving practice, seemed to understand that the culture was richer for spending money on the arts. Those funds supported people who wanted to beautify and better the world, people who protected the old ways of doing things so they wouldn't be forgotten in the rush to mechanize and outsource everything.

"I think you'll be telling the story again," Vaughn agreed as they neared downtown. His shirt stretched around his broad shoulders and muscular upper arms. The cuffs were still rolled from when he'd made them breakfast—huevos rancheros with Tex-Mex flair. "If not to the FBI, then Will's private investigator might want to hear it."

She sighed. As nice as it had been to awaken to breakfast already made for her, she would have preferred to feel his arms around her instead.

"I just hope they find Rich soon." She didn't want these worries hanging over her head when her baby was born.

"They will." He sounded so certain. "Investigators are throwing too much firepower at this for it to drag out." He rolled to a stop sign and glanced over at her. "But in the meantime, I'd like to give you—and your child— a gift that should help you feel more secure at home."

She frowned as he turned town her street. At the far end, in front of her bungalow, she recognized the older model pickup truck that his workers had driven over before. It sat in her driveway now.

"I don't understand." She straightened in her seat, trying to see what Vaughn had in mind. "You aren't responsible for us, Vaughn. There's no need—"

"I know that. I want to help. Consider it an early baby-shower gift." He slowed to a stop behind the red Ford. "At first, I asked Micah and Brandon to meet us here in case you needed help bringing raw material to the hospital." He put his own pickup in Park and switched off the engine while both of his workers hopped out of their vehicle. "But then, I thought it would be a good idea for them to bring some shovels so they could lay the wire for a home security system I'm having installed."

He'd arranged all of that? Stunned, it took her a moment to reply.

"That's far too generous. I can't let you do that." Being independent meant making wise financial decisions on a budget. She could put it on an installment plan.

"You can pay the monitoring fee." He offered that like it was a compromise. "But for today, we'll at least get you up and running so you can sleep here tonight."

Outside on her lawn, she could see the brothers taking measurements of her front yard, stretching a metal tape between them. She let Vaughn's words roll around her brain, trying not to overreact to the implication that she wouldn't be welcome at Vaughn's house on a regular basis. Was she reading too much into it?

Or was that an astute assessment based on how he'd left her bed after their night together?

"In that case, because I wouldn't want to inconvenience you for a second night in a row, I gratefully accept." She turned to lever open the passenger door, unwilling to wait for him.

"Abby, wait—"

She charged into the house to start her day, knowing Vaughn was due at the hospital soon. She had a lot of supplies to gather. Materials he would arrange to transport for her. He remained charming and accommodating. A tender lover and a thoughtful friend.

He was on track to do everything right in making her heart yearn for him. Right up until the moment when he pulled away because he wasn't ready for a relationship.

Especially not a whole family.

She knew all of those things. Had understood them going into last night. It wasn't fair to take her disappointment out on Vaughn, when it was her own fault for letting her guard down around him.

But that didn't stop a whole lot of hurt from flooding through her as she changed her clothes and prepared for a day on the job site. Today, she was focusing on her art.

Her tribute to Alannah.

Any feelings for the sexy doctor were strictly off-limits.

Running a fishtail blade in a long sweep down the tree sculpture, Abigail watched the thin layer of wood peel away as she formed the smooth surface into carved bark.

She'd been crafting the sculpture for nearly twelve hours straight, stopping only to eat a quick bite in the hospital cafeteria a couple of times. And, of course, she'd had to stop to direct Micah's younger brother, Brandon, when he'd arrived with the additional limbs Abigail had requested.

He had been quicker and more efficient than the movers the day before and he'd refused her attempts to tip

him, wheedling that what he really wanted was to work
as her apprentice for the day and learn a new woodworking skill. She'd had reservations, certain Vaughn had
planted that idea in his head. But Brandon had proven
a quick and eager study, paying close attention to her
demonstration for carving the joints to graft new pieces
onto the tree. He'd had an occasional question or ob-
servation based on the kinds of wood she was using,
impressing her with how fast he understood that various grains had different responses to the chisels and
gouges she used.

His help had been invaluable, freeing her up to do
the detail work she really wanted to complete before
the hospital's summer gala. Not that she'd ever fully
succeeded in chasing Vaughn from her thoughts today.
She'd heard him paged earlier and had wondered what
had happened.

If she was distracted from her work, she could always
go back and fix mistakes, but a trauma surgeon didn't
have that luxury. He had to be focused all the time or
the difference could be a matter of life and death. The
thought made her wish she'd tabled this morning's discussion until a later time.

Straightening from her efforts on the bark, she
stepped back to view the texture of the piece.

A little girl in a hospital gown paused beside the
caution tape surrounding the workspace. No more than
seven or eight years old, the patient held hands with a
nurse, trailing an IV cart as she pointed to the trunk.

"Are you carving a tree out of a tree?" she called over
to Abigail. The auburn-haired sprite scrunched her nose
as she looked at the sculpture, clearly perplexed.

"I am." Abigail stepped closer to her, setting aside

the fishtail knife. "I'm starting with one big tree in the center, but I hope to add other trees all around it so you will feel like you're walking through a forest."

The child widened her green eyes and peered up at her nurse. "Wow. So even when it rains, it will be like we can go outside."

The nurse, a tall, willowy blonde in bright purple scrubs, explained, "Zoe is disappointed it's raining today. She likes it when we can go outdoors."

Abigail's chest squeezed in empathy, and she wondered how much time Zoe spent in the children's ward. Her admiration for Vaughn, and every other medical professional at Royal Memorial, notched higher. What a powerful gift to be able to improve someone's health and their quality of life.

"I'm going to hide surprises in the trees so you can spot something new each time you walk through."

Zoe lowered her voice to a stage whisper. "Like fairies?"

Abigail added one fairy to her to-do list.

"Maybe. You'll have to look very hard, though. Fairies are the best at hiding." Abigail wondered if her own child would be as bright-eyed and curious about the world.

Zoe did a happy dance that was sort of like running in place, until her nurse gently touched her head.

"We'd better let the artist return to her work," the nurse suggested, winking at Abigail over the girl's head. "Come on, sweetie."

The two of them strode off down the hall. In the corridor beyond the lounge, Abigail could see another young patient in her bathrobe and slippers, ready for bed.

Night had fallen without any sign of Vaughn since

they'd parted ways this morning—him for the OR and a scheduled surgery, her for the children's ward. She'd been hurt at the time, feeling shunned because of his retreat after their night together.

Yet she'd known even then that her reaction wasn't fair. She had put unrealistic expectations on him when he'd tried to make her aware that he had limitations when it came to connecting emotionally. She'd pushed for more, ready to move on from the disastrous night with her baby's father. But that didn't mean Vaughn had necessarily been ready for what had happened.

"Miss Abigail, are you done for the night?" Brandon called over to her, setting aside the buffer he'd been using to smooth out a rough patch in a peg.

The young man was twenty-four years old. The age her sister would never get to be. His revelation of his age—and the fact that his birthday had been just a few days ago—had been part of the reason Abigail couldn't send him away when he'd offered help. There had been something bittersweet about playing big sister, teaching him something and sharing her craft. But she was glad she'd done it.

"I am." She nodded, knowing she needed to go home and sleep. Put her feet up and take care of her body for her baby. "You've been an incredible help today."

Another gift from Vaughn that he'd shared even though she hadn't been particularly gracious. She promised herself to make it up to him. To do something nice to apologize. Over lunch today, she had finished her sketch of him—the one he'd caught her drawing that first day. She could make a present of that, maybe. They might not be lovers again, but perhaps they could salvage a friendship.

It surprised her how much that idea left her feeling hollow inside.

"Would you like me to come back tomorrow?" Brandon asked her as he straightened all the tools he'd been using, wrapping cords around the handles of small machines, brushing off the sawdust in his hand and tossing it in a waste can.

"I'm sure you have work you should be doing with your brother." She didn't want to take him away from his other duties, and she didn't feel right asking him to work more hours if he didn't allow her to pay him.

"I'll split my time then. Half a day here, half a day there." He laid a hand on the bark she'd carved. "I like working on something that will be in the hospital permanently."

How could she argue with that? She thought it was one of the coolest rewards of her job, too.

"In that case, I will be grateful for whatever help you want to give."

"Can I carry anything out for you? Help you to your car?" Brandon used a rag to wipe off the last blade she'd used before wrapping it on the leather case where she kept them.

"I'll be fine." She wanted to see if Vaughn was still in the hospital. Try to make amends for coming down on him this morning. "But thank you."

Brandon scratched a hand under his ball cap, looking uncomfortable. "Doc C told me to make sure you didn't walk out to the parking lot alone."

Which made good sense. She was so tired she wasn't thinking straight. But before she could offer an alternative—like having Security walk her out later—a familiar voice sounded from behind her.

"That won't be necessary, Brandon." Vaughn stood on the other side of the caution tape, his green eyes locked on her. "I'll make sure Abigail gets home safely."

Eight

Eyes gritty from the worst day he'd had on the job since returning to Royal, Vaughn followed Abigail's car into downtown, making sure she arrived home without incident. She'd tried to wave off his insistence to accompany her into the house the first time she used the new alarm system, but in the end, she'd conceded. He had the feeling she'd only agreed out of concern for the safety of her baby, and not out of any romantic notions about him.

Which was fine. He didn't deserve for a woman like her to think about him that way when he couldn't even close his eyes to fall asleep while they shared a bed. But still, after the day he'd had, the knowledge that he'd hurt her added salt to the wounds he felt hours after he'd failed to save a gunshot victim.

In light of all that had gone wrong today, maybe it had been a mistake to stop by Abigail's work site to see her, let alone follow her home. But after hearing those heart monitors go flat on his nineteen-year-old patient, making sure Abigail was safe had become a priority that somehow carried him through the rest of a gut-shredding shift.

Ahead of him, Abigail's brake lights brightened. She parked in front of the bungalow as he pulled in the driveway behind her. He would simply walk her to the door, follow the instructions from the security company and make sure she knew how to arm the new system again before he left.

One step at a time. He would find a way to get through this day.

Preferably before the flashbacks started bombarding him, reminding him of other gunshots. Other victims. Other young men he had been powerless to heal.

He closed and locked the door behind him before moving toward Abigail's car to help her from the vehicle.

"Thank you." Stepping from the car, she smiled up at him as she took his hand. "You really didn't have to do this. Brandon talked me through how to use the new alarm today."

Vaughn couldn't articulate how much he needed to see with his own eyes that she was safe for the night, so he didn't try. "Brandon and his brother installed the same system at my house last year," he explained, walking her past the phlox, daisies and Texas bluebells she had planted on either side of the walkway.

Her skirt had blooms all over it, too, embroidered sunflowers on a blue background. The hem brushed the encroaching leaves of her runaway garden. She was a vibrant woman in every way, her lush curves making him ache to touch her. Hold her. As she reached the new security panel blinking dimly beside the front door, she turned to him. Waited while he checked his phone for the temporary code she was supposed to reset within forty-eight hours.

With a soft beep, the alarm was disarmed, allowing her to open the door.

"But explaining the alarm system was only a small way he helped me today. He has a gift for woodworking." She raked a hand through her dark hair, sifting curls behind one shoulder as she set her handbag on a table near the door and flicked on light switches that illuminated the kitchen and living area. She drew a deep breath, and her voice took on a different tone when she continued. "He is certainly very sharp and mature for someone who just turned twenty-four."

If Vaughn had forgotten her sister's age, he would have known it by the way Abigail carefully enunciated the number. *She would have been twenty-four*, she'd told him.

And by the way her eyes clouded over with still-fresh grief.

He didn't have much comfort to offer tonight, but he reached to pull her against him. Hell, maybe he did it for his own sake as much as hers. Because having her cheek rest on his chest, the scent of her hair in his nose, managed to steady him as they stood in the soft spotlight from a modern chandelier. He felt a breath shudder from her and guessed she felt the same thing as him.

A momentary ease. Shared strength. Connection.

And yes, undeniable attraction. Desire for her roared through him.

"I'm sorry about this morning," she told him, pulling back to peer up at him.

He frowned, not following. "You have nothing to apologize for."

She slid out of his arms and into the kitchen, pulling two bottles of water out of the small refrigerator and setting them on the breakfast bar.

"I was stressed about the police interview and the possibility of future talks with the FBI." She waved him toward one of the bar stools and then sat down in the other one at the counter. The bright red chair covers and chrome legs looked like the furnishings in a fifties' diner. "I snapped at you about buying the security system because you didn't want me at your place overnight." She sipped from her bottle, then pressed the cold plastic side of it to her forehead. "That was uncalled for."

He slid into the seat beside her, telling himself he'd only stay for another minute. Just long enough to clear up whatever it was she was feeling badly about since she hadn't done a damn thing wrong.

"I have a hard time sleeping at night," he admitted. Haltingly. Because he definitely didn't want to linger on the subject. "If you were getting the vibe that I was retreating, it was because I didn't want to fall asleep next to you and potentially…" Shout and freak her out? Lash out physically while he fought phantom combatants? "Wake you. If I had bad dreams."

Better that he sounded like a five-year-old battling a bogeymen than admit the truth. That his nightmares were flat-out terrifying for him and for anyone unfortunate enough to witness the event. Tonight, after losing a patient, he knew his brain would replay the worst of the worst.

He tipped some water to his dry lips, thinking he should forget about smoothing things over and just get out of her house now. Settle in for a rough night at home with his dog.

"Isn't that something Ruby helps with?" Her dark eyes were compassionate, but—thankfully—held no trace of pity.

Of course, she didn't know how bad it could get.

"Definitely. But I wasn't ready to trust the system with you there." He kept his explanation light on details and hoped it sufficed. Jittery from keeping his emotions in check all day, he speared to his feet, ready to leave. "I'd better let you get some sleep."

"Oh." She stood, too, setting down her water bottle. "I have something for you first."

Slipping past him, she disappeared into the shadows of her studio, where she hadn't turned on any lights. She returned with a thin leather portfolio and passed it to him.

"For me?" he asked, not sure what she'd be giving to him.

"It's just a little something. A gift to make up for the way things unfolded this morning."

"You didn't have to—" he began. Then, he saw the present.

His completed portrait rested inside. The same charcoal drawing he'd glimpsed in her papers that first day he'd come to her house.

The strokes of her pencil were sure and strong, the outline of his face captured indelibly. His hair. His shoulders.

Yet there was something else captured in the drawing. Something beyond his likeness. He saw a weariness in his face. A haunted look in the eyes. Was that how she saw him?

Or was that the reality of how he looked now? A changed man. Inexpressibly older than when he'd left Royal to be a brigade surgeon in Afghanistan.

"Vaughn?" Abigail gently covered her hand with his.

But he still couldn't speak. How could a beautiful young woman—a soon-to-be mother with a wealth of responsibilities on her shoulders—want to go anywhere near him?

Yet there she stood. With unmistakable longing in her eyes.

Tonight, he didn't stand a chance in hell of walking away.

Abigail wasn't sure how the image touched a nerve. But she could see that it had.

Vaughn was different tonight even before she'd shared the drawing with him. Remote. Polite but withdrawn.

Showing him the sketch had allowed her to glimpse behind that aloof mask, however. To darker emotions she knew he wanted to keep hidden. The moment happened so fast, she wondered if she'd seen it at all.

"Is everything okay?" she asked again. "I know art is highly subjective. And I only did a quick likeness, so I understand if it's not—"

"It's perfect. I mean—" He set aside the folder with the picture aside, laying it on the breakfast bar. "It is special to me because you made it."

She didn't want to push the issue. Her ego as an artist wasn't bruised since she knew the value of her work. But it was difficult not to ask a follow-up question when she simply wanted to understand this man better. Know what made him tick.

And yes, what made him pull away so hard.

"I'm glad you like it," she said finally, even though it came out too brightly. "And I didn't mean to keep you when you've had a long day."

He stared at her with an inscrutable look in his eyes. His whole body shifted, restlessly, even though his feet didn't move toward the door.

"I lost a patient this afternoon, Abby."

The words dropped into the room like a stone in a lake. Sinking. Sending ripples through the air that she could feel long after the sound faded.

If the mere idea of it made her ache with empathy, she couldn't imagine how he endured the pain of it.

"I'm so sorry." She clutched his hand, needing him to feel her presence. Her caring. For whatever that was worth. "It never occurred to me. I knew something was off—"

"I don't like to share it." He shook his head like he could deny her that empathy. "It's not your burden to bear. I picked this path. The good and the..."

He didn't finish the sentence. His eyes closed slowly.

"You chose a career that's a noble calling. A selfless one." She couldn't imagine doing his job. Choosing to wade into critical situations armed with education and experience, but knowing that wasn't always enough. "Most people couldn't carry the weight of life or death on their shoulders, but we're grateful to those who try."

She stepped closer to him, spanning his shoulders with her hands. Lightly squeezing her certainty into him as she flexed her fingers.

"The kid has been in the OR before." Vaughn's voice rasped drily. "One of my first major surgeries after I returned to Royal. He'd been shot then, too."

Abigail pressed her cheek against his chest as they stood together.

"You gave him a second chance then. He was fortunate that time."

"Afterward, he joked about it. Said he was getting out of his town while his luck held out. Moving somewhere else. Starting over." Vaughn's chin rested on her head, some small tension seeping away enough for him to relax into her. "He seemed like a decent kid."

"I'm sorry." She wrapped her arms around his waist. Breathing him in.

For a long moment, they stood together in her quiet kitchen with only the sound of Vaughn's heartbeat in her ear. Behind her, the clock ticked. Her refrigerator hummed.

Slowly, she edged away enough to glance up at him again. Their gazes locked. And something shifted between them. A tangible flicker of heat licked over her as the look in Vaughn's eyes changed.

She tried to ignore it since she was offering compassion, not indulging in the chemistry between them.

"Abby." He breathed her name like it was something precious. Something necessary. He focused on her as if he was seeing her for the first time all evening, his eyes turning a shade darker.

His hands gripped her hips. Fingers flexing.

She might have been able to deny her own need, but not his. Not tonight.

She slid her hands to the soft cotton that strained against his torso and let herself feel the tense heat of him. The strength.

He kissed her and she felt the sudden tide of physical desire roll over her like a rogue wave. It all but took out her knees, sending her swaying into Vaughn's arms so he could steady her. Hold her. Answer the plea for more with a demand of his own.

His tongue stroked hers, seeking, urging. She wrapped both arms around his neck, sealing her body to his, wanting the feel of his solid warmth against her.

Her sensitive, aching breasts molded to all that male strength and heat, sending a shiver through her. He lifted her, settling her on the kitchen table so he could step between her legs. A soft moan escaped her lips, a needy sound he sipped from her mouth with another kiss as he placed one hand on the small of her back to draw her hips closer to his.

His free hand traced the column of her throat, sending more sensations racing up her spine. Her skin tightened, tingling, wanting his touch all over her. When his fingers dipped lower, beneath the neckline of her scoop-neck T-shirt, he slipped a hand beneath one lace cup of her bra, palming her breast. Plucking one taught nipple between his thumb and forefinger in a way that sent liquid heat flooding through her.

Desire sharpened. Pushing her higher.

Her world was spinning and she felt dizzy with want. He stripped off her shirt and it wasn't enough. She rolled her shoulders, shrugging off the straps of confining lace on her bra. Anything to be naked sooner. Faster.

So when Vaughn lowered a kiss to fasten around the other taut peak, the sensual swirl of his tongue threatened to make her fly right over the edge.

Need stormed over him.

Hot. Wild. Demanding.

Vaughn couldn't get enough of Abigail. Not her sweet

mouth that he could kiss for days, or her beautiful body that tempted him beyond reason. It didn't matter what drove them together. Only this red-hot blaze of need that burned away everything else. All the reasons they shouldn't be together. All the reasons he wouldn't be right for her tomorrow.

Tonight, there was so much heat, so much hunger, that nothing mattered but the next exquisite touch. The next mind-blowing kiss.

And that she was his.

He wanted her skin against his, her breathy moans in his ear, her legs wrapped around his hips. With impatient hands, he hauled up her skirt, sliding her to the edge of the table so the cradle of thighs met the hard thrust of his need. She felt so good. So right. For a moment, he had to close his eyes against the rising tide of want, fighting for control.

Her breathing was ragged, her hands restless on his shoulders, her nails skimming lightly up his back. He lifted her up, carrying her to a couch in the living room, wanting to be careful with her.

Protective of her beautiful body, he laid her down on the sofa in the far corner.

"Please," she whispered in his ear. "Don't stop."

He met her gaze, bright with desire. He wanted her more than he'd ever wanted a woman. Needed her beyond reason. He worked the buttons of his shirt with ruthless efficiency, shedding the button-down. His every thought of Abigail. Touching her. Tasting her. Filling her.

Making her his.

His belt was next, and his pants, though he had enough forethought to find the lone condom in his wallet. Set it aside.

All the while Abigail's gaze tracked him, her luscious breasts spilling out of the lace cups that his kisses had displaced. When he was naked, he returned to her, flicking open the clasp that held the bra in place. Freeing her to his touch.

His kiss.

She combed her fingers through his hair, arching her back to give him more access. Her skin was impossibly soft everywhere he touched. He raked down the zipper on her skirt, tugging the cotton lower until only a thin scrap of lace kept him from where he most wanted to be.

Seated beside her on the sofa where she was sprawled, he touched the damp lace. Skimmed it aside. Watched her cheeks flush with color, her head thrown back. Her heat flooded through to his fingers until he couldn't resist kissing her there. Licking her again and again until his name was a hoarse shout as she came for him.

Over and over.

Only then did he skim off the lace panties and settle between her legs. He rolled on the condom, his heart slamming inside his chest. By the time he slid inside her, inch by tantalizing inch, she wrapped her legs around him. Her arms. Kissed him with a passion he could taste.

The fire that raged inside him flared hotter. Searing over him. She met him, thrust for thrust, as lost in the moment as him. Each time her breath hitched, her lip caught between her teeth, it drove him higher. He wanted to feel her pleasure—that vibrant glow of her— all around him. It was the only thing that kept him in check when his body demanded release.

He rolled her on top of him, careful of the small curve of her belly. He let her set the pace at first, watching her face while her eyelids fluttered once. Twice.

Reaching between them, he stroked the tight bud of her sex.

Felt the answering shudder that went through her. He sat up just enough to palm one generous breast, guiding her to his mouth so he could kiss her there.

She cried out softly, her body sweetly responsive. He drove into her deeper. Harder. Her fingers fisted in his hair, her lips parted on a silent cry.

And then he felt her release shudder through her, raining sweetness all around him until his own restraint fell away. Pleasure overran him. Inundated him. He couldn't do a damn thing but hold on to Abigail, steadying them both as sensation bombarded them. This time when she called out his name, he shouted hers in an echo of bliss. Total fulfillment.

A devastating oneness than robbed him of breath and left him panting for long moments afterward.

He'd never felt such utter contentment in the silence that followed. His breathing slowed as she fell on top of him, her beautiful body curling into his as naturally as if they'd slept together for a lifetime.

Tugging a lightweight blanket off the back of the sofa, he pulled it around her and kissed the top of her dark hair.

He caressed her shoulder through the veil of curls that fell around her. Breathed in the spicyandcitrus scent of her fragrance.

And wondered how he'd ever walk away.

Nine

Abigail wouldn't allow herself to fall asleep.

Not when she knew how stressed Vaughn had been the last time they had shared a bed together, spending too long wondering if he would have nightmares and how to avoid waking her up. She regretted that he experienced that kind of anxiety, but she empathized even though she couldn't possibly fully understand what he was going through. But she'd seen the agony in his eyes. She couldn't bear for him to go through that again.

So after he'd stroked her hair and kissed her temple for a while, she sat up. Reaching for his shirt, she slid her arms into the fabric that held his scent.

"Aren't you exhausted?" he asked, levering up on his elbow. "Was I keeping you awake?"

"I thought I'd make something to eat before you have to go home." She said it matter-of-factly, like it was no problem that they couldn't share a bed for sleeping. After her brief fling with a man who had deceived all of Royal, Abigail was willing to compromise to be with a man of Vaughn's integrity. "Would you like some chicken? I made a big batch of it on the weekend so I'd have left-overs."

Ten minutes later, they juggled plates of cold fried chicken, raw veggies and hummus and made themselves comfortable on her love seat. Hardly an exotic feast, but it all tasted good after the hospital cafeteria food she'd eaten on the run today while working. Or at least, she thought it tasted good. Perhaps he was used to richer fare.

"This is the best fried chicken I've ever eaten." Vaughn dug into a second piece. He'd dressed again, minus his shirt, since she was wearing it.

It was a good trade in her eyes, since now she had the added benefit of sitting across from a shirtless, sexy doc.

He seemed more relaxed now. His emotions more under control. For that, she was grateful. She hoped it meant he would be able to sleep soundly tonight.

"Thank you. I avoid fried foods for the most part." She swirled a carrot through hummus. "But I draw the line at chicken. This is my grandmother's recipe and my ultimate comfort food."

"This is open-a-restaurant good." He set down a bone and wiped his fingers on the napkins she'd brought out.

His obvious enjoyment pleased her, making her think of happier times with her family. "My grandmother was born and bred in southern Louisiana, but she moved to Texas when my granddaddy swept her off her feet. She taught Alannah and me all her Cajun recipes. But the chicken was always my favorite."

"Cajun?" He sipped the sweet tea she'd poured for them.

"I dial back the pepper in my version," she admitted. "But my grandmother's original recipe was definitely more Cajun than Southern."

"So with all those culinary skills at your fingertips, what made you decide to be an artist?"

"It wasn't a decision, per se." She'd always found it difficult to explain her path in a way that made sense to people. "I feel like I was born an artist. Making things has always been natural to me. When I would go out into the world—on a hike with my sister and to the grocery store with my mother—I would draw a picture of it when I got home."

Vaughn grinned as he reached for another serving. "I guess I did that, too, when I was a kid."

"The difference is, I never stopped. I never got tired of sharing what I saw and how I felt about it." Standing, she picked up one of her sketchbooks from the closest table in her studio and brought it back to the coffee table in front of the love seat. "Even now, if you look through my drawings, they're mostly everyday things. I express myself through my pictures. They're like a journal of what I experience."

Flipping through the pages, she saw the past months flash before her. Images of Royal. Of nature out her window. Of the tiny human being growing inside her.

"Wow." Vaughn set aside his plate and wiped his fingers on a napkin to study the images with her. He pointed to the ultrasound picture, a rough interpretation of her last time there. "That's amazing."

The awe in his voice reminded her how monumentally her life was about to change.

"Isn't it? I'm going back next week for another ultrasound since the baby didn't cooperate for a gender reveal at the twenty-week appointment." She couldn't wait.

But at the same time, it was one of those big moments in the pregnancy that she wished she could have shared with a supportive, excited partner.

Instead, she would be there alone.

"When did you realize you could take the art you make every day and turn it into a career?" He set aside her sketches to finish his meal.

"In college. I pursued art because that's what made me happy. My teachers were supportive and helped me to find outlets at local galleries. I was selling small works even then."

"Because you're incredibly talented," he said without hesitation.

She knew the value of her work, yet still, his compliment made her cheeks heat. "I'm not sure if it's talent so much as my perspective." She'd thought long and hard about that. "I think people like seeing the world through my eyes."

She'd wondered if she would lose that connection when her sister died. If her perspective would become too dark. Too depressing. But she didn't worry about that now. Her art was a reflection of her, no matter what she experienced. She couldn't change that or she would risk alienating her muse.

Vaughn studied her thoughtfully.

"What made you move from drawing to sculpture?"

"A visit to Galveston with my sister. We went exploring on the beach and found some driftwood." That vacation had been so happy. Alannah had been seventeen and Abigail had just turned twenty-two. She'd felt so grown-up taking her sister on a weekend trip to the beach. "I wanted to make something with it when I got home. I discovered I loved working with wood."

She set aside her plate, trying not to get lost in the past as the happy part of the memory faded, bringing with it the darker side. Clearing her throat of the swell of sudden emotions, she continued.

"We used to say that trip was a turning point for both of us. I found the joy of sculpture and she realized a new passion for kayaking." The words hurt her throat as the memory weighted down her heart. "We went together, that first time. She thought it was the best thing, being out on the water with no motor. Just the quiet splash of water off the paddle."

Vaughn set aside his dishes to move closer. Sliding an arm around her shoulders, he pulled her near.

"I'm sorry." He kissed the top of her head. Squeezed her upper arm lightly. "It wasn't fair to lose her so young."

"She was training to work as a firefighter." Her sister had been fearless. "I was so worried about her being the one to run into burning buildings, never thinking she might get hurt doing something recreational. Something that should have been safe."

Tears leaked from her eyes, making her realize how deeply she'd wandered into the past when she hadn't intended to. Vaughn stroked her hair like he could have comforted her all night, but that wasn't fair to him.

She levered herself to sit upright. "I'm sorry. I meant to feed you and let you get back home before it got any later."

"I'm glad to learn more about you." His green eyes followed her as she started scooping up the dishes. "Let me get those."

He plucked them out of her hands.

"I'll go change so you can have your shirt back." She was scavenging for excuses to leave the room, needing to rein in her runaway emotions.

The last time she'd shared her grief with a man, it had all but overwhelmed her. And while she trusted Vaughn not to take advantage of her feelings, she didn't trust herself to maintain control of her boundaries.

Those boundaries were the only way her heart was going to survive this relationship with a man who became more important to her every day.

The hospital summer gala was more than a reception to unveil Abigail's statue, although for Vaughn, that was the most exciting part.

Vaughn had a role to play glad-handing donors to the hospital's trauma center, as well as those who supported the new art installation in the children's ward. He'd visited the barber earlier in the day for a trim, letting the guy shave off his beard while he was at it.

He looked like an entirely different man. More like the military officer he'd been throughout his deployment. He'd been keeping that side of himself at bay, trying to bury his memories, but that hadn't worked.

As he dressed in the requisite monkey suit for the event, he adjusted the bow tie he couldn't get quite right and wondered what Abigail would see when she looked at him tonight. The same world-weary man she'd started sketching that first day they'd met? Or was there more life in his eyes these days, now that she had come into his world with her vibrant outlook?

Vaughn didn't know. He couldn't tell what he saw when he looked in the mirror anyhow. From behind him on the bed, Ruby lifted her head to study him. Apparently she didn't see anything too far off base since she settled her head back on her paws and let her eyes drift closed again.

He was pretty sure the dog missed Abigail.

After that night Abby had spent at his house, Ruby went into the spare room where she'd slept a few times. She'd circled the bed. Nosed the drawer where she'd helped unpack Abigail's few things. Then she'd padded back out into the hall to lie by the door.

Not often. But she'd never done that before Abigail's appearance in their lives.

"Maybe we'll see her again tonight if I'm lucky," he told Ruby, scratching behind her ears.

Since the night when he'd let his guard down at her place, confiding his loss of the patient, he'd been at work two of the three days. He'd finished off those two shifts by visiting her at the children's ward, both times finding Brandon working beside her. Lifting tree limbs into place at her direction, and fastening them onto joints he'd made himself.

Vaughn planned to make a sizable donation to the guy's business start-up fund, although both times he'd mentioned it, Brandon had waved off the suggestion with an assurance that he was learning a lot. That made Vaughn happy even as he wondered what Abigail would have done on her own. Would she have lifted those limbs over her head to extend the size of that tree?

He scowled just thinking about it, but he hadn't wanted to ask her when she was hard at work. She'd texted him last night—on his off day—to show him a photo of her smiling in front of the completed tree. Vaughn had been touched that she'd thought of him, but worried what it meant for them that her primary project at the hospital was finished.

Would he see her after tonight? Sure, her work would continue at the children's ward, but not at this pace. And much of it would be accomplished in her studio and brought to the hospital at a later date. So the days of seeing her regularly were over. The realization nagged at him, pushing him to think of other ways to keep her in his life.

Which made no sense because he'd known from the start that the relationship couldn't really go anywhere. He didn't want a family and she needed to think about her future with her child.

His cell phone chimed before he could leave for the gala, alerting him to a call from a private number. He debated not answering but he was ahead of schedule.

"Chambers," he answered, peering out the back window onto the lawn overlooking the woods where he'd walked with Abigail that day.

"Vaughn, it's Will Sanders."

Just hearing the name sent a weird reaction tumbling through his gut. Abigail had been with a man she believed to be Will the night her child had been conceived. She still thought of that man as "Will." So the surge of jealousy Vaughn experienced at hearing the name was obviously misplaced.

And, considering the hell this guy had been through, would be a slap in the face if he knew.

"It's good to hear from you, Will." Vaughn pulled the blinds on the view and double-checked the lock on the sliding glass doors. Ruby appeared in the room behind him, no doubt remembering it was suppertime.

"I wanted to let you know that I'm putting my personal resources into the investigation of the imposter situation."

"Can't blame you there. Any man would want justice." Vaughn filled Ruby's water and food dishes.

Micah would take the dog out for a walk soon.

"I've hired a detective, Cole Sullivan, from a local private security firm to find Jason Phillips."

"He's with the Walsh Group." Vaughn knew the firm and the man since Cole was a member of the Texas Cattleman's Club. "My father considered hiring him when the oil company executives received some death threats last year."

Cole was a former Texas Ranger and as sharp as they came. But then Vaughn's father had decided to increase his home security system and hand over the threats to the police instead.

"If anyone can get to the bottom of this, I trust Cole to be the man." Will sounded grim. Resolute. "But the first person he wants to talk to is Abigail Stewart, since she may be the last person to have seen him alive besides Rich."

A chill raced up Vaughn's spine.

The thought of Abby being mixed up with guys like that scared the hell out of him. And made him more determined than ever to stick close to her until they figured out where Rich and Jason had disappeared.

"Tonight Abigail will be at the hospital gala with me, unveiling her new statue for the children's ward." He wanted to suggest another day to interview her since Vaughn wanted tonight to be special for her. She deserved the time to enjoy having the spotlight on her work.

"Cole already knows and plans to be there. I'm only

calling to give you a heads-up since I got the impression the two of you are close."

Hell. He was more transparent than he knew when it came to Abigail.

"I appreciate that." Vaughn grabbed his keys, in a new hurry to get to the gala. He didn't want Abigail to face another round of questions alone. "Cole is a good guy but he can be...intimidating to those who don't know him."

Will gave a dry laugh. "Let's hope so. I need him to cut through the red tape and figure out where that bastard Rich went. I feel certain that Jason isn't to blame for any of this, but then again, who knows." He sounded frustrated. Angry. "We need to locate him."

"Thanks for the call, Will."

"I figured you'd want to be with her," he said simply before disconnecting.

As Vaughn slid into the driver's seat of the Mercedes coup he liked to use for work, he wondered how Will Sanders had deduced the truth that he had battled for over a week to deny.

He might have every reason in the world not to pursue this relationship with Abigail. But the plain truth of the matter was, he wanted to be with her. And he didn't see that changing anytime soon.

Scanning Royal Memorial's rooftop garden for any sign of Vaughn, Abigail declined a second offer of champagne from a passing waiter. Since the summer gala was a fund-raiser in addition to an unveiling for her statue, the event planner had spared no expense to make it elegant. Abigail had nearly fallen over when she heard what the tickets to the event cost, but then, the function raised money for much-needed hospital equipment and programs.

White lights had been strung from the trees, creating a fairy canopy overhead. Chamber musicians played for the cocktail hour, which was currently in progress, but she'd heard a popular country band would take the stage afterward to kick off the dancing. Tall sunflowers swayed in the breeze from discreetly placed fans to keep the place cool while the sun set. Even the sky had cooperated for the gala, turning the clouds bright pink and purple.

She longed for her sketchbook and a place to draw, needing to capture this beautiful night in her memory. The unveiling of the statue was a moment that belonged to Alannah as much as Abigail, since she'd dedicated the project to her sister's love of nature. Alannah would love the "Secret Garden" theme of the party, with white tapers flickering in the breeze on a display table of cut flowers that labeled all the blooms taken from the surrounding garden. The floral arrangements ranged from natural wildflower bouquets to more exotic and artful groupings.

The scent of jasmine hung heavy in the air, the profuse blooms lining the railings around the rooftop. The greeters at the door downstairs had given all the women gardenia blooms to wear as wrist corsages, another fragrant note so rich and decadent Abigail wanted to fill her studio with them. Although, not as much as she wanted to see Vaughn tonight.

She plucked a glass of sparkling water with lemon from a tray near the bar, grateful for the nonalcoholic drink options in easy reach. Sipping from the commemorative glass with an etched rose, she scanned the sea of tuxedos while discreetly tugging at her dress hem. She hadn't expected the addition of a baby bump to make finding clothing so awkward. The burgundy-colored dress she'd borrowed from an online rental store was appropriately elegant and a designer she'd never be able to afford outright. But the swell of baby made the dress ride up her hips, where it was snug. Thankfully, a layer of tulle over the sleek satin sheathe still kept her figure a mystery. The dress made the most of her legs and the more curvy breasts that came with pregnancy.

"Abigail Stewart?" One of the tuxedo-wearing guests stepped out of the line at the bar to stalk toward her.

Unfortunately, he was not the handsome doctor she sought.

This man had dark blond hair and piercing blue eyes, his strong shoulders and athletic build the kind of physique she'd seen on local ranchers. There was something about their gait, perhaps. The way they carried themselves.

"Yes?" She set aside her water glass to introduce herself, thinking the stranger might be someone interested in the statue. She'd already fielded a few questions about her work. "I'm Abigail."

"Cole Sullivan." He thrust his hand toward her, his blue eyes fixing on her. "I'm a private investigator retained by Will Sanders."

She stiffened at the name, even as she told herself the real Will Sanders was a perfectly nice man. A man who'd been cruelly impersonated and swindled by a former friend.

"Nice to meet you." She shook his hand, wondering how she could have misread a private eye for a rancher.

"I'd like to ask you a few questions if you have a minute?"

She hesitated, not wanting to ruin her big night with a bout of nerves.

"I'll be sure you don't miss your entrance for the statue unveiling," Cole assured her.

Anxiety fluttered through her. She really needed to help him. To protect her child's future, she was invested in finding Rich Lowell and holding him accountable for everything he'd done. But she regretted the timing for this interview during an important night for her career.

Before she could respond, Vaughn separated himself from the crowd, reaching her side with three long strides. A bolt of relief—and the ever-present desire— shot through her to see him. He looked incredible in his perfectly fitted tuxedo and—more surprisingly—a clean-shaven face that revealed a slight scar along the bottom of his chin that gave his handsome face character. And made her want to kiss him right there.

"You look beautiful, Abigail," he murmured, sliding a possessive arm around her waist and drawing her against his side. Then he turned his attention to the private investigator. "Cole Sullivan, it's been a long time." He shook the man's hand and the two men exchanged pleasantries.

Cole was a member of the Texas Cattleman's Club, apparently, and a local rancher who worked part-time for the Walsh Group. The former Texas Ranger handled the security firm's most challenging cases.

All of which she gleaned in the rapid back-and-forth between the men before Cole repeated his original request.

"I'd like to speak to Ms. Stewart for a few minutes,

Vaughn." The PI's gaze returned to her. "I believe she was just about to agree to that."

Anxiety spiked again. No doubt about it, Cole Sullivan made her nervous. Or maybe it was simply the thought of revisiting that night at the Ace in the Hole and the fight she'd seen there. Knowing how close she might have come to real danger was scary.

"May I join you?" Vaughn turned toward her, the question directed toward her and not Cole.

Vaughn's green eyes searched hers, warming her insides and soothing some of the jitters she'd been feeling.

"I would appreciate that." She'd like his company, his touch, his presence in her life a whole lot more than he would ever know.

But for right now, she was just grateful she wouldn't be facing more questioning alone.

"Fair enough." Cole nodded his satisfaction with the plan. "Where can we speak privately? This isn't a conversation I want anyone else to overhear."

Ten

Vaughn glanced back at Abigail as they left the rooftop garden with Cole, descending the stairs that led toward his office, where they could speak privately.

She looked incredible. The mass of dark hair was gathered at the nape of her neck, the glossy curls spilling down the center of her back. Her scarlet-colored cocktail gown had a floaty fabric around it that gave her the look of an ethereal creature, like one of the winged fairies he'd seen her carve in hidden nooks in the sculpture she'd made.

More than that, she glowed. He'd heard that about pregnant women, but had never noticed it with his own eyes the way he could see it in Abigail. Her skin had the dewy appearance that women tried to recreate with makeup, her cheeks pink with good health. When Vaughn had first seen her at the party he'd done a double take. Not that she was more beautiful in extravagant clothing, because he thought she was perfect in the tennis shoes and T-shirts she favored for work. But seeing her tonight was like discovering a new side of her, another fascinating facet to a woman who intrigued him at every turn.

"Thank you for joining us." She said the words softly as he led her and Cole Sullivan out of the stairwell and into the corridor that led to his office. "I feel better having you here with me."

With Cole a few steps behind her, checking messages on his phone, she probably thought their conversation was private enough. Although Vaughn would lay money Cole didn't miss much.

"I'm hoping to wrangle a dance out of you in return." He wanted to spend every minute of this evening with her, in fact, although some of his evening would need to be devoted to mingling.

Securing donations.

Because while the cost of admission covered the expense of the party as well as some money toward necessary hospital improvements, Royal Memorial counted on this well-heeled segment of the community for more than that. Vaughn was reasonably good at securing those kinds of donations, too. He had sacrificed the easy path in life—taking over his father's business—to make a difference in the world. He walked the walk. So he didn't mind urging people with deep pockets to make a difference by writing a check.

"I'll definitely be ready for a dance afterward." Her eyes glowed with warmth. With awareness.

Vaughn was glad to have distracted her from the

questioning for a minute at least. The stress of those worries wasn't good for her…or the baby. He opened the door to his office with a key card that tracked hours and time of use for the space. The medical arts building was attached to Royal Memorial, but occupied its own wing.

"Come on in." Vaughn flipped on the lights, then held the door for both of them before letting it fall shut behind them. Inside, there was a consultation area with a couch and two chairs, so he wasn't stuck sitting behind a desk when speaking to patients. The dynamic put people more at ease.

He took a seat beside Abigail on the low gray sofa, leaving Cole to take the chair opposite them. Abigail's eyes wandered around the space briefly before Cole asked her to recount the night she'd gone to Ace in the Hole. While she shared the story Vaughn already knew, he wondered what she'd seen when she looked around the office.

He'd always viewed it as functional. But seeing the couple of generic canvases that had come with the room, he wondered what she thought of his complete lack of personal investment in his surroundings. He'd never really thought it before, always fully focused on his work when he walked through the door.

"Did you hear anything specific in the exchange?" Cole asked Abigail now. "Any snippets of conversation or shouted words?"

"There was name-calling and swearing." She shook her head. "I remember some of the more colorful expletives, but I couldn't tell you which voice said what. They were gasping for air, rolling around the floor. It distorted both their voices."

Cole looked up from the notes he was tapping into his phone. He'd asked permission to record the conversation, and he was doing so, but he'd been making notes the whole time, too.

"Could there have been a third voice in that room? Someone else in there that you didn't see?"

"Sure. Maybe." She shrugged, hesitating in a way that revealed her nervousness. "I couldn't see the whole room from where I peered in through a crack in the open door. But I didn't hear any extra set of feet scuffling or anything. And it seems like I would have heard a third person moving around to at least escape the mayhem of Jason and Rich throwing punches."

"Right. Maybe." Cole's forehead scrunched in concentration as he reviewed his screen. "And you're sure of the time and date?"

"Positive." Abigail chewed her lip for a moment. "I kept looking at the calendar that week, trying to tell myself I had plenty of time to tell him about the baby—"

Cole interrupted, "Rich Lowell is the father of your child?"

Vaughn wrapped an arm around her waist, wanting her to feel his presence. To take whatever comfort she could from him being by her side. He understood it couldn't be easy for her to focus on the joy of becoming a mother when the child's father could return to Royal at any time.

The thought sparked a sudden wish that Vaughn could claim her baby as his. Hell, he wished he could claim her, too.

Foolish, fanciful notions.

But she would be safer if both those things were true, damn it.

Abigail's hand shifted protectively to her baby bump. "If Rich Lowell was the man impersonating Will Sanders, then yes." Her voice shook and she drew a deep breath. "Rich Lowell is the father of this child."

"Rich was absolutely the imposter." Cole sat back in his chair, setting aside his phone. "I've stopped recording, by the way. And I appreciate you answering my questions."

A little of the tension in Abigail's body eased. Vaughn could feel it as she relaxed slightly.

"I'm glad I could help. Or rather, I hope I've helped."

Cole nodded. "You're the last person to see Jason besides Rich."

"Can you tell us your next move? What you're doing to push through this stalemate the law enforcement agencies seem to have reached in the investigation?" Vaughn hated not knowing where Rich was. The sooner the imposter was behind bars, the better.

"For starters, I'm going back to the urn that Jason Phillips sent to his sister along with the note she received about Will's death." Cole threaded his fingers together behind his head as he leaned back. "I need to get the contents of the urn retested in case there is DNA present in bone fragments."

"But you know it's not Rich, right?" Abigail asked, her fingers toying with the hem of her dress where it fell over her knee.

"Correct. What I'd like to do next is see if it matches anyone else."

"Jason." Vaughn supplied the obvious answer.

Abigail's hand sought his before she spoke.

"You don't think he killed Jason?" she asked, worry evident in her voice.

With good reason.

"He left Will for dead off Cabo San Lucas." Cole's voice was grim. "And he's spent more of Will's money than he could ever repay. So I'd call Rich Lowell a desperate man."

Vaughn shifted his hold on Abigail, moving his hand to her back to rub soothing circles along her shoulders. She shouldn't have to deal with any of this right now.

"Jason might have found out that Will was a fake and called him on it." Vaughn tried to envision what could have precipitated the brawl Abigail had witnessed.

"Or he could have uncovered missing money and alerted Will," Cole added. "But I'm also having the note that arrived with the urn reviewed by a handwriting expert to see if it's a match with Jason's writing."

Vaughn's finger rubbed along Abigail's back, strands of her hair clinging to his wrist. "Smart thinking."

"Will is committed to getting to the bottom of this mess. He's even flying in some tech genius from Silicon Valley who thinks he's got a software answer for all of this. Luke Weston from West-Tech." Cole shrugged. "And while that may or may not work, I can assure you we're putting every available resource on this."

"Good." Abigail seemed to have regained her composure. She straightened in her seat. "We'll rest easier once we know what happened."

"We'll find out." Cole's smile was predatory. Certain. "We'll locate Rich Lowell, too."

Vaughn noticed the investigator didn't promise the same for Will's right-hand man, Jason Phillips.

Still, the investigation was moving in the right direction. Progress being made. But that didn't mean Abigail and her child were safe. And until they were, Vaughn couldn't walk away.

He couldn't deny feeling relieved that he didn't have to yet. Guilt bit him hard, since he knew that him sticking around could lead to their feelings growing. Deepening.

Frustrated, he bolted out of his office once the interview was over. He would see Abigail at the party, of course. But first, he would throw himself into fundraising and give them both a breather.

Half an hour later, Abigail followed Belinda McDowell, the Royal Memorial development officer, who'd led the meeting the day she was hired. The woman was in charge of the statue's unveiling. An announcement had been made at the rooftop party, inviting guests to join them for a brief ceremony in the children's ward since the sculpture was too huge to transport upstairs.

The whole party didn't relocate, of course, but Abigail was flattered to see how many of Royal's most prominent citizens had turned out to support the hospital and see her artwork. Her career had taken an exciting turn already with this commission and, with any luck, more gallery sales and special projects would follow. She'd told Vaughn that she'd been fortunate to do what she loved for work. But with a baby on the way, she might not always have that luxury. If she couldn't support herself and her child with her creativity, she would end up doing temp jobs again.

When they reached the children's ward lounge, Abigail could see temporary wall partitions had been rolled into place to protect the privacy of the ward and the patients from the unveiling ceremony. An arbor of flowers stood in front of the tree sculpture, which had been partially hidden with a gauzy black curtain. Of course, the statue was so huge the branches spilled out of the top, crawling along the high ceilings where Brandon had helped to secure them. Abigail had carved for hours to add the details she wanted on those high limbs, but she knew she would add more bark and hidden creatures to the hard-to-reach places throughout the coming year when she developed her idea for an interactive forest.

For now, however, the sculpture was impressive enough for the unveiling. Abigail peered behind her for a glimpse of Vaughn, certain he must have come down-stairs with the rest of the attendees who'd chosen to see the statue. He'd been such a steadying presence during her questioning with Cole Sullivan.

She'd been anxious for that dance Vaughn had promised, but he'd been quick to melt into the crowd when they returned from the interview in his office. She knew that was part of his job tonight.

And yet…she wondered if he was also astutely distancing himself from her in front of his colleagues. By the people in the community he hoped would donate more funds to the hospital. Was her presence—an increasingly obvious *pregnant* presence—a detriment to his efforts? Some might view her pregnancy as being on the scandalous side. Especially Vaughn's fellow members of the Texas Cattleman's Club, who were privy to details surrounding Rich Lowell's misdeeds while impersonating Will. While Abigail wasn't the only woman Rich had used and mistreated, she felt like she played a larger role in her own deception than any of the other women. She'd knowingly had a fling with a married man.

She'd been too lost in her grief to question Rich's insistence that he and his wife, Megan Phillips-Sanders, were separated. Although she didn't feel the need to share her personal journey of mourning with the world, she also understood why some people would judge her harshly.

Her thoughts swirling, she almost bumped into the hospital development officer as she paused in front of the flower archway in the children's ward. The older woman wore a black strapless gown with a matching short-sleeve sequin jacket. The long column of simple lines suited her no-nonsense approach.

"Ms. Stewart, if you would stand right here—" she pointed to a spot beside the microphone "—I'll introduce you before the unveiling."

"Thank you." Excited to share her work with the group, Abigail's pleasure was dimmed only by the fact that she didn't see Vaughn yet.

"Do you wish to say a few words?" Belinda asked, testing the sound equipment.

"No. Thank you." She'd dedicated the project to Alannah in her mind. She didn't need to share that story with the group. Besides, she liked for her work to be interpreted individually, without swaying viewers to share her highly personal vision.

"Very well." Belinda took her place on a small platform. "I'm going to get started."

Abigail discreetly lifted up on her toes, trying to see through the crowd for Vaughn. She really thought he'd wanted to see this. To share this with her.

She'd come to rely on him so quickly even though they hadn't known each other long. Now that she would be spending less time at the hospital, would their relationship fade, too? She had an ultrasound appointment at the hospital on Monday—her last trip to Royal Memorial for a while and for a much different reason. She'd thought about asking him to join her.

But was that selfish of her when she knew he wasn't ready for more?

"Ladies and gentlemen, may I have your attention, please?" The hospital administrator took the microphone, quieting the assembled guests before briefly discussing the commitment of the hospital staff to excellence, right down to providing a nurturing environment for patients.

She introduced Abigail as the artist of the hospital's latest attempt to create an uplifting retreat for patients and their families. As the crowd clapped politely, she heard a soft but unmistakable whistle of approval from the back of the room. A few chuckles followed, along with people turning to spot the source of the whistling.

Those turned heads allowed her to spot Vaughn. For a moment, their eyes met and her heart turned a somersault.

He was here.

He lifted a hand in a wave of acknowledgment.

No matter that she was worried about how people would react to them together, apparently he had no such reservations.

"Without further ado," Belinda McDowell continued, "I present to you our very own *Tree of Gifts*."

The black gauzy curtain fell to the ground at her verbal cue, revealing the sculpture in spotlight.

There were appreciative oohs and aahs that sounded genuine to Abigail's hopeful ears. Even the applause that followed was deeper, louder and more prolonged than the earlier polite smattering. And if she'd had any doubt about the positive reception, Belinda McDowell's wide smile told her she saw the unveiling as a success.

Then, just as the clapping began to die down, Belinda returned to the microphone. "Before you leave, ladies and gentlemen, make sure to spot a few of the gifts inside the tree."

Behind her, the spotlight darted to one of the carved owls perched in an obvious nest on a low limb. Then to a more subtle face in the bark.

"You can tell us which one of these surprises you love best," Belinda continued. "And you can bid on the chance to have your name carved on your favorite."

Event volunteers began passing out white cards for guests to make bids on the small pieces of art in the tree, the surprises Abigail had installed for bored and restless children to find as they walked through the lounge. She had to hand it to resourceful event staff for making the most of the statue at the gala. It was a quick, easy way to earn more donations and give guests buy-in on the project.

Seeing her part in the unveiling finished, Abigail stepped away from the flower arch and out of the way of guests who were excited to find new creatures hidden in the limbs. She, on the other hand, was looking through the crowd for Vaughn.

She spotted him at last, speaking with a distinguished-looking older man and woman, still standing at the back of the room. She debated returning to the party upstairs, not wanting to interrupt him if he was speaking to friends or touting the merits of the hospital's mission to potential donors.

But before she could dart away for the stairs, he spotted her. Waved her over to join him.

"Abigail." His smile seemed strained. "I'd like you to meet my parents."

Eleven

Vaughn saw his mother's eyes zero in on Abigail's pregnant belly like a laser beam.

Her look made him belatedly realize this meeting was bound to be awkward. At the time he'd waved Abigail over, he'd been more concerned she would leave the event if she didn't see him. And, selfishly, he'd been grateful for an excuse to dodge his parents' questions about his mental health. They'd been hammering on about the importance of keeping Ruby close by whenever he wasn't working. Hell, they'd brought up switching to a less demanding job, suggesting he come back to the family business, where there would be less stress.

As if he would waste the skills and education he'd spent almost a lifetime acquiring.

Unfortunately, he'd probably made the leap from frying pan to fire. And chances were good he was taking

Abigail with him into the hot seat. Her eyes darted toward him as she made her way over, her uncertainty quickly masked as she reached his side.

He had no choice now but to forge ahead.

"Mom, Dad, this is Abigail Stewart, the artist who created the *Tree of Gifts*." He wasn't sure how else to introduce her. He certainly hadn't thought to ask her ahead of time about their first public appearance together.

They weren't a couple. And yet…to say nothing about their relationship denied her importance to him.

"Hello." Abigail shook their hands, smiling warmly while Vaughn kicked himself. "It's so nice to meet you."

The moment had passed to clarify a relationship. He could see his parents' avid curiosity while they murmured polite greetings.

"Abigail, my parents, David and Bronwyn Chambers." Vaughn knew the burden was on him to extract Abigail from the conversation quickly and efficiently.

He'd never intended to spring a meet-the-parents moment on her tonight. Abigail's gaze flashed to his for a moment. Questioning.

"Your sculpture is beautiful, Abigail." His mother waved the white donation card that she held, along with a small pencil. "I was just going up to take a closer look so I could see what we should bid on. Perhaps you'd steer me toward one of your favorites?"

"Of course." Abigail stepped back, opening up a path toward the sculpture for his mother. "Let's go see."

Vaughn was ready to sprint into action right behind them, but his mother turned back with a steely look in her green eyes. "Gentleman, excuse us," she said firmly. "We'll be right back."

He wanted to concoct a reason to join them. But

Abigail narrowed a look at him that he couldn't quite interpret. Was she hurt that he hadn't claimed a relationship with her? Aggravated? Either way, her expression warned him that she would handle his mother on her own.

He wasn't certain how he knew that. But he understood her silent message just the same. He must be starting to know Abigail very well that they could communicate so acutely that way. Still, he felt defeated as he watched his mother sail off toward the sculpture, her navy blue caftan billowing behind her.

What the hell would they be discussing?

"You walked right into that one," his father observed at his elbow. He clapped a hand on Vaughn's back.

"I disagree, Dad." He ground his teeth together. "I never saw it coming."

"Is the baby yours?" Dad asked. No judgment. Just a question.

Albeit a loaded one.

Vaughn hissed out a breath between his teeth, wondering if his mother was being just as tactful right now with Abigail.

"No." He lowered his voice, making sure they weren't overheard. "I would have mentioned it before now if I was going to be a father."

His dad's hand slid away from his shoulders. "There was a time I would have thought that, too. But we don't hear much from you these days."

Emotions piled on his chest, one after the other. Regret. Frustration. Worry for Abigail. Resentment that their time together was going to end and he wasn't any closer to figuring out how to be a fully functioning half of a couple anymore.

"I'm working on it, Dad," he said finally, not sure what else to say. "That's all I can do."

His gaze landed on Abigail—where she stood beside his mother. She was shaking her head. Emphatic denial. His mother was touching her shoulder. Reassuring her?

It was too much for him. He had to intervene in case his mother was making assumptions about their relationship. Or about Abigail herself. She certainly didn't owe anyone any explanations about her choices or her future. And there was a chance his mother was trying to wheedle both of those things from the woman he cared about.

He might not be the right man for Abigail, but if she was still speaking to him by the time he arrived at her side, he was going to find a way to make it up to her.

"Honestly, Mrs. Stewart." Abigail was trying to make her point another way, hoping to reassure Bronwyn Chambers as they stood under the sprawling branches of the *Tree of Gifts*. "I don't know why Vaughn didn't bring Ruby with him tonight. I was so caught up in my own role in the evening, I didn't think to ask him."

Hoping to redirect her companion, Abigail pointed to a rabbit tucked into a nook between tree roots.

"I think the bunny would be a fun carving to bid on. All the younger kids will find him since he's low to the ground like them." Abigail glanced in Vaughn's direction, ready for rescue before his mother's questions became more personal.

He'd been heading their way at one point, but he'd been intercepted by an older man, who held him in deep conversation now.

The party around the tree had grown, with some additional guests from upstairs joining them as the original group still searched the branches for surprise forest critters to bid on in the fund-raiser.

"Perfect." Mrs. Chambers passed over her card to Abigail. "Would you mind penciling in the necessary details, my dear? I left my reading glasses at home tonight." She grinned ruefully as she held up a beaded evening bag. "I ask you, how could I fit more than a lipstick in this?"

"Of course." Abigail wrote the name of the carving on the card.

"And I don't mean to put you on the spot, Abigail, but I'm so very glad to see you with my son. Together."

Abigail looked up slowly, unsure how to respond. "We're not really together."

His mother attempted to smile but there were worried lines etched around her eyes. "But there was something in his manner when he called you over. He likes you, Abigail. I can tell."

Abigail could see how much his mother wanted to believe that, but she couldn't afford to bear the weight of anyone else's hope. She could hardly corral her own runaway feelings when she knew that Vaughn wasn't ready for more. She'd almost made the mistake of inviting Vaughn to the ultrasound and gender-reveal appointment with her. It wouldn't be fair to his mother to let her think that Vaughn was interested in anything long-term with Abigail.

"We've struck up a friendship, Mrs. Chambers," she assured her as she returned the bid card, her heart in her throat. "But…" She blinked fast. Took a breath to steel herself. "That's all we will ever be."

Needing to leave before her emotions spilled over, she excused herself. Turning, she ran squarely into Vaughn.

He must have overheard her. Although why her words would make his expression turn so thunderous, she couldn't say. She'd simply told his mother the truth, which Vaughn had stressed from the beginning of their relationship.

It wasn't destined to go anywhere. The sooner she began to realize that, the better.

Vaughn wasn't sure what had transpired between Abigail and his mother before she denied having a relationship with him. But the hurt in Abigail's eyes spoke for itself. She was upset.

She edged past him now, taking fast strides toward the exit. Thankfully, Vaughn's father had joined them, so he didn't have to leave his mother standing all alone in the middle of the gala fund-raiser.

"I need to speak to her," he informed his parents, leaning in to give his mother's cheek a kiss. "Thank you both for coming."

He charged through the crowd and headed up the stairs to the rooftop party, where the country band had taken the stage under the canopy of white lights. Steel guitars and fiddles had the dance floor almost full as the party turned lively.

His gaze scanned the tables, searching. Finally, he spotted a flash of scarlet-colored tulle near the sparkling water station by the bar. Abigail had a wrap over one arm and her evening clutch in her hand as she paused to take a drink.

Relief filled him. She hadn't left.

"Abigail." He reached her side, realizing as he approached that she was more upset than he realized. Her eyes looked shiny. Too bright.

He didn't think it was a coincidence that she chose that moment to set aside her glass.

"I was just leaving." She slipped the sheer black wrap she carried around her shoulders, tying it in front. "I'm more tired than I realized. I think the long days of working on the statue are catching up with me."

He heard the exhaustion in her voice. And while he had no doubt this week had been hard for her, he couldn't help but wonder if the conversation with his mother had more than a little to do with her sudden departure.

"I'd like to drive you home." He needed to speak to her. Wanted to keep her safe.

"Thank you. But I'll be fine." She opened her bag and pulled out her keys while the country band shifted the music for a slow number.

"Abby, please." He put a protective arm around her as a new rush of people lined up at the bar nearby. He drew her farther from the noise of the party, toward the display of flowers at one end of the rooftop garden. "I'm sorry if my mother made you feel uncomfortable in any way. She means well."

"Of course she does." Abigail shook her head. "Your parents were both lovely. I just—" She hesitated. "I'm ready to leave."

"And I don't like the idea of you going home alone at night with Rich Lowell still at large."

"You were kind enough to install an alarm system to keep me safe," she reminded him, sliding her key ring over her finger while the metal jangled softly.

"But I'll sleep better if I see you walk inside." He couldn't seem to remove his hand from the small of her back, and wished he had the right to hold her in front of the world. To kiss her here and now. "The conversation with Cole Sullivan put into perspective just how dangerous Rich might be."

She chewed her lip. "I will be careful. But I have to consider another danger, Vaughn, and weigh it against the threat Rich poses." Her voice lowered as she spoke.

"I don't follow." He tipped his head closer to hear her. "What other danger could you possibly be worried about?"

"The emotional kind." Her dark brown eyes locked on his for a long moment. "The danger of falling for you has become very real for me. I can't take that lightly, and I can't allow myself to forget that only a foolish woman would lose her heart to someone who has no intention of ever returning it."

His gut sank. Or maybe it was his heart. He didn't know. Couldn't navigate his own emotions on the best of the days, and this was turning out to be far from his best day. His hand fell away from where he'd been touching her. He tipped his head back to glance up through the canopy of lights to see the night sky. Winking stars.

"Is that why you told my mother that we'll never be more than just friends?" The last snippet of conversation he'd heard returned to chastise him.

Sucker punch him.

"It's what you've been telling me from the very beginning." She toyed with her keys, flipping one back and forth on the ring, a nervous movement. "I simply tried to be honest with your mom before she got excited seeing us as a couple."

He deserved that kind of kick to the stomach. He'd set himself up for it, making sure Abigail knew he couldn't play a bigger role in her life, but wanting more anyway.

"I would still call us more than friends." When he thought about everything he'd shared with this incredible woman, he knew she was much more to him than a mere word like *friend* could ever express.

Her hand fisted around her keys, her jaw tensing. "Which is why you introduced me as *the artist* to your parents." She straightened, taking a step back. "At least I labeled us *friends* as opposed to implying we were merely professionals who briefly worked in the same building."

"That's not fair." His pulse quickened, and he sensed her pulling away. He wasn't ready for that. Especially when he needed to keep her safe while Rich was still on the loose. "I purposely tried to keep the introductions light so I didn't put you on the spot. We hadn't talked about how to deal with situations like that. I didn't want to make assumptions about what you would prefer, so I erred on the side of being less personal."

She closed her eyes for a moment. When she opened them, she met his gaze head-on, her expression serious.

"So you were protecting me." She nodded. "I can accept that, and thank you for it even. But it doesn't change the fact that my life is about to get very complicated. I can't afford to have feelings for someone who isn't ready to be a part of that."

A shout went up from the dance floor as the band announced a popular line dance starting. Even in tuxedos and evening gowns, a group of partygoers responded to the call.

"A baby is not a complication." His gaze dropped to the small swell of her pregnancy. He recalled the thought that crossed his mind when he'd introduced her to his parents. That he wished he could claim both Abigail and her child as his own. "You're going to be an incredible mother."

Her smile was shaky. Sad. "That doesn't change the fact that you don't want to be a part of this."

"How can I be when I can barely sleep through the night on my own? I'm a grown man limping through life with the help of a dog. Working tirelessly because I feel my professional skills are all I have to offer anyone."

Frowning, Abigail reached out to lay a hand on his chest. "That's not true."

"Every word of it is accurate." He wouldn't lie to her and he refused to lie to himself. "And it's not that I don't want to be a part of your life, Abigail. I just won't be the dark cloud hanging over you when you're ready for a vibrant, happy future."

He thought about her artwork and the way people loved it because of her perspective. Part of that perspective was optimism. Joy. Her world was a place where fairies and forest creatures hid in the trees, waiting to be found. His world was a place that made him afraid to fall asleep.

"I can't make you take a gamble on us if you're not ready to." Straightening, she let her hand fall away from where she'd touched him. "I had hoped you might attend the baby's ultrasound appointment next week and be there when I find out the gender." She caught her lip between her teeth. "But I understand you're struggling with other things. And I don't want to cause you more stress."

"That's…" He couldn't even express how much that meant to him. That she'd wanted him there.

Too bad he'd already told her how much of a deficit he would be in her life.

"It's all right." She backed up a step. "You don't have to explain. I'm going to head out now."

He read between the lines.

Heard her saying goodbye to him loud and clear.

"I'm sorry, Abigail."

"So am I, Vaughn. More than you know."

Twelve

We want to be there with you.

On the morning of her ultrasound appointment, Abigail sat in the exam room in her cotton gown and reread the text Vaughn had sent her after the hospital summer gala. The text had a photo attached of him and Ruby. When she'd left the party that night—left him—her heart had felt like it was cracking in a thousand pieces. Spider cracks in every direction, like tempered glass before it falls apart.

And then his message had arrived, asking to be a part of this very big next step in her pregnancy. In her future.

The words made her smile now as she pulled the note up on her phone. She clicked on the photo of him and Ruby to enlarge it, a man-and-dog selfie of the two of them sitting in the spare bedroom, where she'd slept the night she went to Vaughn's house. The photo touched her in a million ways. Made her think she was missed. Gave her hope that Vaughn was ready to tackle his PTSD even more aggressively since he'd been reluctant to bring Ruby into his workplace before now.

Because her ultrasound was in the medical arts wing of Royal Memorial, close to Vaughn's office, surely his colleagues would see him with Ruby today, even though he'd traded shifts with another surgeon in order to be here. He'd texted her he was on his way a few moments earlier. As she waited in the exam room, she wondered who would walk through the door first. The ultrasound technician, or Vaughn and Ruby.

When a quick knock sounded, she set aside her phone.

"Come in." She'd been left alone to change, but the technician—Leslie—had given her more than enough time to slip off her dress and put on the hospital gown.

"All set?" Leslie asked, stepping into the room.

"I'm ready." Abigail's heart sank for a moment, however, her eyes greedy for a sight of Vaughn.

"That's good, because you have a hospital celebrity joining us today." Leslie held the door open wide, admitting the sexy doctor Abigail had been hoping to see.

Ruby's nails clicked softly on the floor as she entered the room with Vaughn, who was dressed in street clothes. Dark pants and a fitted blue polo shirt. Abigail's breath caught just seeing him. He had an undeniable physical effect on her. She couldn't have pulled her gaze away from him if she tried.

"Thank you for letting us be here," Vaughn said quietly as her bent to kiss her cheek, his fingers lingering on her face for an extra few moments.

"It's good to see you. Both." Her skin tingled pleasantly where he touched her, a shiver tripping down her spine.

"We missed you." His eyes held hers while the technician logged in to her machine.

"I'm ready when you are, Miss Abigail," Leslie called to her. "Doctor Chambers, bring whatever chair is more comfortable for you."

Excited and oddly nervous, Abigail laid down on the table, then Leslie quickly covered her legs with one blanket and gave her a second if she wanted it for her breasts. After sliding her gown open, the technician squeezed the gel on Abigail's stomach to help her slide the wand for a good picture.

Vaughn leaned over to grasp her hand, his expression serious. Was he nervous, too? She thought her anxiety came from not knowing what her future held with a man she was falling for. Did his presence here mean he wanted to have a role in her life and the life of her child? But she wasn't sure why Vaughn appeared so... stoic. Quiet.

Perhaps bringing the dog into the hospital had already opened him up to comments and questions from Royal Memorial staffers before he even set foot in the exam room. But she was just guessing, unsure of so many things when it came to Vaughn.

The ultrasound screen lit up with images of the tiny life inside her, drawing her attention away from the worries to focus on the joys.

"Here we go," Leslie said cheerily, using the wand to hover over different parts of Abigail's belly as she pointed out parts of the baby. "Smile and wave for the camera, little one."

"Can you tell the sex?" Abigail asked, marveling over

the images on the display monitor that would give her a video file afterward. "I'm hoping we'll know this time."

"I like to be really sure before I say anything." Leslie smiled, moving over and over one small spot on Abigail's stomach. "But by now, I feel certain." She glanced over at Abigail. "It's a girl."

A little girl. The words made happy tears fill Abigail's eyes. A lump formed in her throat as she looked toward Vaughn, wanting to share the moment.

He stared at the monitor, eyes narrowed. Worry etched between his eyebrows. Ruby leaned heavily against his side, far more in tune with her handler's moods than Abigail had been.

"Vaughn?" she said uncertainly. "I'm so excited."

His face cleared, but it seemed as though it took some effort on his part. He rubbed her arm. "Me, too." He swallowed. Scavenged a ghost of a smile. "That's incredible news."

Something was bothering him, though. And it upset Abigail that she didn't know what, but she tried to let it go and just enjoy the moment. She closed her eyes, listening to the sound of her heart beating over the monitor and the click of the technician's fingers on the keyboard as she zoomed in on various parts of Abigail's baby. The antiseptic scent of the paper-covered exam table distracted her, and she opened her eyes with a start, her senses sharpening rather than relaxing. She couldn't shake the sensation that Vaughn wasn't fully present with her on this important day.

"What's wrong?" she asked, needing him to be supportive or…to not be here at all. She'd really thought they'd moved past this and he was looking forward to being a part of today with her.

He didn't answer. He moved around the bed and approached the display monitor, as if to take a closer view. To Leslie, he asked, "Can you go back here for a second?" He gestured to a point to the left of the center.

Worry stirred inside her.

Real worry.

Ruby must have felt it, too, because the dog lifted her head away from Vaughn's thigh long enough to nuzzle Abigail's calf for a moment. A nuzzle of comfort.

Was this the way Vaughn felt when the golden retriever pressed herself to him? She couldn't imagine feeling this kind of anxiety all the time. Through her own fears, she couldn't deny a pang of renewed empathy for Vaughn.

The ultrasound technician circled the same spot over and over as both of the medical professionals in the room leaned closer to the screen, freaking Abigail out.

"Excuse me for just one second, okay?" Leslie stood, already moving toward the door. "I'm going to have our radiologist join us so she can give you the official reading."

Leslie patted Abigail's calf on her way past the bed, too. An absent gesture, imparting more comfort. Something wasn't right with her baby. She could feel it.

"Vaughn, is my baby okay?" Fear clogged her throat. She stared at the screen, willing her eyes to find whatever it was that they were seeing.

"This is a long way from my field of expertise." He shook his head, deflecting what should have been an easy question. "The radiologist will tell us more."

Vaughn looked pale. Distressed. His eyebrows knit.

"More about what?" Levering up on her elbows, she felt truly scared.

She had already lost her sister. She couldn't possibly lose her baby girl, too.

Vaughn's green eyes turned to meet hers. Serious. Unwavering. "I don't know. But if anything is wrong, you will have the best care in the world. I promise."

He gripped her hand in his, his assurance helping her to catch her breath even as it reinforced her fears. What was wrong?

When the radiologist stepped into the room, tucking a pen into the pocket of her lab coat, the specialist's eyes went briefly to Ruby in her service vest before glancing up at Vaughn and Abigail.

"Dr. Chambers." The woman—Dr. Oma, according to her badge—nodded at him as she took a seat in front of the ultrasound display and rolled the chair up to the work station. "Miss Stewart, I'm going to take a few more photos," she announced, moving the wand over Abigail's belly again. "I ran into your OB in the hall since he delivered a baby this morning, and I was able to consult with him briefly."

"Is he coming in?" Abigail wanted someone, anyone, to give her answers about what was happening.

Vaughn remained by the head of the bed with Ruby, his hand on Abigail's shoulder as he studied the screen behind the radiologist.

"Dr. Prevardi asked me to have Doctor Troy Hutchinson join us instead. If he has time." The ultrasound wand moved back and forth, pressing. The machine paused frequently for screen captures, zooming in on parts of Abigail's baby she couldn't possibly identify without someone explaining what she was seeing.

Beside Abigail, she heard Vaughn's sharp intake of breath.

"Who is he?" Abigail's eyes went from Vaughn to the radiologist.

"Dr. Hutchinson specializes in maternal-fetal medicine." Dr. Oma turned the display monitor toward Vaughn and Abigail. "We want to get his take on this." She circled a spot with her finger—dark blobs on the screen as far as Abigail could tell. "It's a small abnormality in the kidneys and we want to either rule out a problem or address it if there is one."

The radiologist continued to speak. Abigail knew because the woman's mouth moved, but the blood rushed in her ears so loudly that it drowned out everything else. Her brain couldn't process the news.

There was an abnormality in her baby. Her beautiful little girl might have something wrong with her.

Abigail felt like she was being sucked down a tunnel, a dark swirl of fears that blocked out everything else. By the time the specialist, Dr. Hutchinson, strode into the room, she was a mess.

She'd never been so grateful for Vaughn's presence, since he spoke the same language as the rest of the room, giving her the option of closing her eyes for some of the discussion about monitoring the defect. She swiped at the tears leaking down the side of her cheeks. Tears that Ruby must have noticed because she laid her doggy head right by Abigail's shoulder, her dark brown eyes filled with concern.

Later, when Abigail had calmed down some, she would ask Vaughn for his perspective on everything that happened today. He would give her an idea of how worried she ought to be. For now, she held his hand tight while Dr. Hutchinson promised to run more tests and get back to her soon.

* * *

Fixing Abigail something to eat back at her house that afternoon, Vaughn acknowledged he had overestimated himself. Overestimated how much he could change in order to be with Abigail.

Still reeling from the ultrasound appointment, he knew he hadn't been the steadying presence she deserved. Knew he'd failed her when she needed him to be strong. But the news that something might be wrong with her baby had wrecked all his defenses. He wasn't ready to be the man she needed and deserved in her life.

He recognized it as soon as he'd seen the tiny shadow on the ultrasound screen. His failure ate away at him now as he peeled a cucumber to add to the salad he was making for her. Ruby stalked back and forth between the living room, where Abigail rested on the couch, and the kitchen, where Vaughn prepared a light meal.

This morning he had felt a connection to the life inside of Abigail. And he had wanted to be there for her today. That text he'd sent her after the gala came after a lot of soul-searching. He didn't want to be without her. But already, he could see how short of the mark he was falling as a partner. In the exam room, he'd been more than rattled—he'd been afraid he would shut down on her completely, retreat from her emotionally at a time when she needed more support than ever.

If Ruby hadn't been there, keeping him focused and engaged, he might not have gotten through the strained meeting with Hutch. The news that Abigail's baby might have a serious health defect terrified him.

Drying his hand on a dish towel, he tossed the vegetable peels in the trash and set the salad on a tray with flatware and a drink for her. He wanted her to rest and had insisted on driving her home, knowing she was in no shape to drive herself after that scare.

She was rightfully upset.

Vaughn would have Micah bring her car home from the hospital for her. Make sure she had everything she needed. Hell, he'd do anything she wanted to be sure she was safe and cared for during her pregnancy. Especially since Rich Lowell was still out there.

But Vaughn could no longer fool himself that he was doing her or her child any good by sticking around. The darkness inside him wasn't going away.

It would hound him for the rest of his life.

He'd felt it roar to the surface as soon as he'd seen the abnormality on the ultrasound display, his fears so strong he'd been afraid to share his concerns with Abigail, knowing he might overstate the need for further testing. Hutch had handled the news well, remaining positive at all times before making a date to see Abigail again.

That was a good thing. Vaughn was ready to admit her and monitor her 24/7. Not because the baby's issue was so severe. But because he couldn't fathom anything ever happening to Abigail or her child.

He would not be the man who dimmed Abigail's vibrant spirit with his anxiety.

As he entered the living room, Ruby glanced up at him, her tongue lolling out one side of her mouth before she lay down beside Abigail. The dog's vest was off for the day. She'd already worked hard.

Now, however, another stressful moment was upon them.

Steeling himself for the discussion that had to happen, Vaughn settled the tray of food on the coffee table.

He hoped Abigail understood how much this was going to rip out his heart.

Ruby lifted her head again, sensing the tension. She got to her feet and padded over to him, sitting beside him.

"Abigail." Vaughn wished he was better with words. Wished he had some way to make this hurt less for both of them. Already his chest ached like a weight sat there, crushing his ribs.

"Aren't you going to join me?" Her gaze went to the single tray. The single plate of salad.

Time to make sure she understood.

"I can't." It was that simple. And that complicated. "I know I asked to be there with you today." He stepped closer to her, dropping into the seat by the sofa. "I wanted to be a part of this next phase of your life."

Her dark hair spilled over the wide straps of a sundress she wore, red with white polka dots.

"I couldn't have gotten through that appointment without you." She reached for his hand and threaded her fingers through his.

Regret carved a deep hole in him.

He couldn't imagine going through the rest of his life without touching her again. Without feeling this connection.

But he untwined his fingers and stepped away.

"I can't do it, Abigail. I'm only going to end up hurting you and this sweet little girl that's arriving this fall."

Her jaw dropped as she stared up at him. Then she snapped it shut. Her eyes sparked. "I don't understand."

"You mean too much to me for me to check out on you when you need me most." He shouldn't have let the relationship go this far. He'd been weak when he'd sent her that text saying he wanted to be at the ultrasound appointment. "It's better for you if we end things now."

Hurt and anger wrestled inside her, battling for dominance.

They elbowed her insides harder than any unborn child ever could.

Setting her feet on the floor, she rose to stand in front of him, not even trying to rein in the feelings after the scare she'd had today.

"You're walking away now? After you told me how much you wanted to be by my side today?" She'd been prepared to walk away after the gala on Saturday.

Yes, it had torn her apart to let things end. But she'd been ready to respect his wishes. She really thought he'd come to terms with the demons he battled so far. *He'd* been the one to insist on more, after all, knowing how hard it had been for her to let him into her life. And now, he was backing away. It hurt. So damn much.

"I thought—I hoped—I could be a part of your future." The anguish in his eyes was real enough. Ruby walked around him once, then leaned into him hard, pressing her head to his hip. "But I saw today how fast this facade I try to hold together could fall apart." He snapped his fingers. "Like that, Abigail." He shook his head. "That's not the kind of support system you deserve."

"That news would devastate anyone with a pulse!" She didn't want to raise her voice, but she felt it notching higher. "And you still have one, Vaughn, unless you've forgotten. Your life is a gift—something you should see better than most people after the service you gave your country. But you're frittering it away like it means nothing to you."

He looked stunned silent.

Said nothing.

And she realized she wasn't close to done.

"Don't you owe it to the brothers in arms you lost not to take your life for granted?" She blinked hard against a surge of grief for her sister, the wave so strong it threatened to level her. "My sister died, and I hate that. But if she had pulled through, Vaughn, she wouldn't squander her days, scared to live."

Vaughn's shoulders were tense. His features frozen. Expressionless. She'd lost him already, she could tell. And her angry words were only making him retreat further.

Ruby shifted her weight on her front paws. A tiny hint of her own anxiety. Abigail felt like the worst kind of heel, but if she didn't call out Vaughn for taking his happiness for granted, who would?

"I've given my life to my work," he said finally. "I'm making a difference the best way I can."

"A noble sacrifice." Who wouldn't admire the way he'd given up everything to be the best surgeon possible? The most giving? "But you're still breathing, Vaughn. I hope one day you take the time to enjoy it and find happiness."

He studied her with remote green eyes, the way he might study a case file or a difficult patient. Assessing.

"I'm sorry, Abigail." The simple words revealed the huge, yawning divide between them. "I wish it was that simple. But it's not. And I'm...so damn sorry."

She had no words to express how much that hurt her. How much *he* hurt her.

When she failed to speak, he gave a small nod. An acknowledgment that there was nothing more to say. "I'll show myself out."

He turned on his heel, Ruby following behind him.

Abigail covered her mouth with her hand to make sure she didn't call after him. Ruby, at least, spared her a glance back before they walked out of her house.

She felt something wet hit her collarbone and realized tears were sliding down her face. She swiped at them impatiently. No way would she spend tears on a man who hid behind his work at the expense of a real connection with anyone.

At the expense of love.

Closing her eyes, she didn't want to acknowledge that thought. She couldn't have possibly let herself fall in love with a man who would never risk his heart for her. And if she had, she wanted to go on denying it until her own heart stopped breaking.

Thirteen

The next morning, Abigail stared listlessly at her sketchbook.

Charcoal in hand, she hoped to draw something—anything—to take her mind off her worries for her baby. She hadn't slept all night, fear for her unborn child sending her to the internet to read everything possible about kidney defects detectable in utero. That, of course, only frightened her more.

And while it was wrong of Vaughn to join her for the ultrasound if he didn't plan on sticking around, she could recognize today that her reaction had been fueled by fears for her little girl. Emotions had been running high yesterday.

Now, she also had to contend with the hole in her own heart over losing Vaughn. She gripped the charcoal tighter between her fingers and sighed. She'd been in her seat by the studio window for almost twenty minutes now, and she had nothing to offer the blank page. No inspiration. No emotion.

She wished she could at least express her anger. Her frustration. But her tears were spent now after a sleepless night. Even the anger had faded since she'd vented her emotions on Vaughn the day before. She still felt the same crushing disappointment about what he'd done, yet, she sure did regret the way she'd expressed those things to him. Setting down the charcoal, she shoved aside the sketchbook and stared out the window instead, her gaze tracking a hummingbird bobbing around the special red feeder she'd installed so she could watch them drink. Bright emerald and blue, the bird darted in to press its long beak into the sugar water.

Not even the sight of her favorite feathered friend inspired her.

She regretted accusing Vaughn of not living his life. And, knowing how hard he battled his PTSD, she regretted suggesting how he should honor his fallen comrades in arms. It hadn't been her place. She would have bristled if someone told her how she should or shouldn't be honoring Alannah's memory.

There was no right way to grieve.

Restless, she moved to her carving tools instead, taking a seat at a table where she did detail work to play with a thick piece of hickory that hadn't spoken to her yet. The grain was wavy and warped, the lines moving in unexpected directions—maybe a branch had fallen away, giving the tree a lumpy knot to heal over. She traced the misshapen bits with her finger before tugging on a pair of gloves and picking up a gouge.

There was interest in the misshapen. Unlike things that were traditionally beautiful—perfectly formed with symmetry that pleased the eye—there was a different kind of beauty in nature's scars. The odd line that made you look a second time. The unexpected angle that forced the eye to linger.

The healed-over scars were strong. The lumpy branch had gone on long after a part had fallen away. Tough but thriving.

Abigail gouged deeper and deeper. Around and around. She formed circles, not sure where they were going but liking the feel of the wood in her hands. The smoothness she brought to the wood without taking away the erratic look of the grain. She had moved onto the chisel, finding figures in the wood as she worked.

A baby in the middle of it all.

Just a tiny form, but a uniting presence in the center. And arms going around it. Fluid, slender arms. Then, around those, another pair. Strong and muscular.

The chime of her phone beside her dragged her from intense concentration, making her realize that she'd found inspiration at last. Over an hour had vanished without her realizing it. For a moment, she nursed a foolish hope that it might be Vaughn.

But she didn't recognize the number on her caller ID, dashing the idea right away.

"Hello?" Straightening from her worktable, she juggled the phone to her ear and peeled off her gloves.

"Abigail?" a male voice asked. "This is Dr. Hutchinson."

She tensed, waiting to hear more news about her baby. "Thank you for calling," she said, managing to get the words out even though she felt like she'd been robbed of breath. Fear and hope made her neck prickle as she prayed the news was good. "Did you learn anything new?"

She'd been uncertain of his next steps when she left the hospital the day before, thinking she'd quiz Vaughn about it more when they got home. But after their argument, Abigail realized she'd never gotten to do that.

"Nothing definitive." His voice was even, the sounds of the hospital around him—monitors beeping, a phone ringing, the PA system making an announcement in the background. "But I spoke to a colleague who specializes in hydronephrosis—the condition I suspected your child might have."

She'd read about that, too, a dilation of the kidneys. The problem could range in seriousness and required monitoring after birth, but it wasn't life-threatening to her baby.

"Did you rule it out? Or do you think that's what it could be?" She drew in a breath. Held it.

"We haven't ruled it out." He sounded matter-of-fact, but not gravely serious. Was that a good sign? "But my colleague agreed with me that if there is hydronephrosis, it is only to a slight degree."

Swallowing the lump in her throat, she struggled to follow what he was saying. "That's good, right? How serious do you think it is?"

Gazing out her studio window, she hoped for good news with all her heart.

"We are always glad to know about things like this ahead of time," he explained as the background noise from the hospital behind him quieted. He must have stepped into an office or private hallway. "That's why we look carefully at the scan. But to answer your question, we are not concerned about your baby's development and don't need additional scans."

The air rushed out of her lungs so fast she had to hold on to the windowsill. Relief flooded through her.

"We will want to monitor the baby carefully at birth through the first few days to be sure the kidneys function properly so we can intervene quickly if necessary," Dr. Hutchinson continued, "but treatment would be a short or more prolonged course of antibiotics. Nothing surgical."

Abigail felt like a boulder of worry had just rolled off her shoulders. Her baby would be fine. Healthy.

"Thank you so much." She wanted to shout it from the rooftops that her baby girl was all right. "I'm so happy I don't know what to say."

On the other end of the call, the doctor surprised her with a warm chuckle. "As a new father to triplets, I assure you, I can identify with what you're feeling. Nothing is more important to a parent than the health of their children."

As she disconnected the call, feeling like she had a new lease on life, her first thought was to contact Vaughn. He would want to know the baby was healthy.

But would that be fair to him after the way she'd lashed out at him for drawing away? Her chest ached with the knowledge that it wouldn't be right to call him now. No matter what, she loved Vaughn. She couldn't deny that in the clear light of day now that she'd had more time to process the shock and hurt of the breakup. Yes, she still hurt from losing him. Yet she wanted him to be happy, even if that meant living the isolated life he'd chosen.

She pulled her gloves back on and slid her safety goggles into place, taking her seat at the workbench. She would lose herself in her art for a little while, needing to give a voice to the knot of emotions inside her.

At least she knew what she was sculpting now. A little statue that she would send as a gift to Vaughn. A small way to apologize for hurting him. It didn't begin to patch the hole in her heart. But maybe, with any luck, it would help bring him a measure of peace to know that she and her baby still cared about him.

And always would.

Vaughn smashed a tennis ball across the net on the courts behind the Texas Cattleman's Clubhouse, venting his frustration with his racket.

His opponent, Hutch, the same doctor who had read Abigail's ultrasound scans, shocked him by returning the ball with an athletic backhand from the line.

A return shot Vaughn couldn't possibly reach.

Damn.

That meant he'd lost the game and the set along with it.

"Nice shot," he admitted grudgingly, sweat dripping down his back in the unrelenting Texas sun.

They'd started playing early to get ahead of the heat, but they'd tied in game after game, extending the set far longer than Vaughn had imagined they would be playing. He had finally tracked down Hutch for a round of tennis, selfishly hoping to reassure himself about Abigail's ultrasound. Vaughn knew better than to violate her privacy, not that Hutch would have allowed it. But since Abigail had invited him to be in the room during the scan, he thought that at least allowed him to know if he should be worried—if he should stop by and see

Abigail or lend his professional weight to finding the best specialist the country had to offer. He would call in every favor he had to make sure she had the care she needed—even if she didn't want him around.

"I surprised myself." Hutch grinned. "I think that burst of speed was fueled by the fear I was going to have to forfeit if we tied another game." Shaking his head, he stalked toward the bench on one side of the courts, where there was a canopy for shade. "I'm not going to be able to move tomorrow."

Vaughn joined him at the bench where they'd left their bags and Ruby, in full view of the court and inside the fenced area for her safety. He dug in his cooler for a fresh water bottle and cracked open the cap, topping off Ruby's dish before he released her to play, giving her one of his old tennis balls. The retriever could catch almost anything in midair.

"I seriously doubt that." Vaughn yanked off his headband and tossed it in the bag along with his racket. "Recover fast so I can have a rematch and restore my honor."

"Sure thing." Hutch found his own cold drink and dropped onto the bench. He took the ball Ruby had already returned and tossed it to her again, the dog happily chasing it after her quiet time in the shade during the tennis match. "Have you spoken to Abigail recently?"

Regret mixed with guilt. "No."

A situation he planned to remedy immediately.

"I think you should get in touch with her." Hutch's eyes met his.

Vaughn sank to the bench beside his friend, thoughts of Abigail—of how he failed her—a weight on his shoulders. On the tennis court next to them, a foursome set up for doubles. The club was quiet, even for a weekday, the immaculate grounds mostly empty. A couple of young mothers sat poolside with small children in floaties, a lifeguard helping them keep the youngsters safe.

That would be Abigail one day, playing with her baby girl. Vaughn wanted to be in that picture of the future with her. With her child.

"I will."

"She deserves your support." Hutch swung to face him, mopping a towel over his head while Ruby waited for another turn to retrieve the old tennis ball, her tail wagging slowly.

"I—" He didn't know how to admit how badly he'd screwed up. "I wanted to make things work with her. She's the most…" He couldn't even come up with the words to describe Abigail. She was so beautiful, inside and out. So warmhearted and generous. A bright light to everyone around her. "The most incredible woman I've ever met. But I panicked when I heard about the baby."

Shame and remorse filled him. She deserved a better man than him. That was the only facet of the breakup he didn't regret. She should be with someone who would be there for her no matter what.

"What do you mean?" Hutch pulled two oranges out of his cooler and passed one to Vaughn. "As in, you're not ready to be a dad?"

"No. That's not it." Taking the orange, he started to peel it, understanding in retrospect what had made him run. "I am already attached to that baby. But what kind of partner will I make for Abigail when I need to run home and hide out with Ruby every time life gets tough?" Breaking off a section of the orange, he shook his head, more certain than ever of his decision. "If

Ruby hadn't been there during the ultrasound, I might have lost it."

He didn't understand how to deal with his emotions anymore. They came at him too fast, too hard, and they carried memories of times he didn't want to remember. And no matter how much therapy he underwent, he couldn't imagine his future being any different.

"But you didn't," Hutch reminded him. "And if there's anything in life worth breaking down over, it's your kids." The toughest competitor on any Royal Memorial sports team pounded his fist lightly against his chest. "I don't mind telling you I would lose it if someone said my kids were in danger. That's the worst life can dish out, man. And you dealt with it."

Hutch took pity on Ruby and threw her another ball. The dog ran like the wind and leaped to catch it.

Vaughn hung his head, wishing he were a different man. A better one. "I dealt with it by telling Abigail I wasn't ready for more. By walking away when she needed me most."

"It didn't come easy for Simone and me, either," Hutch admitted while the doubles match nearby got underway. "All I know is that if you regret breaking things off, you should tell her."

"How would she trust me after that?" Vaughn would not hurt her again. He couldn't do that to someone he loved. The thought stopped him up short.

Loved?

Hell yes, loved.

On some level he'd known it this week when he'd felt like his heart had been ripped out of his chest with missing her. But now, there was no more hiding from the truth. He loved Abigail.

Hutch said nothing. Waited.

"I wouldn't trust me," Vaughn answered the question for him. He couldn't ask that of her, either. "Not after how I walked out on her."

"Maybe not," Hutch agreed easily, packing up his bag and tossing his orange peel in the trash. "But you're not Abigail. She might see something in you—something better—that you can't."

Promising a rematch soon, his tennis partner strode away from the courts toward the clubhouse.

Leaving Ruby and Vaughn alone.

He needed to shower and head into work. He was taking another doctor's afternoon shift—the trade for having the day off when he'd gone to the ultrasound appointment.

Packing up his tennis bag, he noticed a clubhouse staff member headed his way, carrying a package.

"Dr. Chambers," the younger man called to him. "I'm one of the valets."

"Is there a problem with my car?" Vaughn asked. He couldn't afford to be late for work.

"No, sir." The liveried staffer thrust the package toward him. "Someone named Brandon dropped this off for you. He said he thought it might be important."

Vaughn took the brown-wrapped paper box and noted the return address that had come by special shipment. Abigail Stewart.

Curious and trying not to feel too hopeful, he handed the valet a few bills and started tearing open the paper.

"Um. Sir?" The valet hadn't gone away.

Vaughn kept tearing the paper, finding a box inside. "Was there anything else?"

"You gave me all twenties." The valet looked perplexed as he stared at the tip.

With good reason. Vaughn hadn't even noticed what he was giving him.

"Keep it." The package in his hand represented the only bright spot in the last week, and he wasn't the kind of man who took money out of the hands of someone who'd helped him. "This was important."

The guy—a local college student, he guessed—grinned from ear to ear. "Thank you, sir. I'll share it with my partner out front who covered for me."

Once he was alone, Vaughn turned back to the box, dropping onto the bench again to open it. Ruby stared at it with him, setting aside her tennis ball, as if she knew how important a package from Abigail might be.

His throat burned, emotions creeping up on him fast. What if she was simply returning some personal possession he'd left behind? Something that fell out of his pocket at her house?

But it felt too heavy to be something he would have ever left at her place. Shoving aside the tissue paper, he found a note penned in careful, artistic calligraphy.

We are here for you.

The words—so unexpected—made his eyes burn along with his throat. Only this time, the burn was good. Hopeful. Hope-filled.

Tearing through more tissue, he saw a wood carving inside. He lifted it out with both hands, holding whatever she'd made like the treasure it was.

The sculpture was of two sets of arms—one male, one female—encircling a baby. A family.

One Abigail somehow still seemed to want him to be a part of, despite everything.

Hutch had suggested Abigail might be a more forgiving, trusting person than Vaughn. That she might still be able to move forward with him even though he didn't feel whole. His friend was right.

Vaughn had a second chance at happiness. At the life Abigail warned him he was squandering.

He wouldn't waste this one.

Fourteen

Abigail reeled in her measuring tape as she stood against the east wall of the children's ward lounge. She tried to imagine what limbs she had at her studio that would work for the treehouse she had planned for phase two of the interactive art installation. The play space would be a raised platform just a few feet off the ground, but it would be surrounded by fabric leaves and a sculpture that looked like a giant nest, enhancing the sense of being high in the air.

The hospital hummed with activity nearby, now that the partition had been removed so patients could enjoy the tree sculpture. She would have to plan her future installation dates carefully, waiting to assemble the rest once she had significant portions prebuilt in her studio. Brandon had left her messages already, hoping to help.

His kind offer had seemed so genuinely motivated by

an interest in her work that she couldn't refuse. And she had fun sharing her craft with someone so obviously intrigued. Even if seeing him would remind her of Vaughn and all that she'd lost.

Blinking away the thought of him that she knew would only add to her heartache, Abigail tried to focus on the work she adored instead of the man she loved. She had promised herself that—for her baby's sake—she needed to find joy and happiness again. She'd told Vaughn to do that, so she felt like she needed to at least try to follow her own advice, even if it was easier said than done.

"There's a fairy!" a youthful voice shouted nearby, the thrill of discovery obvious in the raised, excited octave.

Abigail smiled, grateful for the distraction from her sad thoughts. Turning, she spotted a familiar redhead pointing high up in the tree.

Zoe. The patient she'd met when she'd been sculpting the *Tree of Gifts*. Only this time, the little girl was no longer in a hospital gown or attached to an IV. She held the hand of an auburn-haired older woman whose features were startlingly similar to her own. It could only be the child's mother.

Abigail retrieved her purse and walked toward the pair. A handful of other children and their families dotted the lounge. A few of the kids were in pajamas or hospital gowns, wearing hospital ID bracelets. Others seemed to be visiting siblings or friends. But it pleased Abigail to see that all of them were interacting with the tree in some way. Admiring it, touching it, searching for creatures or reading the placard the hospital had let her install after the gala.

For Alannah, the brightest bird of all.

It made Abigail happy to think of her sister that way—a part of nature. A continuing presence in Abigail's art. A joyous aspect of her own perspective.

Arriving near the little girl and her mother, Abigail smiled at the redheaded pixie who had wanted to know if she was really carving a tree from a tree.

"Hello, Zoe." Abigail tucked her measuring tape in her handbag before introducing herself to the girl's mother. "I'm Abigail. Zoe and I met when I was working on the tree."

"I found a fairy, Miss Abigail!" Zoe announced in a very loud, excited whisper, as if she didn't want to give it away for the other children. "Just like you said."

The girl's mother smiled warmly. "I'm Rita." She stuck out her hand and shook Abigail's. "Zoe told us all about your tree. She wouldn't rest until we came back to search for fairies since she was discharged before you were finished."

Touched, Abigail was very glad she'd made something special for Zoe. After the health scare with her own little girl, she had renewed empathy for the hardship of families with children who battle illnesses. "I enjoyed meeting her. And I've been meaning to ask one of the nurses if they had a way to get a small gift to her."

Zoe had been staring up into the tree, perhaps seeking more creatures. But at the word *gift* she edged closer.

"For me?" she asked, green eyes bright.

"Yes." Kneeling down to Zoe's height, Abigail withdrew a small carving wrapped in a purple bandanna. "You inspired me to add fairies to the tree. They are there because of you. So I thought you should have one of your own to keep."

Zoe's eyes went cartoon-wide as she peered up to her mother, as if seeking permission to take the gift. At Rita's nod, the girl carefully cradled the carving in her hands, peeling aside the bandanna. Her eyes met Abigail's over the sculpture, her gratitude and wonder the most moving tribute to Abigail's work that she could imagine.

For a thank-you, the girl flung her arms around Abigail's neck and squeezed her, still clutching her fairy tight.

"I love her," she said, still in a whisper, but this time more heartfelt and sweet. "I'm going to call her Abigail."

"I'd like that." She wondered if the last statue she'd made—the one she'd sent to Vaughn—had been received with nearly as much enthusiasm.

With an effort, she pushed aside thoughts of him to say goodbye to Zoe and Rita.

Now that she had the measurements she needed for the play area nest, she could leave Royal Memorial, too. Her feet were only reluctant, she knew, because there was always a chance of seeing Vaughn here.

Forcing her way toward the stairs, she turned to see Vaughn leaning against her tree in the lounge. Watching her.

Startled, even though people were coming and going in the lounge all the time, Abigail's mouth went dry.

In the few days since she'd seen him, she'd forgotten how devastatingly handsome he was. Still clean-shaven, he wore scrubs, the same as the day they first met. Awareness pricked over her skin. Her breath catching.

"That was a beautiful thing to do." Levering his shoulder off the tree, he stalked toward her. "You made that little girl's day."

Abigail's tongue stuck to the roof of her mouth, no matter that she'd wanted to see him. Hoped to see him. Played in her mind a thousand times what his reaction might be to her gift.

She hadn't anticipated how much she'd pinned her hopes on this man even though he'd walked away from her. She told herself to wait and see what he said. To listen with an open heart.

To be a better person than she'd been the last time they spoke. If nothing else, she would have the chance to apologize.

"She made mine, too." Her voice sounded funny in her own ears.

Vaughn halted a few steps from her. Close enough that she could reach out and touch him. Her pulse quickened, the way it always seemed to when he was near her.

"As much as she liked the statue you made her, I am willing to bet I liked the one you made for me even more." His gaze was steady. Sincere. "Thank you for that, Abigail."

Pleased he enjoyed the gift, she couldn't deny that she'd hoped for...more than that. A part of her had envisioned it as a peace offering. A way to heal things between them. She glanced around the lounge, wishing they could speak someplace privately. Then again, maybe it was better this way. She couldn't fall apart with an audience nearby.

"I'm sorry for the way I—" She had to clear her throat. "I shouldn't have come down on you so hard that day. I was hurting, and I took it out on you."

Vaughn pointed toward the chairs in the far corner of the lounge. "Would you sit with me for a minute? If you have time?"

Nodding, she walked beside him on wobbly legs.

She sat in one of the high-backed leather seats while Vaughn took the one opposite her.

"Abby, every single thing you said to me that day was true." His hands fisted where they sat on his knees, as if fighting an impulse. "I have been going through the motions of an existence that hardly counts as living. Going to work. Fighting off bad dreams. Rinse and repeat."

"You can't help that." She had read more about PTSD since their split, educating herself specifically about the problems veterans suffered. She wished she'd taken time to research more thoroughly sooner in their relationship. "That's why I shouldn't have pushed—"

"You had every right to push. Because I told you I wanted to be there with you." He unclenched his hands now and reached for hers. Held them tightly in his. "And maybe that's what needed to happen for me, Abigail. I've worked hard to live a normal life. And Ruby's been great. But it's like I hit a plateau and that was all I expected from my future. More of the same."

She stared down at where he held her hands, trying to make sense of that urgent touch in relation to his words. "I don't understand."

"When you came along, you pulled me off the plateau, bringing me higher and closer to whole. And it was great. I thought life might open up for me. That I could do more. Be more." He gentled his hold on her, smoothing his thumbs over her knuckles. Soothing them. "But when I froze up in the exam room—I knew I needed to be there for you and I felt like a blank slate. I was scared for you and that tiny child you carry inside you, but I knew it didn't even show on my face. It's like this filter goes up between me and how I feel."

"I remember." She thought back to that day, seeing it in a different light. Remembering how remote he'd seemed. "It didn't seem like you."

She'd been hurt even then, before she heard about the abnormality.

"Exactly. I came face-to-face with my own failing and I know you deserve better." He sounded too certain.

"What if I don't want better?" She thought about how happy it made her to fall asleep in his arms, even if he wasn't ready to share a bed with her for the full night. How much she loved enjoying a meal with him under the stars. Or sharing her artwork and seeing his eyes light up, like he understood what she was trying to create. "Vaughn, what if I want you, just the way you are?"

"Abigail. You deserve better, and that's what I want you to have." His voice brooked no argument.

Her heart fell. She dragged in a raw breath, ready to fight for him. For them.

But he spoke first. "If you'll give me another chance, I can promise you that I will never, ever walk away from you again."

She blinked at the unexpected words. Had he really said what she thought he just said?

"Another chance?" Her voice sounded just like Zoe's had minutes before, a whisper that said she hardly dared to believe what she'd heard.

Vaughn let go of one hand to cup her cheek in his palm.

"I know I don't deserve you, but I do love you, Abigail. So much. And if you'll have me, I will spend the rest of my days making you and that little girl happy." His thumb stoked along her cheek.

Her heart swelled with love for him. Happiness beckoned and she wouldn't ever turn that away. She trusted his sense of honor. His commitment to what he said. She had been hurt so deeply by Rich that she had been guarding her heart carefully, fearing being taken advantage of again. But Vaughn Chambers was nothing like Rich Lowell. The doctor who sacrificed his career to help injured soldiers overseas was a selfless, caring man, and the oath he'd taken as a physician was something he took deeply to heart.

Now, he'd made a vow to her. And she trusted it implicitly.

"When I sent you that note, Vaughn, I told you we were here for you." She tugged their joined hands to her growing baby bump and placed his palm there. "I meant it. I love you."

His hand spanned the curve of new life and the baby fluttered with her own acknowledgment. His eyes widened. A hint of wonder inside the man who thought he didn't show anything to the world. Her heart melted.

"I'm here for you, too, Abby." He drew her close, kissing her with the tender promise of forever. "Both of you."

Her head tipped forward, touching his. She'd never felt so cherished. So precious. So loved. For a moment, she forgot everything else but him. When his lips claimed hers the next time, she clung to him, answering his kiss with a passion that simmered just below the surface.

From the opposite side of the children's ward lounge, someone started to clap. Someone whistled.

Turning as one with Vaughn, Abigail saw Dr. Hutchinson at the nurses' station just beyond the tree sculpture. He seemed to be the ringleader, still whistling, as other nurses and staffers peeked out of patient rooms to see what the fuss was about. A couple of cheers went up. Even a few parents in the lounge joined in the applause.

Vaughn gave the group—his colleagues—a thumbs-up that seemed to quiet them. He turned back to Abigail and kissed her again.

"Everyone loves a happy ending."

"I guess so." She laughed, a sound of joy spilling over. She couldn't be happier. And then she remembered she had even more good news. "Dr. Hutchinson said the baby is going to be fine, you know."

The raw emotion in Vaughn's eyes told her how scared he'd been. How much he already cared for this baby.

"That's the best news I could have asked for." His shoulders relaxed, his smile huge, lighting up the room. "I was prepared to call in every specialist nationwide to help Hutch with your case." Vaughn turned serious again, his commitment to her baby as deep as the one he'd made to her.

He would love and protect them both.

"Thank you." She laid a hand on his chest, grateful to have him back in her life. For good. "That means so much to me."

Vaughn stroked her hair. "Hutch told me it was okay to be terrified for the sake of your child. Normal." He squeezed his eyes closed. "I don't know why it helped to hear it from him, but I needed that different perspective to make me see I wasn't just detaching because of the PTSD."

"I'm all about seeing things through different eyes." Abigail had a career in art that she loved because of it. "And I'm so happy you think of this baby that way. As your child."

He was signing on for much more than being her partner.

"I can't wait to have you both in my life every day. To grow a family and find happiness together."

"What are we waiting for, exactly?" she asked. "I'm ready to start now."

His smile warmed her to her toes. She wanted to see it each day, even for a little while.

"Well, first, I need for my shift to end." He stood, drawing her to her feet with him. "I'm hoping no one noticed I went AWOL to flirt with the hot artist working in the children's ward."

"I won't tell," she promised, thinking about all she wanted to share with this man.

All she still wanted to find out about him.

"But I could pick you up on my way home tonight. Maybe bring you to the ranch for the night? Or forever?"

The question brought tears to her eyes on a day that had already brought her so much hope and promise.

"I would like that." She couldn't wait to be alone with him. To celebrate in private.

"Then I'll pick you up at eight thirty." He kissed her forehead, swiping a finger along her cheek to catch a happy tear. "And start the rest of our lives together."

She brushed her lips to his, standing on her toes. "It's a date."

* * * * *

HIS BEST FRIEND'S SISTER

SARAH M. ANDERSON

To the ladies of the YMCA water aerobics classes. Twice a week, you all listen to me babble about plot points and encourage me to keep moving, even on days when I hurt. Thanks for all your support and for laughing at my silly stories!

One

"I thought you hated the rodeo."

That voice—Oliver Lawrence knew that sweet voice. Except it was richer, deeper. It sparked memories—memories of smiling, laughing. Of having fun. When was the last time he'd had fun?

He couldn't remember.

"But here you are, surrounded by pictures of the rodeo," she went on. He could hear the smile as she spoke. She'd always smiled at him. Even when he hadn't deserved it.

Oliver jerked his head up from where it had been buried in his hands. It wasn't possible. *She* wasn't possible.

But there Renee Preston stood, just inside the door to his office as she studied the framed pictures of the All-Stars that Bailey had artfully arranged along one wall of the office.

Although her back was to him, he was stunned to realize that he recognized her anyway. The pale gold of her hair fell halfway down her back in artful waves, the curve of her backside outlined by a dark blue dress.

How long had it been? Years? He shouldn't even recognize her, much less have this visceral reaction to her. Seeing her now was a punch to the gut, one that left him dazed and breathless. And all he could think was, *I hope she's real.* Which made no sense. None at all. But given the headaches he'd had running Lawrence Energies— why were Mondays so awful?—he wouldn't be surprised if his sanity had taken a breather.

He stared but she didn't move. Bad sign. "Renee?" He blinked and then blinked again when she didn't turn around.

Okay, he was having a bad morning. Because the truth was he did hate the rodeo—the Lawrence Oil All-Around All-Stars Pro Rodeo. He'd hated it ever since his father had won the circuit in a poker game thirteen years ago. But there weren't many people who knew it. It was bad for business if the CEO of Lawrence Energies, parent company of Lawrence Oil—and, by default, the All-Stars— publicly announced how much he hated his products.

So how did Renee know?

His assistant, Bailey, came charging into the room, looking flustered. Finally Renee moved, tilting her head to look at him. "Mr. Lawrence—I'm sorry," Bailey said, breathing hard. He gave Renee an accusing look. "She's *quick.*"

Thank God Oliver wasn't hallucinating the arrival of the last person he'd expected to see today. Renee Preston was actually in his office in Dallas in the middle of a Monday morning.

"It's all—"

But just then, Renee turned the rest of the way around

and Oliver got a look at her in profile. Her little button nose, her sweetheart chin, her gently rounded stomach that curved out from the rest of her body…

Wait.

Was she *pregnant*?

Slowly, Oliver stood. "Renee, what's going on?"

Bailey hung his head. "Should I call security?"

Oliver waved away. "No, it's fine. Ms. Preston and I are old friends." That was not exactly the truth. Her brother, Clinton, was an old friend. Renee had always been an obnoxious little sister who, when she teamed up with Oliver's sister, Chloe, had been a real pain in the butt.

The full impact of her appearance hit him. She gave him a soft little smile that barely moved a muscle on her face. He didn't like that smile. It felt unnatural somehow.

He looked at her dress again. Maybe it wasn't dark blue. Maybe it was black. She looked like she'd decided to stop by his office—some fifteen hundred miles away from New York City—on her way to a funeral.

"No calls," Oliver said to Bailey. If Renee Preston was here, wearing a funereal dress while pregnant, something had gone wrong.

Suddenly, he remembered the email from Clint Preston. Had it been two months ago? Or three? Ever since Oliver's father, Milt, had uprooted the family from their Park Avenue address in New York City and relocated them to Dallas, Oliver and Clint hadn't exactly kept up a friendship. But he remembered now—that odd email that had been sent at four in the morning. *Look after Renee, will you?*

Oliver had never replied. He'd meant to, but…honestly, he'd been confused. Why did *he* have to look after Renee? She had a family. She was a grown woman. It hadn't seemed urgent, not at this time.

Clearly, it was urgent now.

Just when he thought things couldn't get any worse, they did. Served him right for thinking that in the first place.

"Actually," she said after Bailey had closed the door after him, "it's Renee Preston-Willoughby now."

Instead of pulling his hair out, he attempted to smile at Renee. "Congratulations. I hadn't heard." Although… hadn't Chloe said something about Renee getting hitched? It'd been a few years ago and Oliver had been in the middle of what was basically a corporate takeover of the business from his father.

That particular piece of information did nothing to shine a light on why she was in his office. He hadn't seen her since…

Five years ago at her brother's wedding? And Renee had still been in college. He remembered being curious because she hadn't been the same little girl in pigtails.

In fact, she'd been gorgeous, her smile lighting up the room even in the hot-pink bridesmaid's gown. But she'd had a boyfriend and Oliver wasn't going to poach another man's girl, so he'd appreciated the way she had grown into a lovely young woman from the safety of the bar, where he'd been getting sloshed with a bunch of Wall Street financiers who wanted to know if *everything* really was bigger in Texas.

Oliver dimly recalled his growing frustration that no one had believed him when he'd said he'd give anything to be back in New York City. To those idiots, Texas had sounded like a vacation. Barbecue, babes and bulls—as if that was all anyone did in Texas. All the cowgirls in the world hadn't made up for being stuck running the family businesses—and the family—then and it didn't make up for it now.

Besides, cowgirls tended to go for Flash, his younger brother. Not serious Oliver.

He almost hadn't come back to Dallas after that wedding. He'd woken up with a killer hangover and a new resolve to tell his father where he could shove the All-Around All-Stars Rodeo and his ten-gallon Stetsons and his stupid fake Texan accent. Oliver was going back to New York, where he belonged.

But he hadn't. He couldn't go back on his word to his mother. So he'd done the next-best thing—wrestled control of Lawrence Industries away from his father. The old man was still chairman of the board, but Oliver was CEO of the whole thing. Including the damned rodeo.

His attempts to relocate corporate headquarters to New York after the takeover had failed, though. Some days, he thought he'd never get out of this godforsaken state.

Had he and Renee spoken at the reception? Had she asked about his rodeo? Had he been drunk enough to tell the truth? Damn.

Even in that sad sack of a black dress, she was still the most stunning woman he'd ever seen. He wanted to sink his hands into her silky hair and pull her against his body and *feel* for himself that she was really here. Even her skin seemed to glow.

But as he looked closer, he saw other things, too. Beneath her tastefully understated makeup, he could see dark shadows under her eyes. Was she not sleeping? And even as she stood there, submitting to his inspection, her left hand beat out a steady rhythm on her leg, a *tap-tap-tap* of anxiety.

He was staring, he realized. He had no idea how long he had been staring at her. Seconds? Minutes? When had Bailey left?

He cleared his throat. "Well. This is unexpected. What brings you to Dallas?"

Her stiff little smile got stiffer. "Actually," she said, taking a deep breath, "I'm looking for Chloe." Her voice cracked on Chloe's name and she turned around quickly, but not quickly enough. Oliver just caught the way her face crumbled.

He took a step forward before he knew what he was doing. He had the oddest urge to put his arms around her shoulders, to take some of the weight from her. But he didn't. It wasn't like she'd come for him. And he couldn't imagine that she'd welcome what was essentially a stranger giving her a hug. So instead he pulled up short and said, "It's rodeo season."

She was silent for a moment, but she nodded. "And Chloe is the Princess of the Rodeo," she said in a wistful way.

Renee had been the tagalong little sister and then the bridesmaid. He knew nothing of her life. But she was clearly in distress and that bothered him.

His job was to solve problems. He'd promised his mother, Trixie, on her deathbed that he would keep the family from falling apart. That's why he was the CEO of Lawrence Energies instead of taking another job—one that didn't involve managing his father and his siblings. That was why he was still in Texas instead of going back to New York City. That's why he sucked it up and managed the damned rodeo.

Renee Preston-Willoughby was a problem and he had no idea how to solve her.

"She's in Lincoln, Nebraska, right now—and after that, it's Omaha. And after that…" He shrugged, although Renee couldn't see it. "It's rodeo season," he finished lamely. "I think she'll be back in Fort Worth in a month."

Chloe opened and closed every show in the All-Stars circuit. She had for years. She lived out of a suitcase for months on end, all because she liked to dress up in a se-quined cowgirl top and ride her horse into the arena, car-rying the American flag.

Oliver didn't know how his sister could stand it. He *hated* the rodeo. The swagger of the cowboys, the smell of the horses and cattle, the idiocy of people who vol-untarily climbed on the back of wild horses and angry bulls—yeah, that included Flash. There was nothing he liked or even tolerated about the All-Stars.

Now more than ever—what with Chloe demanding that she should be given a chance to prove she could run the thing and his father digging in his heels and insist-ing that only Oliver could do it. Never mind that Oliver absolutely didn't want to do it or that Chloe would do a better job because she actually *liked* the damned rodeo.

"I should've guessed," Renee said, her voice a little shaky. He saw her shoulders rise and fall with a deep breath and then she turned around, her face curiously blank. "I'm sorry I barged in on you," she said, her voice placating. He liked that even less than the fake smile. "Thank you for not calling security on me. It's been good seeing you, Oliver."

This day just got weirder and weirder. She had her hand on the doorknob before he realized that she was waltzing out of his office just as quickly as she had waltzed in.

He moved, reaching the door just as it swung open. He slammed it shut with his hand, causing Renee to squeak. "Wait," he said and then winced as his voice came out in a growl.

He was too close to her. He could feel the warmth of her body radiating through her clothes, through his. He should step back, put some distance between them. She was pregnant, for God's sake. Who knew what else was going on?

Slowly, she turned. Close enough to kiss, he dimly realized as he stared down into her soft blue eyes. She gasped, her eyes darkening as she looked up at him through thick lashes. He was powerless to move away. "Renee," he said, and his voice came out deeper than normal. "Why are you here?"

He wasn't sure what he expected her to do. He wasn't all that surprised when her eyes got a wet look to them—it went with the dress. But then her mouth opened and instead of a sob, a giggle came out. "You don't know," she said, her eyes watering even as she laughed harder. "Oh, God—you really don't know?"

So he was out of the loop on the New York scene. "Know what?" A tear trickled down her cheek and he lifted his other hand to wipe it away. When it was gone, he didn't pull his hand away. He cupped her cheek and kept stroking her skin. It was almost like a hug, right? "What's happened?"

"Oh, nothing," she said, an edge of bitterness creeping into her voice. "It's just…" The giggle ended in a hiccup that sounded suspiciously like a sob. "It was all a lie, wasn't it? My entire life has been a lie."

He caught another tear before it could get far. "I don't understand."

"Don't you? I can't believe you haven't heard." She closed her eyes and he could feel the tension in her body. "They're calling it the Preston Pyramid. My family's investment company was nothing but a pyramid scheme and it's all come crashing down."

How could he *not* know? The collapse of Preston Investment Strategies wasn't just a New York scandal. Renee's father—with the help of her brother and her lying, cheating husband—had bilked hundreds of thousands of investors out of millions of dollars all across the country. She'd thought everyone knew about the Preston Pyramid.

But then again, wasn't that why she was in Dallas instead of New York? She just needed to get away. Away from the reporters camped out in front of her apartment building. Away from the gossip and the threats. She needed to go somewhere where people might not look at her like she was the Antichrist's daughter. And Clint had told her to trust the Lawrence family. He'd said Oliver would take care of her, but Renee was done with people telling her what to do.

Chloe had been her best friend, once upon a time. Chloe never took crap from anyone. Chloe would help her.

Except Chloe wasn't here. Oliver was. And Renee was out of options.

This was how far she'd fallen. Slipping past his executive assistant, barging into his office and doing her level best to keep it together.

Which was hard to do when he was touching her so tenderly. Not that those tender, sweet touches would last when he realized the true magnitude of what had happened. She stared at him as he processed the news. She saw her own emotions reflected in his face. Shock, disbelief—a lot of disbelief. "Your father ran a pyramid scheme? How?"

She shrugged. She should move away from him. He basically had her pinned against the door and was staring down into her face with his intense brown eyes. But he kept stroking her cheek and she couldn't break the contact. It took everything she had not to lean into the touch, not to ask for more.

It had been Clint's wedding, hadn't it? The last time

she'd seen Oliver Lawrence? She remembered Crissy Hagan, another one of the bridesmaids that Renee had thought was a friend until about six weeks ago. Crissy had gushed about how gorgeous Clint's old friend was, but… Renee had blown Crissy off. Oliver wasn't hot— he was irritating. He'd always looked down upon her. He'd been serious and grumpy, even as a kid. He'd never liked her and he'd made it difficult for anyone else to like him. Why he and Clint had got along, she'd never known.

When Renee had found herself next to him at the bar, she'd tried to strike up a conversation by asking about the rodeo. He'd promptly informed her he hated the damned thing in the meanest voice she'd ever heard.

Oliver Lawrence was not someone she could rely on. At least, he hadn't been.

She still didn't know if he was or not.

But Crissy had been right. Oliver had been hot then— and he was hotter now. He was one of those men who was just going to get better looking with age. How old was he? Twenty-eight? Twenty-nine? Clint had turned twenty-nine in jail, so Oliver was around there.

He was not the same boy she remembered. He had four inches on her and he seemed so much…*more* than she remembered from five years ago. Taller, broader. More intense.

Stupid hormones. She was not here to lust after Oliver Lawrence, of all people. She was here to hide.

"Apparently," she said, remembering he had asked a question, "very well. No one caught on for years. Decades. He generated just enough returns that people believed the lies he sold them. Reinvestment, they called it. He convinced everyone to reinvest the profits they made, sometimes investing even more than the original amount. Of course there were no real profits," she said, her emotions rising again. She struggled to keep them in check. "There were never any profits. Not for the investors. It all went to him." She swallowed, forcing herself to look away from Oliver's intensity. "To us. I didn't know anything about it, but there's no denying that I benefited from his schemes. I can't *believe* you haven't heard," she repeated.

Anger and shame burned through her. She was so damned mad at her family—and she hurt for all the people who'd been swindled. Her father had ruined lives so he could buy a fourth vacation home. It was evil, what he'd done.

But worse than that—how could she have gone twenty-six years without realizing that her father was nothing but a glorified con artist?

When Oliver didn't say anything, she glanced back up at him. His jaw was hard and there was something dangerous in his eyes. "Okay," he said. "Your father bilked investors out of a lot of money. I'm going to guess that your brother had something to do with it?"

"Of course." She sighed. "Clint and my husband were both involved."

Abruptly, Oliver stepped back. "I'm sorry I missed your wedding. How long have you been married?"

"I'm not anymore." She took another deep breath and squared her shoulders. She wouldn't let this fact hurt her. She wouldn't let Chet hurt her, not ever again. "Chet Willoughby is dead."

Oliver recoiled another step as if she'd slapped him and then turned and began to pace. "I understand that it is unforgettably rude to ask, but are you…" He waved toward her midsection.

She almost smiled. After the last two months, his apologetic question was the least rude thing she'd heard. "Four and a half months."

Oh, the press had had a field day with that. Preston Pyramid Princess Pregnant! had blared from every newspaper and website for days. *Weeks.* The media loved a good alliterative headline.

Oliver burrowed his fingers in his hair, causing his brown hair to stand up almost on end. "Right. Your family's fortune was stolen, and your husband, who worked for your criminal father, is dead, and he left you pregnant. Am I missing anything?"

The fact that there was no judgment in his voice, no sneering or laughter—that was when Renee realized she'd made the right choice. Even if Chloe wasn't here, getting out of New York was the best thing she could have done. She could breathe in Texas. That's all she wanted. Just enough space to breathe again. "Those are the basics. Oh, my mother took what was left of the money and ran away to Paris. That might be an important detail."

It was an *extremely* important detail to the authorities.

"Yes, I can see how that might be significant." He launched a wobbly smile at her, as if he couldn't tell if he should laugh or not. When she couldn't so much as manage a chuckle, he leaned against his desk and pinched the bridge of his nose.

If she'd had any other options, she wouldn't be here. He'd looked like he was already having a terrible day and that was before she unloaded her tale of woe upon him. Her life wasn't his responsibility.

But she had no place else to go. Getting permission to come to Texas had used all of her remaining political capital.

"Did you know about the scheme?"

She shook her head. "I am fully cooperating with the

investigation. The authorities know where I am and I may be summoned back to New York at any time. I am not allowed to leave the country under any circumstance." That had been the deal. She didn't have much testimony to offer because her parents had maintained that Renee's entire job was to make the family look good. Her appearance was the only thing of value about her. At the time, it had bothered her deeply. How could her own father look at her and see nothing but a pretty face? How could he ignore her and leave her to her mother?

But now? Now she was glad that her father had kept her separate from his business dealings. It was literally the only thing keeping her out of prison.

Her main value to the authorities at this point was convincing her brother to testify against their father. And Clint was in no hurry to do that. He was holding out for a better deal.

Oliver studied her closely, his arms crossed and his hair wild. He stared for so long that she was afraid he was going to kick her out, tell her to go back to New York and deal with this mess by herself. And she couldn't. She just couldn't. If Oliver wouldn't help her, she'd...

She'd go find Chloe. Not for the first time, she wished that her so-called friends in New York hadn't turned on her. Because really, what kind of friends were they? The kind who went running to the gossip websites, eager to spill anything that would make the Preston family look worse than they already did. Not a single one had stood by her. She'd been neatly cut out of her social circle, an object of derision and scorn.

So if Oliver called security, it really wouldn't be that different. She wouldn't blame him at all. She was nothing to him, except maybe a distant childhood memory.

"You need to hide?" he asked just as she had given up hope.

"Yes," she said, her heart beginning to pound faster.

He shook his head and muttered something she didn't catch, something about Clint, maybe? Then he looked at her and said, "I'm sorry about your husband."

One should not speak ill of the dead. It was one of the last things her mother had said to Renee before she'd disappeared with three million dollars of other people's money. But Renee couldn't help the bitter laugh that escaped her. "I'm not."

He thought on that for a moment, his gaze lingering on her stomach. Her skin flushed warm under his gaze. Stupid hormones. Oliver Lawrence was not interested in her. No one in their right mind would give her a second glance.

In fact, it was definitely a mistake that she'd come. She was toxic to everyone and everything surrounding her. Here he was, a good man, and she'd all but thrown herself at his feet.

She was desperate. But she hoped the taint of Preston scandals didn't smear him.

Please don't lie to me, she found herself praying. Even if the truth were brutal—like he was going to throw her out—all she wanted from him was the truth. She couldn't handle another person looking her in the eye and telling a bald-faced lie.

"All right," he said, pushing off the desk and crossing to her. He put his hands on her shoulders, but he didn't draw her in. He just looked at her and even though it was a risk to him for her to be here, she still knew she'd made the right choice—especially when he said, "Let's get you hidden."

Two

He did not have time for this. He was skipping out on important meetings that were guaranteed to draw his father out from his hunting lodge and stick his nose back into Lawrence Energies's business—and for what?

To rescue a damsel in distress. There was no other way to describe Renee. She had one piece of luggage: a carry-on suitcase. That was it. If she was going to be here longer than a week, he was going to need to arrange for her to get some more clothes.

"Is it very far away?" she asked, sounding drained.

He was not a gambling man, but he was willing to bet that Renee was going to be here for much more than a week. "We're going to Red Oak Hill," he told her as they drove away from the Lawrence Energies corporate headquarters on McKinney Avenue and in the opposite direction of his condo on Turtle Creek. "It's my private ranch. The traffic's not too bad this time of day, so we should be there in less than an hour and a half." By Dallas standards, that was practically right next door.

"Oh," she said, slumping down in her seat.

"The way I see it," he said, trying to be pragmatic, "you have two choices. You can either rest on the drive out or you can explain in a little more detail what's going on." Because he thought he had a decent grasp on the basics. Corrupt family, financial ruin, dead husband, four and a half months pregnant.

But a lot of details were missing. He'd told Bailey on his way out to pull up what he could find on the Preston fraud case and send him the links. He'd read them when he got to the ranch. He couldn't help Renee unless he knew what the extenuating circumstances were.

She made an unladylike groaning noise that worried him. "I still can't believe you haven't caught at least some of this on the news."

Worrying about her was pointless. He was doing the best he could, given the situation. Bailey had canceled his meetings for the rest of the day and had been given instructions in case anyone came sniffing around—and that included Milt Lawrence, Oliver's father. No one was to know about Miss Preston or Mrs. Willoughby or Ms. Preston-Willoughby.

"We're acquiring a pump manufacturer, the rodeo season just kicked off and my father is out of his ever-loving mind," Oliver said, trying to keep the conversation light-hearted. "I've been busy."

Besides, none of the Lawrence Energies family fortune was invested in Preston Investment Strategies—or their damned pyramid scheme. And he would know, since he had wrestled financial control of Lawrence Energies away from his father four years ago.

"Is he really?"

Oliver shrugged. "There are days I wonder." His father was only sixty years old—by no means a doddering old man. But the midlife crisis that had been touched off by the death of Trixie Lawrence had never really resolved itself.

He could've explained all about that, but she wasn't here to listen to him complain about his family. She was here because she was in trouble.

Look after Renee, will you?

He should have replied with questions to Clint's email then. If he had, he might have answers now.

He waited. Out of the corner of his eyes, he could see her rubbing her thumbnail with her index finger, the constant circle of motion. Otherwise, she seemed calm.

Too calm.

Oliver did not consider himself the family expert on women. That honor went to Chloe, who was actually a woman—although Flash, their younger brother, gave Chloe a run for her money.

Nevertheless, he had grown up with Chloe and a healthy interest in women. He was not comfortable with the idea of Renee crying, but he was prepared for the worst.

She surprised him with a chuckle. "A lot of it is in the news."

Knowing Bailey, Oliver would have several hours of reading material waiting for him, so there was no point in making her relate something he could just as easily read—with a healthy sense of detachment, instead of listening to her shaky voice and fighting this strange urge to protect her.

"Tell me the part that's not in the news."

"The part that's not in the news," she said softly, still rubbing her thumbnail anxiously. "You know, I don't think my husband was ever faithful to me."

O…kay. "Then why did you marry him?"

"My parents said we looked good together. He worked for my father and my mother thought we'd have gorgeous babies, as if that was the only thing that mattered. He was suave and sophisticated and hot. We were featured on the *Vanity Fair* weddings page online. 'A Storybook Dream' was the name of our photo essay." She laughed, but it definitely wasn't a happy sound. "I wanted a small ceremony, but no. I had to have ten bridesmaids and the craziest party favors ever." He lifted an eyebrow at her without taking his eyes off the road. "Oh, yes. Everyone got a custom engraved pair of Waterford crystal champagne glasses, a bottle of Dom Pérignon with a custom label and a Tiffany & Co. silver ice bucket engraved with our names and wedding date, as if people cared." She sighed heavily.

It wasn't that the elite in Dallas couldn't be just as ostentatious in their displays of wealth—they could. Hell, his condo was worth a few million alone and the ranch was easily worth twice that. Dallas was not a two-bit town by any stretch of the imagination.

But it was different here. As cutthroat as Dallas high society could be, there was just more heart in Texas.

He must have been having one hell of an off day if he was mentally defending this state. He hoped his father never found out that there were things Oliver actually liked about the Lone Star State. "It sounds a tad over-the-top."

"Oh, it was—but it was a beautiful wedding. Just beautiful," she murmured and he remembered what she'd said.

It was a lie. Her husband had never loved her, never been faithful.

"I am *such* an idiot," she said miserably, and that bothered him. Strange how it did. He hadn't thought of her in so long but now that she was here, he found he needed to do something.

"Hardly. You were always smart enough to get the drop on me and Clint, weren't you? I'm thinking of a specific incident involving water balloons off a balcony. Remember?"

That got him a shadow of a smile. "That was Chloe's idea—but I did have pretty good aim."

That shadow of a smile made him feel good. The world was bleak—but he could still make her feel better.

He drove his Porsche Spyder faster, whipping in and out of traffic. The best—and only—thing he could do for her was get her safely out to Red Oak Hill. There, she could have some peace and quiet and, most important, privacy. Once he had her settled, he could get back to town and try to deal with his schedule and his family.

"I don't know if this part is in the news yet or not," she went on, sounding resigned. "I'm sure people have been doing the math ever since I began to show—and I began to show very early, to the disgust of my mother. But do you know?" She paused for a second and Oliver tried to get his head around the fact that her mother was disgusted by her pregnancy. She looked stunning, showing or not.

But that was the sort of thing that he couldn't just blurt out. This was a rescue, sort of. He wasn't whisking her away for a weekend of seduction or anything. Definitely not a seduction. So instead, he just said, "What?"

"He woke me up early that morning and we..." She cleared her throat. "And afterward, he told me he loved me. I normally said it to him—he rarely said the words. Usually he just said, 'Me, too,' as if he also loved himself. But he was different that morning and he surprised me, and I didn't say it back."

This was far more than Oliver wanted to know. He kept his mouth shut like his life depended on it.

"And then he went to work, screwed his secretary, gave her the rest of the day off and blew his brains out, coward that he was. By my count, there were at least three—possibly five—women at the funeral who could have been current or former mistresses."

"That seems like a lot." One would've been too many, but to think that man had had that many women on the side in a year and a half of marriage?

Chet Willoughby was clearly a bastard of the highest order. Or he had been anyway.

"And the thing was I didn't even know I was pregnant for another two and a half months. When I missed my period, I thought it was due to the stress. Isn't that hilarious?"

She turned to him and he glanced over to see a huge, fake smile on her face. "Not really."

Her smile froze. "Some people think it is. Some people think it's the funniest thing they've ever heard. That I'm getting exactly what I deserve. There's also a lot of speculation that I was cheating on him and drove him to his death." Her voice cracked.

His heart damn near broke for her. "Those people are heartless cowards." It was a good thing that Chet Willoughby and his suave face were already dead because otherwise, Oliver would've strangled the man himself. What kind of asshole did this to his wife?

"He knew the pyramid was going to fall and he was going to go with it. My mother tried to paint this as a noble thing. He wouldn't turn on my father. Wasn't that thoughtful of him? Not like Clint's going to, maybe. And the baby?" She shook her head. "She said the baby would be a living reminder of Chet. As if I want to remember him or his betrayal," she finished bitterly.

She was crying, he realized. Softly, quietly—but tears were trickling down her cheeks.

He didn't want to know how everyone she'd ever trusted had betrayed her. Even Clint, who Oliver had thought was a good guy. It was physically painful to know that she was hurting and, worse, to not be able to do much of anything about it.

"I don't think your child would be a reminder of betrayal," he said, feeling his way as he went. "I'd think that the baby would be a testament to your strength, your courage. Others may have cut and run, but you stood strong, Renee. That's what's going to make you an amazing mother."

She gasped and he could tell she was staring at him with huge eyes. He kept his gaze firmly locked on the road in front of him. "Do you really think so?"

He nodded like he was certain, instead of shooting compliments like arrows and praying to hit the mark. "You're welcome to stay at Red Oak Hill as long as you want," he went on. Because, aside from a lucky compliment or two, shelter was the only thing he could offer her. "I'm usually only there on the weekends. I do have a housekeeper, but I can give her some time off if you'd rather be alone."

She nodded, surreptitiously swiping at the tears on her cheeks. "Will anyone else in your family be there?"

Oliver laughed. "Absolutely not. Red Oak Hill is mine. No one will know you're there."

"Thank you," she whispered and there was so much pain in her voice that, without thinking, he reached over and wrapped his hand around hers. She clung to him fiercely. "You won't even know I'm there, I promise."

Somehow, as his fingers tangled with hers, Oliver doubted that.

It would be impossible to be around Renee and not be aware of her every movement.

As soon as he got her settled, he was driving right back to Dallas. He didn't have time to comfort Renee Preston-Willoughby.

No matter how much he might want to.

Three

Renee had not expected this. Red Oak Hill wasn't a long, low-slung ranch house in the middle of dusty cow pastures. In fact, she didn't see any cows anywhere as Oliver pulled up in front of what was undeniably a grand mansion at the top of a small hill. Towering trees she assumed were red oaks cast long shadows against the sweltering Texas sun.

The house looked like something out of a magazine. And she knew quite a bit about that. Something white caught her attention on the small lake on the other side of the driveway. "Are those...swans?"

"Fred and Wilma? Yes. They came with the house."

Renee had had a terrible day. Well, given the last five months of her life, that wasn't saying much. But somehow, the idea that Oliver had inherited a pair of swans made her giggle. "Did you name them after the Flintstones or did they come with those names?"

He quirked an eyebrow at her. "Don't know if you can

really name swans, per se. They don't come when called. But…" He shrugged again, a mischievous glimmer in his eyes. "They seemed like Fred and Wilma to me. They have cygnets this year. Pebbles and Bamm-Bamm."

She didn't remember Oliver having a sense of humor. Had he always been this funny? She remembered him being uptight and grumpy. A stick-in-the-mud, she and Chloe had decided once. That was Oliver Lawrence.

But was he, really? She thought back now to the water balloon fight he'd mentioned. She and Chloe had got the drop on them from the balcony—that'd been Chloe's idea. But Oliver and Clint had retaliated with a garden hose. And Oliver had been aiming the hose.

"Renee? You all right?"

She blinked and realized that he was standing at the passenger door of his sporty red convertible, hand out and waiting for her.

His lips curved into a small smile when she realized she was staring at him. Oh, heavens—she was probably making a fool of herself. Then again, that was nothing new. "I don't know." It was the most honest thing she'd said in so long…but somehow, she knew she didn't have to put on a brave face for him.

"Here." Taking both of her hands in his, he helped her from the low-slung car. But instead of letting go of her or stepping back, he stayed where he was. Close enough to touch. "I got an email from your brother a couple of months ago," he said, staring down into her eyes. "All it said was to look after you. Renee, I'm sorry I didn't follow up. If I had realized…"

She didn't know whether to laugh or cry. Oliver Lawrence was *apologizing*. To her! She didn't need his apologies, but all the same, she felt something in her chest loosen. Everyone else had abandoned her. But this man—

an old acquaintance, a childhood friend at best—was sorry that he hadn't got to her sooner.

Or was this one of those things people said to smooth over the unpleasant truths? Was he saying this because he meant it or because it was a cover?

God, she hoped it was real. She blinked hard and wondered at this strange urge to throw her arms around his neck and lean into his touch. Would he hug her back? Would he wrap his arms around her and press her against his chest? Would the heat of his body reach her through her clothes and the ironclad armor she hid behind?

Or would he stand there stiffly for a moment and then disentangle himself as politely as possible to protect her feelings? She didn't know.

Just then, one of the swans—Wilma, she decided—made a weird whooping noise that broke the moment. "Let me show you around," he said, releasing her hands and getting her luggage out of the car.

She turned to look back at the mansion. There was no other word for it. Three and a half stories of warm red brick welcomed her to Red Oak Hill. On this side, a huge wraparound porch of pristine white wood faced the lake. Trellises of yellow roses ran up the side of the wraparound porch, their sweet fragrance filling the air with every breeze.

The Preston real estate, like everything of value the family had owned, now belonged to the feds. She supposed, once all the trials were over and the sentences had been handed down, the properties and jewels and art would all be sold at auction and the money returned to the investors her family had scammed. It wouldn't be enough, but she certainly didn't have a spare billion or so lying around.

She hadn't even kept her wedding ring. They'd offered to let her hold on to the three-carat diamond in a princess setting—for now anyway—but Renee had been happy to hand it over. It had never stood for love and honor. All it'd been was another lie. Hopefully, however much they could get for that ring would help make things right.

The entrance hall of the mansion gleamed with warm polished wood—red, of course. The sweeping staircase led up to the second floor. The doorway on the right led to what appeared to be Oliver's office, with a massive desk in the center of the room and rich brown leather sofas arranged around the Persian rug.

He gave her a brief tour and started up the stairs but then he stopped and waited for her. "Doing all right?"

In that moment, Renee wished she hadn't come. Yes, Oliver was being a perfect gentleman—and a surprisingly compassionate friend. Yes, this mansion by a pond with a pair of swans was the perfect place to hide.

But she couldn't shake the feeling that she'd put Oliver at risk by coming here. She'd done nothing wrong, but her name was ruined and everything she did—everything she touched—was tainted by the sins of her family and her husband.

She didn't want to do anything that might hurt Oliver or Chloe. She didn't want to hurt anyone anymore.

"Renee?" He came back down the stairs and stood before her. When he lifted his hand and cupped her cheek, she knew she should pull away. It wasn't right to let him care for her.

It wasn't right to care for him.

"I'm sorry," she said. Sorry for all of it.

"It's been a long day," he said, misunderstanding. And, fool that she was, she wasn't strong enough to correct him. "Let me show you to your room. You need to rest."

And even though she knew she shouldn't, she leaned into his touch and asked, "Will you be here when I wake up?"

His thumb caressed her cheek so tenderly that she had to close her eyes. When was the last time someone had touched her like they cared? Chet Willoughby had not been capable of tenderness unless it benefited him directly. Nothing about her presence here benefited Oliver, directly or indirectly. She was nothing but a risk. And yet he was still being kind to her.

She almost exhaled in relief when his hand fell away, breaking that connection. But then he set down her suitcase and the next thing she knew, she was cradled in his arms. "I've got you," he said as he carried her up the stairs. "It's all right. I've got you."

All she could do was rest her head against his shoulder. It wasn't all right. It might never be okay ever again.

But right now, he had her.

And that was good enough.

Somehow, Oliver got Renee's heels off her feet and her legs swung up onto the bed without thinking about her bare skin against his palms too much. He couldn't get her under the covers, so he laid her on the bed, where she promptly curled on her side and shut her eyes.

Blankets. He hurried into the next room and grabbed the coverlet off the bed. By the time he made it back, she was breathing deeply and her face had relaxed.

He tucked the blanket around her shoulders, pausing only when she sighed in her sleep. But she didn't stir.

He could feel his phone vibrating in his pocket—he left the sound off because the chimes interrupted his thinking. Bailey was undoubtedly forwarding him news articles. Oliver should get some work done. He'd need to smooth ruffled feathers from canceling his meetings this afternoon.

Especially the one with Herb Ritter. Ritter had been in business with Lawrence Energies for close to thirty years. He was mean and crotchety and, unfortunately, a damned good oilman. And he'd been Milt Lawrence's best friend ever since the Lawrence family had relocated to Texas, which only made things worse. It was bad enough he had to manage his father, but also dealing with Ritter felt like a punishment. And the hell of it was Oliver had no idea what he'd done to deserve it.

He'd kept his promise to his mother. He ran the family business and kept his father from going completely off the deep end and Chloe as much in the loop as he could and Flash—well, no one could tell Flash a damned thing. Oliver managed the damned rodeo instead of doing something for himself. Even if he wasn't sure what that *something* might be anymore.

He did his job and kept his word. Wasn't that enough? Would it ever be enough?

But even this urgency wasn't enough to pull Oliver away from Renee's bedside.

God, she was beautiful. Tired and worried and pregnant, but beautiful all the same. He wished he could go back to Clint's wedding all those years ago. If only he'd struck up a conversation. If he had reconnected with her then, maybe he would've been able to spare her some of this heartbreak.

He brushed a strand of hair away from her forehead.

His phone vibrated again. Crap. He leaned forward and brushed the lightest of kisses against her cheek before he forced himself to walk away.

He had eighteen emails waiting for him by the time he got rid of his tie, grabbed a beer and sat down at his desk. The cold, heartless truth was that he did not have the time to take care of Renee Preston-Willoughby. He was running a major oil company, overseeing expansions into solar, wind and hydropower—expansions that he had fought his father for and finally won. And the damned All-Stars had just kicked off.

Business that required his full attention.

Will you be here when I wake up?

That heartfelt plea was the only reason why he was sitting in his office at the ranch instead of heading right back to his office in downtown Dallas.

She had asked.

This was only until she was settled in, he reasoned. She hadn't even seen the kitchen yet. He wasn't comfortable leaving her, not until he was sure she would be all right. He couldn't abandon her.

So he would stay.

Two hours later, Oliver had a much better grasp on the Renee situation.

It was a hell of a mess. Preston Investment Strategies was accused of bilking investors out of over forty-five billion dollars over the course of twenty years. Renee's father, Darin Preston, had been in jail for the last two months, unable to make bail since his wife had run off with the remaining money. Clinton Preston was also in jail, although it appeared that negotiations for his testimony and a lighter sentence were ongoing. Chet Willoughby, Preston's son-in-law, had committed suicide four and a half months ago. It didn't appear that the public had made the connection between that suicide and the pyramid scheme until Clint and his father had been arrested, along with most of the other people who worked at Preston Investment Strategies.

Bailey was thorough in his research. In addition to articles from the *Wall Street Journal, Business Insider* and *CNNMoney*, he also forwarded articles from the *New York Post* and even the *Daily News*. Those articles were filled with sly quotes from friends and acquaintances, all taking swipes at Renee and her mother. It only got worse after Renee's mother disappeared. It seemed there was an open debate as to whether or not Renee knew that her family was corrupt or if she'd been too dim to figure it out. Either way, the pieces were not flattering. Neither were the pictures posted with them. Awful paparazzi shots, catching her with red eyes, making her look far more pregnant and jiggly than she was in real life.

Disgusted, he stopped reading the articles because they were only pissing him off. How the hell had this happened? How had Darin Preston managed to get away with this pyramid scheme for this long? How had Clint—a guy Oliver knew was a good guy—allowed himself to be sucked down to these levels? It didn't make sense. None of it did.

His phone buzzed insistently. He picked it up—hell. His father was calling.

"Yeah, Dad?" Oliver said, closing the windows on all of the information Bailey had sent him.

"You done pissed off Herb Ritter, boy," his father drawled in a thick Texas accent. "I thought you knew better than to do that."

Oliver rolled his eyes. His father had been born and raised in New York City, although his family did come from Texas. Oliver's grandfather Mitchell had abandoned Texas when Lawrence Oil Industries—the forerunner to Lawrence Energies—had made him a multimillionaire.

Milt had lived in New York full-time until he was in his forties. Before thirteen years ago, he spent no more than a few weeks in the fall in Texas every year. The Lawrence family had maintained a house here for tax purposes and because this was where Lawrence Energies was based—but his father was *not* a Texan.

He sure liked to pretend he was, though. "I've made my apologies to Ritter," Oliver said, keeping his voice level. "We've already rescheduled the meeting."

"That's not going to be good enough."

Oliver gritted his teeth and decided to change the subject before this call devolved into a shouting match. "Dad, have you heard about Darin Preston?"

Milt was silent for a moment. "That con man? I never did trust his get-rich-quick schemes." He paused, making a low humming noise in the back of his throat. He always did that when he was thinking. "Wasn't he in the news recently?"

"He was." Oliver didn't want to tell Milt that Renee was asleep upstairs. He had promised her privacy, after all.

It was the only thing he could promise her.

"Why do you ask?"

Oliver decided to hedge the truth. "I had a strange message from Clint. It seemed he was helping his father scam people."

"Now, that's too danged bad," Milt said. "Clint was good people. And his sister—what was her name?"

"Renee."

"Yeah, Renee. She and Chloe got along real well. Trixie…" He paused and cleared his throat. Oliver knew that his father's eyes were watering, not that he would ever admit to it. Even after all these years, the mention of his beloved wife choked Milt up. "She thought the sun rose and set on Renee. She used to take the girls shopping. Always made sure to include that girl whenever she could. Hell, she always included Clint when she could. But she had a soft spot for Renee." He hummed again. "Your mother, God rest her soul, didn't think too highly of Rebecca and Darin Preston. And you know she was an excellent judge of character."

Oliver considered this. He honestly had no memories of his mother doting on Renee. But then again, it did seem like the little girl had always been underfoot, hanging out with Chloe and plotting how next to irritate Oliver and Clint.

The Preston kids had eaten a lot of meals at the Lawrence table—and Oliver didn't remember going over to Clint's house very much. Hardly at all, actually. There'd been a few times he and Clint had sneaked into Clint's house to get some trading cards or the latest video games…but they always sneaked right back out and hightailed it to Oliver's house.

It hadn't struck him as odd then. But what if it'd been more than that? Clint had told him they had to be quiet—no, not quiet, but *silent*. He hadn't wanted his mother to know they were in the house. No noise and no touching anything.

Looking back now, Oliver had to wonder—had Clint been afraid of his mother?

"I read that Mrs. Preston ran off to Europe with the rest of the money."

"Hell. What a family, eh? The Preston kids were good kids, but there's only so much a kid can do when they're raised in a pit of vipers. It's a shame that they got caught up in this. At least you had your mother and me. For a while anyway." He cleared his throat again.

It was a damned shame. "I did. We all did." Most days, dealing with his Tex-ified father left Oliver frustrated and bitter. But it was true. Before Trixie Lawrence's death,

Oliver had loved his parents. Both of them. For fifteen years, the Lawrence family had been happy and healthy and stable. Not everyone had that.

He'd promised his mother that he'd take care of his family. They may not be as happy or as stable—thank God they were all healthy—but at least they hadn't all been arrested and indicted. That had to count for something.

But it wasn't enough for his father. It never was. When Milt spoke again, Oliver could hear the forced cheer.

"Have you finished negotiations with ESPN about running the All-Stars?"

"I had to reschedule that meeting today. Something came up." And unlike Herb Ritter, Oliver was in no hurry to get back to this one. "You should let Chloe take the meeting. She'd do a great job."

"She's the Princess of the Rodeo and she's doing that clothing line," Milt reminded him, as if Oliver could ever forget. "I don't want that Pete Wellington anywhere near her."

Oliver rolled his eyes. He didn't like Pete Wellington any more than his father did but the man was too much a born-and-bred cowboy to ever lay a hand on a woman. As evidenced by the fact that he hadn't killed any members of the Lawrence family yet. And he'd had plenty of opportunity. "He wouldn't hurt her."

Not for the first time, Oliver considered signing a minority stake in the rodeo back over to the Wellington family. It'd been their damn rodeo before Pete's father, Davy, had lost it in that poker game. Pete had never forgiven either his father or Milt. Which meant he bore one hell of a grudge against anyone with the Lawrence last name. Oliver would be more than happy to cede a little control of the All-Stars back to Pete. Hell, if Oliver thought it would help, he'd just outright hire Pete to run the damn thing.

The only problem was Pete's pride wouldn't settle for merely working for the All-Stars. He maintained Milt Lawrence had stolen the All-Stars and he wanted it back. All or nothing.

Which meant he got nothing. Funny how winning here felt a lot like losing. "Chloe would be great in the meeting." She'd have the marketing team eating out of her hand and they both knew it.

As usual, though, Milt ignored Oliver. "She's already doing her part. You make sure you do yours." With the final *hmph*, Milt hung up.

The rodeo was good for the business, Oliver repeated silently, just like he did every single time he had to deal with the damn thing. The All-Around All-Stars Rodeo was 60 percent of their marketing and had been consistently in the black for the last six years.

That didn't mean Oliver had to like it.

He pushed the All-Stars out of his mind and focused on the problem at hand. He didn't have to like anything about the Renee situation. He wasn't enjoying this trip down memory lane, where he couldn't remember if his mother had taken Renee under her wing or not. Hell, for that matter, he still hadn't recalled how Renee knew he hated the rodeo.

He *hated* not knowing. Starting from a place of ignorance—about his childhood memories of the Preston kids, about the Preston Pyramid scam, about the woman currently upstairs in bed—that was how bad decisions got made. No matter how the saying went, ignorance was not bliss. It was disaster. And he was tired of this day feeling like a runaway train about to crash into the station.

He couldn't get off this train and continue to let it barrel down on Renee like everyone else had. Her brother and father? They hadn't so much abandoned her as they'd been taken into federal custody. But her husband, her mother—hell, even her friends—all had. No one had stood by her.

He couldn't add himself to that long, long list. Not when he thought back to the way he'd coaxed a small smile out of her when he'd told her the names of his swans. Not when she'd looked at him, trying so hard to be strong, and asked if he'd still be here when she woke up.

Not when his own father remembered Renee as a little girl who'd needed a friend.

Something had to give. He hit the number for Chloe. "What?" she said, sounding breathless.

"And good afternoon to you, too. Listen," Oliver said, bracing himself for the lie. He was not naturally good at deception. "You get to deal with ESPN. The contract negotiations are yours."

There was a pause on the other end of the line. "Is this a joke? Because it's not funny, Oliver," she snapped. "You know Dad would never let me do anything beyond carry the flag."

"No joke," he assured her. "Consider it a…" His mind scrambled for a reasonable explanation that wasn't simply *I don't have time for this*. "A test run. You do a good job on this, and we'll give you more responsibilities. Because I think the rodeo should be yours." That, at least, wasn't a lie.

"And Dad agreed to this?" she asked, doubt heavy in her voice.

That was the problem with Chloe. She was too perceptive for her own good. "He wants the deal done." He hedged. "He wants to see how you handle this and the clothing line."

It'd been Chloe's idea to capitalize on her popularity as the Princess of the Rodeo by launching an eponymous clothing line. She'd been overseeing the development of jeans, tailored T-shirts and sequined tops with the intent of launching with this year's rodeo season. So far, so good.

But could she keep up that success and handle high-level negotiations? God, Oliver hoped so.

She was quiet and Oliver wondered if she'd say no. If she did, Oliver was screwed. "You're sure this isn't a joke?"

He was surprised at how young she sounded. "Chloe, you know I don't have a sense of humor."

"Ha. Ha. Fine." She blew out a long breath. "I can do this, you know."

"I know. I'll forward you the information and let the ESPN people know you're handling the account from here on out. And Chloe?"

"Yeah?"

He almost told her Renee was upstairs and maybe Chloe could come home for girlfriend time so he could get back to work? But at the last second, Renee's face floated before him again, a single tear tracing down her cheek. He remembered the way her skin had felt under his hands as he'd wiped that tear away.

Renee needed him. Chloe needed to prove herself with the rodeo. And maybe it was wrong or selfish, but Oliver would rather help Renee than negotiate a TV distribution deal. Besides, all he needed to do for Renee was get her settled and see what he could do to help her out. How hard could that be?

He'd keep Renee's presence here a secret just a little bit longer. He told Chloe, "Keep an eye out for Pete Wellington. Dad's concerned he's going to pull something."

"Oh, wonderful. There's nothing I love more than unspecified threats from disgruntled cowboys." Oliver heard something in her tone beyond annoyance. But before he could figure out what that was, Chloe went on, "Fine. Anything else?"

"And keep Flash out of trouble," he added, because that was what he always asked her to do. Not that it ever worked. No one could keep that man on the straight and narrow.

"You're up to something," she said, but he could hear the smile in her voice. "And when I find out what it is, you're gonna pay." With that parting shot, she hung up.

He looked at the clock on the wall. It was already three thirty. He had no idea how long Renee was going to rest but there was no shot in hell of him making it back to the office during the workday at this point.

She needs a friend. Oddly, the little voice that whispered this in his mind wasn't his own or even Chloe's—it was his mother's.

Renee was not family. She wasn't grandfathered under the long-ago deathbed promise Oliver had made. He didn't *have* to take care of her.

And yet…

She needs a friend.

Had Trixie Lawrence said that once upon a time, perhaps when Oliver had complained about how much Renee and Chloe were bugging him and Clint?

He didn't know. But one thing was clear. If he didn't do his level best to help Renee out of this situation, his mother would be disappointed in him. Or she would've been anyway.

He stared at nothing in particular and then made up his mind. If he was going to get to the truth of the matter, he had to go straight to the source. He hit his lawyer's number. "Miles? It's Oliver. I need—"

"No, no—let me guess. Did you finally strangle your father? Or your brother? I've got twenty bucks riding on the answer," Miles Hall replied with a laugh.

"Neither." Oliver shouldn't be doing this, shouldn't be doing any of this. Funny how that wasn't stopping him. "I need to talk to Clinton Preston. He's in jail in New York City on fraud charges for—"

"The Preston Pyramid guy?"

He scowled. Did everyone know about the scam but him? Sheesh. He'd have to have Bailey add "major scandals involving people I used to know" to his morning news briefs. "Yeah. Well, the son anyway. I need to talk to him on the phone. Can you make it happen?"

Miles was quiet for a moment. "Give me thirty."

"Thanks."

Clint had a hell of a lot to answer for. Starting with why he'd helped his father steal that much money and ending with why he'd asked Oliver to look after Renee.

Then, once Oliver had his answers and made sure Renee was comfortable and safe, he could get back to work.

But the thought of making Renee comfortable, of carrying her back to bed and this time, staying with her...

Hell. He definitely had to get back to Dallas tonight.

Four

Renee came awake slowly. It was so quiet here. New York was never quiet. There was always someone shouting, horns honking, sirens blaring. A person could barely think in New York City.

She couldn't remember the last time she'd slept so deeply. Usually, it was because terrible nightmares woke her up every few hours, panting and crying. Right now, she felt surprisingly calm. She wouldn't go so far as to say peaceful, but she was thrilled with calm.

A *thunk* from somewhere below her finally got her eyes open. She started when she focused her eyes on the clock. Was it four thirty already? She had been asleep for hours. She needed to get up and…do something. What, she had no idea.

But it wasn't like her to laze the day away. Even back when she'd been little more than a trophy wife, she'd still kept busy. She'd been on the boards of several charities, including her favorite, One Child, One World. She liked helping kids but…since the Preston Pyramid collapsed, she'd resigned from all those boards rather than taint their good works with her family's scandals.

Which left her at loose ends. But it was fine. No one was missing her in New York, that was for sure. This was part of her plan to hide in Texas. If she wanted to nap, she would nap, by God.

She tossed back a blanket and forced herself from bed. It was tempting to go right back to sleep, but…

Oliver had said he would wait for her to wake up.

She was hungry and she had to pee. She stretched, trying to get the kinks out of her shoulders. Over a dresser there was a large mirror and she recoiled in horror when she caught sight of her reflection. Her hair was lopsided and her makeup had not survived the nap. Plus, her dress was wrinkled horribly, and besides, it really wasn't very comfortable.

But her lawyer had recommended that, if she went out in public, she maintain a somber, mourning appearance. It wouldn't do anyone any favors if she were seen looking frivolous or, God forbid, *happy*. Not that there was a lot of risk of that, but Renee understood the point.

Her entire life had been about keeping up appearances. The bereft widow, the horrified daughter—they were all just another role to slip into.

She tore the dress off and kicked it under the bed. She couldn't wear it for another moment, couldn't maintain the fiction that she mourned her husband.

She looked around the room. Had she fainted? She didn't remember coming into this room. She only remembered… Oliver's arms around her, holding her close. His deep voice rumbling in her ear, although she couldn't remember the words. A light touch on her forehead, then her cheek. The smell of his cologne.

She remembered feeling safe and cared for. That was all she needed.

But this was a nice room. There was a small sitting area with a low coffee table—her bag was on it. The love seat ran along one wall and a fancy desk that looked like it belonged in the parlor instead of a guest room was on the other side. The walls were a pale green and the bedding was pristine white. It was calm and peaceful and reminded her of a garden in the early-morning sun.

She took a deep breath and let it out slowly. She could breathe here.

She dug into her bag. Along with her wedding ring, she had left most of her couture and designer clothing for the feds. Her wardrobe had been worth hundreds of thousands of dollars—but it had been just another prop in her never-ending role as the adoring wife, the picture-perfect daughter. She was tired of living that lie.

She dug out leggings and a slouchy tunic. This was her normal outfit for yoga classes—but it was forgiving enough that she could still wear it comfortably. She might even get several more months out of the top. She'd love to take her bra off because the damned thing barely fitted anymore and sleeping in it had not been a good idea. But the thin, creamy cotton of her shirt wouldn't hide anything from anyone. Especially Oliver.

A chill raced over her and her nipples tightened, which was exactly why she had to keep the bra on. She really hoped Oliver wasn't involved with someone else. But the moment that thought crossed her mind, she scowled at herself in the mirror. Okay, he was amazingly hot. And yes, he was being really sweet to her. That didn't mean there was any mutual attraction here and even if there was, what was she going to do? Seduce him? Please. She was the hottest of hot messes and almost five months pregnant.

Fine. It was settled. No seduction. At least…not on her end anyway.

Purposefully *not* thinking of what Oliver might do if she paraded around braless, she used the en suite bathroom and fixed her hair and face, opting for a simple ponytail and just enough under-eye concealer to hide the worst of the dark circles. When she was done, she took stock again.

She looked not-quite-so-pregnant in her loungewear and the nap had helped a lot. She didn't look like the woman she'd been six months ago. The salon-perfect hair was gone, as was the expertly contoured foundation. And she could see the pregnancy weight rounding out her face and her arms. Her mother had called her fat right before she'd run to Paris.

No, Renee was not the same woman she'd been six months ago. Was that such a bad thing? She'd been a mannequin then. Someone to be seen and coveted but not heard. The problem was, she wasn't quite sure who she was now.

She wouldn't allow her voice to be silenced again. As she stroked her stomach, she made a promise to herself and her child—she would do better. Better than her mother. Better than Renee herself had been. She'd be… someone like Oliver's mother. Renee would be the fun mom who made cookies with her child and friends or took them for ice cream in the park. Whether she had a boy who liked fashion or a girl who played soccer, it didn't matter. Just so long as Renee was a better mom. A better woman.

She dabbed at her eyes. Stupid hormones. If there was one thing she'd learned growing up, it was how to keep her emotions on lockdown to avoid getting into trouble. But suddenly she was pregnant and hiding and she couldn't keep her stupid eyes from watering stupidly. Gah.

Besides, there was no need to get teary now. She had a long way to go before tea parties and sports. She had to start being this new, improved woman before the baby got here and it wasn't likely to happen in the bathroom. She needed something to eat and… Well, food first. Plans second.

Quietly, she made her way downstairs, listening hard for the sounds of people. A low hum seemed to be coming out of Oliver's study. He was talking to someone, she realized—probably on the phone. A wave of relief swept over her. He'd made a promise to her and he'd kept it—even if it was an inconsequential promise to hang around for a few hours. He'd still kept it.

Guilt wasn't far behind. She'd pulled him away from a workday. He was probably trying to get caught up. She shouldn't interrupt him. He'd said the kitchen was in the back of the house, right? She should go.

But then, in a voice that was more of a shout than a whisper, Oliver clearly said, "You are, without a doubt, the most vile, abhorrent, morally bankrupt *idiot* I have ever had the misfortune to know and that's saying something. You know that, right? I mean, what the hell were you thinking, Clint?"

Renee stumbled to a stop. Eavesdropping was not exactly on the moral up-and-up, but was he talking to her *brother*? How the hell had he pulled that off?

She moved to stand just on the other side of the door to his study. There were some pictures here, so she pretended to look at them. But really, her entire attention was focused on one half of the phone conversation happening in the next room.

"Yeah, she's here. What the hell, man? You send me a one-line email with no other explanation, no other context—no, I didn't know your entire family had crashed and burned. I'm busy!" This time, he was shouting. "I have my own family to manage, my own business to run—a business that does not steal money from investors! So you'll excuse me if I haven't kept up with all the ways you've destroyed your life!"

A wave of nausea roiled her stomach and she didn't think it was morning sickness.

"No, I know." He said this in a weary voice, and Renee honestly couldn't tell if it was better or worse than him shouting. "Yeah, she told me. How could you let her marry someone like that?"

Renee bristled. Her brother was not her keeper. She was a grown woman capable of making her own decisions and her own mistakes, thank you very much.

That, however, hadn't stopped her from wondering the exact same thing a hundred times over the last few months. Clint had known who Chet was. They'd both worked for her father for several years before the wedding. And yet her own brother had done nothing to warn her that she was marrying a serial cheater and a con artist.

It was hard not to be bitter when there was so much to be bitter about. Growing up, she and Clint had stuck together. So much of her childhood had been the kids against the parents. Even when they'd fought—and they *had* fought—they'd still protected each other from the icy punishment of their mother and the casual neglect of their father.

But when she'd really needed her brother, he hadn't been there for her.

Instead, it was Oliver who was mad on her behalf. Oliver who was defending her.

"That's a shitty excuse and you know it," Oliver snapped. "She trusted you. Your investors trusted you. Hell, I trusted you. And you did nothing to earn it... No,

I'm not going to take it out on her. I'm not a monster, unlike some people I know… Yes," he said, sounding defeated. "She did? I thought you two were going to go the distance. But I guess she couldn't live being married to a snake oil salesman." Another pause. "Renee really didn't know, did she?… I didn't think so. Look, I said I'd take care of her and I meant it. Enjoy your time in jail, buddy."

Renee sagged against the door frame as relief pushed back against the nausea. Oliver believed she hadn't been a part of the scheme. He understood, at least on some level, how badly the betrayal by her family had hurt her.

She shouldn't have come here. She shouldn't have listened to the phone call, either. She didn't want to put Oliver at risk for being a decent human being to an old friend and she didn't want to put either of them in a position where he felt like he had to lie to her.

But she was so glad she was here.

"Renee? Will you come in here?"

She jumped, her heart racing. Had he known she was listening the entire time? Oh, heavens. *Busted.*

She swallowed and felt her face go pleasantly blank, felt her shoulders square up and her chin lift. The reactions were hard-wired at this point and she was helpless to stop them.

With one final deep breath for courage, she stepped into the study.

And stumbled to a stop.

Oliver was leaning against his desk, his ankles crossed and his arms folded in front of his chest. He looked very much like he had earlier—had it only been this morning?

But the differences. Oh, the differences! He'd lost his suit jacket and his tie. His white button-up shirt was now open at the neck and he had cuffed the sleeves, revealing strong forearms. And strangely enough, he was barefoot.

Oh, dear God. He'd made business professional look good but he was making casual look positively sinful. Her mouth went dry and for a moment, she forgot how to speak.

Then everything got worse and better at the same time because he notched an eyebrow at her at the same time the corner of his mouth curved up into a smile, revealing a dimple she didn't remember being there before. Had she ever really seen him smile like that? He was so impossibly gorgeous that her mouth disconnected from her brain, and she blurted out, "I wasn't listening," like an idiot because obviously she had been.

That got his other eyebrow in on the action. But instead of calling her on her juvenile defense, his gaze swept over her. Her skin flushed as he took in her shirt, her leggings, her own bare feet. When he lifted his eyes, Renee could tell that, even from across the room, they were darker, more intense.

Was it hot in here or was it just her?

"I see the nap did wonders for you," he said, his voice low and serious and nothing like how he had sounded on the phone with Clint.

It was broiling in here. She was starting to sweat. "I hope you don't mind that I changed into something more comfortable. Since I have no plans on going back out into public today. Or tomorrow," she finished lamely.

"Or even the day after that?" he teased, pushing off the desk and coming to stand in front of her.

Renee knew not to show fear. Showing guilt was even worse. She had trained herself to keep her head up and her eyes open, no matter what cutting comments or terrifying punishments her mother had decreed.

But this was Oliver. Serious, grumpy, stick-in-the-mud Oliver. And he was smiling down at her, warmth and humor in his face and maybe just a little concern as he said, "My house is yours for as long as you need it. I want you to be comfortable here. I want you to be yourself," as he settled his hands on her shoulders.

Wonderful. Her eyes were watering *and* she was sweating. Maybe she should've stayed in bed a little longer. "Do you know—" and she was horrified to hear her voice waver "—that no one has ever wanted me to just be myself?"

His smile faded. But then his thumbs began to rub little circles on her shoulders and she didn't know if she was getting closer to him or if he was getting closer to her. Maybe they were both moving, drawn together by strange circumstances and an even stranger attraction.

Whatever it was, she found herself in his arms, her breasts pressed against his chest, her chin tucked in the crook of his neck—and her bare toes brushing his. The contact felt shockingly intimate, and for a moment, she forgot how to breathe.

It wasn't right, how much she sank into his touch. It certainly wasn't proper, the way she wrapped her arms around his waist and held on as if her life depended on it.

"I'm sorry I eavesdropped," she muttered against the collar of his shirt. "And I'm sorry I lied about it. I'm… still getting used to honesty." It didn't sound any less lame, but at least it was the truth.

"It's all right," he said softly, and one hand began to rub her lower back in small, delicious circles of relief that made her sigh.

"How did you know I was listening?" She'd thought she'd been quiet. But not quite enough, apparently.

"I heard you get up. I'm sorry you heard me call your brother a vile idiot."

"Even if he deserved it?"

Oliver chuckled, a rich sound that rumbled out of his chest. "Especially if he deserved it." He leaned back and Renee looked up at him. This close, she could see the flecks of gold in his brown eyes like hidden treasure. Something in her chest tightened as he stroked the finger over her cheek and down her chin. "Renee..."

She held her breath. God, she needed...something. She needed to hear the truth.

But then again, what was the truth here? She was naive and gullible at best? Complicit? An idiot, vile or otherwise?

She'd work on facing the truth soon. Tomorrow. Right now, she desperately changed the subject. "Thank you for being here when I woke up."

"I gave you my word. I keep my promises."

She shouldn't, but she couldn't help herself. She buried her face against his shoulder and automatically, his arms tightened around her. "That's...that's good to know," she mumbled against the collar of his shirt. "Not everyone does that."

"I'm not everyone."

Thank God. But she didn't say it out loud. Instead, she said, "Now what?"

"Hmm." She could hear the steady thrum of his heartbeat. That was what made him safe.

But what made him dangerous was the way his body began to rock almost imperceptibly, pulling her along into a rhythm. What made her weak was the way his hand splayed out against the small of her back, pushing her into his solid chest.

Her nipples went painfully hard and given how very little separated him from her, she was sure he could feel those hard points against his chest. Her cheeks flushed and she shivered at unbidden images of her in Oliver's arms, but with far less clothing and far more moving.

Oliver was everything and nothing she needed right now. She absolutely was not thinking about sex, especially not with him. She still hadn't determined if he was involved with anyone else, for crying out loud! She wasn't interested and she wasn't looking to get lucky. End of story.

Good lord, it was hot in here.

And he still hadn't answered her question. That *hmm* didn't count, especially not when she was breathing in the scent of his cologne—something light and spicy and warm that smelled perfect on him.

Then, so slowly she almost missed it, he began to pull away. His arms loosened around her chest and he leaned back to look down at her again. But even then, he kept letting go of her, one moment at a time. "I need to get back tonight," he said, his voice low and serious and perfectly Oliver. She didn't know if that was supposed to be a good thing or not. Was he happy he was getting out of here before she lost her composure again? Or was she only imagining that there was a hint of regret in his tone?

"That's…" She cleared her throat and broke the contact between them. "That's fine. I'm sure you have someone waiting on you to get home." She had to turn away when she said it.

It was for the best if he left. She'd come here for the peace and quiet, right? And she definitely didn't feel peaceful when Oliver was around. Far from it.

He snorted. "Renee."

She put her face back together. She could do this. She didn't want to worry him and besides, she was probably just hungry. And pregnant. It wasn't a great combination. "Yes?"

He'd retreated back to his desk. She could feel the distance between them and, irrational as it was, she hated it. "I won't leave until you're settled."

She bit back the laugh. She might never be settled again. But instead, she said, "I appreciate it."

"I won't be able to get back out here for a few days," he went on, sounding nothing like the man who'd been holding her moments ago. "But if you need anything—clothes, medicines, weird foods—just let me know. I'll plan on spending at least part of the weekend out here."

Was he coming to see her or to babysit her? "All right."

He looked at something on his computer and then put his phone in his pocket. "And to answer your other question," he said, walking back toward her, "no, there's no one waiting on me at home. But I do have to work tomorrow. It's…"

"Rodeo season," she finished, trying hard not to smile. It shouldn't matter that he was available and that she was—well, maybe not available. But certainly unattached.

But it did.

"Dinner?" he said, a friendly smile on his face. His dimple didn't show.

Right. He was being friendly because they were friends and nothing more.

"Dinner," she agreed.

At the very least, it was good to have a friend.

Even if he was Oliver Lawrence.

The whole drive back to Dallas, Oliver tried to solve the problem that was Renee Preston-Willoughby.

He failed.

Instead of running through viable solutions to keep Renee safe and secure for the short and medium term—possibly up to and including the birth of her child—he was thinking of how she'd looked when she'd stepped into his study this afternoon. Gone were the hideous black dress, the dark hose and the understated black pumps. And in their place...

Oliver did not know a great deal about women's fashion, but he recognized the kind of clothes Renee had been wearing. Chloe loved to knock around in the same kind of leggings and loose tops.

It was safe to say that he had a vastly different reaction to Renee in leggings than he did his sister.

The top had come to just below her hips, leaving every curve of her legs outlined in tight black fabric. It'd taken everything in his power not to picture those legs wrapped around his waist at the time. The last thing anyone needed was for him to get a raging hard-on at the exact moment she'd needed to be comforted by a platonic friend.

Now? He adjusted his pants. He had a long drive ahead of him.

Damn, this was ridiculous. He had a million things he needed to do and none of them involved replaying the way Renee's body had fitted against his over in his mind. What he should be doing was talking to Bailey and getting caught up on everything Oliver had missed while he was out of the office today. Yeah, his executive assistant had probably already left work for the day, but Oliver was the CEO and if he needed Bailey to work late, then Bailey worked late.

Then again, Bailey was always talking about his wife and the latest adorable thing their two-year-old son was doing and Oliver would feel bad interrupting his dinner. A man should spend time with his family. He should be involved in the lives of his children.

No, Oliver couldn't in good conscience bother Bailey after work hours.

Which apparently meant he was going to think about

Renee. She had looked so much better after her nap. Still tired, still worried—but she'd been softer. Not as brittle.

That made him feel good. He had given her that.

But that was all he could give her. It didn't matter how much his body responded to hers, how much it hit him in the chest when she smiled—or how much it killed him when her eyes watered but instead of crying, her whole face went oddly blank. What he wanted didn't matter.

He would repeat that sentiment until he got it through his thick skull.

Because it didn't matter that he had finally given in to his impulse and pulled her tight in his arms in the office. It made no difference when he'd felt the tension drain out of her body and it didn't matter that, a moment or two later, he felt the different tension begin to work its way through her. It had no bearing on anything that being around Renee was a slow burn of torture.

Oliver was no angel. He'd been caught up in the throes of lust from time to time. Those affairs had always burned white-hot but fizzled out after a matter of months, if not weeks. He and his lady friends had parted ways with a smile and a fond farewell.

So he knew this attraction wasn't just lust. His whole body was *not* on fire for Renee Preston-Willoughby.

Had he seriously told her that he wouldn't be back until maybe the weekend? That wasn't right. She was all alone in the middle of nowhere in a strange house. Yes, he'd shown her how to operate the stove and where the pantry was and walked her through the remotes for the televisions. He'd even left her with keys for his ranch truck, in case she needed to get to Mineola, the closest town.

But what if something went wrong? What if she had a medical emergency? What if someone figured out where she was—someone who did not think kindly of the Preston family?

He almost turned his Porsche around. He could stay the night and make sure everything was okay and then get up and…

Okay, getting up at four to slink out the house wouldn't help anyone. And she was a grown woman who could navigate New York City by herself. She wasn't a child or an invalid. She'd be fine.

At least for the night.

Maybe he'd go back out tomorrow night, after work. Just to make sure she was doing all right.

Yeah. He'd do that.

That's what friends were for.

Five

She was going to bake.

Renee stood in the massive kitchen at Red Oak Hill, surveying the row of copper pots hanging from a pot rack over a massive island in the middle of the kitchen with stools tucked along one side. The countertops were a cool gray granite and the cabinets were cream with an aged patina. A Subzero fridge, better suited to a restaurant than a house with only one person living in it part-time, commanded almost half of a wall.

She didn't know how to cook. Or bake. No one in her house had cooked growing up. On the few occasions they'd suffered through dinner as a family, either Rosa, the undocumented Guatemalan maid her mother had constantly threatened with deportation, had prepared a meal for them or they'd had food delivered in. Nothing good ever happened at those family dinners. She shuddered at the memories and absently rubbed her leg.

Otherwise, her parents ate out—separately, of course. Breakfast had been cold cereal to be eaten as quickly and quietly as possible before she and Clint made their escape to school because waking her mother up before noon was a surefire way to suffer.

Instead, she had happy memories of boisterous meals with the Lawrence family where everyone bickered and told jokes and only sometimes did she and Chloe switch out sugar for salt or drop peas in Clint and Oliver's milk. If anyone yelled, they were laughing when they did it and no one ever jabbed silverware into someone else's legs.

She had afternoon teas with Chloe and Mrs. Lawrence after they'd gone shopping or seen a show or even just because. She had fun afternoons with Mrs. Lawrence teaching her and Chloe how to bake cookies and cakes. Then Renee and Chloe and sometimes even Mrs. Lawrence would eat their creations with a big glass of milk while watching cartoons. Those times were all the more special because...

Because of Mrs. Lawrence. She'd been warm. Loving. *There.* How many times had Renee dragged her feet when it was time to go home? How many times had she prayed for Mrs. Lawrence to be *her* mother, the Lawrence family *her* family? Her and Clint's. They could've been happy there. They *had* been happy there, all the happier because it was such an escape from home.

Mealwise, not much had changed when she'd married and moved into her own condo with Chet. They'd eaten out most of the time, often separately because Clint was working late or entertaining clients or dating other women, probably. And Renee hadn't seen the point in cooking just for herself, so she'd gone out with friends. Everything else had been delivered. Cooking wasn't a priority, not with some of the best restaurants in the world just a short phone call away.

Renee Preston-Willoughby didn't do anything so menial as prepare food.

That was going to change, starting now. Besides, she was dying for some cookies. Giant gooey chocolate chip cookies, just like she'd made all those years ago with Chloe and Mrs. Lawrence. With ice cream. Did Oliver have ice cream? If he were here, she'd ask him. But she wasn't going to wait around for someone else to solve her problems. Even if that problem was just ice cream related. She'd check the freezer herself.

Besides, what else was she going to do with her time? She could sit around and feel sorry for herself, but that was self-indulgent in the extreme. In addition to her nap yesterday, she'd had a solid night's sleep. She'd eaten breakfast, lunch and dinner for the first time in…a while. Last night Oliver had made these amazing burritos that he had had seemingly pulled together out of thin air and there'd been leftovers. Marinated chicken and steak and a corn salsa that was possibly the best thing Renee had eaten in months, plus tortilla chips and cheese. Lots and lots of cheese. It wasn't true cooking, but she'd assembled her own food today and that was a start. A *good* start.

It helped that, for the first time since her husband's funeral, food tasted good. Suddenly, she was starving.

She scrolled through Pinterest, looking for a recipe that promised both delicious and easy cookies.

It took a long time to assemble the ingredients. She had no luck tracking down baking soda, but baking powder was close, right? They both had *baking* in their names, after all. And it said *1 tsp* of both baking soda and salt. How much was a tsp? She found a measuring spoon that had a *T* on it. *That must be it.*

At least there were chocolate chips. Really, that was all that mattered.

She wished Oliver were here. The peace and quiet of this big mansion out on the countryside was wonderful, but she'd love to share it with him. This morning, she'd walked around the small lake, watching Fred and Wilma as they cut gracefully through the water with two baby swans trailing after them. Oliver had a small dock on the far side, so she'd kicked out of her flip-flops and sat with her toes in the water, watching the breeze ruffle the leaves of the huge red oaks.

This afternoon, she'd sat on the porch with a big glass of iced tea and, surrounded by the scent of roses, watched dusk settle over the land. She'd watched a few episodes of her favorite TV show—the animated one about a diner Chet had thought was stupid. And she'd taken another delicious nap.

No one had yelled at her. No one had accused her of horrible things. No one had mocked her appearance or told her that her husband had got exactly what he deserved. All in all, it had been a nearly perfect day.

Except she wished Oliver had been here. Which wasn't fair. He had to work, she knew that. As she dumped the sugar onto butter, she knew she didn't need Oliver by her side. But she wanted to show him that she was doing all right. Better than all right.

She'd been fragile and shell-shocked when she walked into his office, exhausted with worry and drained from the flight. But that didn't define her. It bothered her that he might think that was all there was to her.

But then again, she had a hazy memory of him telling her that she was strong for her unborn child. So maybe he knew? Or maybe he'd just been polite.

No matter. He would be here this weekend and by

then, she hoped to have figured out the secret to perfect chocolate chip cookies.

The sugar blended into the butter—at least, she hoped that was what *creamed* butter and sugar was supposed to look like—she checked the recipe again. Dang, she'd forgotten to turn on the oven. The recipe said it was supposed to preheat—maybe she should crank it up? Would it preheat faster that way? It was worth a shot. She set the oven to five hundred and then went back to her recipe. It called for one cup of chocolate chips, but that didn't seem like enough. So she doubled it. One could never have too much chocolate.

There. She had something that reasonably looked like chocolate chip cookie dough. If she wasn't pregnant, she'd test it, just to make sure it tasted right. But raw cookie dough was one of those things that pregnant women weren't supposed to eat, so she resisted the temptation. She scooped out the dough and set the sheets in the oven.

It was ridiculous, how proud she felt of this small accomplishment. Putting cookies in the oven to bake barely counted as an accomplishment at all. But still. She'd done it. God, she hoped they were good.

"What's going on in here?"

Renee screamed in alarm as she spun, losing her balance and bouncing off the corner of the island. Seconds later, strong hands had her by the arm, pulling her against a warm, solid chest. Tingles raced down her back and she knew even before she got a look at his face that, once again, Oliver had caught her before she fell.

She shouldn't be this happy to see him. But she was anyway. "You're here!" she said, breathless as she wrapped him in a big hug. *Now* the day was perfect.

"I am," he said, as if he were just as surprised to find himself back at the ranch—and in her arms—as she was.

Oh. *Oh!* She was hugging him, feeling every inch of his hard body against hers. She took a quick step back and let her hands fall to her sides. "I didn't think you were coming back tonight."

He leaned against the island, his mouth curving into a smile that sent another shiver down her back. "I wanted to make sure you were doing all right."

Something warm began to spread in her chest. "You could've called." After all, it wasn't like he'd popped next door to check on her. He had driven a solid hour and a half out of his way. He wasn't even in his suit. He was wearing a purple dress shirt but he had on dark jeans that sat sinfully low on his hips today. God, he looked so good. Better than chocolate chip cookies.

"I could've," he agreed.

His dimple was back and Renee had an inexplicable urge to kiss him right there on that little divot.

"Is everything all right?" If there was bad news, she could see him wanting to deliver it in person because that was the kind of man Oliver Lawrence was.

He wouldn't hide from the unpleasant truth. But instead of lowering the boom, he said, "Everything's fine."

They were words she'd heard hundreds, thousands of times. Chet had said them constantly, including in those last months when their lives had begun to unravel, even though Renee hadn't known it at the time. But she'd been able to tell that things weren't fine. But that's all Chet—or her brother or her father—had ever told her, like she was a toddler who'd bumped her head and needed a simple reassurance.

Those words coming out of Oliver's mouth were different. She was pretty sure. God, she hoped he wasn't that good of a liar. "You're sure?"

He lifted one shoulder. "I have Bailey scanning the

headlines for any mention of you in the greater Texas area, but nothing's cropped up. A few New York headlines are wondering where the pregnant Preston Pyramid Princess has disappeared to, but it's more because they're sad you're not providing them with clickbait fodder. Your brother hasn't accepted a deal yet. Your soon-to-be-former sister-in-law gave an interview to the *Huffington Post* where she eviscerated Clint, as well as your husband and your father, but only mentioned you to say that she'd always thought you were sweet and she really hoped you hadn't had anything to do with the scam. She didn't think you had."

A breath Renee hadn't realized she'd been holding whooshed out of her lungs. "Really? That's…that's great. I should send Carolyn a thank-you card. That's the nicest thing anyone's said about me in months."

"I can think of a few nice things to say about you." His voice was low and sweet, like dark honey and, as he looked her over with something that seemed like desire, her body responded. "More than a few."

Sweet Jesus, she wanted to melt into him. The space between her legs got hot and sensitive and her stupid nipples went all tight again. Which was the exact moment she remembered she didn't have on a bra.

Oh, hell! She didn't have on a bra and she'd hugged him and now he was making her blush. She crossed her arms over her chest and hoped he hadn't noticed.

He lifted an eyebrow and her face got even hotter. Of course he'd noticed.

But he had the decency to refrain from pointing out the *pointedly* obvious. Instead, he looked around the kitchen. "Baking?"

She was not disappointed that he hadn't lavished her in compliments. She was relieved, dang it. "I thought I'd give chocolate chip cookies a try. But fair warning," she said, desperately trying to keep her voice light, "I haven't baked anything in years."

He began to round up the dirty dishes without protesting or anything. "And you wanted to get back to it?"

"I do." She took a deep breath, thankful to have something to talk about that didn't have anything to do with her nipples or their willingness to turn into hard points around this man. "I have these wonderful memories of your mom taking the time to bake with me and Chloe and sometimes it was awful and sometimes we actually made something good and it was always so much...fun. Do you remember?"

Because now that she thought about it, she remembered that although Clint and Oliver hadn't been baking with them, sometimes Renee and Chloe had shared the cookies or cupcakes with them. But only when they were feeling generous.

He paused in the middle of dumping the mixing bowls in the sink. "Yeah, I do."

"Good." It made her happy to know that he still had those shared moments in an otherwise-fraught childhood relationship. "I want to have fun again. I want to be the kind of mom who enjoys making cookies and won't scream if the cookies don't turn out perfect. I want to be the kind of mom my kid looks up to, who'll..." Her voice caught in her throat. "Who'll be there for her kids. And her friends' kids."

Not like her mom had been.

The bowls clattered in the sink and Oliver turned. He studied her with that smoldering intensity of his that sent flashes of heat down her back.

But he didn't say anything. "Yes?" she finally asked nervously. She kept her arms crossed.

"I know my mother loved you. She considered you another daughter."

The sense of loss that hit her was more painful than she'd expected, mostly because she hadn't been expecting it at all. "Oh," she said, her throat closing up and her eyes watering. "That's…that's sweet. I was…" She swiped at her cheeks. "I was sorry we couldn't come to her funeral." Her mother didn't look good in black and funerals were dreary. Which meant Renee hadn't got a chance to say goodbye.

Oliver nodded. "And then we moved to Texas right after that."

It had been a one-two punch and honestly, Renee wasn't sure she'd ever got over it. She'd not only lost the wonderful mother of her best friend, she'd lost the entire Lawrence family. She'd lost the feeling of home that day.

But she hadn't been a little girl anymore. When Mrs. Lawrence had died, Renee had been thirteen and better equipped to deal with her mother's insanity. She'd joined more after-school clubs, found new friends.

Nothing had ever replaced the Lawrence family.

"Hey," Oliver said, stepping forward and pulling her into his chest. "I'm sorry. I didn't mean to upset you."

"It's okay," she replied, her words muffled by his shirt. "Sorry. Hormones. It doesn't take much these days."

"No, I'd imagine not." He leaned back, stroking his hand down her cheek and lifting her face so she had no choice but to look him in the eye. "Renee…"

Her breath caught in her throat again but this time, it had nothing to do with a spontaneous overflow of powerful feelings. Instead, Oliver's one hand was tracing slow circles around the small of her back, pushing her closer to him. To his lips. His thumb dragged over her cheek, sending sparks of electricity across her skin.

"I'm so glad you came back," Renee whispered, even as she lifted herself on tiptoe, closing the distance between them.

"I'll always come back for you," he murmured against her mouth.

Dear God, please let that be the truth. She didn't want easy lies. She couldn't bear the thought of him lying to her at all. Not him. Not now.

His lips brushed over hers, the touch a request more than a demand. She inhaled deeply, catching his scent— spicy and warm, with his own earthy musk underneath and a faint hint of something burning.

Something burning?

She jolted as he asked, "What's that smell?" at the same time a loud beeping filled the air.

"The cookies!" She twisted out of his arms and raced to the oven.

By the time she got there, smoke was beginning to curl out of the oven door. "Oh, no!" She frantically looked around for the oven mitts or…something. Anything, before she set his house on fire! But she didn't know where anything was!

Oliver picked her up and physically set her to the side. Then, as cool as a cucumber, he turned off the oven and produced the missing oven mitts. In short order, he had the cookie sheet and the nearly black puddles that had once aspired to be cookies out of the oven, a fan running and windows open to clear the room, and he was…

Laughing?

He was, the wretch. He was mocking her failed attempt at baking while he pulled the battery from the smoke detector and for a moment, it felt like they were kids again, always poking each other until the other responded. She wondered if she could hit him with a water balloon—

and what he might do in retaliation. Renee tried to scowl at him, but she was suddenly giggling along with him.

"Why, in the name of all that is holy," he sputtered, dumping the ruined cookies into the sink, "was the oven set to five *hundred* degrees?"

God, she was an idiot. "Oh! I forgot to preheat it so I thought I'd turn it on high to make up for it and I must have forgot to put it back down to the right temperature."

He laughed so hard that he slapped his thigh. She had to wrap her arms around her stomach to make sure she didn't accidentally wet her panties. When she thought she had herself under control, she eyed the mud puddles. They clearly had spread beyond the ability of the cookie sheet to contain them—but now that they were charred, they weren't going anywhere. "I may owe you some new cookie sheets," she said, which set off another round of giggles.

"What did you do to those poor things?" He grabbed the spoon she'd used to scoop out the dough and poked at the closest mud puddle.

And then they were off again. God, when was the last time she'd laughed?

She couldn't remember when. How sad.

But she was laughing too hard to let self-pity take control. She sagged into Oliver's arms and he buried his head against her shoulder, which didn't do a whole lot to muffle the almost unholy noises of glee he was making. They both were making.

Eventually, the giggles subsided. But her arms were still around Oliver and his arms were around her and he'd promised he'd always come back for her and then he'd almost kissed her, and she still wasn't wearing a bra.

"It's a good thing I came out here to check on you," he murmured against the skin of her neck.

"It is," she agreed, holding her breath. Would he kiss her again? Or let her kiss him? She shifted against him, bringing her breasts flush against his chest again. "I'd feel really bad if I'd burned your house down."

"That would've been tragic." Then she felt it, the press of his lips against the sensitive skin right below her ear.

She exhaled on a shudder as his mouth moved over her jaw. Then his lips were on hers and this time, it wasn't a hesitant touch.

This time, he kissed her like he wanted her.

Even though she knew she shouldn't because *complicated* would never be a strong enough word to describe her life, she kissed him back.

Months of sorrow and anger drifted away under the power of Oliver's kiss. Because it was an amazing kiss, sweet and hot and a seduction, pure and simple. His hands circled her waist, his thumbs tracing a path along her lower ribs. All the while, his lips moving over hers, his tongue lapping at the corners of her mouth. She opened for him and his tongue swept inside, claiming her.

Branding her as his own.

Because he wanted her. Not because she was her father's daughter, but in spite of that, Oliver Lawrence wanted her.

God, it was so good to be wanted.

So Renee kissed him back. She looped her arms around his neck and lost herself in the rhythm of their mouths meeting and parting and meeting again. Her body went hot and soft and hard all at once and she wanted him with a fierceness that left her dazed.

She wanted this to be real. She needed it to be honest and true.

But the niggling doubts in the back of her mind

wouldn't be quieted. Because what if it wasn't? She couldn't bear another person lying to her.

She pulled away. Slowly, but she did—and just in time, too, as Oliver's hands had begun a slow but steady climb up her ribs and toward her aching breasts. She wanted him to touch her, wanted him to soothe the tension with his touch. With his mouth.

But she wasn't going to throw herself at him. She wasn't going to do anything until she was sure.

She had no idea what that certainty would look like, however.

He let her pull back, but he didn't let her go. Instead, he clutched her to his chest, breathing hard. She curled into him, unwilling to break the contact.

"We should…" His voice cracked and he cleared his throat. "We should do the dishes."

"Yeah."

Neither of them moved.

He stroked her hair. "I'll need to head back tonight. I have an early meeting tomorrow."

That was a good thing. Because if she knew Oliver was asleep right down the hall, she might do something stupid, like slip into his bed in the middle of the night and pick up where they'd just left off.

Funny how him leaving didn't feel like a good thing.

"You can't miss your meetings," she said, her voice wavering just a little. "Not for me."

He made a snorting noise. "I might be able to come back out tomorrow night. Just to see how you're doing. But I can't make any promises."

She smiled and hugged him tighter. "I'm going to try cookies again."

"Maybe this time, you could follow the recipe?"

"Maybe," she agreed.

They laughed and, as if by silent agreement, pulled away from each other. "Then we better wash the dishes."

She grinned. The ways she'd messed up those cookies... "And find the baking soda."

Six

He really didn't have time for yet another three hours in the car, round-trip, plus however long it took to make sure Renee was doing okay and hadn't set the oven on fire. He'd cut out of work an hour early today in an unsuccessful attempt to beat rush-hour traffic, which meant yet another meeting with Ritter had been pushed back. That wasn't going to make his father happy.

Oliver needed to be focusing on his job. His jobs—he needed to check in on Chloe and see how the negotiations with ESPN were going.

Funny how that to-do list wasn't stopping him from making the long drive out to Red Oak Hill again.

He pulled up in front of the house, grabbed the groceries out of the trunk and bounded—bounded!—up the front steps and into the house.

The first thing he noticed was the smell. Instead of burning, something that smelled suspiciously like chocolate chip cookies wafted through the house.

Oliver grinned as he hurried back to the kitchen. Hopefully, she'd followed the recipe this time. But he made up his mind—he was going to eat the damned cookies and tell her they were great, no matter what.

Well, almost no matter what. He wasn't eating charcoal.

He pulled up short when he walked into the kitchen. The place was an utter disaster. Flour coated almost every surface and the sink was overflowing with mixing bowls. Ah—she'd found the stand mixer, as well. Cookies covered every square inch of countertop that wasn't taken up with baking supplies.

Racks and racks of cookies. There had to be eight, maybe ten dozen in all. Some were noticeably darker and some were almost flat and a few looked like they hadn't spread at all.

That was a hell of a lot of cookies.

"If we eat all those cookies at once," he said, trying to find a place to set his bags, "we'll get sick."

"Oliver!" Renee popped up from where she'd been bent over the oven. "You're here!"

He grinned at her. "I am. You've been busy, I see."

She glanced around at all the cookies, her cheeks coloring prettily. "You're out of chocolate chips. Sorry about that."

For a moment, all he could do was stare at her. The longer she was at Red Oak, the better she looked. The shadows under her eyes were a distant memory now and the lines of worry at the corners and across her forehead had faded away. True, she had a smear of flour across her forehead, but that just made her look even more adorable. She was wearing yet another pair of soft leggings and a loose turquoise T-shirt that made her eyes shine. Her hair had been pulled back into a messy braid and all he wanted to do was mess it up further.

He didn't. All he did was look. Because for the first time, Renee looked like she was meant to be—a young, beautiful woman enjoying herself.

God, she took his breath away.

To hell with his restraint. The grocery bags hit the ground and the next thing he knew, she was in his arms and he was kissing her like she was the very air he needed and he'd been holding his breath for the last twenty-four hours.

"I brought more chocolate," he murmured against her mouth before he plundered it ruthlessly with his own.

He hesitated, but she didn't pull away. Instead, her body molded itself to his, her lips parting for his tongue, her fingers sinking into his hair as she tilted his head for better access.

"More chips are good," she agreed, but Oliver had already forgotten what they were talking about.

All he could remember was that this was why he had come. To hold Renee and discover her secrets one long, leisurely kiss at a time.

"Tell me to stop," he muttered as her hands slid down from his hair, over his back and down to his butt. She squeezed and what was left of his self-control began to fray. Badly. "Tell me to stop and I will."

She pulled away, her eyes closed, and he damn near fell to his knees to beg for her. Him! Oliver Lawrence!

But if she wanted him to beg, by God he would, because at some point, his best friend's irritating little sister had become a gorgeous young woman he couldn't walk away from.

He wasn't going to walk away from her.

"Oliver." His name on her lips was soft but he didn't miss the undercurrent of need in her voice. God, he hoped it was need.

"Yeah, darling?"

She opened her eyes and the force of the desire reflected back at him threatened to unman him right then and there. "Don't stop."

This was crazy. Worse than crazy. Dangerous, even.

She couldn't let Oliver sweep her off her feet and carry her up the stairs—again.

She shouldn't let him kick open the door to his bedroom and set her down on her feet. And under no circumstances should she let him kiss her as if she were his last chance at redemption.

There would be no redemption. Not for her anyway. It was selfish and shallow but she just wanted to feel good again. Even if it were just for an evening in Oliver's arms. Nothing permanent. She wasn't looking for another 'til-death-do-us-part. She'd done that already.

But was it so wrong to want to feel desirable? Was it bad to want a man to look at her with naked want in his eyes, to need her so badly that he kept driving halfway across Texas to see her?

Was it an awful thing to take what he was offering?

"Renee," he murmured against her lips as his hands slid underneath her loose tunic. The touch of his bare fingers to the skin at the small of her back made her groan.

How was he doing this to her? She was no innocent—she was almost five months pregnant, for heaven's sake. She'd known desire and want in her time.

But nothing had prepared her for *this*, she realized as Oliver pulled her shirt over her head and cast it aside.

"Oh, dear God in heaven," he said, his voice revenant as he stared down at her bare chest. Because she hadn't been able to bring herself to put a too-small underwire bra on again if she were going to be alone in the house all day.

She'd planned to put the blasted thing on before he got here. She'd had the best of intentions. But Oliver had shown up earlier than she'd expected and it was rapidly becoming apparent that the bra was pointless in more ways than one.

"They're not always this big," she told him. "In the interest of full disclosure." Because no matter what, she didn't want anything that happened in this bedroom to be a lie.

Then she waited. Really, she wasn't afraid of what he might think about her new and improved breasts. Men liked big breasts, after all. Chet certainly had.

But it was the rest of her that had her worried. Her belly had started rounding out by the time she was three months pregnant and, aside from her loose tunics and leggings, nothing fitted. Not even close.

"I've put on a lot of weight." She managed to say it in a level voice, without any of the hurt bleeding into that statement. But if he were going to say something…less than perfect, she wanted to be braced for the worst. She wouldn't let it hurt.

"Hmm." The noise rumbled out of his chest as his fingers trailed over her ribs, their destination unmistakable. "It suits you."

What the heck did he mean by *that*? But before the words got off the tip of her tongue, his fingers were skimming over the sides of her breasts, circling around her nipples.

Which were, of course, tightening to hard points. Of course they were.

His thumbs swept over the tips and Renee stopped thinking about her weight, about Chet Willoughby and how perfectly average he'd been in bed. Instead, her head dropped back and she had to steady herself as the sensation of being touched—tenderly, sweetly and oh-so-hotly—overwhelmed her.

Then something warm and wet swept over her right nipple and her eyes flew open just in time to see Oliver lick it again. "Okay to suck or not?" he murmured against her flesh.

Heat flooded her body, making her shift anxiously. The pressure between her legs was so intense that she could barely think. All she could imagine was his mouth on her. "I... Gently, I think?" Was she more sensitive because she was pregnant? Or just because this was Oliver and he was seducing her like she'd never been seduced before?

She watched in fascination as he fell to his knees before her, his hands around her waist to hold her steady. Then he looked up at her and, holding her gaze with his own, he took her right nipple in his mouth.

She couldn't have held back the moan if she tried—and she did try. But it was a pointless exercise because sensations crashed over her like waves breaking over a jagged shore.

And this was Oliver being gentle. In control. Cautious. She had a sudden urge to see him beyond all reason, wild with need and crazed with desire. For her.

As his mouth drew down on her, his thumb continued to flick over her other nipple and that pressure between her legs crested and then crested again. She dug her hands into his hair and held on tight.

She didn't want to think about all the times she'd faked this kind of reaction, nor did she want to think about all the times Chet had skipped the foreplay to get right to the sex.

So she didn't. She made a conscious effort to put those unpleasant disappointments into a box inside her mind and shut the lid tight. Chet was dead and she wasn't. She was here and she was coming back to life under Oliver's skilled touch.

"You taste like vanilla and chocolate," he murmured as he kissed the space between her breasts before moving to the other one. "God, Renee, you taste so damn good."

She sighed and gave herself over to him. It wasn't selfish if he was giving himself freely, right? He wanted her. She wanted him. They were both consenting adults. There wasn't anything wrong with any of this.

A thought in the very back of her mind tried to remind her that, if anyone put her and Oliver in bed together—or even near the bed—there would be many things wrong with this. Her toxic reputation might very well damage his own, which might affect his business and his family.

All those lovely feelings threatened to turn sour in a heartbeat and she almost pulled away from him. She couldn't risk hurting the Lawrence family and, selfish as it was, she couldn't risk tainting all those wonderful memories from her childhood with loathing and recrimination.

But that was the exact moment that Oliver relinquished her breast and began kissing down her stomach. Renee froze, torn between the need to do the right thing, the urge to hide her belly or the marks on her legs from him and the unleashed desire still crashing through her system. "Oliver…"

He kissed the top of her belly, where it rounded out. And as much as Renee detested it, she was powerless to stop her mother's voice echoing through her thoughts.

Look at you. It's disgusting, how you've already let yourself go. It's embarrassing to be seen in public with you when you're this fat and ugly.

She moved to cover herself but Oliver caught her hands

in his. "Don't hide from me, Renee," he said, his mouth moving lower. "You have no idea how gorgeous you are right now, do you?"

"I'm not." Her whisper was shaky, even to her own ears.

"You *are*." He looked up at her, that intensity shining through the lust. "Let me show you how much I want you." Then, before she could stop him, he hooked his fingers into the stretchy waistband of her leggings and her panties and pulled down.

He had to work the fabric over her hips but he was making that humming noise that seemed to come straight from his chest as he bared her. She balanced herself on his shoulders as she stepped out of her clothes and then she was completely nude before him.

He stared at her in what she desperately hoped was wonder and not something less…savory. He hadn't noticed the scars yet, so she fought the urge to slap her hands over the tops of her thighs. Maybe he wouldn't notice. Chet never had, after all.

God, why was she like this? Why couldn't she let go? Why couldn't she get lost in Oliver's eyes, Oliver's touch? Why was her mother's sneering voice cutting through this moment? Why were memories of Chet lurking just behind that?

Why couldn't this be perfect? No, that wasn't the right question, she realized as she blinked back tears.

Why couldn't *she* be perfect?

Then Oliver leaned forward and pressed a kiss to her belly button, his hands stroking up and down her thighs before moving back to cup her bottom. He squeezed as his mouth moved lower and his teeth skimmed over the space just above the hair that covered her sex. Because she hadn't been able to bring herself to keep up with her waxing. Being naked on a table before a near stranger?

That was a gossip disaster waiting to happen, and besides, who was going to see her like this?

Oliver.

He crouched down a little more and nudged her legs apart. She should let go of his hair, tell him to stop. At the very least, she should insist they pull the drapes and turn off the lights. Then she would be able to hide her belly and her thighs from him and she might be able to let go.

Because she needed to let go. She needed to prove those voices in her head wrong.

She needed this. She needed *him*.

"Beautiful," he whispered and he seemed so damn sincere that she had to believe he meant it, had to believe this was real. That was when his hand slid between her legs, brushing over her core with such tenderness that she wanted to cry. Stupid hormones. Then he leaned forward and pressed a kiss right there and, miracle of miracles, her mind emptied of all the hurt and criticism and pain and there was only Oliver and his mouth and his hands and *her*. He wasn't in Dallas with anyone else. He was here because he chose her.

His tongue moved over her sensitive flesh and it was the same and it was different and it was everything all at once. Because she didn't remember all these sensations crashing over her in a flood that couldn't be held back. She didn't remember making these noises without being able to control them. And she sure as hell didn't remember being so swept away by the rising tide that her legs shook and she suddenly was in danger of falling over.

"Oliver," she begged, pulling on his hair. "I can't stand."

He looked up at her, one arm locked around her legs and that was when she saw it—the raw hunger in his eyes. It took her breath away.

Then he surged to his feet, catching her in his arms. When he kissed her again, she didn't taste vanilla or chocolate, but instead she was on his tongue and he was marking her as his own.

She couldn't think. All she could do was act. So she yanked at the buttons on his shirt and jerked at the zipper of his pants because if she was naked, she wanted him naked, too.

He kicked out of his pants as she hauled his undershirt over his head and then there was nothing between them. She stepped back to see what he looked like underneath his button-up shirts and suit jackets. She got the impression of broad and lean and muscled with a smattering of chest hair. But she barely had time to say, "Oh, Oliver," before he was kissing her again, his hands pulling her hair from her braid as he backed her up.

So she let her hands explore. His chest was hard and warm and he hissed against her lips when she caught his nipples with her fingernails. His stomach rippled with muscles as she moved her hands lower and then...

"Oh, *Oliver*," she moaned against the skin of his neck as she gripped his erection. He was rock hard under her touch and she could feel his muscles shake as her hand moved up his impressive length and back down to his base.

He stilled against her, his head on her shoulder, his breath coming hard. "Woman," he growled, skimming his teeth over the delicate skin where her neck met her shoulders, "if you don't stop that right now, you'll have to wait at least five minutes before I can be inside of you."

She did that. She made him react like that. It was powerful, knowing that she could bring him to the edge, just like he'd done to her. God, it felt good to be in control of something again.

She smiled and stroked him again. "Five whole minutes?"

He groaned against her skin and then he bit her. Not too hard, but it was primal in its own way. "Maybe only three." He grabbed her hand when she squeezed. *"Renee."*

Then he picked her up. But instead of throwing her down on the bed, he spun and sat hard on a sofa. Renee blinked. She'd been so caught up in her own thoughts and in Oliver that she hadn't even realized that his room was set up similarly to hers. There was a large—and inviting—bed done up in deep blues and a sitting area with two love seats and a simple coffee table between them.

They were on the love seat that faced the big mirror over a dresser. "I need to watch you on top," he groaned. He rolled on a condom—where had that come from?—and then lifted her up so she could put her knees on either side of his legs. "I need to see you come apart, babe."

His erection brushed against her center and she shuddered. "Awfully confident, aren't you?"

She shouldn't tease him. But this was Oliver, dang it. She'd been teasing him for as long as she could remember and she had a feeling that he wouldn't dare turn a hose on her right now. It was safe to poke at him, to smile and laugh with him. He wouldn't demand to know what was so funny or, worse, who else she was thinking of.

He caught her face in his hands and touched his forehead to hers. "Renee," he said and she didn't hear any anger or insult in his voice. "I promise you, I won't leave you behind." There was a touch of sadness in his eyes as he said it.

Her throat closed up and her eyes watered. But she put on what she hoped was a sensual face. "I know."

He pressed a kiss to her lips that, considering their position, was surprisingly sweet. "Don't tell me what you think I want to hear, babe. Tell me what you need. Because I won't leave you frustrated." His hips flexed, dragging his erection over the folds of her sex and instinctively, she lifted herself up. His tip lodged firmly against her center and she gasped, her legs shaking again. "One way or another," he promised, "I'm going to make you scream with need." And there was nothing sweet about *that*.

It was hard to breath. Because he meant it. He meant every last word and in that moment, she fell in love with him. How could she not?

She lost her half-hearted battle with gravity and sank down onto him. For a long moment, they both sat still, breathing hard. Renee couldn't think, couldn't feel anything but Oliver inside of her, Oliver filling her. He was a part of her now. He always had been, but this?

"Woman," he growled again. "I can't—I need—oh, God." His fingers dug into her hips and he lifted her up before guiding her body back down again. She moaned as he filled her.

"I had no idea," he ground out, the cords on his neck standing out as he held himself in check. Then he caught her left nipple in his mouth and tugged, ever so gently, while she rose and fell and rose again. Each pull of his lips drew an answering pull from where they were joined and she was helpless to hold on to anything but him. "That's it, babe," he growled, moving to her other breast. "Take what you need."

And she fell a little bit more in love with him because he was waiting for her. And even if he came first, he'd still take care of her. He wouldn't leave her behind. She wasn't just here for his pleasure. He was here for hers, and *that*? That made all the difference in the world.

She lifted his face and kissed him with everything

she had. He groaned into her and that sound of pure need was her undoing. Renee came apart in his arms, her body going tight around his as the wave crested and broke over her.

She collapsed against his chest, unable to do anything but breathe hard as he thrust up into her, his hips moving harder and faster. "Renee," he said, somewhere between a groan and a shout. "Babe!"

She clenched her inner muscles at the same time she bit him on the shoulder and he made a noise of pure animal pleasure, so raw and desperate that she came a second time as he gave her everything he had.

Legs and arms everywhere, they didn't move, except for the panting. "I had no idea," Oliver said, his voice shaking. He leaned back and looked at her. "Okay? Or do you need something more?"

How could she not love him? Because no one—not a single one of her previous boyfriends—had ever asked. And if she'd tried to ask for something else, they'd taken it as an insult to their manhoods. It was her fault if she hadn't come, not theirs.

But Oliver was a different man. A better one.

God, it'd be hard to leave him when the time came.

But that was still a ways off. Hopefully at least a few more weeks. She didn't dare look further ahead than that.

Right now, she was going to live in this moment for as long as she could.

"Better than okay," she said, kissing him again as she lifted herself free. "So much better."

Oh, she liked that grin on him. Then, because on some level, she was apparently still ten and he was still thirteen, she added, "But we might need to try that again later, just to be sure this time wasn't a fluke."

His eyes popped open in surprise and she tried not to

laugh, she really did—but that was a battle she lost. A second after she started giggling, he narrowed his eyes to slits and he would have looked dangerous if he hadn't been smiling. "Why, you little tease. You know what I'm going to do?" He caught her in his arms and she wondered if maybe he hadn't been exaggerating when he'd said five minutes—maybe even just three—earlier.

"What?" She barely got the words out because he took her breath away.

"I'm going to…" He cocked his head to the side. "Do you hear something?"

"What?" That wasn't romantic. Or seductive. That didn't even count as basic flirting.

But then she did hear something. A steady, insistent beeping. Then another beep joined in with the first one, louder. Closer.

Her mind was still sluggish from the climaxes, so it took her a second before the beeping penetrated. Oliver got there first. "The smoke alarms!"

"The cookies!"

Seven

Renee scrambled off his lap and grabbed her top, but Oliver didn't even bother with clothes. He went streaking out of the bedroom at a dead run, his legs still a little wobbly from the sex.

Dear God, if she burned the whole damned house down…

He went skidding into the kitchen. For the second night in a row, smoke was curling out of the oven and hanging in a low cloud against the ceiling—but no flames. Thank God for that.

Oliver moved fast. He grabbed the oven mitts and turned the oven off before he snatched the cookie sheet out of the oven. Still no flames. Just carbonized cookies. Again.

These smelled even worse than the ones from last night. He didn't want to dump them in the sink and there were still dozens of cookies covering every flat surface.

Thankfully, Renee came running into the kitchen.

"Door!" he barked, the oven mitts getting hotter the longer he held on to the cookie sheet.

Coughing, Renee turned and ran. Oliver had to wonder where the hell she was going—there was a perfectly fine door on the other side of the island that opened onto the backyard, but then she yelled, "The pond!"

Right—water would be good. Oliver's hands were growing dangerously hot despite the oven mitts so he took off after her.

She jerked the front door open and stood to the side while he ran outside and barreled straight into the pond. With a silent apology to Fred and Wilma, he threw the whole damn mess into the water before tearing off the oven mitts and letting them fall to the water. He bent over and let the water cover his hands. It wasn't cold because the day had been sunny and warm but compared to the hot cookie sheet, the water felt amazing.

A few yards away, the cookie sheet hit the water with a sizzle, as if he'd been forging iron. He looked up to see the whole thing floating, the hockey pucks formerly known as cookies still smoking.

On the far side of the pond, Fred and Wilma made a lot of noise and flapped their wings in displeasure at having their evening swim disrupted.

"Tell me about it," he muttered, turning his attention back to his palms. They were red but not burned. He didn't see any blisters forming, nor any white skin that signaled a severe burn.

He dunked his hands back in the water, just to be sure.

He heard a strangled noise behind him and he looked over his shoulder. Renee was standing a few feet up the bank. She'd managed to grab her T-shirt and it hung down to the top of her hips, the hem fluttering in the breeze. Backlit by the setting sun, he could see every inch of her silhouette outlined and that was when his brain chose to re-member that, less than ten minutes ago, he'd been inside her, feeling the shocks of her body releasing a climax upon his.

But something wasn't right. Her hands covered her mouth, her eyes were huge and her shoulders were shak-ing. It about broke his heart to see her like that.

They were just cookies. It wasn't like she'd burned the house down or scarred him for life. He didn't like her looking so fragile, so scared.

But then she asked, "Are you okay?" in a voice that was strangled—but it wasn't horror or misery that laced her words.

He recognized that voice. He'd heard it countless times back when they'd been kids and he and Clint had fallen for one of Renee and Chloe's pranks—he was think-ing specifically of clear tape strung across his bedroom door that Oliver had walked into it so hard that he'd been knocked off his feet, tape stuck in his hair.

And Renee had stood over him then, looking almost exactly like she did right now—trying so hard not to giggle at the raging success of her trick. Trying, instead, to look worried and she'd uttered the exact same words.

She hadn't succeeded then and she wasn't succeeding now. "Are you *laughing* at me?"

"No!" she answered way too quickly. "I'm…" She took a deep breath, visibly getting herself under control. "I want to make sure your hands aren't burned."

The smoke detectors beeped from deep inside the house. Fred and Wilma continued to express their dis-pleasure on the other side of the pond, with Pebbles and Bamm-Bamm joining in. But all he could hear was the barely contained amusement in her voice. "Fine," he said coolly, because it was the truth and he didn't want her to worry. "Just a little warm. No burns, no blisters."

"Good." Her gaze cut to his backside at the exact same moment a stiff breeze rippled over the surface of the pond. And his butt.

His bare butt. The one that was sticking straight up in the air because he was bent over at the waist. Everything was hanging *all* the way out.

"Do you think," she said, dropping her hands and trying to look serious, "that there'll be a full moon tonight?"

Holy hell, this woman. She was easily going to be the death of him, and quite possibly his house. But honestly? He was so damned relieved she was okay, that the same mischievous, hilarious Renee who'd driven him up a wall when they'd been kids was still in there that he wanted to laugh with him.

But this was Renee after all, and he wasn't about to let her off the hook that easily. Turning, he scowled at her as he walked out of the pond. "You think this is funny?"

"Maybe." She sobered and took a step back as he advanced on her. "Maybe not."

"This is the second night in a row you've nearly burned down the house, Renee. I don't think I'm going to let you bake anymore."

The light in her eyes dimmed as she paled and she crossed her arms over her stomach, almost curling into herself even though she didn't so much as bend at the waist. Shit, he'd taken it too far. He wanted to make her sweat a little but he didn't want to beat her down.

Fight back, he thought as he got nose to nose with her. *Fight for yourself.* "You, ma'am, are a menace to baked goods the world over," he intoned in the most pompous voice he possessed. "I'd even go so far as to say you're a monster to cookies everywhere, to say nothing of how you're terrorizing my kitchen, my swans and myself!"

Behind him, Fred—or maybe it was Wilma—whooped

from much closer. Involuntarily, he flinched because no one wanted to be bitten on the ass—or other exposed parts—by an angry bird with a six-foot wingspan. He looked over his shoulder. The swans and cygnets had swum over to investigate the now-sinking cookie sheet, so his butt was safe. For now.

He turned back to Renee. She stared up at him, confusion written all over her face. "Did…did you just call me a cookie monster?"

"If the shoe fits." He snarled. Well, he tried to snarl. But suddenly the effort of not laughing was almost more than he could bear.

She blinked at him and then blinked again before pointedly looking at their feet. "We're not wearing shoes."

"Fine. If the shaggy blue fur and googly eyes fit, wear them!"

Fight back, Renee.

Then, miracle of miracles, she did. She gave him a fierce look and poked him in the chest. "I've got news for you, mister." *Poke.* "You're not the boss of me." *Poke.*

"Oh, yeah?" It was not the snappiest comeback he'd ever uttered.

But it did what he wanted it to do. Her eyes lit all the way back up as she smiled and then tried to scowl and frankly, she took his breath away again. This was a game. Maybe not one she'd played in a long time, but she hadn't forgotten the rules. Thank God for that. She was going to give him everything she had and that, more than the explosive sex or the questionably edible baked goods, made him feel ten feet tall. She wasn't afraid of him. He was worth the fight.

She was worth the fight. It was high time she knew it.

"Yeah!" *Poke.* "If I want to bake cookies—" *poke* "—then I'm going to bake cookies. And furthermore—" *poke*

"—I'll have you know that I was doing just fine before you showed up, both nights." *Poke.*

"Ow," Oliver said, backing up a step. She wasn't poking him hard, but she was hitting the exact same spot over and over again.

"You're the reason the cookies got burned." *Poke.* "You distracted me with amazing kisses and the best sex I've ever had." *Poke.* "If you hadn't distracted me, we could be eating the perfect chocolate chip cookie right now."

Amazing kisses? The best sex? He wasn't one to brag but hell, yeah, that was good for his masculine pride. To hell with cookies. He'd have her back in bed. Or on the love seat. Hell, any semiflat surface would do just fine, as long as he could hold her in his arms and feel every inch of her body against every inch of his.

Oliver was grinning his fool head off but he didn't care. There was something so right about Renee defending herself and putting him in his place that it made him want to sing.

Sing! Him! Oliver!

He didn't burst into song. However, he did say, "Were they edible cookies?" just to drive her nuts.

It worked. "The last batch was!" *Poke.*

Stumbling backward, Oliver looked over his shoulder. The cookie sheet had sunk now, but a few hockey pucks formerly known as cookies floated on the surface of the pond. Fred and Wilma and the kids seemed mildly terrified of the things. He couldn't blame them. "The *last* batch?"

"You know what I mean—the batch before that!" *Poke.*

Oliver retreated another step. She was in fine form, his Renee. Her eyes blazed and the breeze molded the thin T-shirt to her body, highlighting her breasts and the gentle swell of her stomach and all he wanted to do was pull her into his arms and kiss the hell out of her.

"I swear to God, if I had a water balloon—" *poke* "—I'd throw it right at your head. But you know what?" *Poke.*

He grabbed her finger before she bruised him. "What?"

A victorious smile graced her face, making her look like an avenging angel. He wanted to fall to his knees and worship before her. She pulled her hand back and said, "I don't need a water balloon."

This time, she didn't poke him. She put both hands on his chest and Oliver had just leaned down to take that kiss from her lips when she shoved him. *Hard.*

He fell backward and the next thing he knew, he was sitting on his butt in the pond, wiping water from his face while Renee stood safely on the bank, staring at him.

"You…" he sputtered, wiping water from his face. The mud was squishing up his butt and around his important parts and, judging from the noise, the swans had declared DEFCON 1 behind him. "You pushed me!"

For a second, she looked just as shocked as he felt. Then her face cracked into a huge smile and it was like the sun breaking through clouds after days of endless rain.

"You. Pushed. Me," he said in his most dangerous growl and then he splashed as much water as he humanly could at her. He missed, of course. From this angle, he could see under the hem of her long T-shirt and, as she danced out of the way of the water, he caught glimpses of her bare body that made him hard all over again, despite the mud.

She laughed, loud and free, and clapped her hands in delight. "Don't move," she giggled, pointing. "I'm going to get my phone. I think Chloe needs to see a picture of this—the high-and-mighty Oliver Lawrence stuck in the mud!"

"The hell you will," he said, trying to get to his feet. But the mud was slippery and he lost his balance and splashed back down again. He couldn't even keep a straight face this time.

The sound of her happiness was worth it, he decided. He'd be cleaning mud out of his crack for a week but he'd take the fall for her again, just to hear her laugh as if she didn't have a care in the world. She wrapped her arms around her waist and bent forward, tears of joy rolling down her cheeks.

"You win this round," he yelled, aiming for his best villain voice—high-pitched and nasal. "But I'll be back!"

Then, just like she always had years ago, Renee jammed her thumbs against the side of her head, waggled her fingers at him and stuck out her tongue, yelling, *"Nyah, nyah na nyah*, you can't catch me!" before she spun on her heels and bolted back to the house. Her legs flashed in the dim light, her bottom peeking out from under the shirt with every step she took.

All he could do was watch her go, an unfamiliar lightness settling around him even as the sun sank behind the house and shrouded the pond in shadows. He hadn't felt this lightness back when they were kids. She'd driven him nuts and he'd done everything he could've to return the favor. But now?

They weren't kids anymore. Life had changed them both but he could still give her those moments of joy.

"Are you coming?" she yelled from the front door.

He rolled onto his hands and knees and made sure he had his feet under him before he stood. Pond water sheeted down his body, leaving muddy rivulets all across his legs. "Hell, yeah," he called back.

Because she wasn't going anywhere without him.

Eight

"These aren't bad," Oliver said around his sixth attempt to eat one of Renee's cookies.

"Really?" Renee ducked her head, a delicate blush pinking her cheeks. "That was the last batch. That survived anyway."

He wanted to cup her blushing cheek in his palm and kiss her again and again. But then again, earlier he'd wanted to pull her back upstairs and try out a few other positions with her, but he couldn't.

Just like always, Oliver had bowed to the demands of reality. Stupid reality.

Frankly, he was lucky he hadn't mooned half of Mineola. Because that's about how many people had suddenly appeared on his property.

While Oliver had been splashing in the pond and doing everything in his power to make Renee laugh and fight back, his housekeeper, Lucille, had called three times to see if the house was on fire or not. When she couldn't get ahold of anyone at the house, she'd called the fire department. The fire trucks had shown up about five minutes after he'd got his naked butt back inside the house, with Lucille hot on their tail. And then she'd scolded Oliver like he was a schoolboy and demanded to know why he'd installed a houseguest without telling her because she could have brought over some more food.

"Or at least some better desserts," Lucille had grumbled when she'd got a good look at the kitchen.

But Oliver had introduced Lucille to Renee and, after her initial shock, Lucille seemed to be warming up. She picked up a cookie from a different batch and took a small nibble. "Good heavens, you're not supposed to use that much salt!"

"Well, I figured that out," Renee said defensively—but at least she said it with a smile. "Eventually. Why would anyone label *teaspoon* and *tablespoon* so similarly?"

Lucille gave Renee a look that made it clear the older woman didn't know if Renee was joking or not.

Oliver snagged another edible cookie and handed it over to Lucille. "The important thing is she figured it out."

Lucille was not one for effusive praise, but even she nodded and said, "That's not half bad," which made Renee bust out another one of those luminous smiles. "Honey, I can teach you to bake, if you'd like." She eyed the mess again. "Might be easier. Or at least safer. When are you due, honey?"

"Oh." Renee turned a pretty pink and stared down at her belly. Oliver couldn't figure out if she was embarrassed by this question or not. "September 27."

Because of course she knew the exact date of conception. The day her husband took his own life. Oliver didn't like the way Renee seemed to pull back into herself. He shot Lucille a look that he hoped communicated *say something nice.*

And Lucille, bless her heart, did. She wasn't a grandmother of six for nothing. "Pregnancy suits you," she announced a tad too loudly.

"It does?" Clearly, Renee didn't believe her.

"You've got that glow, honey. Some women look tired or drained, but you?" She waved her hand near Renee's belly. "Some women were born to this. You're one of them, you lucky duck."

Renee looked doubtfully down at her stomach. "But I'm fat."

Lucille looked truly insulted by this. She patted Renee on the arm. "Oh, honey—who told you that? They were nothing but jealous. You're gorgeous." She turned a hard stare to Oliver. "Isn't she?" It was not a question.

"I already told her that. Multiple times—because it's true," he replied, watching Renee's cheeks color even more. Which meant he almost missed the look Lucille gave him, one that had him realizing that he might have overplayed his hand.

Thus far, he and Renee had attempted to stick with their original story—they were childhood friends and he'd given Renee free use of his ranch while she was hiding and he was working in Dallas.

But that story wasn't holding water, so to speak, and Oliver knew it. It was the middle of the workweek and yet he was at Red Oak Hill. And not only was he at Red Oak Hill, he'd also barely got out of the shower and got pants on before the place had been crawling with firefighters. At least Renee had located her leggings. They'd told the fire crew that he'd fallen into the pond trying to deal with the carbonized cookies—which, again, was true.

But it wasn't a huge leap to get from him naked in the

shower to him naked with Renee. He'd even caught two firefighters nudging each other with their elbows and winking at Oliver's story.

Yeah, no one was buying that half-truth here. Worse, he'd screwed up and used Renee's real name when he'd introduced her to Lucille within earshot of at least three firefighters and now there was no going back.

For all intents and purposes, Renee's presence at Red Oak Hill was now common knowledge.

Especially because Lucille was no idiot and it was clear Oliver had screwed up again. Damn it. This was all going wrong. Lucille, he trusted, but the firefighters? And now Lucille was giving him The Look?

To avoid Lucille's sharp gaze, Oliver snatched up another cookie and immediately regretted it. Coughing, he spit the too-salty one into the trash. "I think we can get rid of these," he sputtered, scraping the whole batch off the cooling rack and directly into the trash. "We're lucky no one else tried these."

"*You* were lucky you weren't caught with your britches down," Lucille said, dumping another batch into the trash and stacking the dirty dishes in the sink.

Oliver froze, the blood draining from his face. A quick glance at Renee told him that the opposite was true for her. She was turning an unnatural shade of scarlet. She shot him a helpless look.

Oliver wanted to bolt but he couldn't abandon Renee to Lucille's questioning. "You should ask Lucille for some tips," he said, ignoring the status of his britches. "She does most of the cooking for me. And she makes an amazing cinnamon roll. I know it's not a cookie but…"

Bless her heart, Lucille said, "You should try a sugar cookie, honey. Once you get the basic dough recipe down, then you can start messing around with it."

"I saw some recipes but they looked really complicated—lots of detailed icing," Renee replied. "I don't think I could do that."

"You only need that much icing if you've got a boring cookie." The older woman eyed the kitchen counters. "I don't think anything you bake could ever be boring."

Oliver could have kissed the woman. Renee looked relieved and that was the most important thing. "I did see some really cute things on Pinterest I wanted to try…"

And they were off. "I'll be in my study—Bailey is emailing me," Oliver mumbled, making a break for it. He didn't know if it was a lie or not. Bailey probably *had* been emailing him.

He dropped into the chair and put his elbows on his desk. He was tempted to yank his hair out of his head, if only to make sure he hadn't hallucinated the last two hours. Renee was right. None of this—the smoke alarms, the fire department, Lucille—would've happened if he'd been able to stick with the plan. He should've stayed in Dallas. Barring that, he should've kept his hands off her. And barring that…

He shouldn't have teased her in the pond. But he hadn't been able to help himself. A jumble of emotions churned in his chest. He wasn't thinking straight and he knew it.

He wanted Renee. One time with her wasn't going to be enough. If anything, he wanted her more now than he had before he'd stripped her bare and slid into her body.

He did not want her to burn his house down. Thus far, they'd had two close calls and he didn't want to find out if the third time would be the charm.

He needed to make her laugh again, to see that joy lighting up her face. He didn't want to see the shadows that hovered around her anymore.

And he'd completely failed her because people knew where she was now.

What a freaking mess.

So he did what he always did when things went sideways on him. He worked. He logged in and attacked the twenty-one emails that Bailey had sent him since 3:45 p.m. this afternoon with a fervor that bordered on possessed. He sent a message to Herb Ritter that he absolutely would make their 9:00 a.m. tomorrow morning. He reviewed the messages from Chloe summarizing how negotiations with ESPN were going. He ignored the ones from his father.

"Oliver?"

He jumped. How much time had passed? It wasn't enough. Seeing Renee in the doorway to the study, her head tilted to the side, light from the hallway settling around her shoulders—he was terrified to realize it might never be enough. "How's everything going?"

"Good. Really good." She stepped into the room, but not very far. He could feel the distance between them. "Lucille's going to bring over some recipes on Friday. I helped her with the dishes. There's a right way and a wrong way to wash dishes, apparently."

He knew that, but he said, "Who knew?" in a teasing tone.

She took another small step into the study. "I'm going to go take a shower. For some odd reason, I smell a little like a pond and charcoal."

"Do you now?" Oliver couldn't fight back the grin.

She nodded, putting together a reasonable appearance of innocence. "Will you..." She paused and straightened her shoulders, her chin coming up. Oliver didn't like that look on her. But he was starting to recognize it for what it was—Renee putting her armor on. "Will you be here when I get out of the shower?"

Screw this distance. Oliver was out of his chair before he could think better of it, crossing the room and pulling her into his arms. "I won't leave you without saying goodbye."

That wasn't what he wanted to say. Hell, he didn't know what he wanted to say. It wasn't like he was going to tell her he loved her. He cared for her, yes. He worried about her. He wanted her happy and well and safe. But that wasn't love.

The problem was, he didn't know what it was.

She looked at him, her eyes round with something that looked too much like fear. "Is this goodbye?"

This was *not* love. But it was definitely something more intense, more focused than he was used to feeling.

"No," he said, brushing his lips over hers. "It's not."

She exhaled against his mouth and he deepened the kiss, clutching her tighter so that her body was pressed against his chest. His hands moved down her back, cupping her bottom and pulling her against him. She gasped as the hard length of his arousal made contact with the soft flesh under her belly.

He lost himself in her. That's what this was. It wasn't love and it wasn't lust. He was simply lost to her.

God help him, he didn't ever want to be found.

He already had her shirt half-off when a loud clatter echoed from the kitchen, followed by some of Lucille's more creative language. Oliver and Renee broke apart, both breathing hard.

"I…" Blushing furiously, Renee backed away. "I need to shower."

Oliver begged to disagree. What she needed was to stay right here in his arms. Preferably with less clothing between them. But he didn't say that out loud. He needed to put more space between them. He needed to get his thoughts—and his dick—back under control. Hell, he needed to drive back to Dallas tonight so he could meet with Herb Ritter in the morning.

But he just might need Renee more.

So all he said was "Sounds good," as if that could've even begun to make things right.

He wouldn't have thought it possible but Renee blushed even more. "Okay."

"Good," he repeated dumbly, his arms beginning to shake with the effort of holding them at his side. But he fought those baser urges because the moment his control slipped, he'd do something foolish like pull her back into his arms and tell her to wait because he was absolutely going to join her in the shower. And then the bed. And everywhere in between.

With a smile, she turned and fled. It wasn't until he heard her steps overhead and the door to her bedroom shut that he exhaled and staggered back to his desk on weak knees.

"She's something." Lucille's gravelly voice made him jump again. "I like her."

Oliver pulled himself to attention. "Sorry about the kitchen. We, uh, lost a cookie sheet to the pond." He was real proud of the way his voice was level. Strong. Less…*shaken*.

Sitting in front of the desk, Lucille stared at him long enough that Oliver began to shift uncomfortably. Like the swans, the older woman had come with the house. She had been cleaning Red Oak Hill for almost twenty years. It had only made sense to keep her on when Oliver had bought the place six years ago.

He'd run a background check on her and got to know her, of course. He wasn't stupid. But the fact was, Lucille was so good at maintaining Red Oak Hill to Oliver's standards that he paid for her to come to Dallas one day a week and clean his condo, as well. And because he valued loyalty, he paid her well.

He was just about to open his mouth and tell her not to mention anything about Renee to anyone, but she beat him to the punch. "That's the Preston Pyramid Princess, right?"

"Right." He could feel himself deflating. "She was best friends with my sister when we were growing up. Her brother was my best friend. They were practically family."

"Darn shame about her husband. He shot his fool head off, right?"

"Right. She's had a rough go of it since then. I'm just giving her a place to lie low for a bit."

"That girl reminds me of me," Lucille announced.

"Really?" Lucille had three kids by three different fathers, but Dale was only her second husband.

Lucille gave him a smile that made it clear she knew what he was thinking. "Different circumstances, same story. Like recognizes like. I love my kids and I love my grandkids. I'm not saying I'd want to change anything because all of it—the good and the bad—gave me them. But I'm an old woman now."

"Hardly," he muttered. Lucille was all of fifty-five.

She ignored that interruption. "I can look back with a little distance. I had a rough childhood—my mom wasn't around much and my dad was a mean drunk. I spent years doing whatever the hell I wanted because who was going to stop me? No one. At least, that's what I told myself."

Okay, so maybe a picture was slowly starting to emerge of a less-than-happy childhood for Renee. But that wasn't anything comparable to what Lucille was talking about. However, discretion was the better part of valor, so Oliver kept his mouth shut.

Lucille went on, "But I didn't know what I wanted. I'd meet someone and suddenly, whatever they wanted was what I wanted. Drugs, alcohol, sex—did I ever really want any of that? Or did I just go along with it because I needed the approval? Who knows, if I'd met Dale earlier…" She let that trail off, her gaze getting soft.

He was about to argue with this assessment of Renee—but then he remembered something she'd said about her wedding. She would have been perfectly happy with something small and intimate but she'd wound up with something like ten bridesmaids and custom-engraved crystal and it was all wildly over-the-top.

Was that what Lucille was talking about? Hell, he didn't know. "As nice a guy as Dale is, I don't think he's Renee's type."

He didn't expect Lucille to scowl. "Do you know why she's been destroying my kitchen? Because she's trying to figure out what she wants. Not what her father, or I assume her mother, wants, not what her husband was willing to give her. Not even what you want, Oliver Lawrence. What *she* wants."

"Is that supposed to be difficult?" He didn't mean to sound flippant. But he didn't see how this was some sort of lifelong struggle. Okay, Renee was still in her midtwenties. And she was going through a rough time in her life. But most people got a handle on life by the time they got out of college.

After all, he knew what he wanted. He wanted to leave Lawrence Energies and his family behind and get back to his real life in New York and…

Didn't he?

Lucille leveled a look at him that, if he'd been a younger

man, would have made him drop his head in shame. As it was, he had to look away. "If you spent your entire life being told that what you want is useless and worthless," she said in a tone that walked a fine line between understanding and disappointed, "that what makes you happy is stupid, then yeah, it's difficult."

"I don't think she's stupid." In fact, he knew she wasn't. God knew he didn't tolerate fools. She was bright and charming and vivacious and gorgeous and... he wanted her.

"You know she's not stupid. I know she's not stupid. But does she know that?"

"Of course she does. Why wouldn't she?" But even as he said it, he had to wonder.

She *did* know, didn't she? That Oliver thought she was all of those amazing, wonderful things? That he never considered her stupid or worthless, not even back when they'd been children tormenting each other? She might've been a pain in his backside, but he had always known that she was smart and talented.

Lucille stood. "She can't stay here. Too many of those boys recognized her."

"You're the one who promised you'd teach her how to bake." The idea of sticking Renee in some soulless hotel where she wasn't allowed to wander around or even attempt a simple sugar cookie left him feeling vaguely ill.

"It's going to take me at least a day to put that kitchen back in order," Lucille grumbled, but she smiled as she said it. "Take her to your condo. I'll be there on Monday anyway. The building has decent security. They won't be able to sneak up on her like they would here."

Oliver had been worried about reporters but what if someone heard that the Preston Pyramid Princess was here and decided to take matters into their own hands?

What if someone came here looking not for a scoop, but for revenge? "You raise a valid point."

Lucille smirked. "Good. Tell her I'll see her Monday." She headed for the door but paused and looked back at him, a knowing smile on her face. "Besides, that would save you a lot of driving."

Yeah, Oliver wasn't fooling anyone.

"Tell her I'll bring my grandma's snickerdoodle recipe," Lucille called over her shoulder and then the door opened and shut.

Oliver dropped his head into his hands, trying to get a handle on the jumble of thoughts all clamoring to be heard inside his mind at the same time.

What did she want? What did he want? Well, he knew the answer to that.

He wanted to go upstairs and sweep Renee into his arms and fall into bed and spend the next twelve to twenty-four hours forgetting about cookies and firefighters and housekeepers and scams and family. He wanted to revel in her body and show her how good he could be for her. He wanted her with a fierceness that was a little frightening, if he were being honest.

Did she want him? Or did she want what he wanted?

He shook his head. None of that mattered, because neither of them was going to get what they wanted. Instead, they were going to get what they needed and right now that was to leave the seclusion of Red Oak Hill and head back to the anonymity of Dallas.

This was a problem. If word got out that Renee was here, then the only reasonable conclusion would be that Renee was with him. Even if she were safely tucked away in his condo, people might still try to get to her. And they might try to get to her *through* him.

He wanted to join her in the shower but he couldn't

risk being caught with his pants down for the second time in one night, so instead he composed an email to Bailey, updating him on the change in circumstances and directing him to order extra security for the condo and the office. Then, when Oliver had gauged enough time had passed that Renee was probably at least partially dressed, he went upstairs to break the news to her.

Damn it all to hell.

His father was going to find out sooner or later.

Oliver prayed it wasn't sooner.

Nine

This was not how she'd planned on spending her evening—making a late-night mad dash back to Dallas for the safety of Oliver's condo.

It wasn't like Red Oak Hill was hers. She'd spent the equivalent of a long weekend there. But she was sadder than she wanted to admit to leave it behind. She been able to breathe there and even though she was a born-and-bred city girl and should be relieved to be back in a big city, she wasn't.

It was true it was easier to hide in the city. But she hadn't had to hide for a few days. She'd been able to sit on the porch and take a walk around the pond and be herself. No worries about who was going to get a terrible photo, no thoughts as to what the next headline would be. Just…peace.

If only she hadn't ruined that.

"Did you enjoy baking the cookies?"

Renee turned her attention back to Oliver. His gaze

was focused on traffic. She didn't recognize where they were, but it wasn't like she'd spent a lot of time driving around. She'd had a taxi take her from the airport to Oliver's office. That was all she knew of Dallas. "I did. There was something soothing about mixing up the ingredients and hoping for the best. And when they were awful, I could try again."

God, she sounded pathetic. But that was the truth. Wasn't that why she'd come to Dallas and to Oliver? All she could do right now was mix things up and hope for the best.

She braced herself for a cutting comment, an affirmation that she wasn't capable of anything other than a Pinterest fail, a warning that cookies would make her fat—something. Oliver couldn't be happy that his house smelled burned. He couldn't be thrilled about bringing her to yet another home on such short notice. He couldn't enjoy the way she kept upending his life again and again.

So when he reached over and lifted her hand to his lips, pressing a tender kiss to her palm, her mouth fell open in surprise. "Then bake cookies. I won't distract you anymore."

Then he kissed her hand again. Sweet warmth spread from where his lips touched her bare skin and she wanted to revel in it.

Because underneath the worry and anxiety that had become her constant companion in the last few months was something new.

She and Oliver had made love. No, that felt too soft to describe what they'd done. They'd had hot, sweet, block-out-the-rest-of-the-world sex that had been a gift because he'd made her feel amazing and then, when it was over, he'd asked if she needed more. Because he was willing to give her more.

Oh, how she wanted to take him up on that offer. She'd wanted him to come upstairs and climb into the shower with her and pick up right where they'd left off before the fire department had shown up.

Instead, they were back in Dallas and any of those hot, sweet feelings had been put aside in the name of practicality.

"In fact," Oliver went on, "we should have a new rule—the moment we feel *distracted*, we have to turn off the oven before anything else happens."

Anything else? Did he mean wild, crazily satisfying sex, or did he mean an actual, full-fledged fire breaking out? Because it would've been tragic enough burning down Red Oak. It would be horrific to set fire to a high-rise building that housed hundreds of other people.

Good heavens, what would the press do to her *then*?

But that was the moment when Oliver tugged on her hand and suddenly his lips were skimming over the delicate skin of her wrists. "Or maybe you should just turn the oven off the moment I walk in the door. Just to be sure," he murmured and even though it'd been a long day, heat still flooded her body.

"Oh. Okay. Good plan." Renee knew she should say something grateful or appreciative. But there was a lump in her throat that made breathing, much less talking, difficult.

With a final nip at her skin, Oliver lowered her hand and laced his fingers with hers. "I can't promise that things won't get even crazier and there are certain realities we can't overlook. But I want you to be comfortable. If there's something you want to try, somewhere you want to go—tell me. I'll do my best to make it happen. Because I want you to be happy, Renee."

She took a long, slow breath. It wouldn't do to burst

into heaving sobs at that, even though it was one of the most beautiful things anyone had ever said to her. She was going to blame the hormones for all of this tearfulness.

On the other hand…what had that meant, if there was something she wanted to try? Were they talking about baking or…

Surely he wasn't talking about her fantasies. They were already making excellent headway on them. The knight in shining armor riding to her rescue? Yeah, that alone covered a lot of territory.

But before she could come up with any sort of reasonable response, she was saved by Oliver withdrawing his hand and turning into an underground garage. "We're here."

As he entered the access code and parked in his assigned spot, Renee felt old doubts creeping in. Oliver was being wonderful—there was no question about that. In fact, before he had come upstairs to tell her she was coming back to Dallas with him tonight and her baking lessons were being postponed because she wasn't safe at Red Oak Hill anymore—before all of that, she had been having the most wonderful day she could remember.

And it wasn't just the cookies.

She could *not* remember the last time she'd had a conversation with anyone that didn't involve the phrase "You should…" in one way or another.

Because everyone had an opinion. Of course her lawyers were going to say that—she was going into debt for their legal advice. But her parents? Her brother? Her husband? Her friends? It was for the best. Wasn't that what they all said? No one had said it louder than her mother. Her *suggestions* were thinly veiled orders she expected to be followed.

When was the last time anyone had asked her what

she wanted? Promised to make it happen? When was the last time anyone had gone *this* far out of the way for her?

When was the last time someone had done something as simple as make her laugh? Because she couldn't remember laughing as hard as she had at the sight of Oliver, butt naked, jumping out of the water while a pair of perturbed swans made menacing noises. For as long as she lived, she would never forget the sound of Oliver's laughter when he'd landed on his butt in the pond. And there'd been that moment when she'd thought he was furious that she'd nearly ruined everything—and instead he'd been teasing her.

Cookie monster, indeed.

She'd stood up for herself. She'd laughed so hard she'd got a stitch in her side. She'd come out on top—literally, she'd come on top of him. When was the last time she'd enjoyed sex so much?

Today had been magical. She hadn't climaxed like that in so long that she had almost forgotten what it was like. And then, instead of telling her she was getting fat, Lucille had told her that she had a glow about her. That she would get better at cookies if she kept practicing.

She hoped that, one day, she'd get back out to Red Oak Hill. Back out to that place out of time where she could be free, even if it were just another short visit.

Carrying her bag, Oliver led her toward a private elevator that required a key code to open. "The security here is good. The lobby is open, but all of the elevators are coded and guards are on duty twenty-four hours a day. No one should be able to slip in."

She nodded as the doors closed behind them. This was important information—necessary, she was sure. But she didn't want to hear about safety and privacy because that was a constant reminder that she was the pregnant

Preston Pyramid Princess and her family had hurt people and, even if she wasn't responsible, she was still at fault.

Her stomach lurched as the elevator began to climb. It'd been easy this evening to forget that simple truth that Oliver was risking not just his home but his reputation and his entire business by protecting her. It wasn't ruined cookies that drove Oliver out of his ranch house tonight. It was her.

Now he was bringing her here? This was a terrible idea. Why couldn't he see that she was a risk to him?

But he couldn't. "I'll request that you not leave the building without me. I know you can handle yourself, but I don't want to worry." He cupped her face in his palm. "I'm…" He took a deep breath. "I'm not used to worrying. I don't like it."

She leaned into his touch. "I'm sorry." Sorry for making him worry, sorry for setting off smoke alarms, sorry for upending his life. She was sorry for things that hadn't even happened yet but were still highly likely to occur.

"Don't apologize." His voice was deep as he lifted her face. "Not to me," he said against her lips.

She shouldn't lean into the kiss. She shouldn't want him and she certainly shouldn't take what he was offering. If she had half a brain, she would catch a ride to a nice hotel and spend the next week or so ordering room service and watching television. If she watched enough Food Network, she'd probably learn a lot about cookies.

But she didn't want to. It was selfish and greedy, but she wanted to kiss a man who wanted her—only her. So she did. She wanted to wrap her arms around his waist and pull him against her so that her breasts were pressed against his hard chest, so she did that, too. And when the elevator dinged to a stop and the doors opened, she didn't want to end the kiss.

But she had to when Oliver pulled away from her, his eyes dark with desire. "We should get inside," he said, but he didn't let her go. He slid his free arm around her waist and guided her down a short hallway with only three doors. "My condo is half the floor. Of the other two condos, one is an oil baron who only sleeps here when he's in town on a business meeting and the other family, I believe, is summering in Paris. So the only people who come off the elevator should be me or Lucille."

She suppressed a sigh. "All right." Like Oliver had said—there were certain realities that neither one of them could ignore. Oh, how she wanted to ignore them.

Wouldn't it be lovely to pretend that they were coming home after an evening out, just the two of them? That this was an everyday occurrence, kissing on the elevator and struggling to keep their hands to themselves until they were behind closed doors? Oh, how she wished that this were her real life instead of a brief, wonderful interlude.

He'd said that all she had to do was ask and he would do his best to give it to her. Somehow, she didn't think he'd been talking about the rest of their lives.

Because she couldn't ask that of him. Sooner or later, her family's scandal would catch up with her. Even if nothing came up about their misadventure with the fire department today, eventually word would get out. That was just the nature of scandals. She'd be called back to New York to testify, kicking off a fresh round of gossip and hatred, especially because she was more noticeably pregnant every single day. When that happened, it wouldn't be just her caught in the cross fire. It would be Oliver.

She shouldn't have barged into his life. If she were smart, she'd bail now.

But then he opened the door to his condo and ushered her inside. When the lights came on, she gasped. "It's beautiful."

The apartment she had lived in with Chet had been worth close to six million, but in reality it had been a smallish two-bedroom apartment. Chet had hated it, hated that they hadn't been able to get the place he'd really wanted, which had gone for ten million and had four bedrooms and a formal dining room. Renee had always considered their snug condo to be perfect and she'd known that, sooner or later, they would move out. But that had never been good enough for Chet. He hadn't looked at it as a starter home. He'd looked at the smallish condo with only four windows and no balcony and seen nothing but failure because it wasn't the very best.

Renee had always feared that he'd had the same feeling when he'd looked at her.

But Oliver's place? There were floor-to-ceiling windows that wrapped around a wall behind a dining table set for six and continued around the corner to another full wall of windows with plush leather sofas and chairs that was interrupted only by an elaborate fireplace and mantel. She glanced around, but she saw no signs that this place was occupied by more than one person.

The place looked…lived-in. Like his study out at Red Oak Hill. Everything in here was of the highest quality. She knew an expensive Persian rug when she saw one and there were three scattered around with various seats grouped around them. All that wealth was understated.

This was his home, on the top floor of a thirty-story building with a view that encompassed half of Texas.

Nothing could touch her here. No other windows looked down into his apartment because this was the tallest building for blocks. She was above the fray here—

literally. "You can see for forever," she said in a sigh, drifting to a window and staring out at the twinkling lights of the city. It wasn't as perfect as Fred and Wilma swimming in the pond but it was *amazing*.

Oliver came up behind her. Her breath caught in her chest when she saw the look in his eyes. Even the hazy reflection in the window couldn't blur away the desire in his eyes. And she was still in her leggings and a T-shirt. After everything that had happened today—and especially with her looking like she did—how could he still look at her like that?

"The view is always spectacular," he said as his gaze dipped to her chest. Her nipples hardened to tight points and she heard him suck in a deep breath. Then he stepped into her and rested his hands on her shoulders. "But it's even better now."

Oliver watched Renee's reflection in the glass as he rubbed her shoulders. He should be giving her a tour of the rest of the condo. He should be showing her to the guest room and giving her plenty of space. It was late and they'd had a crazy afternoon and she was pregnant and…and…

And none of it mattered when he touched her. Despite the air-conditioning and her clothes, he could feel her body's warmth under his touch. When she leaned back into him?

Yeah, this was what being lost felt like.

He wrapped his arms around her waist. "Tell me what you want, babe. I want to give it to you."

Her reflection smiled a saucy smile at him and reached up to lace her fingers into his hair. He went hard for her, harder than he'd ever been in his life. Which was saying something, considering it'd only been a few hours since he'd buried himself in her body.

"I don't want to talk about safety and security," she said, giving his hair a tug to pull him down to her.

"Done." He didn't want to deal with those realities anymore, either. He had her here now and he sure as hell wasn't going to let her go.

"I want to make cookies tomorrow."

He slipped his hands underneath her T-shirt. Bless these loose shirts and doubly bless her for going without a bra. Did she know how much it tortured him to watch her walk around, her beautiful breasts swinging freely? "I'll show you where the fire extinguisher is before I leave for work," he said, cupping her in his hands and stroking the undersides of her breasts.

She inhaled sharply, but he didn't want to rush this. Earlier, he hadn't been able to hold back, to hell with the consequences. But now? They had the rest of the night. If he was dragging at his meeting with Ritter tomorrow, that was a price he was willing to pay. As long as he had Renee in his arms tonight.

So he took his time fondling her breasts and teasing her nipples. He focused on listening to her breaths and watching her reactions in the glass.

When her body bucked in response to his gentle tug on her nipples, he felt it down to his toes. When she moaned as he rolled those nipples between his thumb and forefinger, he moaned with her. He couldn't help it. Her pleasure was his.

She was his.

"Look at you," Oliver breathed as he stared at Renee's reflection in the window. Her mouth was open as she panted, her eyes heavy-lidded. It had almost killed him to watch the light in her eyes die a little when, instead of taking her right back to bed, he'd told her they were leaving.

He wanted to see the Renee who managed to get the upper hand on him, who laughed at his corny jokes, who wasn't afraid of anything—she was the Renee he wanted back. He'd do anything to make her smile again.

The moment the thought crossed his brain, he was stunned by the truth of it.

He would do anything for her.

"You feel so wonderful," he told her as he let the full weight of her breasts fill his palms. "But I need to see these. I need to see all of you."

She inhaled sharply as he skimmed his hands down her ribs and over her hips to the hem of her T-shirt. But when he started to lift, she stopped his hands. "I don't… What if someone sees?"

"No one can see in these windows. That's one of the reasons I've bought this condo."

She didn't let him strip off her shirt. If anything, her grip on his hands tightened. "But…"

Oliver dragged his attention away from the reflection of her chest in the window and looked at her face. The sensual glaze of desire was gone, leaving her face drawn and tight. Then, somewhere far in the distance, a light blinked. It was probably a helicopter or something that was at least a few miles away, but Renee gasped as if someone had flown a drone into the window and started snapping pictures.

Right.

He kissed the side of her neck and then bent over, sweeping her legs out from under her. "Oliver!" she squeaked in alarm.

"I'm being a terrible host," he said, holding her tight against his chest. "I haven't even given you the tour yet."

"Oh?" She relaxed into him, her arms going around his neck. "I saw the living room."

"But not the kitchen," he said, walking right past the doorway on his left.

"It's lovely," she murmured and then her lips were against his neck. "I look forward to spending time there."

"Office," he ground out through gritted teeth as he carried her past the dark doorway on his right.

"It suits you perfectly," she agreed without looking. Then she began to suck.

His knees almost gave. "Guest room." Another fifteen steps—he could make it.

"Is that where I'm staying?" Her teeth skimmed over his skin with the barest hint of pressure.

Take what you need, he wanted to tell her. Hell, he wanted to shout it. "No," he groaned, all but staggering into his master suite. Dimly, he was aware this was supposed to be a slow, steady seduction where all the focus was on her. "For as long as you want, you're staying here with me."

"I…"

"Tell me," he all but begged. His body was on fire for hers but he didn't want to presume a single damned thing. "Tell me what you want."

She leaned back and gave him that smile, the exact same grin she'd launched at him seconds before she'd shoved him into the pond. It made him want to yell with victory.

"I want you." Then she bit him—not hard, but it sent a jolt of need through him unlike anything he'd ever experienced before.

He couldn't even make it to the bed along the far wall. He all but dropped her in front of the door to his walk-in closet.

The door covered with a full-length mirror.

He paused only long enough to reach over and flip on the light. The drapes were pulled and no one would be able to see anything he did to her.

And he was going to do it all.

When the lights flickered on, she gasped. But he was already pulling her T-shirt over her head. "God, Renee," he whispered, starting where he'd left off at her breasts. This time, he tugged on her nipples a little harder and was rewarded with a shudder. "You truly take my breath away."

"I do?"

It just about broke his heart to hear the doubt in her voice. She truly didn't see it.

This was a problem—but he had the solution. He'd make her believe she was the most beautiful woman he'd ever seen or he'd die trying. And given how much he was aching for her, she might be the death of him.

With the last of his control, he spun her around. For the second time today, he hooked his fingers into her pants and pulled, baring her. "Do you have any idea what you do to me?" Because the sight of her bottom begging for his touch really was going to kill him.

So he touched. He slid his hands down her full hips and then to her backside, where he dug his fingers into her generous flesh. She shuddered at his touch. Good. "I'm… I'm getting an idea."

"Not good enough. You need to know how badly I want you."

But when he looked in the mirror, he could see her struggling. "Oliver…"

"Babe." It was rude to interrupt her but he could see that she was going to do something terrible, like ask if they could turn the lights off and hide under the covers

and he couldn't let her think that there was a single thing about her he didn't want. "Watch," he commanded, falling to his knees so he could skim his teeth over the soft skin of her bottom. "Watch what you do to me. Watch what I do to you." Then he bit her. Not hard enough to bruise. He'd never hurt her. But he needed her to stop thinking and start feeling.

It worked. She sucked in a ragged gasp as he kissed the sting away and slid his hand between her legs.

Slow. He needed to take this slow. Because…reasons. Good ones, he was pretty sure.

But those reasons were lost to him as Renee shifted her legs apart for him. She put her hands on the mirror, her gaze moving from Oliver to where he was touching her and back again. He could see her surrendering to her needs—her eyes growing darker, her chest heaving as her breath came faster and faster.

He dug deep for words that were more than just *mine*. "Do you see how pretty you are?" he asked quietly, kissing his way up her back. "Do you see how luscious you are?" He cupped her bottom and squeezed. "God, I love your body."

"Even though…"

If she was trying to convince him that he couldn't want her because someone had told her she was fat, he was going to lose it.

He surged to his feet. "Renee. *Look*." He gripped her by the chin—again, gently—and turned her face so she had no choice but to look in the mirror. "I don't care what anyone else says. I only see you. I see your beautiful eyes and your delicate collarbone," he said, letting his hand drift down to that bit of skin. "And your breasts. God, your breasts." He cupped them again. Since he couldn't kiss them from this angle, he settled for kissing her neck—which he did without breaking eye contact in the mirror. "You are the sexiest woman I've ever seen."

"Don't tease," she said but at the very least, it came out as a breathy sigh. "I'm sorry I pushed you in the pond."

"I'm not." That moment when she'd fought for herself had been glorious.

That was what she needed to do right now—fight for herself. "This is the only way I'd tease you, darling." He slid one hand over the swell of her stomach again and down between her legs. "God, do you see how pretty you are? See how your eyes darken with want?"

"Yes," she moaned, her head dropping back on his shoulder. But she didn't look away as he tormented her nipples, her sex.

He thrust his hips against her backside, his erection chafing behind his pants. "Do you feel what you do to me?" This was where they'd been earlier at the window before she'd allowed doubt to crowd out desire. She sagged against him, bearing down on his hand, but he wrapped his free arm around her waist and held her up. "Look at you," he said, breathing hard as he stared at where he was touching her. "Look at us."

"Oliver," she said, her voice straining.

He pulled back only long enough to shove his pants aside. "Feel what you do to me?" he moaned against her skin.

Then she reached back and circled him with her hands. When she gripped him tightly, he had to brace himself against the mirror to keep from falling to his knees again. "Who else gets you like this?"

"You. Only you."

Her hand slipped lower to cup him. "No wife? No mistress or…" She squeezed and he made a noise that might be considered undignified, but he didn't give a single damn. "Or a girlfriend?"

He shook his head, trying to think. But what she was doing to him—there was no thinking. "Nine months— no, eight. Eight months since my last lady friend." Her grip shifted again and he was helpless to do anything but thrust into her hands.

"What am I, Oliver?" Her voice was so soft that he had to look at her. "What am I to you?"

Not a wife, obviously. But the moment that thought crossed his mind, he had to close his eyes against it.

He'd never wanted to get married. Never wanted to bring someone into his messy family life. He had enough responsibilities—how could he add a wife or children to managing his father and running Lawrence Energies and, who could forget, the damned rodeo? How much more did he have to give, when there was so little of himself left over?

But Renee was already a part of his family. She had been for years.

"Am I your mistress?" she went on and he heard an edge to her voice, one that made him want to weep with joy.

She was fighting back.

"No," he ground out when she gave him an extra-firm squeeze. Not that he wanted to think about her cheating, lying ex right now, but he realized on a fundamental level that she had to make sure. "Not a mistress. Not a… Oh, God," he groaned as she stroked him. "Not a girlfriend, either." That wasn't a strong enough word for what she meant to him.

"Then what am I?" Her voice was quiet but there was no mistaking it—she had him in the palm of her hand. Literally.

When she reached back with her other hand, Oliver's restraint cracked. He grabbed her by the wrists. "I can't wait," he growled as he pushed her hands against the mirror. "Don't move."

He grabbed the condom from his pants and frantically ripped it open. He nudged her legs apart and then slid into her warmth with one long thrust. They both moaned.

Mine. It was all he could think as he grabbed Renee by the hips and buried himself in her over and over again. It wasn't slow or sweet or tender. The way he took her was raw and hard and heaven help him, he loved it.

She loved it. Her hands on the mirror, she bent forward at the waist and thrust her backside up and out, just enough that she could see his face unobstructed in the mirror. And holding her gaze while he furiously pumped into her body was the singularly most erotic thing he'd experienced in his life.

She moaned and then shouted, "Oh, God—Oliver!"

"Renee," he growled, digging his fingers into her skin, fighting the urge to mark her as his.

She pushed back into his thrusts and cried out, her muscles clenching him so tightly that he couldn't hold anything back. Not with her. She would always push him past the point of reason, past the cold grip of logic.

He needed to do something. Something romantic, like whisper sweet words of promise in her ear. Something practical, like *take care of the condom. Something*, for God's sake.

"You destroy me, Renee" was what he came up with. "You simply destroy me."

Because Renee Preston-Willoughby had walked into his office and thrown everything ordered and planned about his life right out the window. His organized days of meetings? Gone. His long-term plans to grow Lawrence Energies—including the damned rodeo? Cast aside. His careful management of his family? Forgotten. His promise to his mother that he'd keep the family together? A distant memory.

All that was left was this fierce need to be with Renee and protect her—and her unborn child.

The destruction was complete.

Because she was his, by God. And he was not letting her go.

Ten

Renee focused on keeping her breath steady and even. Okay, it was a little heavy because sex with Oliver was proving to be so much *more* than she was used to.

That man had scandalously stood her in front of a mirror and made her believe—really believe—that she was pretty and desirable and worth the risk. He was worried about her and he wanted and needed her and he couldn't keep his hands off her and it was perfect.

Or it had been, right until he'd ruined it.

Oh, she knew he hadn't meant it as an insult or even a warning. But there was no mistaking that "you destroy me" for what it was—the truth.

Because she would. Sooner or later, she would ruin him. Not on purpose. Never on purpose. But it was inevitable, wasn't it? Either she was going to do something accidental, like set fire to one or more of his homes, or word would get out about their connection and his reputation would be dragged through the mud.

Knowing her luck, probably both. He thought he understood her messed-up family. But even if things went perfectly from here on out—the press left her alone or her baby's delivery was textbook or Oliver continued to be wonderful?

Her family would go on trial or her mother would find some way to ruin everything all the way from France because there was no way Rebecca Preston would approve of what Renee was doing. Preparing food? Doing the menial work of washing dishes? Doing something unladylike like pushing a friend into a pond and laughing out loud?

She hoped no one from that fire department went to the press. If her mother could find a way to ruin the little bit of peace Renee was struggling to hold on to, she would. Just out of spite.

She and Oliver were fogging the mirror up with their breaths. She didn't want to move. She wanted to pretend like everything was fine.

But she was tired of that, too. She'd spent years pretending and she wasn't going to anymore. At least, she was going to try to not do it as much. She might have to ease into this whole total-honesty thing.

But she definitely wasn't going to let thoughts of her mother into this room. Rebecca Preston had abandoned Renee long before she'd decamped to Paris. It was high time Renee returned the favor.

She pushed against the mirror and thankfully, Oliver backed up. She shivered from the loss of his body covering hers.

She turned to go to the bathroom just in case she fell apart, but Oliver caught her hand.

"Will you stay with me tonight?"

The smart thing to do would be to say no. He had a guest room. She was a guest.

But then he added, "It's whatever you want," and her resolve buckled because honestly, she wanted to spend the night curled in his arms. Whatever this was, it would end badly for all parties involved—she didn't have any doubt about that.

But the fact was it was going to end badly no matter what. Maybe it was selfish and definitely shortsighted, but she wanted to hold on to this little bit of happiness while she could.

So she brushed her lips against his and said, "I'll stay," because he'd done everything in his power to protect her. He'd made her feel good again. For heaven's sake, he hadn't even been that upset about the ruined cookies.

By the time she finished in the bathroom, Oliver had carried her bag in. "You're going to need more clothes," he said absentmindedly as he stared at the solitary piece of her luggage.

She didn't exactly have the money for new things, so she said, "It's not a big deal. I can do laundry."

Actually, she wasn't sure she could but that had to be one of those things that came with instructions. At the very least, Lucille should be able to walk her through the process while minimizing fire hazards.

Oliver looked up at her like she might be crazy. He must've taken advantage of the other bathroom because, while he had taken off his button-up shirt, he was still in his trousers and undershirt and she was completely nude. There was no missing the appreciative gleam in his eye but she was suddenly tired and feeling self-conscious. Her hands dropped to her thighs, covering the scars, but she thought she did so casually enough that he hadn't noticed.

If he wasn't naked, she wasn't going to parade about. The nightstand on the right side of his bed had the alarm clock, so she walked around to the other side and slid under the covers. She immediately felt better.

"You're just going to walk around braless? What happens when you need to leave the house?"

That was a good question. Suddenly, she had a feeling that Oliver was going to insist that she allow him to buy her clothes.

Because that's who Oliver was. If he saw a problem, he was honor-bound to find a solution. She had enough clothes for a week—but in another few weeks, she'd be pushing her luck with the underwear. She had a month, tops, in her yoga pants. Maybe another month in her loose tunic tops. And Oliver was right—eventually, she'd need a bra again. But if anyone caught wind of Oliver buying maternity clothes…

Destroyed. That was the only word for it.

To distract him, she arranged herself on the bed in what she hoped was an inviting way, making sure to suck in her stomach while the sheet fell down off her hips— but stayed above the scars on her thighs. "I thought you requested I not leave."

"You're not Rapunzel. I'm not going to lock you in a tower." His eyes darkened as he looked her over. "Although it's damned tempting to keep you all to myself for the weekend, at least."

Tempting. She liked that. She could still be tempting. And she could have him all to herself for the next few days. "What was that about the weekend?"

He made a noise that was part growl, part groan and all need. But then he paused. "Can I get you anything before I join you? Water? A snack?"

And that, in a nutshell, was why she was in Oliver's bed. "Just you."

She didn't have to ask twice. He flung his clothing

off and was between the sheets within moments. When he pulled her against his chest and pressed a kiss to her forehead that would've been tender if there hadn't been so much heat packed into it, Renee sighed with pleasure. As soon as she settled in his arms, though, her eyes began to drift closed. It had been a very *long* day...

When Oliver spoke, she startled back awake. "I have to go to work tomorrow and Friday," he said apologetically. "I've put this meeting off twice and there's no avoiding it. By Sunday we should know if anyone has connected you to Red Oak Hill. If not, I'd like to take you out. We've got museums or movies or the theater or—"

"Gosh, like a real city?" she couldn't help quipping. She ruined the sarcasm by yawning, however.

"Smart-ass." But as he said it, he began to stroke her hair. "There's a pretty park with a pond and ducks about a block away—we can just take a walk. Although I wouldn't recommend that at high noon, unless you enjoy sweating. Whatever you want—I'm yours for the weekend."

"I'll think about it." She was too damned tired to make any sort of decision right now. It was probably for the best that Oliver was going to work tomorrow. Today had been wild on about six different levels and she needed to recover.

But...there was something she wanted to do before Saturday. "Would it be all right if I called Chloe tomorrow?" So much had happened in the last week—which was saying something, because a lot had happened in the last five months. If she vented to Oliver, she knew he'd listen—but she also knew that he'd try to solve the problem. And she didn't want to be his problem.

She really needed a girlfriend, which meant Chloe. Frankly, there wasn't anyone else.

She felt the tension ripple through Oliver but as quickly

as it had appeared, it was gone. "I don't see why not. I'm sure if you explain the situation, she'll keep your whereabouts quiet. And she's launching a new clothing line, so she might be able to help with the clothes."

She smiled against his skin. Even when he wasn't solving the problem, he was still solving the problem. Men. *This* man.

Mine, her brain whispered as she yawned again. She was his and he was hers…wasn't he?

"I'll call her. But I won't tell her about us," she murmured against his chest. She wished Chloe were here, although…if she were, there would be no hiding the fact that Renee and Oliver were sleeping together. Or they were going to, shortly. Very shortly.

As she drifted off to sleep, she thought she heard him whisper, "I doubt that'll make much of a difference."

"You're *where*?" Chloe Lawrence squealed in Renee's ear.

"At Oliver's condo." Renee thought it best to leave out any mention of Oliver's ranch house. "It's a really long story, but I needed a place to lie low and you're… Where are you?"

"Omaha." Then Chloe's voice got muffled and Renee got the feeling she was giving instructions to someone. "Sorry. Oliver has given me a lot more control over the rodeo—which is great. But it's a lot of responsibility and combined with the Princess clothing launch…"

Renee exhaled in relief. "Which was exactly why I didn't try to track you down. I figured I would just hang out here until you came to Dallas and then we could catch up."

There was a long pause. "I told you not to marry that asshole."

"You were the only one," Renee said, trying to keep the bitterness out of her voice and failing. It wasn't Chloe's fault she'd been right—or that Renee hadn't listened. She deserved that *I told you so*. And probably a few others.

"Oliver would've told you not to marry him, too," Chloe said, because even as a kid, she'd never been able to let anything go.

Because this was a telephone call and not a video call, Renee rolled her eyes. "Tell me about the clothing line." Nothing like a change of subject to dance around the Oliver issue. "Couture or cowgirl?"

"Cowgirl," Chloe said so firmly that Renee had to wonder if she was insulted by the couture suggestion. "Why?"

So Renee laid it all out as quickly as she could. It was odd that Chloe was more up-to-date on the situation than Oliver had been. But she knew of Chet Willoughby's suicide—she'd sent flowers. She knew about the pyramid scheme and had sent emails—not a lot, but some—offering Renee support and help if she needed it.

What she didn't know was how the prosecutors had seized anything that was even remotely close to an asset.

"So all of the designer clothes are gone and even if I still had them, they wouldn't fit. I'm pregnant. I only brought two bras with me and neither works anymore." The words *your brother doesn't seem to mind* danced right up to the tip of Renee's tongue, but she bit down on them before they could escape. "Nothing's going to fit in a few weeks and I might be here longer than that."

"Man, I long for the days when I can wear nothing but yoga pants," Chloe said with a sigh. "But I understand the problem. I bet it's driving Oliver nuts that you're not in a suit or something. I hope he's not being a total butthead."

"He's…fine." Which was not a lie. He certainly wasn't

being a butthead. But that left a lot of room around what *fine* meant. "It's not like anyone will see me in his condo."

"Wait—why did he take you to the condo? Why didn't he take you to the ranch?"

Renee bit her lip. "He did. But I decided I wanted to bake cookies and there was...an incident. The fire department showed up."

"Did you burn Red Oak Hill down?" Chloe asked in a panic. "He loves that place! And those stupid swans!"

"No, no." Although just thinking about it—again— made her stomach flip. "It was only some cookies. The swans are fine. It was just smoke."

Unexpectedly, Chloe began to laugh. "Was Oliver mad? He's *such* a stick-in-the-mud."

That was the thing Renee kept coming back to—he had been upset. But he hadn't taken it out on her. Instead, he'd treated it more like she'd pulled off a successful, funny prank and he was impressed. She told Chloe the whole story.

Chloe hooted with laughter. "I would've paid good money to see that. I knew he was hiding something! If he'd told me you were there, I would've tried to get there, even if only for the day."

"Yeah? I'll admit, it'd be great to see you." Of course, Chloe was too smart by half. She'd take one look at Renee and know for sure that she was sleeping with Oliver. "But Oliver's taking care of me. So you don't have to worry."

Chloe made a humming noise and Renee realized she might have overplayed her hand. But then Chloe said, "Hey, the rodeo is coming to Dallas—well, Fort Worth, which is practically the same thing—in three weeks. I'll be in town for at least five days—longer if I can swing it. You, my friend, are going to spend a few days with me and we are going to catch up. I'm going to take you to the rodeo," Chloe said in a tone of voice that made it clear this was nonnegotiable. "A pitcher of sangria, unhealthy snacks and—"

"I'm pregnant." As if anyone could forget that small detail.

"I don't mind. That's more sangria for me." She was quiet for a moment. "Renee, are you sure you're doing okay? I know Oliver can be grumpy. And rude. And bossy. And—"

"It's fine," Renee interrupted. True, Oliver could be all of those things. But far more often, he was encouraging and kind. When he teased her, she could tease right back and feel safe that, instead of telling her she was wrong, he'd laugh with her instead. "And are you sure going to a rodeo is the best idea? I'm supposed to be lying low."

"It'll be fine! I'll send you some Princess clothes to tide you over but when we're at my place, we'll try everything on. We'll get you a fab hat and I'll tell Oliver to keep an eye on you." She sighed heavily. "As long as we keep you away from Flash, it'll be fine."

"Well…" She remembered Flash being an extremely irritating little brother. There had been lizards involved. But maybe he'd changed. After all, she wasn't the same little sister she'd been back then, either. "I'd actually love to go to one. I've never seen the Princess of the Rodeo in all her glory." Chloe snorted. "But only if Oliver agrees…" She was pretty sure he wouldn't.

"Oh, he will," Chloe said, sounding way too pleased with herself. "It's his damned rodeo, too. He doesn't appreciate how awesome it is. If we're lucky, Flash will get stepped on by a bull. But," she went on, apparently cheered by that thought, "in the meantime, try not to kill him. I know he's uptight but it's just because he never has fun."

"He doesn't?" The man who owned a pair of swans named after the Flintstones seemed like he had maybe a little fun at least some of the time.

"He wouldn't know fun if it bit him on the butt."

Renee smiled at the memory of Oliver jumping when the swans took offense to his invasion of their pond.

Chloe went on, "I worry about the butthead. All he does is work and micromanage. He argues with Dad constantly about the business. He orders me to keep Flash out of trouble—as if anyone could keep Flash out of trouble," she added under her breath. "And all he does with Flash is fight. Promise me you won't let him boss you around."

Renee let that thought roll around her head. If she hadn't spent the last few days with Oliver, she would've agreed with Chloe's assessment. Because that's who Oliver had been, at least in her memory.

Frankly, that was who he'd been at her brother's wedding and that'd been five years ago. Because she'd tried. She'd struck up a conversation with him and she would've asked him to dance, if she'd got to before he'd had so much to drink. Oliver hadn't tried to boss her around, but he had been the textbook definition of *grumpy*.

"He's been great," she finally said, hoping that wasn't giving too much away. "Really, I don't want you to worry about us. I'm more concerned about what to wear to your rodeo."

There was a moment when she didn't think Chloe was going to go for that subject change. But then she said, "What size are you?" And they fell into the familiar habit of discussing clothes and sizing.

"I'll send some samples out for you," Chloe said. "It's not what you'd normally wear, but you'll blend in. And they're *samples*. You can't pay me for them," she added.

Because Chloe was a real friend, bless her heart. It

shouldn't feel different, accepting this gift instead of one from Oliver. But it did. "Thanks, Chloe. I can't wait to see you in a few weeks."

"If Oliver gives you any trouble, call me immediately."

Renee almost defended Oliver again, but she decided that would only make Chloe more suspicious so instead she said, "I will. Promise."

She sat there for a moment after the call ended. Chloe's clothing line didn't make maternity clothing, but she was going to send things a size or two up, which would give Renee a couple of more months to figure out how she was going to afford everything else she needed. Which meant the only thing she needed to buy on her own was underwear, and she could afford a bra and a few pairs of panties.

She began to browse on her phone. But instead of basic white or nude underthings, she found herself looking at pretty bra and pantie sets. Because Oliver wanted to take her out and show her the town. But more than that, because *she* wanted to feel pretty. Leggings were great but they weren't doing much for her ability to look in a mirror and feel good about what she saw. She wanted to be *tempting*, damn it. And she had about two hundred dollars left in her bank account from the money the feds had allotted her to travel with. New panties it was.

She still heard her mother's voice, dripping with icy menace as she complained about Renee getting fat. But at least now, she also had the memory of Oliver telling her how gorgeous she was and how he couldn't keep his hands off her.

She had to choose who to believe. And her mother had never loved her.

Not that Oliver loved her. Of course not. He liked her and he worried about her and that…that was enough.

This whole situation was still a mess. Just like her life. But she couldn't stop thinking about what Chloe had said—Oliver never had any fun. That picture of him didn't mesh with him laughing and naked in the mud, or of him insisting that he show her the town.

It was high time they both started having more fun.

Eleven

"Are you sleeping with her?"

It took a lot of work to make sure Oliver's face didn't react to this bald statement. Obviously, Renee had talked to Chloe. He'd known there was no way Chloe wouldn't put two and two together. But he hadn't quite expected her to scream it in his ear. "One moment." He turned to Herb Ritter, praying the older man hadn't been able to make out Chloe's screech. "Thanks again for coming by. I'm sorry our meeting had to be pushed back."

The older man did something Oliver never would've seen coming in million years—he winked. "I hope she was worth it," Herb said in his gravelly voice. "But try not to let it happen again."

Oliver came *this close* to asking Herb to keep the revelation that a woman was involved to himself, but he managed to hold on to his tongue. At this point, he was neither confirming nor denying anything involving Renee to anyone.

Including his own sister. He waited until the door had closed behind Herb before he turned his attention back to his sister, who was humming the *Jeopardy!* theme song on the other end of the line. "Can I help you with something?"

"You are! You're sleeping with Renee! I *knew* it."

Was there anything worse than a little sister gloating? If so, Oliver couldn't think of what that might be. But he had all the plausible deniability in the world when Renee was the subject. "What are you talking about?" Maybe he'd missed his calling in the theater.

"She told me you were being nice to her and frankly, you're not nice to anyone. Especially not her. So clearly you and Renee have hooked up."

He knew better than to fall for the trick of making a blanket denial. Chloe had missed her calling as a lawyer. Instead, he focused on the first part of the accusation. "I am perfectly capable of being polite, as is Renee. We both grew up and are no longer whiny children. Unlike some people I know," he said, hoping that Chloe would take the bait.

She didn't. "Do you have any idea how big of a mess she's in? And you creeping up on her isn't helping anything! You should keep your damn hands off her! Just because she's vulnerable and needy doesn't give you the right—"

"Stop right there," Oliver growled and, to Chloe's credit, she did. "First off, I am not taking advantage of anyone. Second off, I know exactly how big of a mess she's—I spoke with Clint, the ass, over the phone."

"Really? *Whoa.*"

He ignored her. "Third off, whatever happens between consenting adults is absolutely no business of yours—"

"I knew it," Chloe muttered under her breath.

"And fourth off," he ground out through gritted teeth, "she is *not* vulnerable and needy. She is not a helpless damsel in distress or a lost child and it's insulting her to imply she is. She's a woman in a difficult situation doing the best she can to get her life back on track for her and her child and all I'm doing is giving her the space to decide what she wants to do and helping her accomplish those goals, whether it's attempting a cookie recipe or shielding her from the press. And furthermore," he went on, because he was on a roll and Chloe wasn't interrupting him and that was a rare thing, "I am not creeping on anyone. *Really*, Chloe? You know damn good and well that Mom loved Renee like she was one of the family and all I'm doing for her is what I'd do for you or Flash."

Except for the part where he stripped her down and lost himself in her body. But again—he was neither confirming nor denying that.

"Because that's what Mom would want and expect out of me—out of all of us. So don't insult me or Renee, *sis*, because she's had quite enough unfounded accusations and rumors to last her the rest of her life. Are we clear?"

There was a stunned moment of silence. Oliver wasn't sure if the stunned part was coming from him or from Chloe.

Because he might have just lost his temper. There may have been shouting involved—he wasn't sure. Hopefully, Herb had got out of earshot.

"Is Renee why you gave me the negotiations?" All of her righteous anger was gone.

Yes. But he kept that to himself. "The rodeo is yours, you know that. Just because Dad doesn't appreciate all the work you do to make it profitable doesn't mean I don't."

"Did you just compliment me?" Chloe let out a low whistle. "You did! Jesus, she's good for you. And before you yell at me again, I'm not insulting either of you."

He growled.

"There's the brother I know and love. Listen, I invited Renee to stay with me when I'm in town and I'm taking her to the rodeo."

"That is *not* a good idea." But even as he said it—all right, even as he *growled* it—he knew he was being ridiculous. Hadn't he offered to take her to museums and theaters and whatever she wanted? A rodeo wasn't that different, was it?

Then again, it was the rodeo. Ugh.

"Keep your pants on. I'm sending her a bunch of clothes and we'll find a hat. I could give her big hair. Ooh! We'll try new eye makeup. Trust me, when I'm done with her, no one will recognize her."

He would. He'd recognize her in a crowd in the middle of the night.

"Oliver? You know I wouldn't do anything to hurt her. Or you, I guess."

"Thanks, brat." But he let go of the breath he'd been holding all the same. "How are the negotiations coming along?"

The conversation thankfully veered off into business then, but Oliver couldn't get Renee out of his mind. When he ended the call, he couldn't do anything but sit there and stare at the pictures lining the far wall—all those artistic action shots of the rodeo that Renee had noticed the moment she'd waltzed into his office.

He hated the rodeo—the smells and dirt, the bulls, the young idiots who risked life and limb for a belt buckle—and that absolutely included Flash. Oliver hated the whole damned thing. But if Renee wanted to go see one and

Chloe could disguise her appearance…maybe they could pull it off.

He had so much he needed to do. He should have Bailey order some flowers—delivered to the office so that he could give them to Renee in person. And more baking things—he'd make sure Lucille brought plenty of supplies with her. He needed to find out who Renee's lawyers were and make sure they were doing their job. And he should get the name of a trustworthy doctor. He didn't know how long she'd be here, but if there was a problem, he didn't want to take her to the emergency room and hope no one recognized her. A private doctor who would be on call—for a price, of course—was the solution. And…

Well, she'd be here at least long enough to go to the rodeo in three weeks. And after that?

A vision of her rounding out with her pregnancy materialized in his mind. She absolutely glowed, damn it, and he had a powerful urge to tell her she wasn't going anywhere until after the baby was born. But it wasn't like she could just up and relocate with a newborn. She'd need help then, too. And that baby—Oliver would have to make sure that the media didn't descend like locusts and turn that innocent child into nothing but clickbait.

Would she want him to be there when the baby was born? Would she want him by her side, holding her hand and telling her how amazing she was? Would she want him to hold that whole new person that was the best of her? Or…not?

A sickening wave of loss twisted his insides at the thought of Renee giving birth without anyone beside her to fight for her and that baby. Even if it wasn't him, at least he could make sure Chloe was there. Just so long as Renee knew she wasn't alone.

He shook his head. He was getting ahead of himself

by months. *Years*. Doctors and lawyers were all well and good, but it wasn't like he was asking Renee to stay forever. Chloe was right about that, at least. Renee's life was too complicated for anyone to be thinking about anything more long-term. There were still trials and plea deals to work through and the media to avoid. He needed to focus on the next three weeks. After that, he'd focus on the next three weeks.

Right. He needed roses and chocolate chips. And more condoms. But those he was getting himself. Because, while he trusted Bailey completely, there was no way in hell Oliver was asking anyone else to pick up protection.

Because that's all this was. He was protecting Renee, damn it.

And if that meant he had to go to the rodeo, then he'd suck it up.

For her. Only for her.

"Can I ask you a question?"

Breathing hard, Renee managed to open one eye and peer up at him. "I'm going to need five minutes to recover," she wheezed. The man was simply the best—and most intense—lover she'd ever had.

At least this time they'd made it to his bed. There was something to be said for actual sheets and pillows. Plus, the air was scented with roses and the smell of them together.

He'd brought her flowers. It was a ridiculously sweet thing and if she thought about it too much, she might get teary.

He grinned. "Not that." Moving slow, he skimmed the sheet down her body. At first, Renee thought he was going for another seduction—right until he unveiled the scars. "These."

Renee's lungs seized up. How could she have thought that he wouldn't notice them? Oliver was the most attentive, thoughtful and observant man she'd ever know.

But old habits died hard. She felt her chin lift and her shoulders square, which was impressive considering she was sprawled out over at least three of the four pillows on the bed. "These what?"

"Renee," he said, giving her a look. "Don't do that."

"Do what?" But even as the words left her mouth, she winced. Stupid defense mechanisms.

"*That*. When you put on your armor. You don't have to do that with me. And these are…weird." He looked at her thighs, catching her hands before she could cover them. "I thought they were freckles but they're too regularly spaced and all grouped together. And your right leg has a lot more of them."

How, exactly, did someone say, *Oh, those? That's just what happens when you repeatedly jab a fork into human skin. What of it?* She had no idea.

But if she said, *I don't want to talk about them*, then Oliver would wonder. And he'd ask again. He wouldn't take the pat answer at face value because he was the rare man who actually wanted the truth instead of pretty little lies.

And she didn't want to lie to him. She wanted there to be truth and trust between them.

Funny how those things were easier said than done.

Then he leaned down and pressed a kiss to the rows of tiny scars. "You don't have to tell me, if you don't want. But if you change your mind, I'll be here."

Really, the man was too perfect. She exhaled slowly and then, when she was sure her hand wasn't shaking, ran her fingers through his hair. "All right."

He rested his head on her leg, staring up at her with something that sure seemed like adoration. She was just happy he could still see around her belly. Honestly, between the pregnancy and the cookies, she was impressed she hadn't got bigger than she already had. "Do you want to go to the rodeo?"

"Maybe." She relaxed back into the pillows and stroked his hair. "But you hate the rodeo."

He grinned and she almost wished she could take a picture to show Chloe and say, *See? He can have fun.* "I can be mildly inconvenienced for an evening if you want to see the Princess of the Rodeo in action," he said as he moved to lie down by her side again. She couldn't help but think he sounded resigned to the fact. "Who knows—maybe we'll get lucky and Flash will get stepped on."

She burst out laughing.

He notched an eyebrow at her. "What?"

"Chloe said the same thing. I'm sensing a theme."

"It'll be fine. We won't be in the stands—there's usually a separate seating section for the VIPs," he said, stroking a finger down her cheek. "Brooke Bonner is the musical act that night, too. We'll make a date of it. If you want."

She thought about that. "It can't be any riskier than going to a museum, right? And I do like Brooke's music. Country rockabilly or whatever—it's good girl power music."

"Then we'll go." He squeezed her tight.

Her heart ached with a strange sort of happiness. It was such an unusual feeling, knowing that someone was willing to do something they didn't want to just for her.

She curled back against his side. "Oh, I ordered a few things today to go with the clothing Chloe's sending."

"Hmm?"

"A new bra. And matching panties."

Oliver groaned, which made her laugh again.

She hadn't been able to spend the money on her usual brand—La Perla was not cheap. But she'd found some cute sets at a discount site for less than fifty dollars, which was as much as she could comfortably spend. Then she'd done her best to guess on sizes, erring on the side of caution. If they were too big right now, they'd fit eventually.

"I can't wait to see them."

"Well, you'll get to do that before me—I didn't know the address here so I had them sent to your office." It wasn't like she couldn't have found out the street address of this condo. But there was something to be said for upping their pranks to a more mature level. One that included a lingerie delivery to the office.

Oliver rolled onto her, pinning her beneath his weight. The man was amazing—five minutes really was all he needed. She giggled as they struggled to get the sheet out from between their bodies.

Then, holding himself over her, his smile faded and was replaced by a look of such intensity that it took her breath away all over again. "God, Renee, you destroy me," he said before he captured her lips with his and it was a good thing he was kissing her because she didn't know what to say to that.

Oh, what a mess. She couldn't bring herself to tell him about the scars, about why she and Clint had always been at the Lawrence house instead of their own. But the longer she kept quiet, the more he'd feel like she hadn't put her faith in him when he did find out.

And the longer this not-dating thing they were doing went on, the more time he spent with her, the bigger the implosion would be. She knew all of that and, sadly, she was too selfish to put a stop to it.

Because Oliver was the best thing that had happened to her in a long, long time. So she kissed him back and wrapped her legs around his waist and, after he rolled on the condom and plunged into her, she dug her fingers into his bottom to urge him on because she wanted him.

She might not ruin him. Not like she'd been ruined. But his personal life would become public fodder and his business would take a hit. Because of her. Because of *this*.

But at least he knew it.

Hopefully he'd never find out about the rest.

After two and a half weeks of playing house, Renee was more than ready for a change of scenery.

Not that she was complaining. She'd managed to produce not just a decent chocolate chip cookie on a consistent basis, but had also turned out surprisingly edible sugar cookies and even a batch of snickerdoodles. She was giving Lucille a solid 75 percent of the credit for that, but still. Oliver was taking cookies to work to share with his staff on an almost-daily basis. She had no idea how he was explaining that, but no one had died of food poisoning so it must be okay.

The amount of satisfaction she felt when she opened the oven and pulled out a sheet of nearly perfectly round cookies that not only looked right but tasted good was amazing. Even better was when Oliver came home and, after a kiss—okay, sometimes after a lot more than kissing—he'd try a cookie and tell her it was good. The first time he'd pronounced a snickerdoodle she'd made all by herself "really good," she was so happy she'd actually started crying.

Stupid hormones.

The day he'd brought home the underthings she'd ordered, they never made it to the cookies. Hell, they didn't even make it to the bedroom—not at first anyway. The only time Oliver had hesitated was to ask if the oven was off.

It was.

The day the box of clothes arrived from Chloe, Renee spent the whole afternoon playing dress up and video chatting with Chloe about what worked and what didn't, what Renee liked, what she might change. She got two tunic tops that might last her a few months and two pairs of super-skinny-leg jeans two sizes larger than she normally wore that fitted comfortably with the addition of a rhinestone belt. Chloe had even included a pair of boots—*because everyone wears them and you should break them in now,* she'd said.

Which is how Oliver came home one night to find her in boots and not much else.

They barely made it to the hallway that night.

She baked and learned how to wash dishes and do laundry and clean up after herself. She pestered Lucille for information about babies and pregnancy and also how to vacuum when the older woman came every Monday to clean the condo. Renee watched baking shows and kids' cartoons and whatever else struck her fancy, including a kung fu movie with subtitles.

And when Oliver came home from work, they had fun together. There hadn't been any breathless updates on the Preston Pyramid Princess being spotted in Texas so Renee didn't dread leaving the house. They went to late showings of movies and picked up carryout food—she'd never eaten so much barbecue in her entire life but it was glorious—and when she announced that maybe she'd like to learn how to crochet, he took her to a craft store.

He didn't ask about the scars again and she didn't tell him. But then again, he didn't ask about her former husband or her family and she wasn't about to taint their time together by bringing any of that crap up. She was surprisingly, amazingly happy right now. If only they could stay this way.

It wouldn't last. It couldn't. Renee knew this like she knew her name. The way she burned for Oliver was something white-hot and clear—but, like all raging infernos, it would burn itself out soon enough. After all, she'd once believed that Chet loved her beyond distraction, and see how that had turned out?

She knew Oliver wasn't the same kind of person Chet had been. She *knew* that. But it was hard to unlearn a lifetime of lessons. A few really great weeks didn't change things, not in the long term. Her family was still toxic and she might be called back to New York City at any moment and there was still a pregnancy to deal with. She had no idea how long she and Oliver could share a bed and a condo before things got awkward and even less of an idea of where she would go when it did. She couldn't imagine him relishing the idea of a crying newborn upending his world.

But that was months off. Right now, things were good.

And in a few days, Chloe was coming.

Then they were all going to the rodeo.

Twelve

He wasn't wearing a hat and that was final.

Oliver had no problem putting on the boots and the belt buckle, and jeans and a button-up shirt with a sports jacket were fine, but he drew the line at a hat. Yes, Flash looked decent enough in his black felt hat but Oliver was of the opinion—the correct opinion—that his father looked like a life-size Howdy Doody doll in his enormous Stetson.

No hats.

Oliver was fully aware he was being irrational. But he had barely seen Renee for the last few days. When Chloe had blown into town like a twister, she'd swept Renee up and together they'd decamped to Chloe's place for "quality girl time."

Which was fine. He was perfectly capable of entertaining himself. He'd been doing it for years.

But when he came home to an empty condo and no fresh-baked cookies, it bothered him and it had nothing to do with actual cookies. Renee wasn't there to breathlessly tell him about everything she'd accomplished that day. Whether it was successfully baking a loaf of bread or managing to crochet a small pot holder—at least, that's what they were calling that lopsided square of yarn— she did so with such raw joy that he couldn't help it if he wound up wrapping her in his arms before she'd even asked how his day was.

She *glowed*, damn it. Every day, her body changed a little bit and the haunted shadows under her eyes became an ever more distant memory and he was helpless to do anything but stare at her in wonder.

Because she was wonderful. And he'd missed her more than any reasonable man should miss a houseguest for the last two days.

But that was just it, wasn't it? She wasn't a houseguest, not anymore. She was…

His. She was *his*.

Wasn't she?

He was in a foul mood by the time he made it to the Fort Worth Stockyards. He was hours early, but he wanted to talk to security and make sure Renee wouldn't have any problems.

Plus, now that he was here, he was duty-bound to check in with the promoter and the stock manager about how Chloe was doing. The attendance numbers were good and her clothing line was selling well, as were the other souvenirs, but he wanted to hear it from the horse's mouth.

He gritted his teeth and grinned his way through handshakes and back slaps. Everyone had good things to say about Chloe's management, which was great.

Where the hell were she and Renee?

Then, like something out of a damned movie, the crowd of riders and horses and calves all parted and there she was. His breath caught in his throat as he stared. He barely recognized her, but he *felt* it when Renee looked up and their eyes met across the crowd. She gave him a little smile, one that sent a thrill all the way down to his toes, which were firmly wedged into his damn boots.

Chloe had worked magic on Renee. Her hair curled and artfully arranged under the brim of a straw hat, she was wearing a lot more makeup than usual. Her jeans clung to her curves and her button-up top sparkled with sequins. Her curves were more pronounced, her belly rounding out behind a ridiculous sequined buckle. He guessed that, if someone didn't know she was pregnant she might not look it. She looked like a cowgirl, one that could walk in this world.

Even though it'd only been two days, he could still see how much her body had changed and he was pissed that he'd missed a single moment.

Leading her over to where the calves for the calf-roping event were penned up, Chloe said something to Renee and they laughed.

This was how she should always be—laughing and having fun and no doubt making cooing noises to the calf that sniffed her hand.

God, he'd missed her. Too much. He'd done his best to focus on the last three weeks instead of game planning the next few months or years, but he couldn't help the fantasy that spun out of control in his mind.

He could marry her. He could adopt her baby and they could be a family. He'd grow old with her by his side, teasing each other while eating cookies and spending long evenings in bed and doing all those things parents did with kids—parks and soccer games and school plays. All those things that his parents had done with him—and her—when they were kids.

She could make him happy.

Then a thought jolted him almost completely out of his chair. All those happy scenes?

They hadn't been in New York. They'd been in Texas, at Red Oak Hill, here in his condo. His perfect life with her was *here*. Not thousands of miles away.

Reality barged in because, in that vision of happiness, he hadn't seen his overbearing father or loose-cannon siblings or even this stupid rodeo.

Besides, he didn't even know if he could make *her* happy. She was still getting back on her feet and it probably wasn't helping that they were sleeping together. Hell, she hadn't even been able to explain those strange marks on her legs. He was afraid it had something to do with her husband, but he hadn't wanted to push. She'd tell him in her own time. He hoped. And if she didn't...

Hell.

A big man came up to Chloe and, after a second, Oliver recognized Pete Wellington. Damn it, when would he learn that the All-Stars wasn't his anymore? The last thing anyone needed right now was for Wellington to cause a scene. But if he was here—and by the look of it, giving Chloe trouble—then things were about to go sideways. Fast.

Not that Renee knew it. She looked over at him again, joy on her face. She pointed to the calf, as if to say, *See?* He shot her a thumbs-up. Her whole face lit up and damned if that didn't make him stick out his chest with pride.

He began to work his way toward her and Chloe but a rangy cowboy beat him to it. *Flash*. Damn it. He grabbed Renee's hand and kissed the back of it—then startled and stared at her face. Crap, he'd recognized her. Oliver needed to get over there before Flash did something stupid. Well, Flash always did something stupid. All Oliver could do was hope that Flash took a swing at Wellington instead of making a big to-do over Renee.

"Mr. Lawrence? I need to speak to you. Right now."

Groaning, Oliver cast a worried look at the Chloe/Pete, Renee/Flash train wreck in action before he turned. Surely they could all keep from killing each other for fifteen seconds. "Yes?"

A man glared up at him. Next to him stood a young woman with huge hair and a skintight leather skirt that was so short every single cowboy—and a few cowgirls—were staring.

"Brantley Gibbons." When Oliver blinked in confusion, the little man said, "Brooke Bonner's manager? And this is Brooke Bonner?" in a tone of voice that made it clear he thought Oliver was an idiot.

Right. The up-and-coming country singer performing after the rodeo tonight. Oliver cast another worried glance back at his siblings and Renee, but the crowds had shifted and he couldn't see them.

He put on as welcoming a smile as he could. "Yes, hello. It's a pleasure to meet you both." He shook hands. "Welcome to the All-Around All-Stars Rodeo. We're thrilled you were able to be here tonight." The man's eyes narrowed. Oliver knew that look. Something wasn't quite right. "What can I help you with?"

"For starters," Brantley Gibbons drawled, "you could see to Ms. Bonner's dressing room. We very clearly stated in the contract that there was to be—"

"Why didn't you tell me Renee was here!" This shout was accompanied by a punch to the arm that was hard enough to knock Oliver a step to the side.

"Shut up, Flash," Oliver ground out. He spun to see his annoying younger brother with his arm around Renee's shoulders and the world—well, it didn't go red. But it went a little pinkish.

Flash, being Flash, did not shut up. "How long have you been hiding her?" He sidestepped Oliver's attempt to grab him—and in the process, knocked Renee's hat off her head. "I haven't seen Renee since we were little—but maybe I should've checked her out."

"Damn it," Oliver growled, trying to step between Renee and…everyone. Because everyone was staring now. "Flash, *shut up*."

Renee tried to bend over to grab her hat, but Brooke Bonner beat her to it. "You look familiar—have we met?" the singer asked, handing the straw hat back to Renee.

Brooke's manager made an alarming noise. The look of shock on his face wasn't good. And it only got worse when he said, "You're Renee Preston, aren't you?" in a way that made the hair on the back of Oliver's neck stand straight up.

Flash launched the grin that made him a favorite with the ladies. "She was. Got herself married a few years ago?" He had the nerve to look Renee up and down. "Missed my invitation."

"Knowing you," Renee said, her smile stiffening as she cut another glance at Gibbons, "you would've used the wedding to get even for that one prank when…"

Flash held up his hands in surrender, but at least he was laughing. "God, I've missed you, Renee. You never did play fair, did you?"

The only reason Oliver didn't break his little brother's jaw was because the man between them was staring up at Renee with something Oliver wished wasn't rage—but was.

"No, she doesn't," the manager said, menace bleeding into his voice.

Renee looked at him with panic in her eyes. *Shit*. He had to get her out of here before anyone started snapping pictures. At the very least, he needed to shut Flash up.

He moved toward her as Flash went on, "Damn sorry I missed— Ow!"

Chloe beat Oliver to the punch. "Mr. Gibbons, Ms. Bonner, hello. I'm Chloe Lawrence and—" she paused to grind the heel of her boot into Flash's foot again "—we're thrilled you're here. I see you've already met Flash, one of our featured riders and, unfortunately, my brother."

"Son of a— Damn it, Chloe, get off my— *Ow!*" He shoved Chloe aside and glared. "That was unsporting of you."

Brooke Bonner giggled and Flash's head whipped around. "Hello, Ms. Bonner." With an exaggerated limp, he stepped closer, whipped off his hat and executed a perfect bow, somehow managing to get ahold of her hand and kiss it, just like he'd kissed Renee's. "Flash Lawrence, at your command."

Bonner batted her eyes at him. "Why do they call you Flash?"

If there was one thing Flash was good for, it was a distraction. As long as his attention was on Brooke, no one but the manager was paying any attention to Renee. Oliver got between Gibbons and Renee and started backing up. Renee hooked her hand through his waistband and held on tight.

Chloe let out a long-suffering sigh. "Because that's about how long it takes for him to rub you wrong."

"Or right," Flash cut in. He still had Bonner's hand.

Another cowboy—Oliver didn't remember this kid's name—crowded up. "Brooke, baby—" But that was as far as he got before Flash had him by the shirt and shoved him back.

"You don't talk to her like that," he growled, then added in a louder voice, "None of you talk to her like that. She's a lady and you will treat her as one or I will personally make sure you live to regret it."

Normally, Oliver would be irritated by Flash's ability to make any situation about him. But he'd neatly redirected the crowd's attention away from Renee. Gibbons seemed to remember where he was. He pivoted and headed straight to Brooke's side, shooing back the crowd that had started to press in for a better view of the fight. "Brooke will not go on without—"

Oliver wasn't about to look a gift distraction in the mouth. He backed up another step and was beyond relieved when Renee followed his lead. "Chloe will be able to make everything right." She wanted the rodeo? This was her chance to prove she could handle it. Oliver gave his sister a look. "Mr. Gibbons says there's a problem with the dressing room." Chloe nodded and Oliver gave thanks he had at least one intelligent sibling.

"I'd be happy to see what I can do to make you more comfortable," Oliver heard Flash say, which was followed by something that, if Oliver had to guess, was the sound of Chloe punching their twit brother.

Oliver didn't care. He spun, tucking Renee against his side and all but dragging her away from the crowd. He glanced back over his shoulder to see Gibbons peering past people. Crap. Hopefully, Chloe would be able to communicate to Flash—either with words or fists—to keep his mouth shut about Renee if anyone asked questions.

Oliver was so busy looking over his shoulder that he nearly clocked into Pete Wellington. "Lawrence," the bigger man all but spit.

Jesus, what else could go wrong? "Not today, Welling-ton," Oliver growled, shouldering past the man.

"Your sister is ruining this—"

"She's in charge—take it up with her," he called over his shoulder as Renee crammed her hat back onto her head. "We're leaving."

If he'd expected her to shrink and cower, he was wrong. "Slow down."

"What?"

Still holding on to him, she pulled back, forcing him to take smaller steps. "If you run, they chase." She glanced up at him. "And for God's sake, stop scowling."

Confused, he slowed down. "Because…"

She sighed. "Because they're sharks, Oliver. If they smell blood in the water, they'll go into a frenzy." Some-how, she managed to smile up at him. "Trust me on this."

He damn near stumbled over his feet at that smile. It was warm and carefree and, if he didn't know her so well, he'd think she was just another cowgirl having a good time before the rides.

But he did know better. Her shoulders were back and her chin was up and she had every single piece of her armor locked into place. And she was right, he realized. She had a lot more experience dealing with unfriendly crowds than he did.

So he forced himself to go at a snail's pace. "I'm sorry you're going to miss the rodeo," he said, guiding her around a pair of cowboys making a beeline toward Brooke Bonner and her leather miniskirt. "I'll make it up to you, babe."

"It's fine," she lied. And it broke his heart because that lie rolled right off her tongue like he was supposed to be-lieve that things would ever be fine again.

After what felt like a century but was probably only

about ten minutes of semileisurely strolling, they made it to where he'd parked his truck. He helped her up into the cab and then fired up the engine.

Anger boiled through him. He'd told Chloe this was a bad idea, although it wasn't her fault it'd all fallen apart so quickly. No, he had Flash to thank for that. His father was going to pitch a fit over this.

For years—*years*—Oliver had kept his promise to his mother that he'd take care of the family, because Trixie Lawrence had known then that her death would devastate Milt.

She hadn't been wrong. But he'd tried and tried and *tried*, for God's sake, to be the glue that held the Lawrence family together. He'd given up on his dreams of moving back to New York and working for anyone other than his father—because that was the truth. He wasn't going back to New York as anything more than a tourist.

He'd given up so much more than that. He dealt with the damned rodeo and he ran an energy company and he didn't like either one. His whole life had been in service to the Lawrence family name. Yeah, he had money to show for that. Money was great.

But it wasn't a life.

And he wanted his life back. More to the point, he wanted a life with Renee. He wanted to make those daydreams a reality. He wanted to do what he wanted, not what was best for the bottom line or his father.

Maybe he wasn't that different from Renee, after all. He wanted her for himself.

If he lost her because of his brother, so help him God, he would not be responsible for his actions.

They were silent while he navigated through traffic, but he was thinking the whole time. He could deal with his rage and his dreams later. Right now, he had a problem—

a huge one. The Preston Pyramid Princess had been confirmed at the All-Around All-Stars Rodeo by someone who'd probably lost a lot of money in the scheme.

Oliver was a man of means. He had options. He didn't have to put everything and everyone on lockdown. He didn't want Renee locked away. He wanted her to be safe—and free. And more than anything, he didn't want those two things to be a contradiction.

Once they made the roadways, he began to talk. "Here's what I'm thinking."

"Oliver…" she said softly.

He kept going. "I have a vacation home in Colorado—Vail. If I charter a flight, we could leave first thing in the morning."

"Oliver."

"But we could plant some rumors—be proactive. Say you were seen in Florida or something. I know a media specialist and—"

"Stop."

"I see the red light," he muttered as he braked. "If you're not up for flying, we can take a car, but it'll take longer. We should probably still hire the charter and send them in the other direction so—"

"*Oliver.*" Her voice was sharp, hard. It cut through the cab of his truck like a knife. "No."

"You'd rather fly?"

"Jesus, men," she said under her breath as the light turned green. "No, I'm not going to Vail."

"That's fine. Where would you like to go? I can—"

"Are you going to make me keep interrupting you?"

He almost didn't recognize the woman next to him. There was something so cold and remote about the way she spoke, the way she held herself…

It was exactly how she'd been on that first day when she'd waltzed into his office. Had it really been a month?

One month with Renee, watching her grow and change with her pregnancy. Watching her discover who she wanted to be and making sure she had the space to be that new woman.

This was a huge problem. Because there had to be a way to keep her in his life without telling his family to go to hell or resigning. There had to be a way to get what he wanted and still honor his promises. She had to let him fix this because if she thought he was going to hang her out to dry...

"Well," she began and instead of sounding upset or even worried, she sounded...amused? "I knew this would happen."

"Babe..."

She held up a hand to cut him off. "It's fine," she repeated again. Oliver decided that the more times she said that, the less *fine* it actually was. "It was lovely while it lasted. And I did learn how to bake cookies. So that was nice."

The hair on the back of Oliver's neck stood up. He didn't like how everything had suddenly become the past tense, as if the time they'd spent together was a chapter and Renee was closing the book. "It'll be nice again," he said, hating those pitiful words. *Nice* didn't cover waking up in her arms. *Nice* didn't cover laughing with her. *Nice* didn't come close to how he felt about her. "I'll—"

"No, you won't." She all but whispered the words. And then it only got worse because she turned to him and said, "I shouldn't have come and I shouldn't have stayed. I'm sorry, Oliver."

"This is not your fault," he ground out. That did it. Flash was a dead man.

She smiled. It didn't reach her eyes. "That's sweet of you, but we both know the truth."

"The truth? What 'truth' do you think you know? Because here's the truth, Renee—if I thought it'd make things better, I'd marry you today. Right now." She went dangerously pale but otherwise, she didn't react. Oh, hell. "I'd turn this truck around and head right back to the rodeo because there's always a preacher who gives the opening prayer and I'd marry you in front of God, my crazy family and a bunch of livestock because, even though it'd be a huge scandal, it'd be the right thing to do. It doesn't matter what your father or your brother or that ass of a husband of yours did, not to me—just like I hope it doesn't matter to you that Flash is a jackass and my father is lost in his own little world and I've given years of my life trying to help them only to have them fight me on every single damned thing. I don't care about them, Renee. I only care about you."

Her eyes glimmered and her armor almost cracked. *Fight*, he wanted to yell. *Fight for us.*

"I care about you, too." He took it as a good sign that her voice wavered just a little bit. "But I can't hurt you like this."

"Like what?" He stared at her, aware that his mouth was open. "How are you hurting me, Renee?"

She turned to look out the windshield. "Did you ever wonder why Clint and I were always at your house?"

So much for that crack in her armor. "Because we were friends and our house was more fun."

Her mouth moved into something that would have been a smile if it hadn't been so damned sad looking. "Fun. That it was."

When she didn't have anything to add to that, he said, "Renee?"

"Do you know what those marks on my legs are?" she said all in a rush.

"No." He looked at her thighs as if he'd magically acquired the power to see through denim in the last five minutes.

He hadn't. But he remembered those evenly spaced dots clustered together over a few square inches of her skin. They were too perfectly spaced to be random.

"She liked forks," Renee said softly. "Whenever we did something that displeased her, she'd smile that cold smile and insist that we sit on her left side. She was left-handed. But once Clint tried to stick up for me, she stabbed him in the other leg, just because she could."

Oliver blinked and blinked again. "Those are...stab wounds?"

"The scars of them," she said with a single nod.

"Who stabbed you?" He felt an odd sort of relief that at least it hadn't been her husband.

But that relief was short-lived. "My mother, of course."

Oliver let out a slow breath. "Your mother."

Another single nod. "She had these rules. No noise, no mess, obviously. Anything that might embarrass her was not a smart thing to do."

He reached over and covered the spot on her leg about where the scars were with his hand. "I didn't know."

"We didn't talk about it," she said, as if that weren't obvious.

Another long moment passed as traffic streamed past them in the direction of the Stockyards. All those people were putting down good money to see if Flash would get stepped on by a bull or not, and to see Brooke Bonner and her leather miniskirt bring down the house. They'd buy Chloe's clothes and the men would spend money on All-Stars merchandise—all of which also had Lawrence

Oil logos on it. People would buy nachos and beer, and there were games for the kids, who would buy stuffed horses and bulls. The rodeo was an evening of family fun.

He'd pay any price if he could give that to Renee.

He'd do anything to change the past. To do a better job of shielding her from an abusive, controlling mother and the scandals of her father. If he could go back, he'd give Clint a job, one that was legal and legit—one that would keep him out of jail.

"I need to leave," Renee said quietly.

"I'll go with you."

She made a huffing noise that might have been laughter or it might've been frustration. "No, you won't."

"But—"

"You don't get it, do you?" She pivoted in her seat and pinned him with a hard look. "I will ruin you, Oliver Lawrence. I'll ruin you and your business and everyone you love. And I won't do it. I…" Her voice cracked and she looked back out the windshield. "I can't do that to you."

His mouth opened but nothing came out.

"I need to pack," she said, her voice strong and sure again. "And then I need to leave before it all comes crashing down on you. I won't let my family destroy yours like they've destroyed me."

Thirteen

Oliver kept talking. One minute, he was going to charter a plane. The next, a helicopter. Then it was a private yacht leaving from Galveston and heading for open waters because "no one could follow us there," as if determined reporters wouldn't be able to rent a speedboat.

Renee listened with only half an ear as she packed because it didn't matter—whatever harebrained scheme he came up with, it wouldn't work. There was no quick, easy fix that would let everyone live happily-ever-after. Not this time. Not for her.

She knew that. She'd always known that. Funny how thinking it, however, made her heart ache.

She needed to leave quickly before Oliver got it into her head to *make* her stay or, worse, enlist his family. Renee knew what she had to do but if the entire Lawrence family showed up to plead their case, she might not be strong enough to do the right thing.

And the right thing was so obvious. Renee simply couldn't hurt any of the Lawrences. Not even Flash. After all, he hadn't done anything Oliver himself hadn't done. Oliver had just had the good fortune to blurt out her name in front of small-town firefighters instead of a desperate music promoter.

So her mind was made up. She was leaving—alone. She'd see if she could stay with her former sister-in-law, Carolyn, for a few days. It would be awkward and uncomfortable but then again, Carolyn had given that interview where she'd passed on the chance to destroy Renee. And she and Carolyn had always got along before the scandal and divorce and death.

Besides, it wasn't like she could do more damage to Carolyn's reputation. She'd already been married to Clint. In the ruined department, she and Renee were practically equal.

Renee and Oliver would never be equal. Good Lord, he'd proposed. He'd said he'd marry her in the middle of the rodeo and he hated the rodeo.

In another time, another life, it would've been something wonderful.

Except for the *but*. Because there was always a *but*, wasn't there? As sweet as that marriage proposal had been, Oliver had prefaced that declaration with, *If I thought it'd make things better...*

He'd marry her. He'd do his best to make her happy. He might even adopt her child, when the time came, and she knew he'd be an amazing father. It might be good. Great, even.

But it wouldn't be perfect because he couldn't live without her. He'd offer her the protection of his name and access to all his resources because it was the most obvious solution to a problem.

Her.

She might be hopelessly in love with him, but she wasn't his problem to solve. And she wasn't about to marry another man who didn't love her.

Leaving was the only option.

"...one of those big bus-sized RVs that rock stars travel in," he was saying when he growled and spun, pulling out his phone. He never kept the sound on and therefore, she was always startled when he'd answer it at random times. "What?"

She hadn't bothered to pack the funeral dress or shoes—neither fitted anymore. But her lawyers would most likely blow their collective tops if she were spotted walking around in Chloe's fancy rodeo clothes. But the only alternative was pushing her leggings past the point of decency, so sequins it was. Which left the problem of the boots. She couldn't exactly walk around in those things anywhere but Texas. If she showed up in New York in the boots and the sequins, the press would have a freaking field day with her. What a shame. She set them next to the closet door and then closed the zipper on her single piece of luggage.

"Renee?" There was something different in Oliver's tone instead of the desperation that had colored all his grand plans thus far.

"Yes?"

"There are some men here for you."

The way he said it made it clear that he wasn't talking about the press. Even as the bottom of her stomach fell out, she squared her shoulders and lifted her chin. Old habits never died, it seemed. Just because she hadn't had to fall back on them for the better part of a month didn't mean she'd forgotten how to protect herself. "Who?"

But she already knew because Oliver wasn't trying

to arrange a quick getaway in his zippy sports car. "The FBI. Security checked them out. They need you to return to New York with them."

Ah. They must have decided to turn the pressure up on Clint. At least, she hoped that was the case and not that they'd already caught wind of the disastrous rodeo outing.

Again, her stomach tried to turn at the thought of someone snapping a picture of her smiling and laughing—the very things her lawyers had informed her not to do. But Oliver had reminded her how to be happy and she'd almost forgotten what it was like to keep her real self locked deep inside.

She needed to remember. Quickly.

"I see." She tried to smile for Oliver, to show him that she wasn't scared or worried—that she'd be perfectly safe in the company of the Justice Department's best officers.

She didn't make it. "Don't do that," he snapped, throwing his phone down and closing the distance between them. He grabbed her by the shoulders. "Don't act like everything is fine when it's not."

She was leaving. Things might never be fine again. "You can't fix this, Oliver."

"The hell I can't," he said and slammed his mouth down over hers.

He meant it as a kiss of possession. Renee knew that. He wasn't going to let her go without a fight, fool that he was. But Renee knew the truth.

This was goodbye.

She wasn't going to cry.

Once upon a time, the Lawrence family had shown her what love was. They'd given her another life, one where people were sweet and loud and messy and loved. So, *so* loved. If she hadn't had that second childhood with Chloe, she didn't know how she'd have survived.

Oliver might not ever realize it because, knowing him, he'd look back at this moment and see nothing but a failure to fix everything just so. But he'd given her the same gift again. Love and happiness and a glimpse into a future she might one day have. He'd let her find her own way and made her laugh again.

She'd be forever grateful for this month.

But she couldn't tell him any of that without breaking down into sobs and she knew damned well that if she so much as wavered, he'd do something stupid like bust out the high-powered attorneys and call a press conference and all but announce to the world that he'd been sleeping with the pregnant Preston Pyramid Princess, and that?

That would be his downfall.

So, when the kiss ended, she pressed her lips against his cheek and gave him one final hug. "Goodbye, Oliver." Then she grabbed her solitary piece of luggage and hurried for the door before she changed her mind.

"Damn it, Renee, I can fix this! I just need more time," he said, sounding half-mad with desperation. "By the time the FBI is done with whatever they need you for, I'll have this figured out—I promise."

No, she couldn't be his problem.

So she kept walking.

She didn't look back.

Fourteen

Goodbye, Oliver.

Fuck that shit.

After nearly running over two photographers staked out by the garage entrance, Oliver stepped off the elevator. The door to his father's condo swung open seconds later, making it clear that Milt Lawrence had been waiting for him. Just when he thought the day couldn't get worse...

"Beer?" Milt said, holding up a longneck, and Oliver knew he didn't have much say in the matter.

He supposed this wasn't a surprise. Renee's brief appearance three days ago at the All-Around All-Stars Rodeo—brought to you by Lawrence Oil—in the company of Oliver Lawrence, head of Lawrence Energies, had made headlines less than an hour after Renee had been whisked back to New York in the company of the FBI's finest. The whole debacle was exactly the sort of thing that would draw Milt out of his hunting lodge and into the city.

Not for the first time, Oliver wished his father hadn't bought the condo next to his for those rare trips into Dallas. Being called in for a lecture had a way of making Oliver feel like he was twelve again and about to be grounded for another prank gone wrong.

Except this time, it wasn't an elevator and a bunch of balloons filled with shaving cream. This was the family business. Their livelihood. He'd risked an international energy company and his family's financial safety and well-being for...

For Renee. Who'd walked away without a look back.

God, it hurt.

It turned out that Brantley Gibbons, Brooke Bonner's manager, had lost a lot of money to the Preston Pyramid. In fact, he was under investigation because several of his clients claimed he'd inappropriately invested their funds with Preston's firm. Brooke had stuck by him because Gibbons was her uncle.

Family. Was there any bigger blessing and curse than that word?

"Here," Milt said, handing Oliver a beer and motioning for him to sit on the leather sofa overlooking the skyline. Unlike his hunting lodge, Milt Lawrence's condo was as impersonal as a hotel. Probably why he only spent maybe ten nights a year here. "Well, this is a fine how-do-you-do you've got yourself into."

Oliver gritted his teeth. "Do you think that, just once, we could cut the cowboy crap, Dad? Because I'm not in the mood to hear about how I look lower than a rattler's belly in a wheel rut." He took a long pull on his beer. It didn't help. "No offense." Oliver braced himself to be dressed down because with that attitude, he deserved it.

But that's not what happened. "I take it she'd been with you since you first asked if I'd heard about the scam?"

To Oliver's ever-lasting surprise, there was less drawl in his father's voice. Still a little bit, though.

It was enough. "Yeah. A month." A good month. One of the best he could ever remember having.

Because Renee had been there. For the first time in years—maybe decades—Oliver had done something more than look at the family business or his family as just problems waiting to be solved.

He wasn't able to go back to who he'd been before Renee.

"Do you know where she is now?"

"New York." She wasn't responding to his texts, beyond the bare-bones information to let him know she was fine. Everything, apparently, was fine.

He was *not* fucking fine.

"She said she had to leave because she'd ruin me. I think she actually believes that," he said before taking another long swallow of his beer. It still wasn't helping.

"Hmm," Milt said noncommittally.

"She said…" He had to swallow a few times to make sure his throat was working right. "She said she wouldn't let her family ruin mine or my business like they ruined her."

"Ah," Milt unhelpfully added.

"That's it? That's all you've got? *Hmm* and *ah*?"

"I was going to say something about rattlers but that didn't seem to be the way to go."

"Jesus, Dad, are you mocking me?" There were days when his father was every bit as irritating as Flash—and worse.

"Simmer down, son." He held up his hands in surrender. "I'm not here to fight. If you're looking to take a swing at someone, either find your brother or go punch Clint Preston. Doubt either would help in the long run, though."

They sat for a moment. The silence was getting to Oliver, which had to be the only reason why he kept talking. Either that or the beer was actually starting to work and he just couldn't feel it. "I asked her to marry me and not only did she not say yes, she said goodbye." All that armor had been so locked in place that he still couldn't tell if she would've said yes or not had circumstances been different.

If the FBI hadn't shown up, would she still be here—or there or wherever he could have safely hidden her away? Or would she still have walked?

"Did she, now? In general, women like a nice proposal," Milt managed to say without laughing.

Oliver drank some more. Had it been, though? A nice proposal, that was. He'd said...

If he'd thought it would help.

Shit.

"She said she wasn't my problem to solve," he admitted, feeling suddenly stupid.

"Ah," Milt said again.

Oliver didn't dignify that with a response.

But had he actually said those words to Renee? He'd been upset, yeah. Flash had blown Renee's cover and Oliver had been frantic with worry about the best way to keep her safe but...

It hadn't been a nice proposal. Hell, it'd barely qualified as such.

"Do you know," Milt began, and for the first time in years, Oliver heard New York in his father's voice, "what I would give to have another day with your mother?"

Oliver let that thought roll around his head as he finished his beer and got up to get another. "Everything," he said when he settled back on the couch next to his father. "You'd give everything to have her back."

"You're damn right I would. The company, the rodeo, the lodge…" Milt cleared his throat and Oliver made sure not to look because he didn't want to see his father wiping away tears. "*Anything* to have her back."

"I'm sorry it's not going to happen," Oliver said. His mother's death was a problem he'd never be able to fix.

"And you know why I'd give everything for her?"

Oliver did look at his dad then. "Because you love her." There was no past tense about it.

"You're damn right I do." He stood, knocking back the last of his beer. "Herb Ritter's in town and I've got to smooth his ruffled feathers. And don't think I don't know you gave Chloe those negotiations after I told you not to. But Oliver?"

Oliver unclenched his teeth. "What?"

His father stared down at him with love and worry in his eyes. "We aren't your problem, either." He put a hand on Oliver's shoulder. "I know what you promised your mother, and she'd be right proud of you and everything you've accomplished. But we can take care of ourselves." He sighed. "We always could."

Then he grabbed his hat and walked out of the condo, leaving Oliver alone with his thoughts.

He couldn't function without Renee. He loved watching her try a new recipe and sharing in her success. Hell, he loved her failures, too—because they were always hilarious and only occasionally a hazard to home and health. He loved watching her grow and change with her pregnancy and he absolutely hated that she wasn't next door, waiting to welcome him home with a kiss that became so much more.

Holy hell, he loved her. Scandal-ridden family, broke, pregnant with another man's child—he loved Renee exactly as she was.

He hadn't told her that. Instead of treating her like the woman he wanted to spend the rest of his life with… he'd treated her like a problem that he was responsible for solving.

Jesus, what had he done?

Because now she was thousands of miles away, facing lawyers and officers and, worse, her family without anyone to back her up while he sat here and got scolded by his father.

What the hell was wrong with him? She wasn't the problem. *He* was.

He loved her.

That was worth risking everything.

"And have you had any other contact with anyone in your family?" the bored federal prosecutor asked.

Frankly, Renee was bored, too. She'd been sitting in this conference room for the last three hours, answering the same questions she'd answered a few days ago with the same answers, which were the same questions she'd answered a few months ago. She was pretty sure the prosecutor was wearing the same suit.

"The friend I stayed with in Texas spoke with Clint, but only to confirm that I had nothing to do with the scheme."

That got the prosecutor's attention. "He did?"

"Oliver Lawrence was a childhood friend. He runs Lawrence Energies. He wanted to make sure I was being honest." Renee cleared her throat. It hurt to think of Oliver right now. "Trust but verify, right?" The prosecutor didn't so much as blink and Renee felt that old fear of having done something wrong roil her stomach. "I did get permission to go."

The prosecutor conferred with his secretary, who made notes as the prosecutor said, "Anything else?"

Renee unlocked her phone and called up the most recent text message from her mother. "I got this two days ago." She handed the phone over because there was no way in hell she was going to read that message out loud.

Someone had got a shot of her at the rodeo. Renee had actually thought it wasn't as bad as some of the paparazzi shots and she liked the way Chloe's jeans had looked on her. But her mother had, of course, felt it necessary to remind Renee how fat and embarrassing she was—especially in those clothes. Sequins were against her mother's rules, to say nothing of actual blue jeans. The horrors.

Renee hadn't even finished reading it. She was a grown woman, an expectant mother. She did not have to let her mother into her life anymore. Her parents had never loved her—or Clint. She owed them nothing.

The secretary made more notes and Renee forwarded a screenshot to the lawyer's email. "What else do you need from me?" Because no one had escorted her to Rikers or arranged for transportation. She was here to plead with Clint, wasn't she?

The bored prosecutor looked over his notes again and Renee fought the urge to roll her eyes. Finally, the man said, "Ms. Preston-Willoughby, Clinton Preston has accepted a plea deal in which he'll get a reduced sentence in exchange for testifying against Darin Preston."

"Oh." The word rushed out of her. "That's good. If I may ask...how reduced?"

"He'll plead guilty in exchange for a sentence of twelve years at a minimum-security prison with the possibility of parole. He might be out in seven." The prosecutor looked up at her. "I don't plan on letting your father out of prison in his lifetime, even if he pleads guilty to avoid a trial."

"Good." If the man was surprised by this, he didn't show it. "Will you be able to extradite my mother?"

That got her a faint smile. "If we do, will you be willing to testify against her?"

Renee thought about all those terrifying family dinners with forks repeatedly stabbed into her legs and being blamed for getting blood on her ruined pants and skirts. She thought about a lifetime of manipulation and deceit, of being made to feel small and hopeless and embarrassing.

Then she imagined her mother in the defendant's table, being forced to listen to Renee poke holes in her story of innocence one precise jab at a time. She smiled. Let her mother find out what real anxiety was like. "I'd be delighted to."

"I believe we have everything we need," the prosecutor went on. "If your father's case goes to trial, we'll expect your full cooperation." Renee nodded. That was always the deal. "Please don't leave the country and keep my office informed of where you are. Otherwise, you are free to go." He gave her that faint smile again. "Good luck, Ms. Preston-Willoughby."

She sat there for a moment, stunned. "I can go back to Texas if I want?"

Not that it was a good idea—it wasn't. She'd walked away from Oliver, after all. And he had paparazzi watching him now. She'd seen the pictures of him entering and leaving his building and Lawrence Energies's office complex. In every single shot, he was scowling. In all probability, she was probably lucky he hadn't punched anyone. But at least he wasn't running. He'd remembered that.

She'd done that. She'd taken away his privacy, not to mention Chloe and Flash's privacy. The Lawrence family was in the press in a highly public way.

"Of course. Get a job, move on with your life. We

won't be garnishing your wages or any wages of anyone you marry."

Renee's mouth almost, *almost* dropped open at that, but those old damned habits kept her face blank. The prosecutor was just as unreadable but she shouldn't have been surprised. The man was no idiot.

"That's good to know. Thank you."

She and her lawyers stood, as did the prosecutor. Everyone shook hands. "Good luck," the man said.

She almost laughed at that. She'd been born to privilege and she was lucky enough to have known the love of the Lawrence family. But beyond that?

She'd been lucky enough to have a good month with Oliver. To ask for more than that would be too much.

She said goodbye to her lawyers and then hurried to the ladies' room. Her bladder seemed smaller every day. Her baby was growing. She could focus on impending motherhood now. That would be enough.

Lost in thought about what kind of job she might be able to get—something anonymous would be great—she exited the elevators into the lobby and headed for the door. She could see the paparazzi milling around outside but she didn't care anymore.

"I thought you hated the paparazzi."

That voice. *His* voice. "Oliver?" Renee stumbled as she whipped around, searching for him. Please, *please* don't let her be imagining his voice.

"But here you are, about to walk right out into their waiting cameras." He guided her to the side so effortlessly that she wasn't sure her feet touched the ground.

"You're here," she whispered as he pulled her into a waiting elevator. His arm went around her waist and he pulled her against his chest. God, she'd missed him. The five days since she'd forced herself to walk away from him had been a new, different kind of misery. She threw her arms around his neck and held on tight as the elevator doors slid shut. "What are you doing here?"

"Looking for you." He hit the button for the garage level and they began to move. "I made you a promise."

"You did?" She searched her memories and her heart sank.

He'd promised Clint he'd look after her.

Oh, no. He wasn't here because he couldn't live without her. He was here because he had a promise to keep. This wasn't any different than him offering to marry her because it might help. Oliver Lawrence was the most honorable man she'd ever known. Even though she'd walked away from him, he was going to take care of her. Whether she wanted him to or not, apparently.

"You don't have to do this," she said, her voice too soft. She was too soft when it came to him. Because she'd walked away once with her head up and her shoulders back. She wasn't sure she could do it again.

"I do." He lifted her chin so she looked him in the eye. "I promised I wouldn't leave you without saying goodbye."

She reared back, but he didn't let her go. He *had* promised that, hadn't he?

"But…" she said, staring at him. "I said goodbye."

"I didn't." Her breath caught in her throat at the sound of his voice, deep and intense. Oliver's eyes darkened. "What do you want, Renee?"

Before she could come up with an answer, the elevator dinged again and people got on. Oliver shifted so that Renee was standing next to him but his arm stayed locked around her waist and, fool that she was, she leaned into him.

He was really here. He was warm and he smelled like

Oliver and he was wearing cowboy boots in New York with his suit, and if she wasn't careful, she was going to burst into tears.

Her brother had agreed to a plea deal. Her father was never getting out of jail and, with any luck, her mother would be locked up before too much longer.

Renee was free to do whatever she wanted.

So what did she want?

They rode in silence the rest of the way down to the parking garage. He led her to a chauffeured car. The driver hurried to open the back door for her and Oliver guided her inside.

It was only when the door was shut that Renee found her voice. "What…"

"You didn't really think I was going to let you walk into that crowd of sharks and try to hail a cab, did you?" He shook his head like he'd told a joke.

"Oliver," she said, aiming for a sharper tone. His eyes softened as he folded her hand in his. "What are you doing here?"

"Coming for you."

She blinked and then, when nothing changed—he was still staring down at her with those warm brown eyes, still looking at her like he was glad to see her.

How was any of this possible? She'd seen the headlines. The wild—and not always wrong—guesses about the nature of her relationship with Oliver. The firefighters telling how she'd almost burned down the ranch house. Hell, someone had even got Lucille to give a comment. True, it'd been "Private people are entitled to private lives. Now, get off my porch or I'll shoot," but still.

"You know if we're seen together again, it'll only make things worse for you."

Everything soft and happy about Oliver hardened in a heartbeat. "Renee, what do you want?"

Her eyes watered instantly and she had to turn to look out the darkened windows of the car. They were out of the garage now and slowly creeping past the paparazzi waiting for her outside the building. She wondered how long they'd wait. Hopefully hours.

"I don't want to cost you your business," she said because it was the truth.

He snorted. She jerked her head around to stare at him. "Renee. What do *you* want? In the next five minutes or the next five years. What you want. Not what you or anyone else thinks you should do."

Her throat got tight and somehow, a lifetime of training herself not to cry began to fail her now. Because Oliver was the only person who'd ever asked and actually listened to the answer. "I don't want to hurt you."

"Oh, babe." He moved, pulling her onto his lap. She curled into him. "You know what I want?"

She shook her head against his shoulder.

"I want to take long walks around the park and maybe trail rides on the ranch. I want to see first steps and hear first words. I want to come home to fresh-baked cookies and spend nights in bed with you and wake up in the morning knowing you'll be right there. I want to be by your side, in sickness and in health, in scandal and in quiet times—hopefully more quiet than this," he added with a chuckle.

"But why?" She sniffed. "Why would you risk everything for me?"

He tilted her face up and stared into her eyes. "Because I love you."

Her breath caught. She wanted that life, too. She wanted to raise her baby with him and know that he'd always be there for her. He'd never leave her and never cheat on her because he couldn't live without her. Not because she was a promise he had to keep.

"I *love* you, Renee," he repeated again, putting more force on the words. He tilted her chin up so she had to look at him. "And you know what?"

"What?"

"You're worth more than any business or house or even swans. I'd give all of it up in a heartbeat, just as long as you were by my side. My father, my siblings—they're all grown adults. They can take care of themselves. I don't have to do anything for them. I only have to do what I want. And what I want is to marry you. I want to love you for the rest of our lives. That's all I want."

She gasped. As declarations went, that was pretty damned good. Much better than offering to marry her if it'd help. But there was still one giant, huge problem. "I can't be your problem to solve, Oliver. I can't. That's not a life."

She braced for him to start a running list of why he could protect her, how he could take care of her—just like he'd done when she'd been outed at the rodeo. But instead, he touched his forehead to hers. "I'm always going to do my best to make things easier for you. Not because you're my responsibility but because that's what you do for someone you love."

When she didn't say anything, he cupped her face and kissed her. "Tell me what you want. Forget the cameras and our families. Just you and me, babe. We're the only ones who matter."

"I want it all," she sobbed. Stupid hormones. "I want to bake and crochet and take care of my baby. I don't want nannies or chefs or... Well, Lucille is okay. But I just want us. I want to know that you won't lie to me and

I won't lie to you. I want to know you'll come home at the end of the day and we'll spend the evening together as a family. I want to hang out with Chloe and be irritated by Flash. I want…" She was crying so hard she could barely talk. "I want to be a Lawrence. I've *always* wanted to be a Lawrence. I want a big, happy family where everyone is loud and messy and loved and no one hurts anyone. And I want that with you."

"Oh, babe." His voice sounded choked as he wrapped her up in a huge hug and let her cry. When she'd calmed down a little, he looked her in the eyes. His thumbs rubbed over her cheeks, erasing her tears. "Renee, I promise you—I will never lie to you or cheat on you. I will always be there for you and make sure you have the space you need to find your own path forward. I'm not going to give up on you and I'm not about to let a little notoriety drive me away. You know why?"

"Why?"

"Because you—both of you," he added, resting a hand against her belly, "will always be family. Because I love you."

"I love you, too. God, Oliver, I love you so much."

He kissed her again and again and she lost herself in his touch, his taste, his smell. God, he smelled so good. Renee had no idea how much time had passed before the car made a wide turn, startling her back to her senses. "Where are we going?"

Oliver gave her that smile that, had she been standing, would have weakened her knees. "We're going home."

Finally.

Home was with Oliver.

Epilogue

"Up next on ESPN, June Spotted Elk has an exclusive interview with the Princess of the All-Around All-Stars Rodeo, Chloe Lawrence, about how the All-Stars are about to break big."

Pete Wellington's head popped up from the report on cattle prices he was working on. Not that there were many cattle left—but even if there were, at these prices, he'd never be able to pay the mortgage off. "What the hell?"

He caught a glimpse of the one woman who could make his blood boil with nothing more than a smile. Because Chloe Lawrence was smiling at the screen and his blood hit boiling in 0.2 seconds.

The camera cut to June, the world-famous bull rider. "Bull riding brings in the big money. How can the All-Stars compete with the Total Bull Challenge?"

Pete's eyelid began to twitch as the camera cut back to Chloe. She flipped her rich auburn hair over her shoulder, the rhinestones on her shirt—unbuttoned just far enough to hint at the tantalizing curves of her breasts—sparkling in the lights. But nothing outshone her smile. That damned woman simply glowed. "For starters, I'm hoping to get you to ride on our circuit!" The women laughed. "We'll be introducing more women competitors," Chloe went on.

God forgive him, she was nothing short of perfect, which only made his ridiculous attraction that much worse. How many people tossed and turned at night because she haunted their dreams with that smile, those lips, that body? How many woke up hard and aching for her?

Probably too many to count. Pete took comfort that he wasn't alone.

But no one else saw her for what she was. The rest of the world bought into her stupid cowgirl persona.

He didn't want her. Hell, his life would be that much better if he never heard the names Chloe or Lawrence ever again. Pete's body might crave hers, but his brain knew the truth.

Chloe Lawrence was no cowgirl. She was nothing but a thieving, cheating liar, from a long line of cheats and thieves. The Lawrence family were little more than con artists and criminals. They'd stolen Pete's rodeo, his family ranch—his entire life.

Now she was ruining his rodeo. The one her father maintained that Pete's father had lost fair and square in a poker game. But Pete knew better.

When it came to Chloe Lawrence and her damned family, Pete Wellington had one goal and it had nothing to do with the way he ached for her.

He wanted his life back. And he was going to start by getting *his* rodeo back.

Even if he had to steal it out from under her nose.

* * * * *

LET'S TALK
Romance

For exclusive extracts, competitions
and special offers, find us online:

📘 facebook.com/millsandboon

📷 @millsandboonuk

🐦 @millsandboon

Or get in touch on 0844 844 1351*

For all the latest titles coming soon, visit
millsandboon.co.uk/nextmonth